The Modern Library College Editions

PÈRE GORIOT

and EUGÉNIE GRANDET

D1529355

THE PUBLISHERS WILL BE PLEASED TO SEND, UPON
REQUEST, A BROCHURE SETTING FORTH THE PURPOSE AND
SCOPE OF THE *Modern Library College Editions,*
AND LISTING EACH VOLUME IN THE SERIES.

MODERN LIBRARY COLLEGE EDITIONS

PÈRE GORIOT *and* EUGÉNIE GRANDET

BY HONORÉ DE BALZAC

Translated from the French by
E. K. Brown, Dorothea Walter, and John Watkins

With an introduction by E. K. Brown,
Professor of English, University of Chicago

THE MODERN LIBRARY
NEW YORK

Random House IS THE PUBLISHER OF

THE MODERN LIBRARY

BENNETT A. CERF · DONALD S. KLOPFER · ROBERT K. HAAS

Manufactured in the United States of America

CONTENTS

INTRODUCTION

by

E. K. BROWN

No OTHER novelist has had an aim so ambitious as Balzac's. He proposed to paint the entire panorama of French society in his half-century—Paris, the provincial cities and towns, the country-side, the common people, the bourgeoisie, the nobility—and so that his complex pattern might be fully representative he would furnish pictures of types of life he considered to lie somewhat apart from the general movement, political life, for instance, and military life. France was, he believed, the richest subject open to a novelist in that time; in France there was the greatest variety of social types, and in France these types were most sharply defined; in France occurred the dramas of the keenest intensity, and in those dramas the underlying ideas of the age were most fully engaged. He would do for the France of his time, and do systematically, what his admired Scott had done for a few scattered moments of the past. And the disorders and splendors of passionate love which Scott had shrunk from presenting—he made a holocaust of passion, says Balzac, and offered it to the bluestockings of his nation—would take their due place, a large one, in his panorama.

Balzac was born May 20th, 1799, at Tours, "one of the least literary among French cities." His father, self-made, served the Revolution, and then the regime of Napoleon, and did well out of each. Honoré was the eldest of four children; the next, Laure, was his confidante, and wrote his biography. The boy spent the years from 1807 to 1813 at the College of the Oratorians in Vendôme, not far from Tours, without the mercy of a single vacation. He left the college when the family moved to Paris; and in 1816, at his father's insistence, he reluctantly entered a lawyer's office. During his four years as clerk, he found time to attend many courses and to write voluminously. Soon after 1820 he began to publish over pseudonyms; his early stories have small value. In his greediness for a large fortune quickly made, he risked everything many times in fantastic speculations. His debts were enormous; but there was a compensation in the detailed heartfelt knowledge of many sorts of business which adds to the realism of his novels. He had love affairs with aristocratic women, one of them a godchild of Marie Antoinette, and by their kindness he was introduced to the life of fashionable society. "You can guess," he said, "what goes on in kitchens; but you must learn by experience what goes on in drawing rooms—that is something you cannot guess."

It was a story of Brittany during the Revolution, *Le Dernier Chouan* (later called *Les Chouans*), published in 1829, that first showed his great powers. He was aware of its worth: this was the first novel to which he signed his name. He had found his way, after an apprenticeship almost as long as Thackeray's; and the rest of his life was mainly given to blackening reams of paper with the symbols of an inexhaustible imagination. When he was not writing he liked to wander about the streets of Paris, or some other French city, endlessly inquisitive, and was at his happiest when he could add to his vast collections of *objets d'art*. He was never a willing recluse; and enjoyed almost all sorts of society, seeking to make up, when he had some leisure, for the months when he could scarcely leave his desk. Few people have ever known so much of the aspect of Paris, or of the many kinds of life that flourish in France—in city, town, and country.

In 1833 Balzac met the Countess Hanska, a Polish woman who from adoring his works soon came to adore the man; she was the great love of his life. Although her husband died in 1841, Balzac could not persuade her to marry him until he was gravely ill and within a few months of his death, which occurred at his house in Paris on August 18th, 1850.

In his approach to French society Balzac was as serious in method as a professional historian; and the material he dealt with eluded the professional historian and yet was as essential an expression of the inner nature of the period as any constitution or any campaign. Even in the incomplete state in which he left it, dying at fifty-one and incapacitated for fiction two years before, his *Human Comedy* is a precious contribution to French history. The great historian of the French Revolution, Albert Sorel, thought its pages as luminous as those in any archives. Still, to be a historian was neither the whole nor even the heart of Balzac's intention, nor was his interest limited to his own age. Along with its studies in manners, his *Comedy* was to comprehend a series of philosophic studies of which only a few were written. In these his concern with the here and the now would give way before a curiosity about the recesses of human motivation and the determination to construct a theory of human nature in action. Much as we may regret his failure to complete this part of his undertaking—and there was to be a third cycle of studies more rarefied still—we may find in his pictures of his own France the essence of his prophetic vision of man and his universe.

It was the vision of a human biologist. "The leading idea of this human comedy," he tells us, "came to me first as a dream. . . . The idea came from the study of human life in comparison with the life of animals." All animals, he thought, were variations of one essential form of animal life, and the variations were produced by differing environments. So it was with mankind. "Society makes the man; he develops according to the social centers in which he is placed; there are as many different men as there are species in zoology." But between men and animals there is this crucial difference, by which the representation of men becomes immensely more dramatic, more complex, and more interesting: in the individual man there is striking change as his habitat is changed. Throw the rabbit into the ocean, and he is still a rabbit; throw the young provincial into the welter of Paris, and he becomes a being new and strange.

At the beginning of *Le Père Goriot* we meet Eugène de Rastignac, freshly arrived in Paris from a retired and upright life on a small estate in the south of France; we then watch him as he develops unexpected traits of ambition, covetousness and vanity under the pressure of the luxurious and corrupt life of the capital. In later appearance in other scenes of the *Comedy* the process carries him much farther from his initial integrity; and in the end he marries the daughter of his first mistress and is linked in politics and business with the very men whose cynicism and egotism had revolted his youth. Eugénie Grandet's cousin falls to an even lower moral condition by reason of the years he spends in the slave trade and other occupations which petrify the feelings. Eugénie herself, born, as Balzac says, to be magnificently wife and mother, is in her widowed years commonly known as the "old maid," and her twist in this direction is the work of the social forces which had made her father what he was.

For Balzac a character's environment, his "social center," includes not only the material configurations of the place where he lives but the spirit of the age and the persons with whom he has to do. Edith Wharton observed that he was the first novelist to care profoundly about the material circumstances in which his personages lived. He did care profoundly, archeologically, encyclopedically. His characteristic openings—such fatiguing obstacles to most modern readers who prefer a more insinuating exposition—are packed with a thousand facts about the city, the quarter, the street, the house in which the action will occur, even the rooms down to the last grease-spot on the table and the broken rung of a chair. Balzac believed, as Faguet says, that the shell helps to explain the tortoise. The intensity of his care for material environment was new, and the success with which he rendered it helped to make his characters more real to the reader.

What is more notable perhaps, and certainly more interesting, is Balzac's treatment of the less obvious kind of environment, his interest in the social and economic history of his people: how they made or inherited or stole their money—money was never long out of Balzac's mind!—what their occupations had done to their minds and hearts as well as to their bodies, what their opinions were about family, altar and throne. The tragedy of Eugénie Grandet could not have happened if her father had not been a miser; we must know, Balzac thinks, what it means to be a miser, how being a miser affects a man's relations with his family and his associates (as much as it does his attitudes to his furniture and the decoration of his house), how it leads him to spend his days and nights. In the end we have a vivid sense of what it means to live in the formidable shadow of César Grandet. The tragedy of Eugène de Rastignac could not have happened if Paris had not been a corrupt community—and specifically a community corrupted by money. If the old order, represented by the Viscountess de Beauséant had continued in power, or if the new order represented by Vautrin had come into power, the particular temptations to which Rastignac succumbed would not have had their evil strength. He succumbs because of the vast new wealth of a bourgeoisie frantic for display, recognition and enjoyment.

It is often said that modern France may be divided into two sorts of people: those who do and those who do not accept the French Revolution. In his maturity Balzac did not accept it. He considered that the plutocratic regime which followed on the questioning of the authority of the Church, the weakening of the monarchic principle, and the impoverishment and ·dispersion of the old aristocracy, was a moral and social catastrophe. Both Goriot and Grandet were men suddenly enriched in the Revolution and thrown off their balance for the rest of their lives. Nucingen's title and Nucingen's power date, the one from the period of Napoleon, the other from the Restoration.

Profound and suggestive as Balzac's treatment of the lives of individuals in terms of the social structure and spirit of their time may be, it is not chiefly because of this that his novels can still hold us from the chimney-corner. It is above all because of the enormous energy of his imagination. Once we have cleared the obstacle of the opening pages, bristling with details which take on their full meaning only in the sequel, his greater novels and tales sparkle and crackle with life. Much of the life is centered in the one or two dominant characters of the work, huge monoliths, human but carrying a human trait to the extreme, as the Baron Hulot carries sensuality, Gobseck and Grandet avarice, and Goriot paternal love. These dominant characters are not complex; from first to last they are essentially the same, but as the novel develops they express their master-trait with ever-growing force. Grandet on his deathbed, clutching at the crucifix because of its precious metal and dying from the spasm of energy, is a type of the great Balzacian monolithic character in final revelation. It is no wonder that such characters seemed to Balzac more fully alive than the mortals he knew. Jules Sandeau who was his secretary before becoming an author has told how Balzac broke off his condolences on a disaster in Sandeau's family to say that they must return to realities, to *Eugénie Grandet*.

Like most great novelists in the nineteenth century Balzac delighted in the *scene à faire,* the great scene in which a character such as Goriot or Grandet or Vautrin meets some immense obstacle to his master-passion, and throws himself upon it with every atom of his emotional and intellectual power. In such scenes Balzac is at once the realist—who can forget Grandet's stammer or his deafness, the moments when both are brought to a calculated height, or what happens to the wen on his nose when his ire is roused?—and always something more than the realist, infusing into the dominant character an intensity of being which is usually found only in the highest dramatic poetry. The man who has given us so many pages of scientifically precise description now becomes a great dramatic artist, and the dialogue, so exquisitely individualized, so full of pregnant phrases revealing some secret depth in the speaker, so headlong in its energy, is one of the most splendid aspects of his work.

Eugénie Grandet and *Le Père Goriot* both belong to Balzac's early prime. In 1832, with *Le Curé de Tours,* he had first shown with what sustained power he could evoke a characteristic sequence of incidents, a characteristic group of personages, in a provincial town. Appropriately the setting was that of the town in which he was born. In 1833, with *Eugénie Grandet,* he repeated his triumph, with a greater intensity and a more somber mood, but with no loss of simplicity in line. This is the best of his scenes of provincial life. *Le Père Goriot* came a year afterward; written in the summer and early autumn of 1834, it began to appear in the *Revue de Paris* before the year was out, and as a book belonged to the season of 1835. Something of its great dramatic force comes from Balzac's memory of his own early years in Paris, a poor young provincial laden with noble aims and succumbing in his own fashion—which was not Rastignac's—to the seductions of Parisian luxury and Parisian love. He was close enough to his youth to have kept a full imaginative understanding of the appeal in the modes of life which outrage his moral sense. The book is the quintessence of Balzac's vision of the horror of Paris. He himself called it "monstrously sad."

Professor André Le Breton, noting the phrase and the confession that Balzac required weeks to recover from the depression of spirit in which he ended the work, remarks: "In his pictures of the reality of his own age Balzac has equaled the horror in Dante's vision of hell. His characters are demons; they are like Vautrin, the very genius of evil, or like Goriot and a hundred others, those whom passion has damned." Yet they are human still, just as the sufferers in Dante's hell are human. Once set among the scenes of Parisian life, *Goriot* was finally grouped among the scenes of domestic life; and if the retelling of the Lear story has an unquestionable right to a place among the series of domestic tragedies, a study so richly steeped in the atmosphere of the Paris that Balzac loved so much and hated so much ought not to be separated—and in our thought we cannot separate it—from his other disclosures of the city which in a letter of 1844 he named as his only country.

It is a pity to read any master of fiction in a translation, but it is less of a pity with Balzac than with most. He wrote with fevered haste, often for sixteen or eighteen hours at a stretch—from midnight till late the following afternoon; he was desperately put to it to keep pace with the flow of his ideas and impressions; his thought was upon them, and for the language with which he clothed them he usually cared little. When he tried to turn a phrase the outcome was often worse than his worst carelessness. George Moore placed him with Shakespeare, sometimes above Shakespeare, but he declared that it was only when one translated Balzac that one could fully realize his deficiencies. Still, the deficiencies pale and are obscured by the sustained energy of his imagination and the life it imparts so richly to his creatures. We have tried to render him with fidelity; we must have missed some of the nervous force of his dialogue, but in compensation we have tried to untwist some of his sentences, and their meaning will perhaps shine a little more clearly if with less stormy a grandeur.

BIBLIOGRAPHY

EDITIONS

The standard edition is the *Oeuvres Complètes de Honoré de Balzac* (ed. M. Bouteron and H. Longnon), 40 volumes. Paris, Conard, 1910–1940.

The best English translation is *The Comédie Humaine* (ed. G. Saintsbury). Philadelphia, Gebbie, 1899–1900.

BIOGRAPHIES AND INTERPRETATIONS

IN ENGLISH

Benjamin, René: *Balzac*. New York, Knopf, 1927.

Brunetière, Ferdinand: *Honoré de Balzac*. Philadelphia, Lippincott, 1906. This is the best critical book available in English.

Dargan, Edwin P.: *Honoré de Balzac, A Force of Nature*. Chicago, University of Chicago Press, 1932.

Dargan, Edwin P. and Weinberg, Bernard: *The Evolution of Balzac's Comédie Humaine*. Chicago, University of Chicago Press, 1942.

James, Henry: Two essays both entitled "Honoré de Balzac" in *Notes on Novelists*. London, Dent, 1914. Subtly discriminating estimates.

Moore, George: *Conversations in Ebury Street*. New York, Boni and Liveright, 1924. See chapters III and IV, the latter in French.

Royce, William H.: *A Balzac Bibliography*. Chicago, University of Chicago Press, 1929.

Sandars, Mary F.: *Honoré de Balzac, His Life and Writings*. London, Murray, 1904. The best narrative of the life available in English.

Zweig, Stefan: *Balzac*. New York, Viking, 1946.

IN FRENCH

The number of excellent scholarly and critical studies is immense. This list is limited to a few books of general interest.

BIBLIOGRAPHY

Bardèche, Maurice: *Balzac, Romancier*. Paris, Plon, 1947. This profound study of Balzac's fiction up to 1835 is an abridgment of a more erudite work published under the same title in 1940. The final chapter is a close examination of *Le Père Goriot*.

Bellessort, André: *Balzac et Son Oeuvre*. Paris, Perrin, 1924. An excellent supplement to Brunetière's book mentioned above.

Le Breton, André: *Balzac, L'Homme et L'Oeuvre*. Paris, Colin, 1905. A critical account by one of the best historians of the French novel.

PÈRE GORIOT

Translated by E. K. Brown

TO THE GREAT AND ILLUSTRIOUS

GEOFFROY SAINT-HILAIRE

AS AN EXPRESSION OF ADMIRATION

FOR HIS WORKS AND

HIS GENIUS

Honoré de Balzac

MADAME VAUQUER, the former Mademoiselle de Con-flans, is an old woman who for forty years has kept a cheap boarding-house in the Rue Neuve-Sainte-Geneviève, between the Latin Quarter and the Faubourg Saint-Marceau. This boarding-house, known as the *Maison Vauquer,* welcomes both men and women, the old and the young. If no slander had ever attacked the morals of this respectable establishment, it must be con-ceded that no young girl had been seen in it for thirty years, and that if a young man lived there it was because his family assigned him a very meager allowance.

In 1819, however, when our drama begins, a poor young girl was living there. We must use the word *drama* here, despite the discredit into which it has fallen because of the false and distorted manner in which it has been bandied about in these times of gloomy literature. In the strict sense of the term this is not a dramatic story; but before it ends perhaps some tears will have been shed both *intra muros* and *extra.* Will the story be understood outside Paris? It is doubtful. The peculiarities of the scene, abundant in local color and personal notations, can be appreciated only between the hills of Montmartre and the heights of Montrouge, in that famous valley of plaster always on the point of falling, of gutters black with mud; a valley where suf-fering is very real and joy often false, and where life is so ter-ribly agitated that something very extreme is needed to evoke a sensation which lasts beyond the moment. Here and there in

Paris, however, there come to pass agonies to which grandeur and solemnity are imparted by an agglomeration of vices and virtues; at the sight of these the most self-centered pause and feel some pity, although the impression is as transitory as when one eats a delicious fruit quickly.

The chariot of civilization, like Juggernaut's, is barely delayed by some heart which does not break as easily as others, and holds back its wheels; soon the heart is shattered, and the chariot continues its glorious march. And you will do the same, you who hold this volume in a white hand, and, sinking back in a soft armchair, say to yourself: "Perhaps this book is going to entertain me." After you have read of the hidden sorrows of Père Goriot, you will dine with a keen appetite and blame the author for your insensibility, accusing him of poetic exaggeration. Oh, you may be sure that this drama is no work of fiction, no mere novel! It is all true, so true that everyone may recognize its elements within himself, perhaps in his very heart.

The boarding-house belongs to Madame Vauquer. It is situated at the foot of the Rue Neuve-Sainte-Geneviève, where the ground falls away toward the Rue de l'Arbalète with a grade so sharp that horses rarely go up or down the street. This circumstance is conducive to the silence which reigns in these streets confined between the domes of the Val de Grâce and the Panthéon, two monuments which have their effect on the atmosphere, imparting a yellow tone to it and darkening it with the gloomy shadows projected by their cupolas. In these streets the pavement is dry; there is no mud or water in the gutters; grass grows along the walls. The most thoughtless mortal, in common with all the other passers-by, feels the sadness; the noise of a carriage is an event; the houses are somber; the walls make one think of a prison. A Parisian straying through them would see nothing but cheap boarding-houses and institutions, poverty and ennui, old age about to die, happy youth under the curse of hard work.

No quarter in Paris is more horrible, nor, we may add, less known. The Rue Neuve-Sainte-Geneviève, above all, is like a frame of bronze, the only frame appropriate to this story for which the mind cannot be too thoroughly prepared by dark colors and serious ideas; it is like descending into the Catacombs; from step to step the light lessens and the guide's speech sounds more hollow. The comparison is sound. Who shall say which is more horrible to see, empty skulls or dried-up hearts?

The façade of the house fronts on a little garden, so that the building is at right angles to the Rue Neuve-Sainte-Geneviève, from which its depth is visible. Along the façade, between the house and the garden runs a walk six feet wide, paved with cobblestones, and in front of this is a sanded alley, bordered with geraniums, oleanders and pomegranates planted in large vases of blue and white porcelain. You enter the alley by a door over which there is a sign with the words MAISON VAUQUER in large letters and below them in letters of smaller size, *Lodgings for Men and Women, etc.* During the day a door with a noisy bell and a wicket permits a glimpse, at the end of the little walk, of an arch which a craftsman of the quarter painted on the wall opposite the street to simulate green marble. Beneath the recess this painting suggests, there is a statue of Love. In the scaling varnish which covers it, the lover of symbols might perhaps discover a myth of that sort of Parisian love which is cured a few steps from there. Underneath the pedestal there is an inscription half worn away which enables one to date the work of art by the enthusiasm it expresses for Voltaire, who returned to Paris in 1777:

> *Qui que tu sois, voici ton maître,*
> *Il l'est, le fut, ou le doit être.*

At nightfall the door with the wicket gives place to one that is of solid wood. The little garden, as broad as the façade is long, is confined by the street wall and the partition wall of the house next door, along which there is a mantle of ivy that hides it completely, and attracts the eyes of passers-by by an effect which, in Paris, is picturesque. All the walls are covered by trellises and vines. The meager and dusty grapes are the source of annual fears to Madame Vauquer and also of material for conversations with her boarders. Along each wall runs a narrow alley leading to a grove of lindens, a word which Madame Vauquer, despite her noble maiden name obstinately mispronounces in the face of repeated corrections from her guests. Between the two lateral alleys is a square of artichokes flanked by pyramidal fruit trees, and bordered by sorrel, lettuce and parsley. Beneath the lindens there is a round table painted green and surrounded by chairs. There, in the days of the greatest heat, the boarders who are rich enough to treat themselves to coffee come to savor it in a temperature warm enough to hatch eggs. The façade, three stories high with mansards above, is of rough stone, daubed with that yellow which imparts an ignoble character to almost all the houses in Paris. In each story at the front there are five windows with small panes, the blinds drawn up to different heights so that all the lines are at variance. On the sides there are but two windows in each story, and those on the ground floor have the decoration of iron bars. Behind the building is a court about twenty feet square in which rabbits live amicably with pigs and fowls, and at the rear of this is a woodshed. Between this shed and the kitchen window a meat cage is suspended and below it runs a drain for the greasy outpourings from the sink. From the court a narrow door leads into the Rue Neuve-Sainte-Geneviève, and through it the cook sweeps away the garbage, cleansing the drain with great jets of water to avert infections.

Intended by nature to serve as a boarding-house, the Maison Vauquer has on the ground floor a front room which may be entered by a French window, and which has, besides, two other windows facing the street. It adjoins the dining room, which is separated from the kitchen by the staircase, the steps of which are of checkered wood and waxed. Nothing could be more somber than the front room, the salon, where the furniture is covered with horsehair in stripes alternately dull and glossy. In the middle there is a round marble-topped table, with, for ornament, a tea service in white porcelain with half-faded gold bands, of the sort that is to be seen everywhere today. The floor is far from even; the wainscotting rises to elbow-height; and the rest of the wall is hung with a varnished paper representing the principal scenes from *Télémaque,* with the classic personages in color. The panel between the two barred windows exhibits to the guests the feast offered by Calypso to Ulysses' son. For forty years this picture has stimulated the humor of the young boarders who try to forget their poor estate by making fun of the dinners to which it condemns them. The stone mantel, with a fireplace so clean that obviously it is used only on notable occasions, has for ornaments two vases with faded artificial flowers under glass and a blue marble clock in the most atrocious taste.

There is an odor in this room for which the language has no name, and which we must call a boarding-house smell. It is close, mildewed and rancid: it makes one shiver with cold, it makes the nose damp, it penetrates one's clothes; it smells like a room in which dinner has just been eaten: it stinks of the kitchen, the scullery, the hospital. Perhaps it could be described if someone had found the terms for cataloguing the nauseating elements that come forth from the unique catarrhal breaths of all the boarders, young and old.

Well! Despite its being so horrible, if you were to compare this room with the dining room which is next to it, you would think that the drawing room was as elegant and sweet-smelling as a boudoir should be. The dining room, where the walls are paneled to the ceiling, was long ago painted in some color which cannot be discerned today, and is now only a background on which layers of dirt have formed in such a fashion as to present some bizarre designs. The room is surrounded by sticky buffets holding carafes which are dirty and chipped, round mats with a metallic sheen, piles of plates of thick blue-bordered porcelain, manufactured at Tournai. In a corner there is a box with numbered pigeonholes for the stained and spotted napkins of the boarders. The room has those indestructible pieces of furniture, proscribed from every other place, and resting there just as the refuse of humanity come to rest in homes for the incurable. You would see there a barometer with a monk who comes forth when it points to rain, engravings so horrible as to spoil one's appetite and all framed in varnished black wood with gold stripes, a tortoise-shell clock case inlaid with copper, a green stove, Argand lamps, in which dust mixes with oil, and a long table covered with oil cloth so greasy that a merry boarder can write his name on it with the end of his finger. And there are rickety chairs, and little piteous hempen mats which slip away under one's feet but never vanish for good, and broken footwarmers with hinges that no longer work and with their wooden parts burnt away. To explain how old this furniture is, how cracked and rotten and shaky and worn, how deformed, how lopsided, and sick and dying, we should have to embark on a description which would too long delay our start on the story and which hurried readers would not pardon. The red tiles of the floor are full of indentations caused by waxing and painting. In short, this is the kingdom of poverty without poetry: a poverty which is economical, concentrated, threadbare. If it is not yet filthy, it is spotted; if it has not holes and rags, it is about to rot away.

This room is at the height of its splendor when, toward seven o'clock in the morning, Madame Vauquer's cat precedes its mistress, leaps on the sideboards, sniffs at the milk in several bowls covered with plates, and enjoys its morning purr. Soon the widow follows, arrayed in a tulle cap under which is a mass of false hair ill-arranged; as she walks she drags her slippers which have lost their shape. Hers is an oldish, fattish face with a parrot's nose in the center; her plump little hands, her body fat as a church rat's, her prominent pendulous breasts, all are in harmony with this room which is dripping with unhappiness, vacant of all speculation, and full of warm stale air which Madame Vauquer breathes without any sense of disgust.

That face of hers, as nipping as the first autumn frost, those wrinkled eyes, whose expression shifts from the smile required of dancers to the bitter frown of the cashier, indeed her whole person gives the clue to the boarding-house, just as the boarding-house implies such a mistress as Madame Vauquer. You cannot imagine a jail without a jailer. The unhealthy obesity of this little woman is the product of this life of hers, just as typhus fever is the product of the exhalations in a hospital. Her skirt is made of an old dress, and through its rents the wadding projects; beneath it falls her woollen petticoat; and these clothes sum up the drawing room, the dining room, the little garden, explain the kitchen and give an idea of the boarders. The moment she is here, the spectacle is complete.

Madame Vauquer is about fifty years old, and is like all those women who have had a lot of trouble. She has the glassy eye and the innocent air of a procuress who will put on a show of indignation in order to get a better price, but in every other way is capable of anything that will be to her advantage, ready to inform on anyone in hiding. She is all right at bottom, her boarders say, for they believe that she is in difficult circumstances, hearing her groan and cough like themselves. What had Monsieur Vauquer been? His widow never talked about her late husband. How had he lost his fortune? He had had reverses, she said. Toward her he had behaved badly, leaving her only

9

her eyes to weep with, this house to live by, and the right never to sympathize with anyone's misfortunes because, she said, she had suffered everything it was possible to suffer. When she heard her mistress's step, big Sylvie, the cook, hurried to serve breakfast for those of the boarders who lodged in the Maison Vauquer.

Generally the boarders who lived elsewhere took only their dinner at the house, paying thirty francs a month. At the time when this story begins there were seven lodgers. The second floor had the two best apartments in the house. Madame Vauquer lived in the smaller of these, and the other was rented by Madame Couture, the widow of a commissary-general in the time of the Republic. With her she had a very young girl, Victorine Taillefer, to whom she acted as a mother. The bill for these two ladies was eighteen hundred francs a year. The two suites on the third floor were occupied, one by an old man named Poiret, the other by Monsieur Vautrin, a man of about forty who wore a black wig, dyed his whiskers and described himself as a former merchant. On the fourth floor there were four small rooms, two of them occupied steadily, one by an old maid, Mademoiselle Michonneau, the other by a former manufacturer of vermicelli, Italian paste and starch, who let himself be called Père Goriot. The remaining two rooms were kept for birds of passage, for such luckless students as (like Mademoiselle Michonneau and Père Goriot) could scrape together only forty-five francs a month for board and lodging. Madame Vauquer was not much pleased to have students and took them only when she could not do better; they ate too much bread.

At the time which concerns us, one of the two rooms was occupied by a young man from the neighborhood of Angoulême who had come to study law at Paris, and whose large family endured the most severe privations in order to send him twelve hundred francs a year. Eugène de Rastignac, this was his name, was one of those young men whom misfortune has condemned to hard work, who understand in their first youth the hopes that their relatives have set upon them, and who prepare for a great career by calculating the bearing their studies will have upon it and adapting them in advance to the future tendencies of society in order to be among the first to profit by them. Had it not been for his curiosity to observe and the skill with which he was able to secure entrance to the salons of Paris, this tale would have lacked the tones of truth which it will unquestionably owe to his discerning mind and to his wish to fathom the mysteries of a terrible situation, concealed with equal care by those who had created it and by the one who was its victim.

Above this fourth floor was an attic for hanging up the laundry and two rooms with mansard windows, one for Christophe, the man of all work and the other for big Sylvie, the cook.

Besides her seven lodgers Madame Vauquer had year in and year out eight students in law or medicine, and two or three residents of the quarter, who took only their dinners. At dinner there were eighteen at table and there was room for about twenty; but in the morning there were only the seven boarders, and the meal had the air of a family gathering. Everyone came down in slippers and made confidential remarks on the dress or manner of the diners and on the events of the evening before. These seven were Madame Vauquer's spoiled children, and her care and regard for them was in wonderfully exact proportion to the size of their bills. One idea weighed with all these creatures whom chance had brought together. The lodgers on the third floor paid only seventy-two francs a month. Such rates exist only in the Faubourg Saint-Marcel between La Bourbe and the Salpetrière—rates which none but Madame Couture could rise above—and are proof that these lodgers were condemned to carry a load of misfortunes more or less obvious. Accordingly the disheartening spectacle of the appearance of the rooms of the boarding-house was repeated in the costumes of the residents, all of them seedy and worn. The men wore frock coats so faded that their color was doubtful, shoes such as are seen lying in the gutters of the more fashionable districts, linen which had frayed —in a word costumes in which only the idea survived. The women's dresses were out of style, dyed and re-dyed, faded; their old lace had been mended; their gloves had been hardened by long wear; their collars were dingy; and their fichus were frayed. Despite such worn and faded attire, the lodgers had solid frames, bodies which had resisted the storms of life, cold, hard, expressionless faces, resembling coins which have been taken out of circulation. Their ruined mouths were armed with greedy teeth. These boarders gave one a sense of dramas in the past or present—not the sort of dramas played behind the footlights, with a scenic backdrop, but such dramas as belong to the mute reality of life, icy dramas which powerfully stirred the heart, dramas without an end.

Old Mademoiselle Michonneau wore over her weary eyes a dirty shade of green taffeta circled with a thin rim of brass, an object which would have terrified the angel of Pity. Her shawl with its scanty drooping fringe seemed to cover a skeleton; her shape was so angular. What acid had taken away from this creature a woman's contours? Once she must have been pretty and attractive. Was it vice or grief or cupidity? Had she loved too well, had she been a dealer in second-hand clothes, had she been a courtesan? Was she expiating the victories of an insolent youth packed with pleasures by an old age so horrible that passers-by avoided her? Her pallid look was enough to chill you; her shrunken face seemed to express a threat. She had the sharp voice of a grasshopper sounding from a thicket as winter draws on. Her story was that she had looked after an old man suffering from catarrh of the bladder and deserted by his children who believed that he was penniless. This old man had bequeathed to her a pension of a thousand francs which the heirs periodically disputed, assailing her with slanders. Although her face had been disfigured by passions, it retained some vestiges of whiteness and fineness of texture which let one suppose that her body still had some remnants of beauty.

Monsieur Poiret was a kind of machine. Many people wondered if he were not one of the sons of Japhet who flit about the Boulevard des Italiens, as they saw his great length stretch out like a gray shadow in some alley in the Jardin des Plantes, saw his head covered with a shapeless cap, his hand barely able to hold his cane with a knob of yellow ivory, the tails of his frock coat flying behind him and disclosing trousers which seemed to have no flesh within them, his legs encased in blue stockings and staggering like those of a drunken man, his dirty white vest and his crumpled stock inadequately attached to the cravat tightly wound around his thin turkey neck. What sort of work had worn him down to this? What passion had ruined his swollen face, which, had it been a caricature, would have been judged incredible? What had he been? Perhaps he had been a clerk in the Ministry of Justice, in the office where executioners send in their expense accounts, carrying such items as black veils for parricides, grain for the headsman's basket, string for the blades of the guillotine. Perhaps he had stood at the gate of an abattoir, or been a sub-inspector of sanitation. In short, this man seemed to have been one of the donkeys in our great social treadmill, a creature pulling the community's chestnuts out of the fire, a pivot on which the misfortunes and dirtinesses of the people had turned, one of those men of whom it is said when they are seen: Nevertheless we have to have men like that. The handsome side of Paris knows nothing of such faces, pale with moral and physical suffering. But Paris is a veritable ocean. Take as many soundings in it as you will, you will never know its depth. Scour it and describe it with the greatest care you can, no matter how many or how eager its explorers may be, there will always be some unknown cavern, some flowers and pearls and monsters, something unheard of, something forgotten by the literary divers. The Maison Vauquer is one of these curious monstrosities.

Two faces among the boarders formed a striking contrast with the rest. Although Mademoiselle Victorine Taillefer had a white complexion whose unhealthiness resembled that of young girls who suffer from tuberculosis, and moreover had a likeness to the pervading suffering which formed the background of the picture through her habitual sadness, her worried look, her air of poverty and frailness, nevertheless her face was not old; her movements and her voice were quick. This embodiment of youthful misfortune resembled a shrub whose yellowed leaves show that it has just been planted in a soil that does not suit it. With her delicately colored face, her blonde hair and her over-slender figure she was an instance of that grace which modern poets find in the statuettes of the Middle Ages. Her eyes, a gray with some black, expressed Christian sweetness and resignation. Her cheap and simple clothes revealed her youthful contours. By juxtaposition she was pretty. If she had been happy, she would have been captivating; happiness is the poetry of woman, as dress is the ornament. If the happiness of a ball could have given a rosy tint to her pale face; if the charms of an elegant life could have filled out and crimsoned her cheeks already a little sunken; if love could have animated her sad eyes—Victorine would have vied with the most beautiful of girls. She suffered from the lack of what is the second birth of women, fine clothes and love letters. Her story would make a book. Her father considered that there were reasons why he should not admit her legitimacy and refused to have her in his household. He allowed her six hundred francs a year and had rearranged his affairs so that he could leave his entire fortune to his son. Madame Couture was a distant relative of her mother, who had come to her when she was dying of despair. She took care of the girl as if she were her own child. Unfortunately the widow of the commissary of the armies of the Republic had only her dowry and her pension; one day she might leave the poor girl without experience and without resources at the mercy of the world. The good woman took Victorine to mass every Sunday, to confession every second week, in order that she might be sure of the girl's piety. She did well. In the sentiments of religion there was a future for the repudiated child who loved her father and every year went to his house bringing her mother's forgiveness but knocking in vain at a door which was inexorably closed to her. Her brother, her only mediator, had not come to see her once in four years and sent her no help. She would beg God to unseal her father's eyes, to soften her brother's heart, and she prayed for them without accusing them of anything. Madame Couture and Madame Vauquer could not find any word in the dictionary sufficiently insulting to describe such barbarous conduct. When they were cursing the infamous millionaire, Victorine would say something gentle, something which would recall the song of the wounded dove, mingling love with the utterance of pain.

Eugène de Rastignac's face was wholly Southern, with his white complexion, his black hair, his blue eyes. His figure, his manners, his customary demeanor marked him as the son of a noble family and one whose early education had been entirely in the traditions of good taste. If he spared his clothes, if on ordinary days he finished wearing out his last year's garments, he could nevertheless go out now and then dressed like an elegant young man. Usually he wore an old frock coat, an ugly vest, a miserably worn, badly knotted student's black tie, trousers in keeping with such a costume, and resoled boots.

Intermediate between these two and the rest, Vautrin, a man

15

of forty with dyed whiskers, served as a sort of link. He was one of those about whom the man in the street will say: "There's a real fellow!" His shoulders were broad, his chest deep, his muscles conspicuous, his hands thick, square and strikingly marked by red hair on his fingers; his face, seamed by premature lines, gave an impression of hardness which was contradicted by his yielding and supple manners. His deep voice which harmonized with his virile gaiety was not displeasing. He was helpful and given to laughter. If there was trouble with some lock, he would quickly take it to pieces, fix it, oil it, and put it back in place, saying: "I know about that sort of thing." He knew about many other sorts of things, ships, the sea, France, foreign countries, business, men, current events, laws, hotels and prisons. If anyone complained forcefully, he at once offered to help. Many times he had made a loan to Madame Vauquer and to some of the boarders; but his debtors would have died rather than fail to repay the loans, such fear did he inspire, despite his genial air, by a certain deep look which was full of determination. Even in the way he spit he disclosed an imperturbable coolness which would not prevent him from engaging in crime if it would help him out of an equivocal position. His eyes were like those of a severe judge in penetrating to the heart of every matter, of every conscience, of every feeling.

It was his custom to go out after breakfast, to come back for dinner and then to spend the whole evening elsewhere, returning toward midnight and letting himself in with a key which Madame Vauquer had permitted him to keep. He alone had this favor. Further, he was on the best of terms with the widow, whom he used to call "Mama" as he seized her by the waist, an attention it was hard to estimate! Madame Vauquer thought this was an easy thing to do, but the truth is that only Vautrin had arms long enough to go round that heavy circle. One of his peculiarities was to pay liberally for the brandy he took in his coffee at dessert. People less superficial than young boys and girls caught up in the whirlwind of Paris or old folk indifferent to anything that had no direct bearing on their own concerns would have not been content with the doubtful impression that Vautrin made upon them. He knew or surmised the business of those around him while no one could grasp what were his thoughts and concerns. Although he had projected his apparent good nature and his constant consideration for others as a barrier between himself and the world, he would suddenly display the terrible depth of his character. Often he would utter some slashing sentence worthy of Juvenal, in which he appeared to trample on the law, castigate high society, convict it of self-contradiction; and it might have been supposed that he had some rancor against society and that at the bottom of his life there was a carefully buried mystery.

Attracted, perhaps without knowing it, by Rastignac's good looks and by Vautrin's strength, Mademoiselle Taillefer divided her stolen glances and her secret thoughts between them; neither of them, however, seemed to give her a thought, although any day might mark a change in her position and make her a wealthy girl. None of the boarders, however, took the trouble to discover whether the misfortunes the others claimed to have suffered were genuine or mere pretense. They all had for one another that distrust mingled with indifference which arose from their own particular situations. They knew that they could not assuage their own griefs, and they had told them so often that they had exhausted what condolences their companions could offer. Like old married couples they had nothing more to say to one another. All that remained to connect them was the mechanical process of life, and the mechanism operated without oil. They would all have walked right past a blind man standing in their path in the street; they would have listened unmoved to a tale of misfortune; and would have seen in death the solution to a problem of poverty which left them cold to the most terrible agony.

The happiest of these ruined souls was Madame Vauquer, who sat on the throne of this private almshouse. For her alone the little garden, made large and lonely as a steppe by silence and cold, drought and dampness, was a smiling dell. For her alone this gloomy yellow house, smelling of the counter, offered delight and joy. She fed these criminals condemned to life imprisonment, and wielded over them a recognized authority. Where in Paris would these wretched beings have found at so low a price healthy and sufficient food and rooms which were clean and healthy if neither comfortable nor elegant? If she had had a fancy to perform some action of striking injustice, the victim would have bowed beneath it without uttering a complaint.

Such an assemblage was bound to offer and did offer a microcosm of a whole social world. Among the eighteen diners there was, just as there always is in schools, as there always is in the world, one butt, one victim upon whose head the railleries fell. At the beginning of his second year at the boarding-house, Eugène de Rastignac found that this being became for him the most striking of all those among whom he was condemned to pass two more years. This was Père Goriot, the former manufacturer of vermicelli upon whose head a painter, like the present narrator, would concentrate the light in his picture. By what chance had such contempt which was half hatred, such persecution mingled with pity, such indifference to misery, fallen on the oldest of the boarders? Had he aroused such feelings by some of those ridiculous ways, some of those eccentricities which are pardoned less often than vices? Such questions as these are essential in many cases of social injustice. Perhaps it is part of human nature to make a being suffer if, whether from genuine humility, or from weakness, or from indifference, he will endure all. Do not we all like to prove our strength at the expense of someone or something? The weakest of creatures, the street urchin, will ring all the doorbells when the weather is cold, or will clamber up to defile a pure monument by writing his name on it.

Goriot, almost seventy, had retired to Madame Vauquer's establishment in 1813, after he had given up his business. At first he lived in the apartment now occupied by Madame Couture, and paid twelve hundred francs a year as befitted a man to whom a few francs more or less was a trifle. Madame Vauquer had done over the three rooms of which the apartment consisted, in consideration of a down payment sufficient, it was said, to cover the cost of yellow calico curtains, wooden armchairs covered with Utrecht velvet, a few cheap pictures, and wall-paper which was too ugly for suburban cafés. Perhaps the thoughtless liberality which Père Goriot showed in letting himself be taken in—and this at a time when he was still respectfully addressed as Monsieur Goriot—led her to set him down for an imbecile who had no practical sense.

Goriot brought with him a splendid wardrobe, the magnificent outfit of a man who, retiring from business, denies himself nothing. Madame Vauquer admired his eighteen shirts with cambric fronts, whose fineness of texture was the more extraordinary since Goriot wore on his frill two pins each with a large diamond and connected by a chain. His usual costume was a blue coat, with every day a fresh vest of white piqué, beneath which his huge paunch swelled out and tossed back and forth a heavy gold chain with trinkets. His snuff box was also of gold and held a medallion with locks of hair, giving him the air of a man who had had a number of loves. When his hostess accused him of being a lady's man, he displayed the joyous smile of a bourgeois whose weakness has been caressed. The chests in his room were filled with the quantity of silver he had amassed for his household. The widow's eyes shone as she helped him unpack and arrange the soup-ladles, tablespoons, forks and knives, cruets, sauce dishes, plates and breakfast services, in short a multitude of silver pieces, some of them prettier than others, but all weighing a substantial amount, and too attractive to him for separation to be possible. They recalled to him the great occasions of his family life. "This," he would say, to Madame Vauquer, gripping a plate and a porringer on whose cover there were two billing doves, "was the first present my wife ever gave me; it was the day of our anniversary. Poor dear, she spent all she had saved before our marriage. You know, I would rather grub in the earth and break my nails than give that up. Thank God, I can take my coffee in this porringer every morning for the rest of my life. I have nothing to complain of; I won't starve for a long time to come."

Madame Vauquer had seen with those magpie eyes of hers some Government bonds which, loosely added up, pointed to an income of from eight to ten thousand francs for the worthy old man. From the day she saw those figures, the former Mademoiselle de Conflans, who was actually forty-eight and admitted to thirty-nine, began to have ideas. Although the lower rims of Goriot's eyes were swelled and hung down, and he so often had to wipe away the water, she thought he had an agreeable and proper appearance. Moreover, his fleshy and prominent calves and his long square nose appeared to hint at certain moral qualities by which the widow seemed to set great value, and these were confirmed by the moonlike and innocently foolish face of the old fellow. He was, she considered, a beast of solid substance, who would express himself in bursts of feeling. His hair, elaborately dressed—the barber from the École Polytechnique came to powder it every morning—fell over his low brow in five points, and supplied a fine frame for his face. If he was a little of a boor, he was so neatly dressed and took his snuff with such lavishness, sniffing it as if he were a man who would always have a plentiful supply of the best sort in his case, that from the very day that he came to live at her place Madame Vauquer would go to bed burning with eagerness to leave off her widow's weeds and begin a new life as Madame Goriot.

To marry, to sell her boarding-house, to walk arm in arm with this rich and model bourgeois, to become an important woman in the quarter, to go soliciting funds for the poor, to fare forth on little Sunday parties to Choisy, Soissy, and Gentilly, to have a box at the theatre when the mood was on her, and no longer wait for the complimentary tickets which some of her guests would hand to her in the off season—she dreamed the full gamut of the desires of a petty bourgeoise of Paris. She had never confessed to anyone that she had saved up penny by penny the sum of forty thousand francs. With that she could well think she was an eligible choice, in fortune at least. "And as to the rest, I am as good as the old fellow," she would say to herself as she tossed in her bed as if to prove to herself what a fine figure she had—a figure which big Sylvie could read the next morning molded in the bed.

For about three months, Madame Vauquer made use of the barber who came for Goriot and spent some money on her attire, justifying these outlays as necessary if she was to be in harmony with the honorable persons who now frequented her house. She made many plots to improve the quality of her guests, making much display of her claim that henceforth she would take in only those who were most distinguished from every point of view. When anyone called in search of accommodation, she would boast of the preference given her house by Monsieur Goriot, one of the most estimable and notable merchants in Paris. She distributed advertising slips, at the top of the page: MAISON VAUQUER, and below: "One of the oldest and most esteemed boarding-houses in the Latin Quarter, with a most delightful view over the valley of the Gobelins [visible from the third floor] and a *pretty* garden leading to a beautiful ALLEY of lindens." There were references to the healthy air and the quiet.

This advertising brought to the house the Countess d'Ambermesnil, a woman of thirty-six who was waiting until she should receive the pension due her as widow of a general who had died on the *fields* of battle. Madame Vauquer took pains with her menus, lit fires in the downstairs rooms for almost six months, and lived up to her advertising to the point that she was really *drawing on capital*. Thus it came about that the countess told her, calling her "my dear friend," that she would bring to her the Baroness de Vaumerland and the widow of a colonel, Count Picquoiseau, two of her friends whose term at a boarding-house in the Marais quarter, more expensive than Madame Vauquer's, was about to end. These ladies, moreover, would be in easy circumstances when the War Office had dealt with their cases "But," she added, "the War Office is dreadfully slow." After dinner the two widows would go up to Madame Vauquer's room to have a little chat, a glass of cassis and some delicacies that did not appear in the dining room but were for the mistress's private pleasure. The Countess d'Ambermesnil warmly approved of Madame Vauquer's designs on Goriot, excellent designs which she had, indeed, discerned the first day she was in the house; she thought him perfect.

"Ah, my dear," she would say to Madame Vauquer, "such a healthy man, a man who has kept his full strength and can still give a great deal of pleasure to a woman."

The countess abounded in remarks on Madame Vauquer's dress, which she found out of keeping with her aspirations. "You must go on a wartime footing," she told her. After much calculation the two of them went off together to the Palais Royal, where they bought a feathered hat and a bonnet. At another shop, to which the countess led her, Madame Vauquer chose a scarf and a dress. When these munitions were brought out and Madame Vauquer came forth arrayed for battle, she resembled nothing so much as the sign at the Boeuf-à-la-Mode restaurant. Nonetheless she thought her appearance was so much improved that she felt she owed the countess something, and although not much of a giver, she pressed on her a hat which cost twenty francs. The fact is that she was planning to ask her a favor; the countess was to sound Goriot out and praise Madame Vauquer to him. She agreed to do this in the friendliest spirit, and bearded the old manufacturer in the course of a conversation she succeeded in having with him; but when she found him shy, if not actually indeed repelled, when she tried to seduce him for her own purposes, she left him claiming that his coarseness had disgusted her.

"You will get nothing, darling," she told her dear friend, "from that man. He is absurdly suspicious, nothing more than a miser, a brute, a fool, who will bring you only grief."

What had gone on between Monsieur Goriot and the countess made the lady unwilling to associate with him. The next day she left, forgetting to pay for the six months' board and lodging she had enjoyed, and leaving a cast-off dress valued at five francs. Madame Vauquer made a thorough search for her, but nowhere in Paris could she find out anything concerning the Countess d'Ambermesnil. She would often speak of this sad business, lamenting her trustful nature, although she was more suspicious than a cat; the truth was that like many another she was distrustful of her neighbors and yet easily taken in by a casual acquaintance. This is a moral fact which may seem queer but is authentic, and its root in the human heart is easy to see. Perhaps one may have nothing more to gain from the people with whom one lives; to them the emptiness of the heart has been shown and by them silently judged, one feels, with the severity it deserves. But there is a need for the flattery which they do not offer, or there is a longing to appear to possess the qualities that one does not have; and so one hopes to win the regard or the affection of strangers, despite the risk of losing it some day. In short, there are mercenary folk who do nothing for neighbor or friend because to do so would be a matter of obligation and yet they will do a service for someone not known to them because to do so feeds their sense of self-satisfaction. The nearer their friends are, the less they love them; the less the friendship, the more ready are they to help. Madame Vauquer no doubt had something of both faults, both essentially petty, false and hateful.

"If I had been here," Vautrin would say to her, "this misfortune would have not happened. I should have unmasked that rascally countess without mercy. I know their tricks."

Like all narrow-minded folk, Madame Vanquer kept to the little circle of facts and made no effort to discriminate their causes. She liked to blame others for her own faults. When she suffered the loss that has been mentioned she considered that the worthy manufacturer was the source of her misfortune and began at once to see him, as she used to say, without illusions. When she realized that all her tricks and expenditures were useless, she was quick in surmising the reason. She saw that, to use her expression, her guest had his own ideas. In short she considered it proved that the hope she had cherished with such care rested on a basis of complete unreality, and that, as the countess had said —a woman who must have been a connoisseur—she would get nothing at all from that man. Inevitably her aversion was greater than her friendship, which it replaced; her hatred was not in proportion to her love, but to her disappointed hopes. If the heart of man rests now and then as it climbs the heights of affection, it seldom stops in its course down the slopes of hatred.

Still Monsieur Goriot was her lodger, and the widow had to bottle up the explosions of wounded pride, bury the sighs caused by the disappointment, and swallow the longings for revenge, like a monk harassed by his prior. Little minds find satisfaction for their feelings, good or bad, in little things. The widow set to work all her feminine malice to invent quiet means of persecuting her victim. She began by withdrawing all the extras she had recently introduced into her boarding-house. "No more pickles, no more anchovies," she told Sylvie the morning when she returned to her former regimen. "A pack of nonsense, that's what they are!"

Monsieur Goriot was frugal; in him the parsimony which is inevitable in people who have made their own fortune had deteriorated into mere custom. His favorite dinner had always been, and would always be, soup, boiled meat and vegetables. Since it was impossible to annoy a man whose tastes were so simple, Madame Vauquer found it difficult to torment Goriot. In her despair at finding that she had to do with an impregnable character, she set to work making light of him, and thus brought her boarders to share her aversion to Goriot, and for the fun of it, to co-operate in her plans of revenge.

Toward the end of his first year of residence, the widow's suspicions of him had grown to the point that she was disturbed by the fact that a merchant with an income of seven or eight thousand livres a year, to say nothing of superb silver and jewels as fine as those of a kept woman, should be a guest in her house, paying her so small a sum in comparison to his fortune. During the greater part of that year Goriot often dined out once or twice in the week; later, little by little, his dining out fell to twice a month. It was so much to Madame Vauquer's interest that her guest should be absent that the progressive decline in his dining out was noted by her with dissatisfaction. These changes in his habits were attributed equally to a slow decrease in his funds and to a desire to vex his landlady. One of the most detestable habits of Lilliputian minds is to find their own littleness in others.

Unfortunately, at the end of his second year, Monsieur Goriot gave support to the chatter about him by asking Madame Vauquer to move him to the floor above, and to reduce his rent to nine hundred francs. He was now so rigidly economical that he lit no fire in his room during the winter. The widow demanded payment in advance, and this was agreed to by Monsieur Goriot, whom she hereafter called Père Goriot. The reason for his impoverishment was left to surmise; it was difficult to fathom. As the pseudo-countess had said, Goriot was a sly and secretive fellow. In the opinion of empty heads, who talk freely of everything that concerns them since their own affairs are such trifles, anyone who does not talk about his is silent because he has something to hide. The once-distinguished merchant was now a rascal; the old dandy was now an old scamp. One of the fairy tales, put in circulation by Vautrin who came to live at the boarding-house toward this period, represented Père Goriot as one who was always at the Stock Exchange and now was dabbling in the market after ruining himself with speculations. Another story was that he was a petty gambler who risked and won eighteen francs in an evening's play. Another represented him as a spy of the special police; but Vautrin claimed he was not shrewd enough to be one of *them*. Or else Goriot was a usurer who lived by making short-term loans, or else a fanatical follower of the lotteries. In short, he was described as everything mysterious that vice, shame or impotence can produce. But however ignoble his conduct or his vices might be judged, the aversion he inspired was never quite enough for him to be asked to leave: he paid his rent. Besides, it was convenient to have him; everyone could use him as the butt of jests or horseplay.

The most probable of all the stories about him was Madame

Vauquer's, and it found general acceptance. Her view was that this old man who had kept so much of his strength, who was so extraordinarily healthy, and who could still provide a woman with a great deal of satisfaction, was a libertine with perverted tastes. Here are the facts on which she supported her slander. A few months after the countess, who had proved to be such a disaster by living off Madame Vauquer for six months, had vanished, one morning, before the mistress of the house got up, she heard on the stairs the rustle of a silk dress and the light step of a young and frivolous woman who was sneaking up to Goriot's room, the door of which he had opened, doubtless by arrangement. Big Sylvie at once came to tell her mistress that a girl who was too pretty to be respectable, dressed like a goddess, with leather slippers which had no mud on them had slid into her kitchen like an eel and had inquired which was Monsieur Goriot's room. Madame Vauquer and Sylvie listened behind the door and overheard some words uttered in an affectionate tone in the course of the visit which lasted a considerable time. When Monsieur Goriot saw his "lady friend" to the door big Sylvie at once picked up her basket, and so that she might follow the loving couple into the street pretended that she was going to market.

"Madame," she said, on her return, "Monsieur Goriot must be devilishly rich, all the same, to keep them in such style. You won't believe that at the corner of the Rue de l'Estrapade there was a grand carriage in which *that woman* went away."

During dinner Madame Vauquer got up to draw a curtain, so that the sun should not continue to shine in Goriot's eyes.

"Beautiful women love you, Monsieur Goriot, and the sun seeks you out," she said, making an allusion to the visit he had had that morning. "No one can deny you have good taste; she was really pretty."

"It was my daughter," said Goriot, with a sort of pride which the boarders interpreted as the silliness of an old man, keeping up appearances.

A month after this visit Monsieur Goriot had another. His daughter who had before come in street dress, this time came after dinner, dressed for a party. The boarders, who were talking in the drawing room, could see that she was beautiful, blonde, slender, graceful, and much too distinguished to be a daughter of Goriot's.

"That makes two!" said big Sylvie, who did not recognize her.

A few days afterwards another girl came, tall and dark, with black hair, darting eyes and a fine figure. She too asked for Monsieur Goriot.

"And that makes three," said Sylvie.

This second girl who had the first time come in the morning, as the other had done, came a few days later in the evening, and when she got out of her carriage it was seen that she was dressed for the ball.

"That makes four!" said Madame Vauquer and big Sylvie, who could not find in this great lady any trace of the simply dressed girl who had paid a morning visit.

Goriot was still paying twelve hundred francs a year for board and lodging. To Madame Vauquer it seemed perfectly natural that a rich man should have four or five mistresses, and she even admired Goriot's cunning in passing them off as his daughters. She was not outraged by his giving them rendezvous at her establishment. Her only comment upon the visits, which explained her lodger's indifference to his landlady, was in her calling him, from the beginning of the second year, an old rip. But when his bill had dwindled to nine hundred francs, one day seeing one of the ladies getting out of her carriage, she asked him in a very insolent way what he took her house for. Goriot replied that this lady was his elder daughter.

"I suppose you have thirty-six daughters?" said Madame Vau-quer sharply.

"I have only two," the lodger replied with the gentleness of a man whose ruin is so complete that he has accepted all the humiliations of poverty.

Toward the end of the third year, Père Goriot cut his expenses even further, moving to the top floor and paying only forty-five francs a month. He abandoned snuff, ceased to have his barber call, and gave up powdering his hair. The first time that he appeared without powder, the landlady could not repress a cry of astonishment, for his hair was of a dirty greenish-gray color. His face, which had been imperceptibly saddened from day to day by his secret grief, seemed the most desolate of all those gathered about the table. Doubt was no longer possible. Goriot was an old libertine whose eyes had been saved from the effects of the medicines his diseases required only by a doctor's skill. The nauseating color of his hair was the consequence of his excesses and of the drugs he was obliged to take in order to continue them. The mental and physical state of the old man served to confirm such gossip. When he had used up the outfit with which he had come to the boarding-house, he replaced his fine linen with the cheapest calico. One by one his diamonds, his gold snuff box, his chain, his jewels disappeared. No longer did he wear a blue frock coat, or anything of value or charm; winter and summer he wore a frock coat of rough chestnut-colored fabric, a goatskin vest, and thick gray trousers. He became thinner and thinner; his calves lost their curves; his face which had had the plump look of a happy bourgeois became almost unbelievably wrinkled; his forehead had new lines; the contour of his jaw became prominent. During his fourth year in the Rue Neuve-Sainte-Geneviève he was unrecognizable.

The worthy manufacturer of sixty-two who had seemed less than forty, the round fat bourgeois, so foolishly joyous, whose gay appearance had entertained those who met him in the street, who had kept something youthful in his smile, now seemed to be a septuagenarian, torpid, confused, and unsure of himself. Those blue eyes of his which had had so much life in them were now a dull iron gray; they were pale; they did not water any longer; but their red rims seemed to carry tears of blood. Some were filled with horror when they looked at him; others with pity. Young medical students noticing that his lower lip hung down, and measuring the height of his facial angle, pronounced that he was becoming a cretin; but however long they ragged him he made no reply.

One evening after dinner, Madame Vauquer said to him merely as raillery, "Well, well! Your daughters don't come to see you any more, eh?" implying that she did not believe that the relationship was a family one. Goriot started as if he had been stabbed.

"They come sometimes," he replied in a voice full of feeling.

"Ah, ha," shouted the students, "so you still see them sometimes. Bravo, Père Goriot."

The old man did not hear the jests which his reply had prompted, for he had already relapsed into that meditative frame of mind which those who observed him only superficially regarded as senile torpor. If they had really known him, they would perhaps have had a keen interest in the problem presented by his moral and physical condition. But nothing was more difficult than to know Goriot in that way. It would have been easy, to be sure, to learn that he had really manufactured vermicelli, and what the exact figures of his fortune were, but the old folk in the boarding-house who were curious about him never left the quarter and lived in the house as oysters live on a rock. The younger guests, because of the pace of Parisian life, forgot the old man whom they made fun of the moment they left the Rue Neuve-Sainte-Geneviève. For those whose minds were narrow, as for those who had the carelessness of youth, the colorless poverty of Père Goriot and his blank manner were incompatible with any sort of ability or fortune. Concerning the women whom he called his daughters everyone agreed with Madame Vauquer, who said with the strict logic natural in old women who develop the habit of making all sorts of inferences because they spend all their evenings in gossip: "If Père Goriot had daughters as rich as the ladies who have come to see him appear to be, he would not be living in one room on my top floor, paying only forty-five francs a month for board and lodging and wearing the clothes of a poor man." And there was nothing to disprove these inferences.

At the end of November, 1819, when this drama burst into action, the whole company in the boarding-house had the most definite ideas about the poor old man. He had never had wife or child; his sinful excesses had made a poor limpet of him, an anthropomorphic mollusk who should be classed in the genus of cap-wearers, in the phrase of an employee at the Museum who took his dinners there regularly. Poiret was a fighting cock, a gentleman, in comparison with Goriot. Poiret had the powers of speech, reason and reply; to be sure his speech, his reasoning, and his replies amounted to nothing, for it was his way to repeat in different terms what had been said to him; but he did contribute to the conversation, he was alive, he appeared to have his senses; while Père Goriot, to quote the employee at the Museum once more, was always at the temperature of zero.

Eugène de Rastignac had come back to the boarding-house in a state of mind familiar to all young men with ability or with those qualities above the ordinary which can be induced for a period by a difficult situation. During his first year in Paris he had found that the early stages of work in the Faculty of Law were so easy that he was able to enjoy at leisure the tangible pleasures of Paris. Indeed a student can make good use of all his

31

time in getting to know the repertoires at all the theatres, studying the entrances and exits in the labyrinth of the town, acquainting himself with its social usages, learning its peculiar language and accustoming himself to its peculiar pleasures, searching out the haunts of virtue and of vice, attending the interesting courses, making his way through the wealth of the museums. . . . At this stage a student will become excited with follies which will seem great and splendid to him. He has his own special great man, a professor at the Collège de France, whose salary is paid on the understanding that he shall grip his audience. He straightens his tie and strikes a pose to impress women, in the first gallery of the Opèra Comique. By dint of a series of such initiations, the young man removes his husk, broadens his horizon, and finally comes to understand the stratification of society. He begins by admiring the carriages which pass along the Champs Elysées, and before long he craves a part in the procession.

Eugène had in an unconscious way undergone such an apprenticeship before he left for his vacation after graduating as bachelor of arts and bachelor of law. His childish and provincial illusions had disappeared. The change in his point of view and the spur to his ambition which came of his year in Paris gave him the power to see matters as they really were in his family and their manor. On their small estate lived his father and mother, two brothers and two sisters and an aunt whose sole resource was an annuity. The property brought in about three thousand francs a year, subject to the uncertain fortunes of the wine trade; and from this small sum twelve hundred francs had to be painfully set aside for him. The sight of their constant indigence, solicitously hidden from him, the comparisons he could not refrain from making between his sisters who had in his childhood seemed so beautiful and the women of Paris, who were the realization of a type of beauty he had merely dreamed of, the hazardous future of this large family which depended upon him, the sparing hand with which he saw the cheapest produce used, the wine for family consumption made from the dregs of the press—in short a mass of facts, unnecessary to detail here, multiplied tenfold his longing to win success and gave him a thirst to achieve distinction. As is the way with magnanimous spirits, he did not wish to owe his advance to anything but his own merit. But his temper was intensely Southern; and so in carrying out his plans he was inevitably affected by those hesitations which seize on young men when they are launched and do not know into what quarter they should sail, or how to make port. His first idea was to give himself wholly to hard work; then, appreciating how necessary social connections were, he noticed how great was the influence of women, and decided to make his way into fashionable society so that he might find among its members women who would help him to a career. He did not think that he could fail of winning such friends, since he had wit and ardor, and in addition an elegant appearance and that sort of tense good looks so attractive to them.

These ideas beset him as he wandered through the fields in the walks which he took so gaily with his sisters. They found him deeply altered since his stay in Paris. His aunt Madame de Marcillac had once lived there; she had been presented at court; and she had moved on the very heights of aristocratic society. The ambitious young man suddenly appreciated that in the reminiscences which his aunt had so often rehearsed to him there were the elements for many social victories at least as important to him as any that he might win in the Faculty of Law; so he questioned her about the family connections to which he might appeal and thus reopen relationships after so long an interval. She shook out the branches of the genealogical tree and considered that among all the rich relatives who might be able to help her nephew, the least refractory of the selfish tribe would be the Viscountess de Beauséant. To this young woman she wrote a letter in the old-fashioned manner, and giving it to Eugène told him that success with the viscountess would lead to success with his other relatives. A few days after his return to Paris, Rastignac sent his aunt's letter to the viscountess; and she replied by inviting him to a ball the next evening.

Such was the general situation of the boarding-house at the end of November, 1819. A few days later, after a ball at the Beauséant mansion, Eugène came in about two in the morning. To make up for the time he had lost, the courageous student had made up his mind while he was dancing that he would work till morning. This was the first time that he would pass the night in this way in the midst of the silent quarter. The sight of the splendors of society had cast on him the spell of a factitious energy. He had not dined in. And the boarders might well think that he would not return from the ball until dawn, for he had sometimes come in as late as that from the Prado or the Odéon, with his silk stockings muddied and his dancing shoes stretched out of shape.

Before barring the door, Christophe had looked out into the street and Rastignac had come along at just that moment, and could thus go up to his room without making any noise, followed by Christophe who made a good deal. Eugène undressed, put on his house slippers, and a miserable old frock coat, lit his fire and light-heartedly got ready for work, and all so quietly that Christophe's loud steps blotted out whatever little noise he made. For a few moments before plunging into his law books, Eugène remained pensive. In the Viscountess de Beauséant he had just recognized one of the queens of Paris fashion, and the woman whose house was regarded as the most delightful in the Faubourg Saint-Germain. Besides, by her name and fortune she was one of the leaders of aristocratic society. Thanks to his aunt at home, the poor student had been kindly welcomed, without appreciating how great was the favor which had been extended to him. To be admitted to the gilded drawing rooms of the Beauséants was the same thing as having high titles of nobility. By appearing in this society, exclusive beyond all others, he had won the right to go anywhere. Dazzled by the brilliant gathering, after a very brief interchange with the viscountess, Eugène had been content with singling out from the mass of Parisian goddesses in this assembly a woman who was among those a young man must worship from the first moment.

The Countess Anastasie de Restaud was tall and her figure so beautiful that it was thought to be among the best in Paris. Imagine large black eyes, a magnificently beautiful hand, a shapely foot, movements full of fire, a woman whom the Marquis de Ronquerolles had described as a "thoroughbred." Being high strung had not robbed her of any physical charm; her figure was beautifully rounded, without being too full. "Thoroughbred" and "high stepper" were the expressions which were now taking the place of "adorable angels," "women of Ossian," and all the old-fashioned mythology of love which dandyism was rejecting. For Rastignac the Countess de Restaud was simply the desirable woman. He had contrived to write his name twice on the list of partners on her fan, and during the first quadrille he had been able to talk to her. "Where am I to see you from now on, Madame?" he had said to her abruptly, with that strong passion which is so pleasing to women. "Why, in the Bois de Boulogne, at the Théâtre des Bouffons, at my home, everywhere," she replied.

The adventurer from the south had sought to make as swift progress with this delightful countess as a young man can make with a woman in the course of a waltz and a quadrille. Since he was able to say that he was a cousin of the Viscountess de Beauséant, this woman, whom he mistook for a great lady, invited him to call when he would. Her parting smile made Ras-

tignac consider that he could not fail to pay a visit. He had had
the good fortune to meet a man who had not made sport of his
ignorance, as brilliant, impudent men of fashion would infallibly
have done, men such as Maulincourt, Ronquerolles, Maxime de
Trailles, de Marsay, Adjuda-Pinto, Vandenesse, who were all
there in the glory of their smug folly, mingling with the most
elegant women of the time, Lady Brandon, the Duchess de
Langeais, the Countess de Kergarouët, Madame de Sérizy, the
Duchess de Carigliano, the Countess Ferraud, Madame de Lanty,
the Marchioness d'Aiglemont, Madame Firmiani, the Marchioness de Listomère, the Marchioness d'Espard, the Duchess de
Maufrigneuse, and the Grandlieus. Happily for him the inex-
perienced student had fallen in with the Marquis de Montriveau,
the lover of the Duchess de Langeais, a general with the simplicity
of a child, who told him that the Countess de Restaud lived in the
Rue du Helder.

Oh, to be young, to be eager to move in the world of fashion,
to desire a woman, to find two houses opening before one, to set
foot in the Faubourg Saint-Germain in the mansion of the Viscountess de Beauséant, and also in the Chaussée d'Antin in the
Countess de Restaud's, to penetrate at the first trial into the
drawing rooms of Paris! To think that one is fine-looking enough
to win the aid and protection of a woman, to feel in oneself such
ambition that one can take a turn on the tightrope on which one
must walk with the assurance of a gymnast who does not think
it possible that he might fall, and to have found in a charming
woman the best of balancing rods!

It was with such thoughts as these and with the image of such
a woman rising from his miserable fire, between the Code
Napoleon and the evidences of his poverty that Eugène—could
he have done otherwise?—was dreaming of the future and his
dream was full of triumphs.

His wandering thoughts gave such solidity to his future joys that he believed himself actually with the Countess de Restaud, when a sigh, deep enough to have been a death rattle, disturbed the silence of the night and the dreams of the youth. He opened his door quietly, and as soon as he stood in the hall he could see light shining under Goriot's. In the fear that his neighbor was ill, he peered through the keyhole, and saw the old man engaged in an activity that seemed so criminal he thought he would be performing a duty to society if he found out as much as he could of what the old man was contriving in the dead of the night. He must have begun fastening to the cross bar of a table, which he had placed upside down, a silver plate and porringer, and now he was pressing on these richly ornamented objects with a sort of cable, pressing with such enormous strength that he was twisting them out of their original shapes, no doubt with the idea of converting them into ingots. "What a powerful fellow!" thought Rastignac at the sight of the muscular arms of the old man who with only a cord could noiselessly mold that silver as if it were mere paste. Could he be a thief or a receiver, for the greater freedom in carrying on his trade pretending to be stupid and weak, and living like a beggar? This was Eugène's thought as he rose for a moment from the keyhole. He put his eye to it again. Père Goriot had now unrolled the cord, and, taking the mass of silver, stretched out his counterpane on the table and placed the silver upon it. There he rolled the silver into the shape of a bar, an operation in which he succeeded with marvelous facility. "Can he be as strong as King Augustus of Poland?" Eugène wondered as the bar became almost perfectly round. But Père Goriot was looking at his work with sad eyes; tears began to fall; he blew out the miserable candle by whose light he had refashioned the silver; and Eugène heard him going to bed sighing.

"He is mad," thought the student.

"Poor child!" Père Goriot said aloud.

Hearing this, Eugène thought it best to say nothing about this incident, and not to condemn his neighbor without reflection. He was just about to go back to his room when he heard a sudden noise, difficult to put into words, the sort of noise that might have been made by men going upstairs in felt shoes. Eugène pricked up his ears, and could distinguish the sounds of two men breathing. Without his hearing either the opening of a door or the steps of the men, he could then see a little light from Monsieur Vautrin's room on the floor below. "This is all very mysterious for a respectable boarding-house," he reflected. He went down a few steps and as he listened he could hear the sound of gold. Soon the light was put out, and again without a sound from the door two people drawing breath could be heard at once. Then as the men went downstairs the sound grew fainter and fainter.

"Who's there?" Madame Vauquer cried out, opening the window of her room.

"It's only I coming home, Mama Vauquer," said Vautrin in his deep tones.

"This is odd," thought Eugène. "Christophe had slid the bolts." He went back into his room, thinking that one must sit up at night to know exactly what is going on, if one lives in Paris. These little incidents had distracted him from his ambitiously amorous meditations, and he set to work. But the suspicions Père Goriot had aroused were a distraction; the image of the Countess de Restaud was a more powerful distraction, suggesting from time to time that she was the harbinger of a brilliant future. So he ended by going to bed and sleeping heavily. More than half of the nights that young men plan on giving to work, are given to sleep. One must be more than twenty to be able to sit up.

On the following morning there was one of those thick fogs which envelop and hide the city so thoroughly that the most punctual people are deceived about time. Business appointments are not kept. Everyone thinks it is only eight o'clock when it is full noon. It was nine-thirty and Madame Vauquer was not stirring. Christophe and big Sylvie had got up late and were quietly taking their coffee in which they had poured the topmost inches of the milk for the boarders, the balance of which Sylvie was boiling for a longer time so that Madame Vauquer would not know the tax they had levied, illegally.

"Sylvie," said Christophe, dipping his first bit of toast, "Monsieur Vautrin, and he's a good fellow remember, saw two people here last night. If Madame asks about it, she mustn't hear anything."

"Did he give you something?"

"Yes. He gave me the hundred sous he does every month, a sort of way of saying to me 'Keep quiet.'"

"He and Madame Couture are the only ones—and they are not close—who don't try to take back with one hand what they give with the other at New Year's," Sylvie replied.

"As if they really did give us anything," said Christophe. "Always a worn-down coin, and only a hundred sous at that. Why, take Père Goriot, for two years he has blacked his own boots. And that miser of a Poiret wouldn't think of having his blacked. He'd rather drink the stuff than put it on his clogs. As for that fine fellow of a student, he gives me forty sous. That doesn't pay for the wear and tear on my brushes, and he sells his old clothes into the bargain. What a hole!"

"Still," said Sylvie, as she sipped her coffee, "it's better to work here than in any other house in the quarter; we're better off. But, to come back to fat Papa Vautrin, Christophe. Has anyone been speaking to you about him?"

"Yes. A few days ago I met a man in the street who said to me: 'Isn't it at your place that a fat man with dyed whiskers lives?' Well, I said: 'No, Sir, he doesn't dye them. A jolly fellow like him hasn't the time for that.' So I told Monsieur Vautrin.

and he said: 'That was right, my boy. That's the sort of answer I want you to give all the time. There's nothing more disagreeable than to have one's little weaknesses known. That is the kind of thing that stops a marriage.'"

"Well, now, when I was at the market, there was a man who tried to get me to say if I ever saw Vautrin when he was putting on his shirt. What a trick! Come," she exclaimed, breaking the thread of her speech, "there's a quarter to ten ringing at the Val de Grâce, and not a person stirring."

"No wonder! They are all out. Madame Couture and her little friend have gone to communion at St. Etienne, the eight o'clock mass. Père Goriot has gone out with a package. The student will not be back till ten when his lecture's over. When I was cleaning the stairs I saw them leaving; and whatever Père Goriot was carrying must be hard as iron. I know because it struck against me. What can the old man be up to? The others whirl him about as if he were a top, but he's a fine fellow nonetheless, and is worth more than all the rest of them put together. He doesn't give me much; but the ladies he sends me to see now and then come through with splendid tips, and they're wonderfully tricked out."

"Those that he calls his daughters, eh? There are a dozen of them."

"I have only gone to the houses of two, the same ones who've come here."

"There's Madame Vauquer stirring about. She's going to make her bed. I've got to go up. Watch the milk, Christophe. See that the cat doesn't get it."

Sylvie went upstairs to her mistress.

"How's this, Sylvie? Here it's a quarter to ten and you've let me sleep like a dormouse. Such a thing has never happened before."

"It's all because of the fog. You could cut it with a knife."

"But what about breakfast?"

"Oh, your boarders are all full of the old Nick this morning. They were all off at twilight."

"Do get your words right, Sylvie," replied Madame Vauquer. "You must mean at dawn."

"Very good, Madame. I'll say whatever you want. But the fact is that you can have your breakfast at ten o'clock. Old Michonnette and the Poireau haven't budged. They're the only ones left in the house and they're sleeping like the logs they are."

"But, Sylvie, the way you talk, one would think that they were sleeping together."

"So what?" Sylvie replied with a silly coarse laugh. "Two make a pair!"

"It's odd, Sylvie, the way Monsieur Vautrin could get in last night after Christophe had slid the bolts."

"That wasn't at all the way it was, Madame. Christophe heard Monsieur Vautrin, and came down to open the door. That's how you thought . . ."

"Give me my camisole, and go right down and see about breakfast. Fix up the rest of the mutton with potatoes, and serve preserved pears, the kind that cost two liards a piece."

A few minutes later Madame Vauquer came down just as her cat had upset with a little kick the plate which had covered a bowl of milk and was lapping up the milk as fast as he could.

"Mistigris!" she cried. The cat made off, then came back and rubbed against her legs. "Go on, coax away, you old hypocrite," she said. "Sylvie, Sylvie!"

"Well, Madame?"

"Look what the cat's been drinking!"

"It's all the fault of that stupid beast Christophe. I told him to set the table. Where has he got to? Don't worry about it, Madame, that will be for Père Goriot. I'll put water in it; he won't notice. He pays no attention to anything, not even to what he eats."

"Where has that old monster gone?" said Madame Vauquer as she set the plates.

"How can anyone know? He is up to a thousand tricks."

"I've slept too long," said Madame Vauquer.

"But Madame is as fresh as a rose. . . ."

At this moment the bell rang, and Vautrin came into the dining room singing in his heavy voice:

> *J'ai longtemps parcouru le monde,*
> *Et l'on m'a vu de toute part. . . .*

"Ah, ha, good morning, Mama Vauquer," he said, noticing his hostess and then gallantly taking her in his arms.

"Come, stop that!"

"Say I'm fresh!" he retorted. "Come, say it. Will you say it? Look, I'll help you set the table! I'm a nice fellow. Isn't that right?

> *Courtiser la brune et la blonde,*
> *Aimer, soupirer . . .*

I've just seen an odd thing, quite by chance."

"What?" asked the widow.

"At eight-thirty Père Goriot was in the Rue Dauphine, seeing the jeweler who buys old silver and lace. He was selling him at a stiff price a piece of silver plate rather nicely twisted for a man who isn't very skilful."

"You don't say!"

"Yes, indeed. I was on my way back here after saying good-bye to a friend of mine who is leaving the country by the royal mail coach. I waited for Père Goriot just to see what he was up to, just for the fun of it. He came back to the quarter, and went into the Rue des Grès and entered the house of a well-known money-lender. Gobseck his name is, a tremendous rascal, who would make his own father's bones into dominoes. Gobseck is the kind of skinflint who can't be robbed; he puts every cent he has into the bank."

"What can Père Goriot be up to?"

"It's not what he's up to; it's what he's down to," said Vautrin. "He's stupid fool enough to ruin himself out of love for girls who . . ."

"Here he comes," said Sylvie.

"Christophe!" shouted Père Goriot. "Come upstairs with me." Christophe did as he was asked, and soon came down again.

"Where are you going?" said Madame Vauquer.

"On an errand for Monsieur Goriot."

"What have you got there?" asked Vautrin, wresting from Christophe's hands a letter on which he read: *To Madame the Countess Anastasie de Restaud.* "Where are you off to?" he asked, giving the letter back to Christophe.

"Rue du Helder. I am to give this only to the countess herself."

"What's in it?" asked Vautrin, holding the letter up to the light. "A bank note? No." He slipped the envelope open. "A receipted bill," he cried out. "What a gallant the old rip is! Go on, old boy," he said, giving Christophe such a slap with his huge hand that he whirled about like a top, "you'll get a good tip."

The table was set. Sylvie was boiling the milk. Madame Vauquer was lighting the stove, with the help of Vautrin who kept on humming:

> *J'ai longtemps parcouru le monde*
> *Et l'on m'a vu de toute part. . . .*

When everything was ready, Madame Couture and Mademoiselle Taillefer came in.

"Where have you been so early, my dear?" said Madame Vauquer to Madame Couture.

"We have been to our devotions at St. Etienne du Mont, for today we go to Monsieur Taillefer's house. Poor girl, she is trembling like a leaf," Madame Couture continued as she sat down in front of the stove, putting her shoes up so close to its door that they soon were steaming.

"Warm yourself, Victorine, do," said Madame Vauquer.

"You are right in praying that God will soften your father's heart, Mademoiselle," said Vautrin, drawing up his chair to be close to the orphan girl. "But that isn't all that should be done. You need a friend who would make it his business to tell that shark where he gets off. Imagine, a man with three millions, and who won't give you a dowry! In these times even a beautiful girl must have a dowry."

"Poor child," said Madame Vauquer, "some day your unnatural father will suffer terrible misfortune for his treatment of you."

At these words Victorine's eyes filled with tears, and the widow stopped short in her speech at a sign from Madame Couture.

"If we could only see him, if I could only speak to him, and give him his wife's last letter," said Madame Couture, "I have never dared to risk mailing it, for he would recognize my writing. . . ."

"Ah, 'women, innocent, luckless, persecuted'!" cried Vautrin breaking in. "What a plight you are in! In a few days I'll step in and help you, and you will find that everything will turn out right."

"Oh, Monsieur Vautrin," said Victorine, looking at him with tearful and burning eyes—which had no effect on Vautrin, "if you could only find some way to talk to my father, would you tell him that his love and my mother's good name are dearer to me than all the money in the world? If you could soften him a little I would pray for you. I should be so grateful. . . ."

"*J'ai longtemps parcouru le monde,*" Vautrin began to sing in an ironic voice.

At this moment Goriot, Mademoiselle Michonneau and Poiret

came downstairs, drawn perhaps by the smell of the gravy that Sylvie was making for use with the scraps of mutton left over from the night before. Just as the seven boarders sat down, wishing one another good morning, the clock struck ten and Rastignac's step could be heard in the street.

"Well, Monsieur Eugène," said Sylvie, "today you will have your breakfast at the same time as everyone else."

Rastignac greeted all the boarders, and sat down next to Père Goriot.

"I have just had an extraordinary adventure," he said, helping himself to a large serving of mutton and cutting off a piece from the loaf, the exact size of this being carefully eyed by Madame Vauquer.

"An adventure!" said Poiret.

"And why not? Why are you surprised, old boy?" asked Vautrin. "Our friend is just the sort of fellow to whom adventures happen."

Mademoiselle Taillefer gave the young student a timid look.

"Tell us what your adventure was," said Madame Vauquer.

"Last night I was at a ball given by a cousin of mine, the Viscountess de Beauséant, who has a superb house, rooms hung with silk; it was a magnificent party, and I was as happy as a king. . . ."

"Kinglet," said Vautrin, interrupting sharply.

"What do you mean, Monsieur?" asked Eugène sharply.

"I said kinglet because kinglets are a lot happier than kings."

"How true!" said Poiret, in his role of echo. "I should rather be the unworried little bird than a king because . . ."

"Well," said the student, cutting him short, "there I was dancing with one of the most beautiful women in the room, a ravishing countess, the most exquisite woman I've ever seen. She had peach blossoms in her hair; she had the most beautiful bou quet of fresh flowers. How sweet they smelled! But how silly of me to try to describe a woman as animated as dancing could make her! You would have to see her. Well, this morning, I met this divine countess, about nine o'clock, afoot, in the Rue des Grès. . . . How fast my heart beat! I imagined . . ."

"That she was on her way here," said Vautrin, giving the student a look full of meaning. "I suppose she was on her way to Gobseck, the moneylender. If you ever ransack the hearts of Paris women, it's the moneylender you will find there rather than the lover. Your countess's name is Anastasie de Restaud and she lives in the Rue du Helder."

As Vautrin uttered this name the student looked at him fixedly. Père Goriot abruptly raised his head, and looked at the two men with a glance so bright and so anxious that all the boarders were astounded.

"Christophe will have got there too late. She must have gone before he arrived." There was pain in Goriot's voice.

"I've guessed the riddle," Vautrin whispered into Madame Vauquer's ear.

Goriot was eating mechanically, without knowing what he put in his mouth. He had never seemed so stupid and so abstracted as now.

"How the devil did you find out her name, Monsieur Vautrin?" asked Rastignac.

"Oh, come now! Why, Père Goriot knew it well, you see. Why shouldn't I?"

"Monsieur Goriot!" cried Eugène.

"What's that?" asked the poor old man. "And so she was very beautiful yesterday?"

"Who?"

"The Countess de Restaud."

"Look at the old rascal!" said Madame Vauquer to Vautrin. "Watch his eyes light up!"

"Can he be keeping her?" Mademoiselle Michonneau whispered to Eugène.

"Oh, yes, she was fascinatingly beautiful," Eugène went on, while Père Goriot followed with an eager look. "If Madame de Beauséant had not been there, my divine countess would have been the queen of the ball. All the young men's eyes were on her the whole time. I was her twelfth partner. She danced every quadrille. It made the rest of the women furious. If there was a living being happy yesterday, it was certainly the Countess de Restaud. How right the saying is that there is nothing more beautiful than a ship under sail, a horse at the gallop, and a woman dancing!"

"Yesterday at the top of a heap, at a duchess's party; today at the bottom, at a moneylender's shop: how typical that is of Parisian women," said Vautrin. "If their husbands cannot maintain them in their frantic luxury, they sell their bodies. If they can't do that, they'd disembowel their own mothers to glitter before the world. They'd stop at nothing. It's the old story!"

Père Goriot's face, which had shone like the sun on a fine day as he listened to Eugène, darkened again at Vautrin's cruel reflections.

"Well," said Madame Vauquer, "and what about your adventure? Did you speak to her? Did you ask her whether she meant to study law?"

"She didn't see me," said Eugène. "But wasn't it odd to meet one of the prettiest women in Paris in the Rue des Grès at nine in the morning, a woman who couldn't have got home from the ball before two? Paris is the only place where such things can happen."

"Oh, a great many things odder than that are happening," said Vautrin.

Mademoiselle Taillefer had scarcely listened to what was said, so great was her preoccupation with the step she was to take that day. Madame Couture signaled to her to go upstairs and dress. As soon as the two women had left, Père Goriot followed.

"Oh, did you notice him?" Madame Vauquer asked Vautrin and her other boarders. "There's no doubt that he has ruined himself for those women."

"Nothing will ever make me believe," Eugène protested, "that the beautiful Countess de Restaud belongs to Père Goriot."

"Who wants to make you believe it?" asked Vautrin, interrupting him. "You are still too young to understand Paris; later on you will see that it is full of men with *peculiar passions*."

At these words, Mademoiselle Michonneau gave Vautrin a look full of understanding. Her manner was for all the world like a regimental horse hearing the sound of the trumpet. Vautrin stopped short in his discourse to give her a deep answering look and to say, "Ah ha! and so we too have had our odd little passions?" The old maid lowered her eyes just like a nun in the presence of nude statues. "And so," he went on, "people of that sort, once they have picked up an idea, never let it go. They want only a certain sort of thing, often a low and dirty thing, and to get it they'd sell wife and children; and they'd let the devil have their own soul as well. For some the one passion is gambling or the stock market, or a collection of paintings or of insects, or music; for others, it is a woman who knows how to give them just the delicacies they want. If you offered them all the other women on earth, they'd have nothing to do with them; they only want the one particular woman who satisfies their passions. Often this woman doesn't love them at all, is cruel to them, lets them have only a few crumbs and sells these exceedingly dear; but you will find that these rascals never tire, and would pawn their last covering to get a last crown and bring this to her. Père Goriot is one of these. The countess exploits him because he knows enough to be quiet about it. That's the way of the fashionable world! The poor old fellow thinks only of her. Apart from this passion of his, as you can see, he's a stupid fool. But the moment this one subject is mentioned, he begins to sparkle like a diamond. This particular secret is not hard to unveil. This morning he brought some silver to the smelter, and I saw him going into Gobseck's shop in the Rue des Grès. Now follow closely! When he came back, he sent that idiot Christophe to the Countess de Restaud's—and Christophe let us see the address of the letter, which contained a receipted bill. Obviously if the countess also was going to the old money-lender's, it was about some urgent business. Père Goriot has been a gallant and financed her. You don't have to be very smart to get to the bottom of this. This will show you, young fellow, that while your countess was laughing, dancing, going through her tricks, balancing her peach blossoms, and holding up her dress, she was sweating blood, as the expression goes, at the thought of notes of hers or of her lover's which had been protested."

"You make me terribly eager to get at the truth," said Eugène. "I'll go to her house tomorrow."

"Yes," said Poiret, "you must go tomorrow to the Countess de Restaud's."

"And perhaps you will find the old fellow there, cashing in on his gallant deed."

"Why," said Eugène with an air of disgust, "your Paris must be a heap of filth."

"And what a heap of filth it is!" Vautrin went on. "Those who get filth on them, riding in carriages are fine fellows; those who get it afoot are rogues. Try to walk off with something, no matter what a trifle it may be, and you are shown as a monster on the square of the Palace of Justice. But steal a million, and you are pointed at in the drawing rooms as a man of mark. We are paying thirty millions to the Police and the Law to maintain that moral system. It's pretty, isn't it?"

"What's this," said Madame Vauquer. "Could Père Goriot have been melting down his silver breakfast service?"

"Weren't there two doves on the top of one of the pieces?" asked Eugène.

"That's right."

"He must have been very fond of it. He was weeping when he was kneading the porringer and the plate. I happened to see."

"He was as fond of it as of his life," Madame Vauquer replied.

"See what a passionate fellow the old man is," said Vautrin. "That woman can tickle his very soul."

Rastignac went up to his room. Vautrin left the house. Shortly afterwards, Madame Couture and Victorine got into a cab which Sylvie had gone out to find for them. Poiret gave his arm to Mademoiselle Michonneau, and they went out to walk in the Jardin des Plantes during the two best hours of the day.

"Ah," said Sylvie, "there they go, almost married. This is the first time they have gone off together. They're both so dried up that if they knock together, there'll be sparks of fire."

"Mademoiselle Michonneau must look out for her shawl," added Madame Vauquer with a laugh, "or it'll go up like tinder."

When Goriot came back at four o'clock, he could see by the light of two smoky lamps that Victorine's eyes were red. Madame Vauquer was listening to the tale of the fruitless visit to Monsieur Taillefer during the afternoon. Exasperated by the call of his daughter and the old lady, he had had them shown in, and discussed the case.

"My dear friend," said Madame Couture to Madame Vauquer, "can you imagine, he did not even ask Victorine to sit down; she stood through the whole of their talk. He told me, with no approach to anger, with the greatest frigidity, that we should refrain from troubling to call on him. He went on to say that Mademoiselle—he did not call her his daughter—was only getting into his bad graces by pushing herself upon him once a year—the beast!—and that since he had married her mother without a dowry she could not rightly claim anything from him. In short, he said the harshest sort of things, and made the poor dear burst into tears. Then she threw herself at her father's feet and bravely told him that she was so persistent only because of her mother and would obey him without a murmur of protest. She only begged him to read the mother's will, taking out the letter and offering it to him while she was saying the sweetest things you could conceive. I don't know how she thought of them. God must have breathed them to her. The poor child was so inspired that as I heard her I cried like a dumb brute. Do you know what that horrible man was doing while she spoke? He was paring his nails. He took the letter his wife had written amid her tears and threw it into the fire, saying 'very good!' He tried to pull his daughter to her feet; she took his hands to kiss them, but he drew them away. Wasn't that criminal? His big jay of a son came into the room and did not even speak to his sister."

"They must be monsters," said Père Goriot.

"And then," Madame Couture went on, without paying any attention to the old man's remark, "father and son left the room, telling me that they begged to be excused, for they had pressing business. That was how our visit turned out. At least he has seen his daughter. I don't know how he can deny she is his daughter, for she is as like him as two peas in a pod."

Lodgers and boarders came in, greeting one another and uttering those nullities that for some Paris minds constitute wit, in which stupidity is the main ingredient, and gesture and inflection the main merit. This sort of slang is always changing. The jest about which it turns never has more than a month's life. Some political event, some judicial trial, some street song, the carryings-on of some actor—all help to keep up such a sort of wit, which lies particularly in taking ideas and words like tennis balls and tossing them back and forth as if with rackets. The recent invention of the diorama, carrying optical illusion farther than in panoramas, had brought into some of the ateliers the jest of throwing superfluous "ramas" into one's talk. A young painter who took his dinners at the boarding-house had inoculated it with the fever.

"Well, Monsieur Poiret," said the man who worked at the Museum, "and how is your good *healthorama*?" Then, without waiting for a reply, he said to Madame Couture and Victorine, "You have some worries?"

"Are we going to have dinnerrr?" called out Horace Bianchon, a medical student and friend of Rastignac. "My stomach is down in my shoes."

"It's dreadfully *coltorama*!" said Vautrin. "Move over, won't you, Père Goriot. What the devil! Your foot is taking up the whole stove door."

"Illustrious Monsieur Vautrin," said Bianchon, "why do you say *coltorama*? That's wrong; it should be *coldorama*."

"No," said the Museum employee, "*coltorama* is the regular form."

"Ah! ah!"

"Here is his Excellency the Marquis de Rastignac, doctor of outlaw," said Bianchon, seizing Eugène by the neck and embracing him so tightly that he choked. "Come on, the rest of you, come on."

Mademoiselle Michonneau came in quietly, greeted the others without speaking, and joined the three women.

"That old bat always makes me shiver," said Bianchon to Vautrin in an undertone. "I'm studying Gall's system of phrenology and I think she has the bumps of Judas."

"You've known her, Sir?" asked Vautrin.

"Who hasn't met her!" Bianchon replied. "That pallid old maid always reminds me, I swear, of the long worms that can gnaw a rafter through."

"The truth is," said the man of forty, stroking his whiskers:

Et rose elle a vécu ce que vivent les roses,
L'espace d'un matin.

"Ah ha! here's a wonderful *souporama*," said Poiret, seeing Christophe who came in carrying a tureen with respect.

"Excuse me, Monsieur Poiret," said Madame Vauquer, "it's a *cabbage* soup."

All the young men burst out laughing. "You're caught, Poiret! Poiret's caught!"

"Two points to Mama Vauquer," said Vautrin.

"Did any one notice the fog this morning?" asked the man from the Museum.

"It was a feverish and unexampled fog," said Horace Bianchon "a gloomy fog, melancholy, dusty green, a Goriot fog!"

"A *Goriorama,*" said the painter, "for one couldn't see a thing."

"Oho, Lord Goriot, we're talking about you."

From his place at the foot of the table near the door to the kitchen, Père Goriot raised his head from sniffing at a piece of bread which was under his napkin, the relic of an old business habit of his, which still cropped up now and then.

"What's this?" asked Madame Vauquer in a sharp voice which rose above the din of the spoons, the clatter of the plates and the voices. "Have you any fault to find with the bread?"

"Not at all, Madame," he replied. "It's made with the first quality flour."

"How can you tell that?" asked Eugène.

"By the whiteness and the taste."

"By the smell, you mean," said Madame Vauquer. "You're

becoming so parsimonious you'll soon find a way to get along without food by just smelling the air in the kitchen."

"And you'll have to patent that," said the man from the Museum. "You'll make a fortune."

"Drop the subject," said the painter. "He does it just to make us see that he's been a manufacturer of vermicelli."

"Is your nose a corn-sampler?" asked the man from the Museum.

"A corn what?" asked Bianchon.

"Corn-cob."

"Corn-borer."

"Corn-crake."

"Corn-cockle."

"Cornea."

"Cornorama."

All these words burst forth from various parts of the table with the speed of musketry, and seemed the funnier because poor Père Goriot was looking at the boarders with the foolish expression of a man trying to understand a foreign language.

"Corn?" he asked Vautrin who sat near him.

"A corn on the foot, old fellow!" said Vautrin, giving him such a tap on the head that Goriot's cap was pushed down over his eyes.

For a moment, the old man, stupefied by the sudden attack, remained motionless. Christophe took away his plate, thinking that he had finished his soup; so that when Goriot had put back his cap to its right place and began to use his spoon again, it clattered against the table. All the boarders burst out laughing.

"Monsieur Vautrin," said the old man, "you have a poor taste in humor, and if you ever let yourself do that again . . ."

"Well, and what if I do?" asked Vautrin interrupting him.

"Well, you'll pay dearly for it some day."

"I suppose you mean in hell," said the painter, "in the dark little corner where the bad little boys go."

"Well, Mademoiselle," said Vautrin to Victorine, "you are not eating anything? Papa was obstinate, I suppose?"

"A monster," said Madame Couture.

"He must be brought to a more reasonable frame of mind," said Vautrin.

Rastignac, who was sitting quite close to Bianchon, said, "Mademoiselle could bring a case over food, since she does not eat anything. Oh, look, look, at the way Père Goriot is concentrating on Mademoiselle Victorine."

The old man, oblivious of his food, was studying the poor girl whose features expressed the most genuine kind of grief, that of a child rejected by a father and continuing to love him.

"My friend," said Eugène in an undertone, "we've been wrong about Père Goriot. He is neither an imbecile nor a man whose strength has left him. Use your phrenological knowledge, and tell me what you think of him. Last night I saw him twist a silver plate as if it had been wax, and right now his expression shows that he is undergoing some extraordinary emotions. I think that his life is too much of a mystery not to be worth study. Yes, indeed, Bianchon, you may laugh, but I'm not joking."

"The man is a medical fact," said Bianchon. "If he wants. I'm ready to dissect him."

"No, feel the contour of his head."

"Oh, no, perhaps his stupidity is contagious."

The next day Rastignac dressed with unusual care, and toward three in the afternoon went to the Countess de Restaud's, giving free rein on his way to those wildly foolish hopes which lend such charming emotions to the lives of young men. In such moods they calculate neither dangers nor obstacles; everywhere they see only the promise of success, and make their lives poetical by the pure exercise of imagination. They become sad or unhappy simply because of the failure of projects which owe all their life to their wild desires; if it were not for their ignorance and timidity, there would be an end to social life. Eugène took infinite precautions against muddying his shoes or trousers, but even so he could keep in his mind the thought of what he would say to the Countess de Restaud; he was storing up witty remarks, inventing the clever retorts which would find their places in an imagined conversation; he was getting ready his subtle words, his phrases worthy of a Talleyrand, suitable for the declaration on which his hopes of the future were based, and which he would make if certain little circumstances were propitious. He did get muddy and he had to have his shoes polished and his trousers brushed at the Palais Royal. "If I were rich," he thought, as he changed a hundred-sous piece, which he had put in his pocket in case of dire need, "I should have taken a carriage and then I might have followed out my train of thought without a break."

He finally reached the Rue du Helder, and asked for the Countess de Restaud. He felt the cold anger of a man who is certain that one day he will triumph at the disdainful looks of the servants who had noticed his approach across the courtyard on foot, and had heard not a single sound which might have indicated a carriage at the gate. He suffered the more because coming through the court his inferior position had already been impressed on him as he looked at a handsome horse with a rich harness and one of those elegant cabriolets which are the tokens of the luxury of a dissipated life and imply the habit of enjoying all the happinesses of Paris. Suddenly he felt in a bad temper. It was enough to shut up all the treasures of wit in his head and to deprive him of the use of every one of them. As he waited to hear the countess's pleasure while a footman went to tell her the names of those who had called, Eugène stood on one foot before a window in the vestibule, leaned his elbow on a table, and looked vacantly into the courtyard. He felt the length of the time he was kept waiting, and would have gone away had it not been for that Southern obstinacy which brings forth prodigies when it is single-minded.

"Monsieur," said the footman, "Madame is in her boudoir and very busy. She did not answer when I knocked; but if you would like to go to the drawing room, you will find another gentleman there."

With his mind full of the thought of how frightening was the power of servants who by one word can offer a judgment or an accusation of their masters, Rastignac slowly opened the door through which the footman had returned, no doubt with the idea of convincing the insolent tribe that he knew those who dwelt in the house. To his confusion he found himself in a room where he saw lamps, buffets, a gadget for heating bath-towels, and which in turn opened into a dark corridor and a hidden stairway. The stifled laughter in the vestibule brought his confusion to a height.

"Sir, the drawing room is this way," the valet told him with that pretense of respect which seems more insulting than an insult itself.

Eugène retraced his steps so hurriedly that he jostled against a bath, but he succeeded luckily in holding on to his hat which otherwise would have fallen into the water. At this moment a door opened at the end of the long corridor, lighted by a small lamp, and Eugène heard at once the voices of the Countess de Restaud and Père Goriot, and the sound of a kiss. He came back to the dining room, crossed it following the footman, and found himself in a drawing room where he took his place beside a window which, he saw, opened on a court. He wanted to be sure that this Père Goriot really was his Père Goriot. His heart was beating with a strange rapidity, he was recalling the terrifying reflections of Vautrin. The footman was waiting for Eugène at the door when an elegant young man came out, saying impatiently: "Maurice, I'm leaving. You will tell the countess that I waited for her more than half an hour." This impertinent fellow—no doubt he had a right to be!—was humming some Italian air as he approached the window where Eugène stood, as much to see the young student's face as to look into the court.

"The count would be wiser to wait a moment longer. Madame is now free," said Maurice, returning.

At this moment, Père Goriot, who had descended by the private stairway, appeared in the courtyard near the porte-cochère. The old fellow was pulling at his umbrella and was about to open it; he did not notice that the main gate was open and that a young man wearing a decoration and driving a tilbury was about to pass through. Père Goriot barely had time to leap back and escape being crushed. The umbrella had frightened the horse and it balked a little on its way to the entrance. The young man turned his head with an expression of anger, looked at Père Goriot, and then greeted him in the grudging fashion one uses toward a usurer who is a necessity to one's life, or some degenerate personage who can claim from one a respect of which later on one will be ashamed. Père Goriot responded with a friendly little nod, full of good nature. These events occurred with the speed of lightning. Eugène was attending to them so closely that he forgot he was not alone. Suddenly he heard the countess's voice.

"Ah, Maxime, you were leaving!" she said in a tone of reproach, mingled with a little displeasure.

The countess had not noticed the entrance of the tilbury into the courtyard. Rastignac turned around abruptly and saw her, smartly attired in a negligée of white cashmere with rose-knots, and with that sort of careless hair-dress which is usual with Parisian women in the daytime. She was perfumed; doubtless she was fresh from her bath, and her beauty, which had become more supple, so to speak, seemed more voluptuous; her glance was liquid. Young men's eyes take in everything; their minds fix on the glories of women, just as a plant breathes in from the air the substances necessary for its own particular nourishment. Just so did Eugène feel the freshness diffused from the hands of this woman, without having to touch them; he saw, through the cashmere, the rosy tints of the breast which the negligée, not quite tightly drawn, left visible here and there, and on this his gaze was bent. The countess had no need of the help of a corset; her girdle was enough to show how flexible her figure was; her neck was an invitation to passion; her feet were pretty in their slippers. It was when Maxime took her hand to kiss it that Eugène noticed him, and the countess, Eugène.

"Oh, it's you, Monsieur de Rastignac. I'm so pleased to see you," she said in a manner that men of the world understand and obey.

Maxime was looking at Eugène and at the countess in turn, and in so significant a fashion that it should have led the intruder to take himself off. The looks he was giving could be clearly and intelligibly translated in such words as these: "Come, now, my dear, I hope you're going to get rid of this silly young fool." The Countess Anastasie was looking at this impertinent and haughty youth whom she had called Maxime with that submissive expression which gives a woman's whole heart away without her knowing it. Rastignac felt a fierce hatred for this young man. The beautiful blond hair, so admirably curled, made him feel what a messy look his own hair had. Besides, Maxime's boots were of the finest leather and beautifully polished while his, for all the care he had taken in walking, bore a light coating of mud. Finally Maxime was wearing a frock coat which fitted him elegantly and made him look like a pretty woman, while Eugène, past two-thirty in the afternoon, was wearing an ordinary black suit. Eugène was too intelligent not to appreciate the advantage the dandy had in being so perfectly dressed, and in being so tall and slender, so clear-eyed and so pale, in short in being one of those men by whom orphans come to their ruin.

Without waiting to hear what Eugène might say in reply the countess passed into the other drawing room like a breeze, the skirts of her negligée floating in the air with a graceful furling and unfurling motion which made her resemble a butterfly. Maxime followed her. Eugène in his anger followed Maxime and the countess. The three stood in a group beside the mantel in the main drawing room. Eugène knew perfectly well that his presence would annoy Maxime, whom he loathed; but even if he should displease the countess he was bent upon annoying the dandy. Suddenly, as he recalled having seen this young man at the Viscountess de Beauséant's ball, he guessed the relationship which linked him with the Countess de Restaud; and with that daring of youth which leads to great follies but also to great victories, he decided: "This is my rival. I mean to triumph over him." How imprudent he was! He did not know that Count Maxime de Trailles did not seek to avoid an insult; he followed it up by using the first shot to kill his man. Eugène was a skilful hunter, but he had not yet hit twenty out of twenty-two targets in a row. The young count threw himself into an easy chair near the fire, took up the tongs, and prodded the fire with such a violent and angry movement that Anastasie's beautiful face was suddenly covered with annoyance. She turned toward Eugène, and gave him one of those coldly questioning looks which say so effectively: "Why don't you go away?" Such looks make well-bred men discover at once the sort of speeches which enable one to take a quick leave.

Eugène responded by looking more agreeable than ever and began: "Madame, I was in such a hurry to see you that I . . ."

He stopped short. A door opened. The gentleman who had

driven the tilbury suddenly appeared, without a hat, did not greet the countess, looked thoughtfully at Eugène, and gave his hand to Maxime, saying "Good day," with a fraternal manner which greatly astonished Eugène. Young men from the provinces are so far from understanding the pleasantness of a triangular relationship.

"The Count de Restaud," said the countess to Eugène, indicating her husband.

Eugène made a low bow.

"This," she went on, completing the introduction, "is Monsieur de Rastignac. He is related to the Viscountess de Beauséant through the Marcillac, and I had the pleasure of making his acquaintance at her last ball."

Related to the Viscountess de Beauséant through the Marcillac! The countess pronounced the words almost with a special emphasis, with that special sort of pride a hostess has in demonstrating that she receives only persons of distinction. They had a magical effect: the count lost his air of formal coldness and welcomed the young man.

"I am delighted, Monsieur," said he, "to have the pleasure of making your acquaintance."

Count Maxime de Trailles for his part gave Eugène a worried look and dropped his impertinent manner. The stroke of the magic wand, the proof of the power of a name, restored to the youth all the resources of his brain, and made him master once more of all the clever things he had meant to say. A sudden shaft of light had shown him the atmosphere of the high society of Paris, in whose darkness he had been lost. The Maison Vauquer and Père Goriot were then far from his thoughts.

"I thought that the Marcillac line was extinct," said the Count de Restaud.

"It is, Monsieur," Eugène replied. "My great uncle, the Chevalier de Rastignac, married the heiress of the Marcillac. He had but one child, a daughter who married Marshal Clairimbault, maternal grandfather of the Viscountess de Beauséant. We are the younger branch, and the poorer because my great uncle, a vice-admiral, lost everything in the service of the king. The Revolutionary government would not accept our credits when the company of the Indies was liquidated."

"Did not your great-uncle command the *Vengeur* before 1789?"

"That's right."

"Then he must have known my grandfather, who commanded the *Warwick*."

Maxime glanced at the Countess de Restaud, shrugging his shoulders slightly, as if to say: "If your husband begins to talk navy with this fellow, we're lost." Anastasie understood the look. With that wonderful power of women, she began to smile and said: "Come, Maxime, I've something to ask of you. Gentlemen we'll leave you to sail on the *Vengeur* and the *Warwick*." She rose and made a sign full of jesting complicity to Maxime, who accompanied her toward her boudoir. Scarcely had this morganatic couple (a beautiful German expression for which there is no French equivalent) reached the door before the Count de Restaud broke off talking with Eugène.

"Anastasie," said he with a touch of bad temper, "stay here, my dear. You know very well that . . ."

"I'll be back, I'll be back," she said, interrupting him. "It'll only take me a moment to tell Maxime what I want him to do."

She did come back promptly. Like all women who are obliged to study their husband's character in order to do as they wish, and who are able to recognize just how far they can go without losing the trust they need so much, and so never annoy him in the little matters of life, the countess had judged from the inflections in her husband's voice, that it would not be at all safe to remain in the boudoir. Her difficulties were due to Eugène.

So she pointed to him, with an air and gesture of annoyance, and Maxime, for whom she did this, said with epigrammatic conciseness to all three: "I see that you have business. I don't want to bother you. Good-bye." He made off.

"You mustn't go, Maxime," said the count.

"You must have dinner with us," said the countess, leaving Eugène and her husband again and following Maxime into the other drawing room. There they stayed long enough to give the Count de Restaud time to get rid of Eugène.

The latter could hear them, now bursting into laughter, then chatting together, and sometimes there would be silence. However, he mischievously entertained the Count de Restaud, flattering him, getting him started in discussions, all to be able to see the countess again, and to discover what were her ties with Père Goriot. To him there was a mystery in this woman— so clearly in love with Maxime, and her husband's ruler as well— having a secret link with the old manufacturer of vermicelli. He meant to fathom this mystery, and he hoped that by doing so he could dominate one who was so eminently a Parisian woman.

"Anastasie!" the count called out again.

"Come, poor Maxime," she said to the young man, "we'll have to part. I'll see you tonight."

"I hope, Nasie," he whispered in her ear, "that you will see no more of that little fellow whose eyes glowed like burning coals when your negligée fell a little open. He would make love to you, and compromise you, and so you would make it necessary for me to call him out and kill him."

"How stupid of you, Maxime!" she said. "These young students are very useful. They can make excellent lightning-rods. I'll certainly make Restaud take a dislike to him."

Maxime burst into laughter, and went out, followed by the countess, who took her place at a window to watch him get into his carriage, make his horse rear, and wave his whip. She did not come back until the main gate had shut behind him.

"Listen, dear," said the count, when she had rejoined them, "the estate where Monsieur de Rastignac's family lives is near Verteuil on the Charente. His great-uncle and my grandfather were acquainted."

"I'm delighted that there is a link," said the countess in an abstracted way.

"There are more links than you suppose," Eugène said in a low voice.

"What do you mean?" she said sharply.

"Well," he went on, "I have just seen a gentleman leave this house who is in the room next to mine at the boarding house where I live—Père Goriot."

At the use of the familiar term before the name, the count, who was poking the fire, dropped the tongs as if they had burned his hands, and got up.

"Monsieur de Rastignac," he said, "you might have said 'Monsieur Goriot'."

The countess grew pale as she saw how stirred her husband was; then she reddened and her embarrassment was evident. When she spoke it was in a voice she was trying to keep natural, and her manner showed an effort to be artificially easy. "You could not," she said, "know any one of whom we could be fonder. . . ." She broke off, looked at the piano as if she had had a sudden fancy, and said, "Are you fond of music?"

"Very fond," said Eugène, who also had reddened and who had lost his assurance through a confused notion that he had just committed some awkward blunder.

"Do you sing?" she went on, moving to the piano, and quickly sweeping her hand the full length of the keys. T-r-a-l-a-a!

"No, I do not."

The Count de Restaud was walking up and down.

"What a pity!" said the countess. "You have robbed yourself

of one of the great means of success. "Ca-a-ro, ca-a-a-ro, ca-a-a-a-ro, non du-bi-ta-re," she sang.

The name of Père Goriot had been another stroke of the magic wand, but its effect was the opposite of what had followed the words: related to the Viscountess de Beauséant. Eugène's present situation might be compared with that of a man who had been favored with an introduction to a collector of curios and who, by awkwardly jostling against a cabinet of statuettes, makes three or four heads which were loose fall off. He would have liked to bury himself out of sight! The countess's face was now cold and hard, and her eyes, wholly indifferent, avoided his.

"Madame," he said, "I know that you have things you wish to talk of with the count. I beg to take my leave and to ask you whether I may . . ."

"Whenever you come," the countess said quickly, as with a gesture she stopped Eugène, "you may be sure that it will be a very great pleasure for the count as well as for me."

Eugène made a low bow and left the room, followed by the count who insisted on accompanying him all the way to the door.

"Whenever that gentleman calls," said the count to Maurice, "you will tell him that neither the countess nor I are at home."

When Eugène reached the portico he saw that it was raining. "Well," he said to himself, "I have done some awkward thing. What it was, and why, I don't know. Now I'll ruin my coat and hat into the bargain. I ought to stay in a corner and get up my law, and aspire to be nothing but a rustic magistrate. How can I go into society, when I ought to have a set of cabriolets, polished boots, jewels, gold chains, and even for daytime wear doeskin gloves at six francs a pair, and yellow gloves for the evening? That old fool of a Goriot has done it!"

When he had gone as far as the street, the driver of a cab for hire, who had, I suppose, just brought a bridal couple to their destination, and who wanted nothing better than to make

a few trips on his own and pocket the fares, made a sign to
Eugène, seeing that he had no umbrella although he was dressed
in black, and had a white waistcoat, yellow gloves and polished
boots. Eugène was in one of those dull rages which lead a young
man to fall farther and farther into the abyss, as if at the bottom
there might be a lucky exit. By nodding his head Eugène signaled
his agreement and he got into the carriage where there were
still a few petals of orange blossom and a few bits of wire to
attest the recent presence there of the bride and groom.

"Where do you wish to go, Sir?" asked the coachman, who
had already taken off his white gloves.

"Good Lord, since I've started I may as well turn the thing
to some use," Eugène reflected. "Go to the house of the
Beauséants," he said aloud.

"Which one?" asked the driver.

A wonderful question which left Eugène confused. This green
man of the world did not even know the number of relatives
he had who were indifferent to him.

"To the Viscount de Beauséant's, Rue de . . ."

"Grenelle," said the driver, nodding his head and cutting him
short. "There's also the house of the Marquis and the Count de
Beauséant, in Rue Saint Dominique," he added as he raised the
step.

"You have no need to tell me. I know that very well," said
Eugène dryly. And he reflected that on that day everyone was
laughing at him. He tossed his hat on the cushions of the seat
across from him.

"This frolic is going to cost me a king's ransom, but at least
I shall pay my visit to this so-called cousin of mine in a thoroughly
aristocratic manner. Père Goriot has already cost me no less than
ten francs, the old rascal! Good Lord, I'll regale the viscountess
with my adventure and perhaps it will make her laugh. She is
sure to know the mystery of the criminal relations between the

miserable old rat and that beautiful woman. I'll do better to please my cousin than to bang away against that immoral woman —who would be a very costly conquest, I'm thinking. If the beautiful viscountess's name was so potent, what power would her person have? I'll aim high. If I do, it's best to aim at the highest of all."

These words are the gist of the thousand and one thoughts that tossed him about. He got back a little calm and assurance as he watched the rain falling. He told himself that if he was spending two of his few precious hundred-sous pieces, it was a good thing that they were helping to save his coat, his shoes and his hat. He even was buoyant for a moment as he heard his driver call out "Open the gate please!" A footman, resplendent in red and gold, made the main gate to the Beauséant house turn noisily on its hinges, and Rastignac felt a mild satisfaction as his carriage passed under the porch, turned in the courtyard and stopped beneath the canopy which protected the steps. In his heavy overcoat of blue fringed with red, the driver got down and unfolded the step. As he alighted from the carriage Eugène could hear the suppressed laughter from three or four valets who stood jesting at this equipage, which suggested a vulgar wedding party. Just as he was being enlightened by this laughter, he saw, and compared with his own vehicle, one of the most elegant coupés in Paris, drawn by two pawing horses with rosettes at their ears, champing at their bits, whose driver, wearing a powdered wig and a neat cravat, was holding them in as if they were trying to run away. In the Chaussée d'Antin, the Countess de Restaud had in her courtyard the elegant cabriolet of a young man of twenty-six. In the Faubourg Saint-Germain stood the luxurious equipage of a great lord; thirty thousand francs would not have purchased it.

"Who is calling?" Eugène wondered, appreciating a little tardily that in Paris there must be very few women who were not besieged, and that the winning of such a queen would cost more than one's heart's blood. The devil would have it that his cousin too must have her Maxime de Trailles!

He went up the steps to the entry full of despair. As he approached, the glass door opened; the valets were as solemn as an ass receiving a beating. The party he had attended had been held in the large reception halls on the ground floor of the mansion. He had not had time between receiving his invitation and coming to the ball for a visit to his cousin; so he had not seen the viscountess's own rooms. He was now to see for the first time the marvels of that personal elegance which reveals the spirit and the manners of a distinguished woman. The study would be the more interesting because the drawing room of the Countess de Restaud gave him the basis for a comparison. At four-thirty the viscountess was receiving. Five minutes before she would not have admitted her cousin. Eugène, utterly ignorant of the various etiquettes of Paris, was led up a great white staircase with gilded banister and red carpet, and with a profusion of flowers, to the viscountess's apartments. He then knew nothing of her life, of one of these changing histories which are related quietly every evening in the drawing rooms of Paris.

For three years the viscountess had been intimate with one of the richest and most famous noblemen of Portugal, the Marquis d'Adjuda-Pinto. It was one of those innocent relationships so agreeable for those who take part in them that they cannot endure the addition of a third person. The Viscount of Beauséant had set the tone for society by respecting, willingly or unwillingly, this morganatic union. When in the early days of the friendship people came to call on the viscountess at two in the afternoon they found the Marquis d'Adjuda-Pinto with her. The viscountess did not like to refuse to receive a visitor, and it would have been improper for her to do so; but she welcomed callers so coldly and looked so steadily at the cornice that everyone who came understood how unwelcome his presence was. As soon as Paris knew that a call on the Viscountess de Beauséant between two and four in the afternoon was unwelcome, she found her solitude complete.

She would go to the Théâtre des Bouffons or to the Opéra in the company of her husband and the marquis; the viscount, as a man of the world would leave his wife and the marquis as soon as they had taken their places. The marquis was now about to marry. He was marrying one of the Rochefides. There was one person, and one alone, in the society of Paris who did not know of the intended marriage: this was the Viscountess de Beauséant. Some of her friends had made obscure references to it of course; she had laughed, believing that they were trying to disturb a happiness which made them jealous. Now, however, the bans were about to be published. Although he had come especially to speak of the marriage to her, the handsome Portuguese had not had the courage to breathe a single word of it. Why? Nothing could be more difficult than telling a woman that her fate has thus been settled. Some men are less nervous on the dueling ground, standing before a man who threatens to run them through than in the presence of a woman who, after speaking through her tears for two hours, pretends to faint and asks for smelling salts.

At the very moment Eugène was going up the stairs, the marquis felt as if he were walking on hot coals and was trying to take his departure, comforting himself with the assurance that either the viscountess would pick up the piece of news for herself, or he would write it to her, for it would be much more convenient to manage this assassination of a love by correspondence than by conversation. When the viscountess's valet announced that Monsieur de Rastignac was calling, the marquis was filled with joy. It is certain that a woman in love is even more ingenious in shaping doubts for herself than in varying pleasures for her lover. When she is about to be deserted she can divine the sense of a gesture more readily than Virgil's courser scents the distant corpuscles which promise love. Accordingly, there can be no question that the Viscountess de Beauséant caught that alarming start of his, despite its being so slight and so involuntary. Eugène did not realize that one should never call on anyone at all in Paris without having learned from the person's friends the history of the husband and the history of the wife and children; for it is only in this way that one can escape committing one of those stupid blunders so picturesquely described in Poland as "harnessing oxen to your carriage"—perhaps so that you may be drawn out of the mud in which by mischance you have been caught. If such conversational slips have not yet found any precise term in French, it is probably because in France they are thought to be impossible by reason of the immense scale on which malicious gossip is there diffused. After he had foundered at the Countess de Restaud's— she had not even given him time to harness oxen to his carriage —only Eugène could have continued on his stupid way when he was in the presence of the Viscountess de Beauséant. However, if he had been a nuisance to the countess and to the Count de Trailles, he was a godsend to the Marquis d'Adjuda-Pinto.

"Good-bye," said the Portuguese, as he made his way quickly to the door upon Eugène's entrance into the exquisite little gray and rose drawing room where luxury was disguised as elegance.

"We shall meet again tonight," said the viscountess, turning her head and looking at the marquis. "It's to the Bouffons we are going, isn't it?"

"I won't be able to go," said he, with his hand upon the knob.

The viscountess rose and called him back to her without paying the slightest attention to Eugène, who stood dazzled by the brilliance of marvelous wealth and began to believe in the reality of the Arabian Nights; he was also deeply embarrassed that she still took not the least notice of him. The viscountess had raised the first finger of her right hand and, with a pretty gesture, bidden the marquis to return to her side. The gesture was so strong a proof of passion that he took his hand from the door and came back. Eugène looked at him not without envy.

"There," he thought, "is the man with the coupé. Certainly one would need splendid horses, liveries and floods of gold to win the heart of a Parisian woman." Greed for luxury seized his heart; the madness of luxury gripped him; the thirst for gold parched his throat. He must live on a hundred and thirty francs for the space of three months. His father, his mother, his brothers, his sisters, his aunt, among them all did not spend two hundred francs a month. The quick comparison between his present situation and the goal at which he aimed contributed to his stupefaction.

"Why," asked the viscountess with a laugh, "*won't you be able to go* to the Théâtre des Italiens?"

"Business. I am having dinner at the British Ambassador's."

"You can leave."

When a man embarks on a deceit, he is inevitably forced to heap one lie upon another. The Marquis d'Adjuda replied with a laugh. "Is it a command?"

"Yes, of course."

"That is what I wanted you to say to me," he replied, with one of those subtle looks which would have reassured any other woman. He took the viscountess's hand, kissed it, and left.

Eugène ran his hand through his hair, and twisted about to bow, thinking that now the viscountess would turn her thoughts to him. Suddenly she got up, hurried to the gallery, rushed to the window and watched the Marquis d'Adjuda as he got into his carriage. She listened attentively as he gave his orders and heard the porter tell the driver: "To Monsieur de Rochefide's." These words, and something in the way in which the marquis had buried himself in the carriage were thunder and lightning for the poor woman and she came back into the room a prey to mortal fear. The most dreadful catastrophes in the great world are but this. The viscountess went into her bedroom, sat down at a table and took up a piece of exquisite stationery.

"The moment," she wrote, "that you dine at the Rochefides', and not at the British Embassy, you owe me an explanation: I shall expect you."

When she had gone over some letters which had been disfigured because her hand had trembled in making them, she signed with a "C" for Claire de Bourgogne, and rang.

"Jacques," she said to her valet who had come at once, "at seven-thirty you will go to Monsieur de Rochefide's, and you will ask for the Marquis d'Adjuda. If he is there you will see that this letter gets to him, but do not wait for a reply; if he is not there, you will bring the letter back to me."

"There is a gentleman in the drawing room, Madame."

"Oh, so there is," she said, shutting the door.

Eugène was beginning to feel very uncomfortable. Finally the viscountess spoke to him in a tone in which there was so much emotion that it stirred his heart to its depths. "I'm sorry, there was a note I had to write. Now I'm entirely yours." She did not know what she was saying. This is what she was thinking: "He means then to marry Mademoiselle de Rochefide. But is he free then? This evening the marriage will be off or I shall. . . . Tomorrow the matter will have been ended."

"Cousin," said Eugène.

"What's that you say?" said the viscountess, giving him a look so insolent that it froze him.

Eugène understood. In the course of three hours he had learned so many things that he was extremely vigilant.

"Madame," he continued, reddening. He stopped short, then

resumed: "Pardon me, I stand in such need of help that a slight claim of relationship would have done no harm."

The viscountess smiled, but in a sad fashion; she already felt the unhappiness which was about to burst upon her.

"If you knew in what a plight my family is," he went on, "you would delight in the role of one of those fairies of romance who take pleasure in waving out of existence the obstacles which hamper their godchildren."

"Well, cousin, then," she said with a laugh, "how can I be of help to you?"

"How can I say? Just the slender thread of relationship which connects me with you, obscure as that is, is an immense fortune in itself. You have made me nervous. I can't recall any longer what I came to ask you. You are the only person I know in Paris. Ah! what I meant was to ask you to take me as a poor child that wants to cling to your skirt, and would die for you."

"Would you kill a person for me?"

"I'd kill two," said Eugène.

"You child! Yes, you're a child," she said, holding back her tears. "If *you* loved, it would be a sincere love."

"It would, indeed," said he with a toss of his head.

The ambitious reply of the boy had strongly interested the viscountess. He was now for the first time calculating his acts. Between the blue boudoir of the Countess de Restaud and the rose drawing room of the Viscountess de Beauséant, he had completed his full course in that *Parisian law* which is never put in words, although it constitutes a high social jurisprudence which will lead one who really understands and practices it safe and sound to any goal he has in view.

"Now I have it," said Eugène. "I had noticed the Countess de Restaud at your ball. Today I called on her."

"You must have been very much in the way," said the viscountess with a smile.

"Yes, indeed. I am such an ignoramus that I will set every one against me, unless you will help me. I believe it must be terribly hard to meet in this city any young, beautiful, rich, and elegant woman whose heart is free. I need someone to explain for me what you women understand so well: Life. Everywhere I am going to find a Count de Trailles. So I was coming to you to ask you for the key to a riddle, to discover from you what sort of blunder I made. I was talking of an old . . ."

"The Duchess de Langeais," Jacques announced, interrupting the young man who showed by a gesture how much he was annoyed.

"If you want to get on," said the viscountess in a whisper, "don't be so unconstrained, that's a first point.

"Good day, my dear," she went on, getting up to meet the duchess, and taking her hand with as much effusive affection as if they were sisters. The duchess responded with the prettiest compliments.

"There," Eugène reflected, "are two genuine friends. From now on I shall have two women to help me; they must have the same likes, and the duchess will certainly take an interest in me."

"To what happy thought do I owe the pleasure of seeing you, Antoinette dear?" asked the viscountess.

"I just saw the Marquis d'Adjuda-Pinto going into the Rochefide house, and so I thought that you would be alone."

The viscountess did not bite her lips, nor did she blush; her expression was unchanged; her forehead seemed even to clear while the duchess was saying these fatal words.

"If I had known that you weren't free . . ." the duchess added, turning toward Eugène.

"This is Monsieur Eugène de Rastignac, a cousin of mine," said the viscountess. "Is there any news of General de Montriveau?" she asked. "Sérizy was telling me yesterday that he is not seen about any more. Was he at your house today?"

The duchess was madly in love with General de Montriveau and it was supposed that he had abandoned her. The question pierced her to the heart, and she reddened as she replied, "Yesterday he was at the Palace."

"On duty?" asked the viscountess.

"Clara, you must know," said the duchess, with a mass of malignant feeling in her look, "that tomorrow the bans will be published for the Marquis d'Adjuda-Pinto and Mademoiselle de Rochefide?"

This was too strong a blow; the viscountess paled as she replied with a laugh, "This is just one of those rumors which fools like to circulate. Why would the marquis take one of the most splendid names in all Portugal to the Rochefides? Their title is only of last year's vintage."

"Berthe will have two hundred thousand livres in income, people say."

"The Marquis is too rich to make such calculations."

"But, darling, Mademoiselle de Rochefide is a charming girl."

"Indeed!"

"He is dining with the family tonight; the contract has been arranged. It seems very odd to me that you know so little about it."

"What is the foolish thing you have done, Monsieur de Rastignac?" the viscountess asked. "This poor boy is so new to our society that he understands nothing of what we are saying, my dear Antoinette. Out of kindness to him won't you let me put off talking more of this till tomorrow? Tomorrow, you see, everything will doubtless be official, and you will be on surer ground."

The duchess turned to Eugène with one of those insolent glances which take a man in from head to foot, flatten him out and freeze him utterly.

"Madame," he said, "without knowing what I was doing, I plunged a dagger into the heart of the Countess de Restaud. Just that I didn't know, that was my only fault," the student went on, for he had had the wit to see that there were biting implications beneath the affectionate words of the two women. "You do not refuse to see, perhaps you even fear those who knowingly cause you pain, but the person who causes it without knowing what he is doing is set down for a fool and a blunderer who does not see where his interest lies, and every one despises him."

The Viscountess de Beauséant gave Eugène one of those melting looks in which a great soul can fuse gratitude and dignity. Her glance was like a salve soothing the wound that had just been made in Eugène's heart by the cold appraisal the duchess had given him.

"Do you know," Eugène went on, "I had just captured the good will of the Count de Restaud?" Turning toward the duchess with an air which was at once humble and mischievous, he added, "I must tell you that I am as yet no more than a poor devil of a student, very much alone in the world, and very poor."

"You must not say such a thing, Monsieur de Rastignac. We women never have any use for what others disdain."

"Oh, as to that," Eugène retorted, "I'm only twenty-two, and one has to put up with the misfortunes that belong to one's years. Besides I'm making a full confession, and I couldn't imagine a prettier confessional to kneel in. Here the sins are committed that are avowed in the other."

The duchess's expression grew chilly as she listened to this anti-religious speech which she found to be in bad taste. She said to the viscountess, "This gentlemen has just come . . ."

The viscountess laughed heartily both at her cousin and at the duchess, before she replied, "He comes, seeking a woman who will teach him good taste."

"Isn't it natural," Eugène continued, "that one should want to know the secrets of whatever charms one so much?" ("Hold on," he said to himself. "I'm sure that I'm talking like a hairdresser.")

"But the Countess de Restaud is, I believe, the pupil of the Count de Trailles," said the duchess.

"I didn't know anything about that," replied Eugène. "So I was foolish enough to burst in upon them. In short, I had got on quite well with her husband. I was at least tolerated for the time being by the countess herself, and then I had the notion to mention to them that I knew a man whom I had just seen leaving by a private staircase, and who, at the end of a corridor, had kissed the countess."

"Who was that?" the two women asked in the same breath.

"An old man who like myself pays two louis a month for board and lodging in the depths of the Saint-Marceau quarter. He is really down and out, a poor creature whom everybody laughs at and whom we call Père Goriot."

"What a child you are," cried the viscountess. "Goriot was the Countess de Restaud's maiden name."

"The daughter of a manufacturer of vermicelli," the duchess continued, "a little person who was presented at court the same day as the daughter of a pastry merchant. Don't you remember, Clara? The king burst out laughing, and told a Latin joke about flour. People—how did it go?—people . . ."

"Ejusdem farinae," said Eugène.

"That's right," said the duchess.

"So he is her father," Eugène went on, with a gesture of horror.

"Yes, that fellow had two daughters, and he is almost mad about them though they have both practically renounced him."

"Isn't the other one," said the viscountess, looking at the Duchess de Langeais, "married to a banker with a German name, a Baron de Nucingen? Isn't her name Delphine? Isn't she a blonde who has a box on the side at the Opéra, and doesn't she come to the Théâtre des Bouffons also, and laugh very loud, so she will be noticed?"

The duchess replied with a smile, "I marvel at you, darling. Why do you take such an interest in such people? Restaud must have been madly in love to have daubed himself with the Goriot flour. But he will get the worse of the bargain. She's in the hands of the Count de Trailles, and he'll ruin her."

"They have renounced their father," Eugène repeated.

"Yes indeed, their father, the perfect father," the viscountess rejoined "a father who has given them everything he had, so people say, five or six hundred thousand francs each as a dowry so they could be happy and marry well; and who kept only eight or ten thousand livres income for himself, since he thought that his daughters would go on being his daughters, and that he had made for himself two lives, and prepared two houses where he would be worshipped and made much of. Within two years the sons-in-law had banished him from their society as if he had been the lowest of the low. . . ."

Tears were flowing from Eugène's eyes, for it was not long since he had been among his own pure family, and he was still under the spell of youthful beliefs; it was only his first day on the battlefield of life in Parisian society. Genuine emotion is so infectious that all three for a moment looked at one another in silence.

"Good heavens," said the Duchess de Langeais, "yes, I know it seems utterly horrible, and nevertheless we see it every day. Isn't there a reason for it? Tell me, darling, have you ever thought exactly what a son-in-law is? A son-in-law is a man for whom we bring up, you and I, a dear little creature with whom we form a thousand bonds and who for seventeen years will be the joy of a family, its white soul, as Lamartine says, and who will become its ruin. When this man has taken her from us, he will start out by seizing her love, as if it were an axe, and with it he'll cut out of her heart, out of her very life, every feeling which bound her to her family. One day our daughter was everything to us, and we were everything to her; the next day she has become our foe. Don't you see this tragedy taking place every day? Here it's the daughter-in-law showing the utmost impertinence to her father-in-law, who sacrificed everything for his son; and there it's a son-in-law putting his mother-in-law out of his house. I hear people asking what's dramatic in society today: well, the drama of the son-in-law is a terrifying one, and then there are our marriages which have become such very stupid things. I remember very clearly what happened to this old manufacturer of vermicelli. I think that this Foriot . . ."

"Goriot, Madame."

"Yes, this Moriot was president of his section during the Revolution; he was on the inside during the great famine, and began making his fortune at that time by selling flour for ten times what it had cost him. He could get all the flour he wanted. My grandmother's steward sold some to him for immense prices. No doubt like all those people Goriot gave a cut to the Committee of Public Safety. I remember that the steward told my grandmother she was perfectly safe staying on at Grandvilliers because her wheat entitled her to a clean bill of political health. Well, this Loriot who sold wheat to the headchoppers has had only one passion. People say that he worships his daughters. He has slipped the elder into the house of Restaud and the younger he has grafted on the Baron de Nucingen, a rich banker who makes a show of royalism. You can understand that under Bonaparte the two sons-in-law did not make too much of a fuss about having this old revolutionary among them; it was still quite all right. But when the Bourbons were restored the old fellow was an embarrassment to the Count de Restaud, and still more to the banker. Perhaps his daughters still loved him, and they tried to please both sides, their father and their husbands; they had Goriot come when no one else was coming; they alleged that they did so because of their great affection. 'Come today, Papa, it'll be nicer, we'll be alone.' But, my dear, I think that real feeling has eyes and a mind; and the heart of the poor old revolutionary bled. He saw that his daughters were ashamed of him; that if they loved their husbands, he was annoying his sons-in-law. He had to sacrifice himself, and he did sacrifice himself, because he was a father; he decreed his own banishment. And when he saw that his daughters were happy, he knew that he had done right. The father and the children were accomplices in this little crime. The same thing is going on everywhere. Wouldn't this old Doriot have been a grease-spot in his daughters' drawing rooms? He would have been uncomfortable; he would have been bored there. What happened to this father can also happen to the prettiest woman in the world with the man she loves best; if she bores him with her love, he'll leave her, he'll do dishonorable things in order to get away. That's how it is with every emotion. Our heart is a treasure; empty it at one turn and you're ruined. We no more forgive an emotion for showing itself complete than we forgive a man for not having a cent. This father had given everything. During twenty years he had given his love, his very life's blood; and in one day he had given his fortune. Once the orange had been squeezed dry, his daughters left the skin at the street corner."

"What an ignoble thing the world is!" said the viscountess, fingering her shawl and without raising her eyes. The words directed at her by the Duchess de Langeais in the course of the story had cut her to the quick.

"Ignoble, no!" rejoined the duchess. "It merely keeps to its path, that's all. If I say these things to you, it's to show you that I'm not taken in by the world. I agree with you," she went on pressing the viscountess's hand. "The world is a dirt-pile; let us try to keep above it." She rose, kissed the viscountess on the brow and said to her, "You are looking very beautiful at this moment, my dear. I've never seen your color so pretty." Then she left with a slight nod to Eugène.

"Père Goriot is sublime!" said Eugène, remembering how he had seen him twisting the silver at night.

The Viscountess de Beauséant did not hear him; she was lost in thought. Some moments passed in complete silence, and the poor student was too awkward and too bashful to be at ease either in leaving or in staying on or in speaking.

"The world is ignoble and nasty," the viscountess said, at length. "As soon as one meets with a misfortune, a friend always comes to tell of it and to twist a dagger in one's heart, and in the very moment of doing so asks one to admire the beauty of its hilt. Sarcasm and railleries begin immediately! Oh, I shall defend myself!" She lifted her head like the great lady she was and darted fiery glances from those proud eyes of hers. "Oh," she said "you are still here!"

"Still," he said pitifully.

"Well, Monsieur de Rastignac, treat this world as it deserves You want to succeed. I'll help you. You will discover how deeply corrupt women are, and you'll measure the enormous and wretched vanity of men. I have read far in the book of the world, but there were some pages I didn't know. Now I know them all. The more coldly you calculate, the farther you'll climb. If you strike without pity, you will be feared. Use men and women only as horses for your coach, and by the time they've finished the stage they are to carry you, let them founder, and you will come to the very height of your desires. Note that you can achieve nothing here unless you have some woman who takes an interest in you. She must be young, rich and elegant. If you feel any genuine emotion, hide it like a treasure; don't ever let it be suspected, or you'd be ruined. You would cease being the execu-

tioner, and become the victim. If you ever fall in love keep your
secret well! Don't make it known until you're very sure of the
person to whom you open your heart. In order that you may keep
that love, the love that has not yet come into existence, you must
learn to mistrust this world that lies about you. Listen to me,
Miguel" (she naïvely used the wrong name, without noticing),
"there's something even more frightful than the desertion of a
father by his two daughters who wish he were dead. That's the
rivalry of two sisters. Restaud is of high birth, his wife has been
accepted, she has been presented at court; but her sister, her
wealthy sister, the beautiful Baroness de Nucingen, the wife of
a businessman, is eaten up with disappointment; she is dying
of jealousy, a hundred leagues from her sister; her sister has
ceased to be her sister; these two women renounce each other as
they renounce their father. So the Baroness de Nucingen would
lick all the mud there is between the Rue Saint Lazare and the
Rue de Grenelle to enter my drawing room. She thought that
de Marsay would enable her to attain her goal, she has made herself de Marsay's slave, and how she bores de Marsay! De Marsay
cares very little for her. If you bring her to me and introduce her
to me, you will be her favorite, and she will adore you. Afterwards, love her if you can, and if not make use of her. I will see
her once or twice, at my large evening parties, when there's a
mob about; but I won't receive her in the daytime. I'll greet
her; that's all that will be needed. By your mention of Père
Goriot you've closed the countess's doors against you. Yes, my
friend, if you went there twenty times, she'd not be at home
once. Orders have been given not to admit you. Well, let Père
Goriot be your means of introduction to the Baroness de
Nucingen! The beautiful Delphine de Nucingen shall be your
banner! Once you are the man she singles out, women will go
wild over you. Her rivals, her friends, her closest friends will try
to take you away from her. There are women who love a man

82

just because he has been selected by another woman, just as there are poor bourgeois women who by imitating our hats hope to acquire our ways. You will have many successes. In Paris success is everything; it's the key to power. If women think you witty and gifted, men will believe them unless you show them their error. Then you can aim at anything; you will have an entry everywhere. And then you will find out what the world is, a gathering of dupes and rogues. Be of neither party. I give you my name to serve you as Ariadne's thread in making your way into this labyrinth. Do not compromise it." She gave the student a queen's glance and with a graceful curve of her neck added, "Give it back to me unsullied. Now leave me. Women also have their battles to wage."

Eugène interrupted her, saying, "I wonder if you may need a man who is ready to light a fuse for a mine."

"And if I did?" she asked.

He struck his hand against his heart and smiled in answer to his cousin's smile, and then left. It was five o'clock. Eugène was hungry and he was afraid he would not be back at the boarding-house in time for dinner. From this fear he shifted to thought of the pleasure he felt in being driven rapidly through the city. It was a purely physical pleasure and left him free to give his whole attention to the thoughts that beset him. When a man of his youth is the victim of contempt, he becomes angry, he rages, he clenches his fist against the whole of society, he means to be re-venged, and yet he doubts his own powers. Eugène was crushed by the words: The Countess de Restaud's door is shut against you. "I'll go to her house," he said to himself, "and if the Vis-countess de Beauséant is right, if I am refused admission . . . the Countess de Restaud will find me in every drawing room she enters. I'll learn to fence, and to shoot, and I'll kill her dear Maxime." "And where will you get the money for all this?" his conscience inquired. In a moment all the wealth spread out before him at the Restaud house shone before his eyes. He had seen there such costly beauty as a former Mademoiselle Goriot would have desired, gilded walls and ceilings, expensive ornaments conspicuous everywhere, the stupid luxury of the parvenu, the wasteful expense of the kept woman. This splendid image was quickly eclipsed by the grandeur of the Beauséant mansion. His imagination, carried into the high places of Parisian society, planted a thousand evil thoughts in his heart and at the same time enlarged both his mind and his conscience. He saw the world for what it is: law and morality impotent among the rich. In wealth he saw the *ultima ratio mundi*. "Vautrin is right," he decided, "wealth is virtue."

When he had reached the Rue Neuve-Sainte-Geneviève he quickly went up to his room, came down to give ten francs to the driver and then went into the nauseating dining room where the eighteen boarders engaged in feeding met his eyes and struck him as so many animals at a trough. The sight of such poverty and the aspect of the room were horrible to him. The transition had been too abrupt, the contrast was too complete to pass without giving an exorbitant stimulus to his ambitious feelings. On one side the fresh and charming images of the most elegant society, faces young, lively, surrounded by the wonders of art and luxury, passionate heads full of poetic appeal; on the other, sinister tableaux framed in filth, and faces on which the passions had left as marks of their passage only the ugliest traces of their mechanism. The lessons the Viscountess de Beauséant had burst out with in all her wrath at learning that she had been deserted, and her captious offers of help flocked back into his memory and took on a new force because of the poverty round about him. Eugène decided to dig two parallel trenches, both of which should lead him to fortune, one by way of knowledge, the other by way of love; he would be a learned lawyer and also a man of fashion. How young he was still! These two lines are asymptotes which can never meet.

"You are very gloomy, Marquis," said Vautrin, with one of those looks by which he seemed to inform himself of the heart's most deeply hidden secrets.

"I'm not disposed to put up with the pleasantries of those who call me marquis," said Eugène. "To be a real marquis here one must have an income of a hundred thousand livres, and anyone who is living at the Maison Vauquer is not exactly a favorite of Fortune."

Vautrin looked at Eugène in a patronizing way, as if he were saying: "What a child! I could swallow him at one gulp." Then he replied, "You're in a bad temper, perhaps because you weren't successful with the beautiful Countess de Restaud?"

"She's given orders I'm not to be admitted at her house because I told her that her father eats at our table," Eugène cried out.

Glances were exchanged around the table and Père Goriot lowered his eyes and turned away to wipe them.

"You threw some snuff into my eye," he said to his neighbor.

"Anyone who teases Père Goriot will from now on have me to deal with," said Eugène, with a glance toward Goriot's neighbor. "He's the superior of us all. I don't include the ladies," he added, turning toward Mademoiselle Taillefer.

This speech resolved the tension. Eugène had uttered it with an air which imposed silence round the table. Only Vautrin was not silenced, and he said in a jovial way, "If you're going to make yourself responsible for Père Goriot, you'll have to learn how to use sword and pistol like a master."

"I'll do just that," said Eugène.

"So you've begun a campaign today?"

"Perhaps," Eugène replied. "But I owe no one any account of

85

my affairs, since I don't seek to find out what affairs others transact at night."

Vautrin gave him a side glance.

"My boy, if you don't mean to be taken in by the marionettes, you must get right into the booth, and not just content yourself with looking through the holes in the curtains. Let's stop, now," he added, noting that Eugène was about to get angry. "We'll have a bit of a talk together whenever you feel inclined."

The temper of the diners had become cold and somber. Père Goriot, crushed by the intense pain he had felt at what Eugène had said, was unaware that the state of mind toward him had changed or that a young man who could put a stop to persecution had come to his defense.

"Can it be," asked Madame Vauquer in an undertone, "that Monsieur Goriot is really the father of a countess?"

"And of a baroness, too," retorted Eugène.

"That's his only function," said Bianchon to Eugène. "I've studied his head for bumps; there is only one, the bump of paternity. He'll be an *eternal* father."

Eugène was in too serious a mood to laugh at this joke of Bianchon's. He meant to profit by the advice given him by the Viscountess de Beauséant, and he was asking himself where and how he could get money. As he thought of the savannas of the world extending before him empty and yet full, he fell into a brown study. No one spoke to him when the dinner was over.

"So you've seen my daughter?" asked Goriot in a voice full of emotion.

Roused from his meditations by the old fellow, Eugène took his hand and, looking at him with a sort of affection, replied, "You're a very fine person. We'll talk about your daughters later." He got up and, unwilling to listen to Père Goriot, went up to his room and wrote to his mother the following letter.

My dear mother,

I depend as much upon you at this moment as when I was a baby at your breast. I am in a position where I can quickly make a fortune. I need twelve hundred francs and I must have them at any cost. Don't say a word about this plea to my father; perhaps he would oppose it, and if I were without this money I should be in such a desperate state that it would lead me to blow out my brains. I'll explain myself when I see you; I should have to write whole volumes to make you understand the situation I'm in. I haven't been gambling, dear mother, I have incurred no debts; but if you wish to preserve the life you gave me, you must find this sum for me. I am frequenting the Viscountess de Beauséant who has taken me under her protection. I have to go into society, and I haven't a cent to supply me with gloves. I can do with bread to eat and water to drink, I can go without any food; but I can't go without the tools that are needed to plow the land in these quarters. It's a question of my either making my way or sticking in the mud. I know all the hopes you have placed in me, and I want to realize them quickly. Dear mother, sell some of your old jewels; I'll soon replace them. I know enough of our family's situation to be able to appreciate such a sacrifice, and you must believe that I do not ask you to make it vainly, or I should be a monster. Please believe that this prayer of mine is the cry of absolute necessity. Our whole future depends on this sum, with which I must open my campaign; this Paris life is a perpetual warfare. If to make up the sum there is no way of avoiding the sale of my aunt's lace, tell her I will send her lace still more beautiful.

Etc.

He wrote to his two sisters, asking them for their savings, and in order to get possession of these without their telling the family of the sacrifice which he knew they would make with joy, he appealed to their delicacy, playing upon those chords of honor which are so sensitive and so strongly resonant in young hearts. When he had written these letters he felt an involuntary trepidation; his heart beat fast and his frame trembled. The ambitious youth knew the stainless excellence of their spirits so far removed from the press of the world. He knew what pain he would be giving his sisters and also what joy; with what pleasure they would talk together of their dear brother in the privacy of the garden. His conscience set before him in a strong light the sisters counting over their little treasure in secret; he saw them exercising the mischievous ingenuity of young girls in inventing a means of sending this money to him without being found out, for the first time in their lives taking part in a deception—with an aim that was sublime. "A sister's heart is like a diamond for purity, like an abyss for the depth of its tenderness!" he reflected. He was ashamed of having written. How powerful their prayers would be, how pure the elevation of their souls toward heaven! What delights they would find in sacrificing themselves! What sadness his mother would feel if she could not send the full sum he had asked for! These noble feelings, these appalling sacrifices, would serve him as rungs in the ladder that led to Delphine de Nucingen. A few tears started from his eyes, a last tribute to his family feeling. He paced up and down in an agitation full of despair. Père Goriot, seeing him in this state through his door, left ajar, came in and asked what was wrong.

"Oh, my good neighbor, I'm still a son and a brother as you are a father. You have every reason to tremble for the Countess Anastasie—she's in the grip of a certain Maxime de Trailles, and he will ruin her."

Père Goriot withdrew, stammering something that Eugène could not understand. The next day Eugène went out to post his letters. Up to the very last moment he hesitated, but he thrust them into the box, saying, "I'll succeed," the gambler's phrase, the great general's, the fatalistic phrase which ruins more men than it saves. A few days later he went to the Countess de Restaud's and was not received. He went back three times, and three times he was refused admission, and this although he came at times when the Count de Trailles was not there. The Viscountess de Beauséant had been right. He had stopped studying. He went to class only to answer to his name, and as soon as he had done so, he slipped away. He had followed the course of thought that attracts so many students; he would put off studying until examination time. He intended to let everything accumulate till the end of his third year; then he would really set to work to learn the law and do so in one great effort at the very last moment. By this decision he had fifteen months of leisure to swim about in the ocean of Paris, to engage in woman-traffic or to fish for a fortune.

During this week he saw the Viscountess de Beauséant twice, going to her house only as the Marquis d'Adjuda's carriage was driving away. For a few days longer this celebrated woman, the most poetic figure in the Faubourg Saint-Germain remained victorious and held off the marriage of Mademoiselle de Rochefide with the Marquis d'Adjuda-Pinto. But these last days, the most passionate of all because of her fear she would lose her happiness, merely hastened the catastrophe. The Marquis like the Rochefide family had regarded this quarrel and this reconciliation as a happy circumstance; they hoped that the Viscountess de Beauséant would become used to the idea of this marriage and would in the end understand that her delightful afternoons must end in order that a man's natural destiny might be fulfilled. Despite the most sacred promises daily renewed, the marquis was tricking her and she was happy in being tricked. "Instead of nobly jumping from a window," as the Duchess de Langeais put it, "she was letting herself be dragged downstairs." Nonetheless these last gleams kept the Viscountess de Beauséant long enough in Paris for her to help her young relative for whom she had a superstitious sort of affection. Eugène had shown her his devotion and the warmth of his feelings at a moment when a woman finds no genuine consolation or pity in any glance. If any soft and gentle words are said to her by a man at such a time, it is because he is speculating on the future.

In his wish to acquire a full knowledge of the lay of the land before laying siege to the house of Nucingen, Eugène sought to find out all he could about the earlier life of Père Goriot, and collected much accurate knowledge, which may be reduced to this:

Jean-Joachim Goriot had been, before the Revolution, a simple maker of vermicelli, clever, economical and enterprising enough to buy out his master's interest when the latter fell a chance victim of the first rising in 1789. He set up shop in the Rue de la Jussienne, near the grain-market, and had the good horse sense to accept the presidency of the section so that he could arrange for the protection of his trade by the most influential people in that dangerous time. This sense was the beginning of his fortune which dated from the famine, real or pretended, which led to the enormous rise in the cost of grain in Paris. There were murderous riots at the bakeries, while certain people would go quietly to get Italian paste at the grocers'. In the course of this year, Citizen Goriot built up the capital which later enabled him to carry on his trade with all the advantage that a great mass of money confers on the one who possesses it. What befell him was what befalls all men who have only a limited ability. His mediocrity saved him. Besides, since his fortune became known only when there was no longer any danger in being rich, he aroused no one's envy. The grain business appeared to have absorbed all his intelligence. If he had to do with anything like grain, flour or tailings, the appreciation of their quality, their source, their conservation, the foresight into their prices, the prediction whether harvests would be abundant or short, the purchase of cereals at low prices, the quest of supplies in Sicily or the Ukraine, Goriot was first and the rest nowhere. Seeing him managing his business, explaining the laws on the import and export of grain, studying their drift, seeing their loopholes, anyone would have thought he was qualified to be a minister of State. Patient, active, energetic, unchanging, quick in filling his orders, he had an eagle's vision; he forestalled and anticipated everything, knew everything, hid everything, a diplomat in his projects, a general in his actions. Once outside his specialty, his simple dark little shop—in his leisure time he stood on the step during long hours of indolence, leaning his shoulder against the door—he was no more than the rough stupid workman, a man incapable of following any line of reasoning, insensitive to any of the pleasures of the mind, a man who fell asleep at the theatre, strong only in his stupidity.

Such natures are almost all alike. In the heart of nearly every one you could find some sublime emotion. Two all-absorbing feelings had filled the vermicelli maker's heart, had absorbed all its warmth, just as the grain trade occupied his whole brain. His wife, the only daughter of a wealthy farmer from La Brie was for him the object of a religious admiration, of a boundless love. Goriot had admired in her a nature at once frail and strong, sensitive and pretty, in vigorous contrast with his own. If there is one feeling innate in the heart of man, is it not the pride in protection exercised at every moment over one who is weak? Unite with this feeling of love, the lively gratitude which all sincere people have for the source of their pleasures, and you will understand a host of moral oddities. After seven years of unclouded happiness, unfortunately for Goriot he lost his wife; she was beginning to extend her mastery over him beyond the sphere of feeling. Perhaps she would have cultivated that inert nature of his, perhaps she would have imparted to it an understanding of the things of the world and of life.

After his loss the feeling of fatherhood developed in Goriot to the point of madness. His affections, robbed by death of their first object, were thrown upon his two daughters; and at first they fully satisfied all his emotions. No matter how advantageous were the propositions made to him by businessmen or farmers in their eagerness to marry off a daughter, he continued a widower. His father-in-law, the only man for whom he had any liking, claimed certain knowledge that Goriot had sworn not to be unfaithful to his wife even after her death. The people at the market, unable to understand this sublime madness, joked about it and gave Goriot a grotesque nickname. The first of them to utter it—it was when he and Goriot were drinking at the conclusion of a deal—got from the vermicelli maker a blow on the shoulder which sent him head first out into the Rue Oblin. The unthinking devotion, the delicate and susceptible love which Goriot had for his daughters was so well known that one day when one of his competitors wished to get him to leave the grain market so that he might remain and dictate the prices, it was enough to say that Delphine had been run over by a cab. Ghastly pale, the vermicelli maker left the market at once. He was ill for several days as a result of the contending feelings to which this false alarm had exposed him. He did not aim a murderous blow at this man's shoulder; no, he forced him out of the market by ensuring his bankruptcy at a crucial moment.

The education of Goriot's two daughters was inevitably mad. He had an income of more than sixty thousand livres; he spent less than twelve hundred francs on himself, and found happiness in satisfying their whims: the best teachers were engaged to impart to them the talents whose cultivation marks a good education; they had a companion, and happily for them she was a woman of mind and taste; they rode, they had a carriage, they lived like the mistresses of a rich old lord. They had only to express a wish, however costly, for their father to hurry to fulfill it. In return for all he gave all he asked was a caress. He set them among the angels, necessarily far above himself, poor man! He loved even the pain they caused him. When they were old enough to be married, they were free to choose their husbands according to their tastes; each of them was to have as dowry a half of her father's fortune. Anastasie was sought, for her beauty, by the Count de Restaud; she had aristocratic longings which led her to leave her father's house and dash into the spheres of high society. Delphine was fond of money. She married Nucingen, a banker of German origin who was created a baron of the Holy Roman Empire. Goriot remained a maker of vermicelli. His daughters and his sons-in-law were soon upset at seeing him carry on his trade, although it was now the whole of his life. After standing against their appeals for five years, he agreed to retire with what he could make by selling his stock, and with what he had been able to amass during these last years; this constituted a capital which Madame Vauquer (to whose house he then came) had estimated as bringing in from eight to ten thousand livres income. He buried himself in this boarding-house in his despair at seeing that his two daughters were forced by their husbands to refuse not merely to take him into their homes, but even to invite him to appear if there was company.

Such was the sum of knowledge concerning Père Goriot possessed by a certain Monsieur Muret who had bought him out. The suppositions Eugène had heard the Duchess de Langeais make were thus confirmed.

This is the end of the exposition of this obscure but appalling Parisian tragedy.

Toward the end of the first week in December, Eugène received two letters, one from his mother, the other from his elder sister. The well-known handwriting made him at once quiver with pleasure and tremble with fear. On these frail bits of paper was the verdict of life or death for his hopes. The recollection of the poverty of his family made him feel some fear; and he had had such proof of their love that he might well fear that he was draining the last drops of their blood. His mother's letter ran as follows:

My dear child,

I am sending you what you asked for. Make good use of this money, for, even if your life were at stake, I could not match such a large sum without telling your father and so disturbing the quiet of our household. The only way we could get it would be to mortgage our property. I cannot judge the worth of projects of which I have no knowledge; what can they be like when you are afraid to tell me of them? There was no need to go into long explanations; a mother needs only a word, and that one word would have saved me the anguish of uncertainty. I cannot conceal from you the painful impression your letter made upon me. My dear son, what can the feeling be which has forced you to strike such terror into my heart? You must have suffered a great deal in writing to me in such terms, for I have suffered much in reading what you wrote. In what career are you embarking? Are your life and your happiness bound up in your appearing to be what you are not, mingling with a society in which you cannot move without spending money on such a scale as you cannot afford, and without losing time which is precious for your studies? My dear Eugène, believe what your mother tells you from her heart: devious ways lead to nothing great. Patience and resignation are the proper virtues for a young man in your position. I am not scolding you. I don't want to mix any bitterness with our gift. My words come from a mother who is as full of trust as of foresight. If you know your duties, I know, for my part, how pure your heart is, how excellent your intentions are. So I can say to you without any fear: "Go ahead, my darling." I am afraid, because I am your mother; but every step you take will be accompanied by our prayers and blessings. Be careful, my dear boy. You must be as prudent as a full-grown man, for the destiny of five of those dear to you is in your keeping. Yes, our fortunes depend upon you, just as your happiness is our happiness. We all pray that God may help you in your undertakings. Your aunt has been kind beyond conception in this business; she was even able to understand what you said about your gloves in your letter. She has a weakness for the eldest child, as she said gaily. Eugène, you must love her dearly. I will not tell you what she has done for you until you have succeeded, for if I did her money would burn your fingers. You young folk cannot know what it is to sacrifice one's memories! But what would one not sacrifice for you? Your aunt bids me tell you that she sends you a kiss on the forehead, and that she would wish this kiss to give you the strength to be often happy. The dear woman would have written to you herself but she has gout in her fingers. Your father is well. The harvest of 1819 exceeds our hopes. Good-bye, dear boy. I won't say anything about your sisters. Laura is writing to you. I leave to her the pleasure of chattering to you about the little incidents of our family life. May Heaven bring you success. Oh, you must succeed, Eugène! You have made me feel a pain which I could not bear if it were repeated. I have found out what it means to be poor by wishing for wealth that I might give it to my child. I must say good-bye. Don't leave us without news, and here is a kiss from your mother.

By the time Eugène had finished reading this letter he was in tears. He was thinking of Père Goriot twisting his silver and selling it to pay for his daughter's notes. "Your mother has twisted her jewels," he said to himself. "Your aunt must have wept as she sold some of her keepsakes. What right have you to blame Anastasie? You have just done the very same thing simply for selfish concern for your own future that she did for her lover. Which of the two is the better person?" Eugène felt coursing through his body a current of intolerable heat. He yearned to renounce the world, not to take this money. He felt that noble and lofty remorse whose quality is seldom appreciated by men when they sit in judgment on their fellows, but which leads the angels to absolve the criminal whom an earthly judge has condemned. Eugène opened his sister's letter and its words of innocent grace refreshed his heart.

Your letter was very timely, my dear brother. Agathe and I had so many different plans for our money that we could not decide how to spend it. You have done like the King of Spain's servant who upset his master's watches; you have made it possible for us to agree. The fact is that we were constantly quarreling about which of our desires should have the preference, and we didn't foresee, my dear Eugène, the use which would satisfy all our desires. Agathe was beside herself with joy. In a word, we were like two mad things all day long, to the degree that (our aunt's style!) our mother said to us, putting on her severe expression, "What's wrong with you girls?" I think that if she had given us a little scolding we should have been even happier.

A woman must be very happy when she can suffer for the person she loves! I was the only one who was a little disappointed and remorseful in the midst of my joy. I am sure I'll be a bad wife; I'm too much of a spendthrift. I had bought for myself two belts and a pretty little stiletto to pierce the eyelets of my corsets, foolish purchases, so that I had less money than that big lump of an Agathe who is economical and heaps up her crowns like a magpie. She had two hundred francs! And I, my poor darling, had only fifty crowns. It's a proper punishment for me. I'd like to throw my belt into the well; I'll never have any pleasure in wearing it. For I have robbed you. Agathe was charming. She said to me, "Let's send the three hundred and fifty francs from the two of us!" But I didn't take time to tell you before how things happened. Do you know what we did so that we could carry out your orders? We took our glorious money, went for a walk together and as soon as we were on the main road, we ran as fast as we could to Ruffec, where we gave the whole sum to Monsieur Grimbert, who has the local office for the Messageries royales. We were as lighthearted as two swallows, coming home. Agathe asked me whether it was happiness that made us so. We talked of a thousand things which I won't repeat to you, for they had too much to do with you.

My dear Paris brother, how much we love you—that's the gist of it in a word. As to keeping it secret, a couple of deceivers such as we are, our aunt calls us that, are capable of anything, even of keeping quiet. Our mother went off with our aunt on a mysterious trip to Angoulême, and they have both been very secret about the high purpose of their journey, which took place only after long conferences from which we, like our father, were excluded. Great conjectures are filling all minds in the state of Rastignac.

The muslin dress with a flowered pattern which the princesses are making for Her Majesty the Queen progresses in the deepest secrecy. There are only two more widths to do. It has been decided that instead of a wall on the Verteuil side of the property there shall be a hedge. The small holders will lose some fruit, and some lattices by this decision, but foreign persons will gain a beautiful view. If the heir presumptive should need any handkerchiefs, notice is given that the Dowager de Marcillac in going through her treasures and her trunks, designated as Pompeii and Herculaneum, discovered a piece of beautiful Holland linen which she did not know she had; and the Princesses Agathe and Laure have placed at her disposition their needle and thread and *hands that are always a bit too red. The two young princes, Sir Henri and Sir Gabriel, have kept their fatal habits of being too greedy for jam, putting their sisters in a rage, refusing to learn anything, amusing themselves by turning birds out of their nests, cutting loose in general, and chopping down willows to get switches, contrary to the laws of the State. The apostolic delegate, vulgarly known as Monsieur le curé, threatens to excommunicate them if they continue to abandon the sacred canons of education for the warlike staves of the elder. Good-bye, my dear brother, never did a letter carry so many wishes for your happiness, nor so much contented love. You will have so much to tell us when you come back. I'm the elder, and you'll tell me everything. My aunt has hinted that you have had success in society.*

L'on parle d'une dame et l'on se tait du reste.

You can trust us! Just tell us, Eugène, if you wanted it, we could get on without handkerchiefs, and make shirts for you instead. Tell us quickly if you want them. If you had an urgent need for some beautiful shirts, nicely sewn, we should have to set to work on them at once; and if there are fashions in Paris that we mightn't know of, you could send us a pattern, particularly for the cuffs. Good-bye, good-bye, a kiss on your forehead, on the left temple which is mine alone. I leave the remaining sheet for Agathe who has promised to read nothing of what I've written. But to make sure she doesn't, I'm going to stay right beside her while she writes.

Your loving sister,

Laure de Rastignac.

"I must make my fortune at any cost, at any cost at all," Eugène thought. "Whole treasures couldn't recompense devotion like this. I'd like to bring them all kinds of happiness together. Fifteen hundred and fifty francs," he reflected after a pause. "Each one must find its mark. Laure is right. Trust a woman!

My shirts are of coarse linen. In the interests of someone else's happiness, a girl becomes as shrewd as a robber. Innocent in her own life, prudent on my behalf, she is like an angel that forgives the sins of men without knowing what they are."

The world was his! Already he had summoned his tailor, sounded him out and conquered him. From seeing the Count de Trailles Eugène had realized the influence that tailors exercise on the lives of young men. Alas, there can be no middle way; one's tailor is either a mortal enemy or a priceless friend. In his, Eugène had met a person who had a clear view of how his trade could fructify, and appreciated that he was the link between the present and the future of young men. So it fell that Eugène in his gratitude made this fellow's fortune by one of those phrases at which later in his career he excelled: "I know," he used to say "of two pairs of trousers he has made which brought about marriages giving an income of twenty thousand livres."

Fifteen hundred francs, and whatever clothes he wished! At this moment the poor Southerner had lost every fear of the future, and when he came down for breakfast he had that indefinable air that a young man wears because he possesses a little money. When the money slides into the young man's pocket, an imaginary column is created for his support. He carries himself better than he did before, he meets your eye directly, his movements are more agile; the day before, in his humility he would have bowed his back to receive a blow; on the morrow he would slap a Prime Minister. Unheard of phenomena are going on within him; he wants everything and there is nothing he cannot do, his desires are of all sorts, including the fantastic; he is gay, liberal, expansive. In short the bird that was wingless has found its powers. The moneyless student nibbles at a little pleasure just as a dog sneaks off with a bone amid a thousand dangers, breaking it, sucking its marrow on the run; but the young man who can clink a few stray gold pieces in his pocket savors his delights at leisure, counts them one by one, walks on air, no longer knowing what the word poverty means. Paris belongs to him completely. Time when everything is bright, when everything scintillates and flames! Time of joyful strength, and which neither man nor woman knows how to use! Time of debts and sharp fears which multiply all one's pleasures! He who has not frequented the left bank of the Seine between the Rue Saint-Jacques and the Rue des Saints-Pères knows nothing of human life!

"Ah, if the women of Paris knew," Eugène said to himself, as he ate his preserved pears (at one sou apiece) served by Madame Vauquer, "they would come here for love."

Just then a porter from the *Messageries royales* came into the dining room, after ringing at the door. He asked for Monsieur Eugène de Rastignac, and gave him two sacks and a receipt to sign. The searching look that Vautrin then gave him was as sharp as the stroke of a whip.

"You will be able to pay for some lessons in fencing and some sessions at the shooting gallery," were the words that accompanied the look.

"The galleons have arrived," said Madame Vauquer, looking at the sacks.

Mademoiselle Michonneau was afraid to look at them, not wishing to betray her covetousness.

"You have a good mother," said Madame Couture.

"The young man has a good mother," echoed Poiret.

"Yes, Mama has bled herself white," said Vautrin. "Now you can have your fun; you can go into society, and fish for a dowry, and dance with countesses who have peach blossoms in their hair. But mark my advice, young man, learn to shoot!"

Vautrin made a gesture like that of a man who is taking aim at his opponent. Eugène wanted to give a tip to the porter, but could find nothing in his pocket. Vautrin dipped into his and flung twenty sous to the young man.

"Your credit is good," he continued with another sharp look.

Eugène had to thank him although ever since their bitter exchange on the day he had come back from the Viscountess de Beauséant's the man was intolerable to him. During the eight days that had elapsed since then the two men had always been silent in each other's presence and had observed each other closely. Eugène puzzled himself why it should be. One may suppose that ideas are projected in direct ratio to the force with which they are conceived, and speed to their mark by a mathematical law comparable with that which projects the shell from the cannon. The effects are not the same in all cases. There are gentle natures in which ideas penetrate and carry destruction; but there are also tougher natures, skulls with ramparts of brass, against which the wills of others flatten out and fall as helpless as bullets before a strong wall; and there are flaccid and woolly natures in which the ideas of others expire like cartridges that come to nothing in the yielding soil of earthworks. Eugène had one of those heads like dynamite that go off at the least shock. He was too vividly young not to be accessible to the projection of ideas, to the infection of feelings which take hold of us so strangely without our being aware of the phenomena. His moral perceptions had the sharpness of a lynx's eye. His intuitions had, all of them, that mysterious lastingness, that flexibility of movement which astonishes us in superior persons, those who are cunning in seizing upon the weak point in any one's armor. Moreover, in the course of the past month Eugène's growth had been in strength as well as in error. His errors had been developed by the world and by the will to achieve his desires. One of his sources of strength was that Southern impetuosity which leads a man to walk straight up to the difficulty which faces him in order to get the better of it, and does not permit a man who comes from beyond the Loire to remain in any uncertainty. This is a strength, though Northerners consider it a defect; in their view if it was the source of Murat's success it was also the cause of his death. What we must conclude is that when a Southerner can unite the cunning of the North with his natural daring, he is a complete man such as can win and hold the kingdom of Sweden. So Eugène could not stay any longer beneath the batteries of Vautrin without finding out if this man were friend or enemy. At every moment he felt that this singular personage was reading his passions, and penetrating into his very heart, while everything about Vautrin was so carefully hidden that he seemed to have the profound immobility of the Sphinx which knows and sees everything and says nothing. Eugène, now that his purse was full, rebelled.

"Please be so good as to wait," he said to Vautrin, who was getting up to leave the room after sipping the last drops of his coffee.

"Why?" rejoined the elder man, as he put on his wide-brimmed hat and picked up his steel cane, with which he so often went through exercises which suggested he did not fear an assault by four robbers at once.

"I'm going to pay you back," said Eugène, as he undid a sack and handed over a hundred and forty francs to Madame Vauquer. "No debts among friends," he said to the widow. "We're clear now till New Year's. Will you change this hundred-sous piece?"

"No friends among debts," echoed Poiret, looking at Vautrin.

"Here are your twenty sous," said Eugène handing a coin to the bewigged sphinx.

"One would think that you were afraid to be my debtor," cried Vautrin, giving Eugène a look that pierced to the very depths, accompanied by one of those mocking and Diogenes-like smiles that a hundred times had almost angered the young man.

"Well . . . I am," Eugène replied, as, his two sacks in his hands, he rose to go upstairs.

Vautrin went out by the door which led to the drawing room and Eugène was about to leave by that which led to the stairway.

"Do you know, my lord marquis, that what you just said to me is not exactly polite," Vautrin remarked, beating his cane against the door and then coming toward the student who gave him a cold stare.

Eugène closed the dining-room door, and accompanied Vautrin to the well of the stairs, where there was a door which led into the garden, with a long grilled section in the upper half. There, just beside the kitchen, before Sylvie who had just come through, Eugène said, "*Monsieur* Vautrin, I am not a marquis."

"They're going to fight," said Mademoiselle Michonneau, with an air of complete indifference.

"To fight," echoed Poiret.

"No, they aren't," replied Madame Vauquer, as her fingers moved caressingly through the pile of crowns.

"But look, they're going out under the lindens," cried Victorine as she got up to look into the garden. "And the poor young man was quite right."

"Let us go upstairs, my dear," said Madame Couture. "These are matters that are no concern of ours."

Madame Couture and Victorine got up and met Sylvie who barred the way at the door.

"What's going on here?" she asked. "Monsieur Vautrin said to Monsieur Eugène: 'Let's have this out.' Then he took him by the arm and now they're trampling on our artichokes."

At this moment Vautrin appeared. "Madame Vauquer," said he, "there's absolutely nothing to be frightened about," and he smiled. "I'm going to try out my pistols under the lindens."

"Oh, Sir," said Victorine, knitting her hands together, "why do you mean to kill Monsieur Eugène?"

Vautrin took two steps backward and looked at Victorine closely. "Here's another story," he said in a mocking voice which made the poor girl blush. "The boy is very nice, isn't he? You give me an idea. I'll make both of you happy, my child."

Madame Couture had taken her ward by the arm and led her away, whispering to her, "Victorine, I simply can't account for the way you're behaving this morning."

"I don't want any pistols being fired on my property," said Madame Vauquer. "Why, you'll frighten everyone in the neighborhood and they'll call the police at once."

"Come, don't get excited, Mama Vauquer," Vautrin replied. "There, there, everything's all right. We'll go to the shooting gallery." He rejoined Eugène and took his arm in a familiar fashion. "When I've proved to you that at thirty-five paces I can hit the ace of spades five times in succession," he said, "your courage won't fail you, I know. You seem to me to be a little crazy and you'd let yourself be killed like an idiot."

"You're not standing your ground," said Eugène.

"Don't make me angry," Vautrin replied. "It's not cold this morning; let's sit down over there," pointing to the green chairs. "No one can hear what we say there. I must talk to you. You're a very good sort of young fellow, and I don't wish you any ill. I'm fond of you, on the word of Chea . . . Damn it! On the word of Vautrin. Why, I'm fond of you. . . . Well, I'll tell you. And before I do, be sure that I understand you as well as if you were my son, and I'm going to prove it to you. Put your sack down there," with a gesture toward the round table.

Eugène put his sacks down on the table, and sat down, afire with curiosity stirred in him to its very highest point by the change which had suddenly taken place in the manners of this man who after speaking of killing him now came forward as his protector.

"You would naturally like to know who I am, what I've done, or what I'm doing," Vautrin went on. "You're too curious, my boy. Come, don't get excited. You've a lot more to hear! I've had a lot of misfortunes. Listen to what I have to say first; you can reply afterwards. Here is the earlier part of my life in few words: Who am I? I am Vautrin. What do I do? What I please. Now let's get on. Do you want to know my character? I am kind to those who aid me and who appeal to me. They may do anything they like; they could kick me in the shins if they wanted without my saying: *Take care!* But, damn it, I'm as nasty as the devil with the people that annoy me or those who just don't happen to please my fancy. It will be a good thing for you to know that I don't care that—and he spat—for killing a fellow. Only when it's absolutely necessary to kill him I try to make a neat clean job of it. I'm what you call an artist. I've read the *Memoirs of Benvenuto Cellini,* though you mightn't think so to look at me, and in the original Italian. That fellow was a high-class rascal and I've learned a lesson from him, to imitate God, whose hand falls upon the just and the unjust, and to love the beautiful wherever I find it. Isn't it a fine part to play, too, standing alone against all mankind, and having luck on your side? I've done a good deal of thinking about the present frame-work of your social disorder. My boy, dueling is a child's game, a bit of folly. When one of two living men must go, it's idiocy to leave the choice to chance. And good Lord, that's what dueling does. Now I can hit the ace of spades five times in succession, with each bullet landing where the previous one lodged, and I can do it at thirty-five paces! When you have that sort of talent you may think you can feel sure of killing your man! And yet I've shot at a man from only twenty paces, and I missed him. The fool had never had a pistol in his hands before. Look!"

The extraordinary man opened his vest and showed a chest as hairy as a bear's back, with a reddish fell that excited a sort of disgust mixed with terror.

"Well, this tyro left his mark upon me," Vautrin took Eugène's finger and placed it on a hole near his breast. "But in those days I was a child. I was no older than you are now—twenty-one. I still believed in something, in a woman's love, in a heap of silly things in which you are just going to be caught. We should have fought, shouldn't we? You might have killed me. Suppose I were under ground, where would you be? You'd have had to slip away, go to Switzerland, squander your father's money, and he hasn't much of it.

"I'm going to make clear to you just what state you are now in; but I'm going to do it from the superior plane of a man who has examined the condition of things here below and seen that there are only two lines to take: stupid obedience or rebellion. I obey no one, you understand? Do you know what you need, with the sort of life you're leading? A million francs, and right now; without them you might as well go and wander about in the glades at Saint-Cloud and try to find out if there is a Supreme Being. And this sum, this million francs, I'm going to give it to you."

He stopped short and looked at Eugène.

"Ah, ha! Now you are looking at Papa Vautrin in a kinder way! When you hear that word you're like a young girl who hears the words: Till we meet tonight, and who spends the day primping and feeling like a cat that has swallowed the cream. That's the right spirit. Now let's settle this account between us. Here is the way your tally stands, my boy. Back home you have Papa, Mama, Great-aunt, two sisters (eighteen and seventeen) two young brothers (fifteen and ten), that's the list of the crew. Aunty is bringing up the sisters. The curé comes to teach the brothers Latin. The meals are more generous in boiled chestnuts than in white bread; Papa has to watch that his trousers don't wear out; Mama scarcely can have one dress for winter and one for summer; the sisters get along as best they can. I know all about it; I've been in the South. Things are like that in your home if you are allowed twelve hundred francs a year and the property only brings in three thousand. There's a cook and a manservant, for appearances must be kept up; Papa is a baron. As for ourselves, we are ambitious, we are related to the Beauséants, and we go about on foot; we want a fortune and we haven't a sou; we eat the stews of Mama Vauquer and we love the grand dinners of the Faubourg Saint-Germain; we sleep on a straw mattress and we want a mansion.

"I don't blame you for your desires. My boy, everybody hasn't the luck to be ambitious. Ask women which men they seek— the men who have ambition. The ambitious have the strongest bodies, the most iron in their blood, hotter emotions than other men. Women feel happiest and are most beautiful when they are strong, and so they prefer above all other men those who have enormous force, even when they run the risk of having it shatter them. I'm cataloguing your desires because I mean to put a question to you. This is the question. We're as hungry as a wolf; our paws have talons; how are we going to keep the pot boiling? We have first to swallow the law books, that isn't much fun and doesn't teach anything worth knowing! But they have to be dealt with! It can't be helped. We become a lawyer so that we can become the presiding judge at the assize court; we brand poor rascals who are better men than we are in order to prove to the rich that they can sleep quietly in their beds. It's no fun, and it takes a lot of time. To begin with, two years in Paris, hanging around and looking on, but without daring to touch the sweets we want so much. It's very exhausting to be always wanting something and unable to satisfy oneself. If you were thin-blooded, a sort of mollusk, you'd have nothing to fear; but you are as hot-blooded as a lion and your appetite would involve you in a score of foolish acts every day. You'll succumb to this torture—and it's the worst torture there is in God's hell. Let's suppose that you are good, that you drink only milk and compose elegies. Very well, high spirited as you may be, after a lot of trials and privations harsh enough to madden a dog, you'll have to begin by being assistant to some rascal in some dreadful hole of a town where the Government will throw you as your honorarium a thousand francs a year. Why, it's just like setting down a plate of soup before a butcher's mastiff! Go and bark at the thieves, plead the cases of the rich, send the fellows with guts to the guillotine. Many thanks! If you don't have patrons, you can go on rotting in your local court.

"When you're getting on for thirty, you'll be a judge there with twelve hundred francs a year, if you haven't yet thrown your gown into the garbage can. When you're about forty you'll marry some miller's daughter, who has an income of about six thousand francs. Very nice. If you have patrons, you'll be crown-attorney at thirty, with a salary of a thousand crowns, and you'll marry the mayor's daughter. If you go in for some low political tricks, such as reading Villèle for Manuel (there's rhyme, that's enough to pacify your conscience) on some document, by the time you're forty you'll be an attorney-general, and you may even become a member of the Chamber of Deputies. Note, my boy, that we shall have done some tampering with our darling little conscience, that we'll have endured twenty years of tribulations and hidden poverty, and that our sisters will have stayed unmarried. It's my privilege to point out to you, besides, that there only are twenty attorneys-general in France and twenty thousand aspirants to the title, among them some rogues who'd sell their whole family to rise one step. Suppose the profession displeases you; let's see what else there is. Does the Baron de Rastignac want to be an advocate? Very pleasant. You begin with ten years of suffering; you lay out a thousand francs each month; you have an office and a law library; you kiss the robe of a solicitor in order to get briefs; you lick the floor of the Court House. If this turned out well I wouldn't say you were foolish; but just find me in Paris five members of the bar who at fifty make more than fifty thousand francs a year! Bah! Rather than let my soul shrivel in that way I'd be a pirate! And besides, where would you get the money to last the course?

"It isn't very gay, the life I've painted for you. The dowry a wife would bring would help. If you marry there's a stone around your neck; and besides if we marry for money what becomes of our noble feelings, of our sense of honor? You might as well begin your rebellion against social conventions today. It would be nothing to lie down like a snake at a woman's feet, lick her mother's shoes, do things so low they'd disgust a sow, if you found happiness in the end. But you'll be utterly unhappy with a woman you'd have married in this way. It's better to wrestle with men than to match yourself against a woman. Well, there's the battleground of life, my boy. Make your choice. You've already chosen; you've gone to see your cousin de Beauséant, and you've scented luxury at her house. You've gone to the house of the Countess de Restaud, Père Goriot's daughter, and you scented the Parisian woman there. The day you came back from her place one word was graved on your forehead, and I could read it there: it was the word, *Succeed!* Succeed at any cost.

"Bravo, I said to myself, there's a fellow who suits my taste. You had to have money. Where was it to be had? You've taken everything your sisters could give you. It's the way of all brothers to slip away with more or less of their sisters' resources. Those fifteen hundred francs, got together God knows how, in a country where there are more chestnuts than hundred-sous pieces, are going to disappear quicker than a gang of marauding soldiers! And then, when they're gone, what will you do? You'll work? Work, understood as you understand it now, means that when you're old, if you have kept your strength as Poiret has, you'll be able to afford an apartment at Mama Vauquer's in your old age.

"How to make a fortune quickly—that's the problem fifty thousand young fellows in your position are right now trying to solve. You're one unit in that number. You can judge what efforts you'll have to make and how fierce the contest will be. You have to eat one another like so many spiders thrust into a pot, since there aren't fifty thousand good places available. Do you know how a man succeeds here? Either by the flash of genius or the adroitness of corruption. You have to crash into that mass like a cannon ball, or else slip in like a disease. Honesty is of no use. Men will bend beneath the power of genius, hating it, trying to slander it, because it takes all and gives nothing; but in the end they will accept its yoke if genius is stubborn. In a word, they'll worship it on their knees after they've failed to bury it in the mud. Corruption is everywhere; talent is rare. So corruption is the weapon of swarming mediocrity, and wherever you go you feel its edge. You'll see women whose husbands' pay is only six thousand francs a year, and they'll be spending ten on their dress alone. You'll see clerks who make twelve hundred francs buying property. You'll see women selling their bodies to ride in the carriage of the son of a lord, because then they can drive out to Longchamps in the middle lane. You've seen that poor fool of a Père Goriot forced to meet the note his daughter had endorsed, and her husband has an income of fifty thousand livres. I challenge you to take two steps in Paris without coming upon some devilish machinations. I'd bet my head to a head of that lettuce that you'll come on a wasp's nest with the first woman who attracts you, no matter if she's wealthy, beautiful and young. They're all up against some law, all at war with their husbands over everything. I'd never end if I had to explain to you all the shabby tricks that are used to get lovers, to get dresses, to hold children, to keep up the household, or just to satisfy vanity, but very seldom for any virtuous end, you may count on that. So the honest man is everyone's enemy. And what do you think an honest man is? In Paris he's the man who keeps silent, who refuses to make a deal. Of course I'm not talking about those poor serfs who exist everywhere to do the world's rough tasks and are never rewarded for their labor—I call them the confraternity of the wooden shoes of God. In them you find virtue in the fine flower of its stupidity, and their mark is utter poverty. I can imagine the horrible disappointment of these worthy folk if God should play a joke on them, a cruel joke, and stay away from the last judgment.

"So if you want to make a fortune in a hurry, you must either be rich already or else give the appearance of being rich. To get rich you have to do things in a big way, otherwise your gains are just small change, and it's all up. If in the hundred occupations which are open to you there are ten men who get rich quick, they're called robbers. Draw your own conclusions. That's the reality of life. It's no prettier than a kitchen; it smells as bad; and you've got to get your hands dirty if you're going to cook anything. The thing is to know how to get them clean again; the whole morality of our age is in that. If I talk to you like this about the world, it's because I've a right to. I know it. Do you suppose that I condemn it? Not at all. That's the way it's always been. Moralists won't ever change it. Man is an imperfect creature. Sometimes he is more of a hypocrite, sometimes less, and ninnies say he's good when he is more, and bad when he's less. I'm not championing the poor against the rich; man is the same at the top, in the middle, at the bottom of the social ladder. In a million of these high-grade cattle there are ten rascals who stand above everything, even above law. I'm one of them.

"And you, if you're really a superior person, plunge right ahead and hold your head high. But you must expect to contend against envy and calumny and mediocrity, against the whole world. Napoleon had to do with a Minister of War, Aubry was the name, who almost sent him out to the colonies. Take stock of yourself! See if you're strong enough to get up every morning with a firmer will than you had the night before. If you are, I'm going to make you a proposition that nobody would refuse. Listen carefully. You see I've got an idea. I mean to go and live a patriarchal life in the midst of a great estate, a hundred thousand acres say, in the southern part of the United States. I mean to be a planter, have slaves, make a nice few millions selling my livestock, my tobacco, my wood, live like a king, doing everything I crave, leading such a life as isn't imagined here where people creep into plaster burrows. I'm a great poet. But I don't write my poems; they are made of feelings and actions. Right now I have fifty thousand francs, and with that sum I could hardly buy forty blacks. I need two hundred thousand because I want two hundred blacks so that I can satisfy my tastes for the patriarchal life. Blacks, you see, they're like new-born children; one can do what one wants with them, without having some prying prosecutor coming along to ask you for explanations. With this black capital, in ten years I'll have three or four million francs. If I succeed, no one will ask: 'Who are you?' I'll be Mr. Four Millions, an American citizen. I'll be fifty, I won't be doddering for a while after that, and I'll have fun in my own way. Here's my question: 'If I get for you a dowry of a million francs, will you give me two hundred thousand?' A commission of twenty per cent. Is that too high? You'll make your sweet little wife fall in love with you, and once you're married, you'll give signs of anxiety and remorse; you'll pretend to be dejected for a fortnight. And one night, after some monkey business, you'll tell your wife between kisses that you owe two hundred thousand francs, and you'll remember to call her darling. The farce is played every day by the most fashionable young fellows. A young woman doesn't close her purse to the man who has taken possession of her heart. Do you fancy that you'll lose by it? Not at all. You'll find a way to make up the two hundred thousand francs in some scheme. With your money and your intelligence, you'll pile up a fortune as large as you could want. Therefore, within six months' time, you'll have made yourself happy, your lovely wife happy and Papa Vautrin happy, not to speak of your family which is perishing with cold all winter because there isn't enough wood. Don't be astonished by what I'm proposing to you, or by what I'm asking of you. Out of sixty splendid marriages in Paris, there are forty-seven that involve some such bargain."

"What do I have to do?" Eugène asked greedily, breaking into Vautrin's discourse.

"Why, scarcely anything," replied Vautrin, with an involuntary flash of joy such as a fisherman feels when a fish tugs at the line. "Listen carefully. The heart of a poor girl who is both unhappy and in poverty is greedier for love than anything else in the world and the smallest particle of love will make it dilate with joy. You have all the trumps in your hand; you're betting in a lottery with knowledge in advance of the number that will win; you're playing the stock market on a sure tip, when you make love to a young girl whom you meet when she is lonely, poor and in despair, and doesn't have any idea of the fortune she's about to have! You're building a marriage on foundations that can't crumble. When this young girl gets her millions she'll shower them on you as if they were only pebbles. 'Take them, darling! Take them, Adolphe! Alfred! Take them, Eugène!' That's what she'd say to her Adolphe, or her Alfred, or her Eugène, if he had the wit to make sacrifices for her! What I mean by making sacrifices is selling an old suit to take her to the

Cadran Bleu for a meal of mushroom pie, and then to spend the evening at the *Ambigu Comique* theatre; pawning your watch to give her a shawl. I'm not thinking of the trickeries of love, the sort of nonsense by which women are so tickled, things like sprinkling drops of water over a letter to imitate tears when you're far away. I'm sure you know all about the special idiom of the passion. Paris, you see, is like a forest in the new world, peopled by twenty different tribes of savages, Illinois and Hurons and so forth, each living on the results of its own particular kind of hunt; you're hunting millions. To get them you have to use snares, and pipes and bait. There are a lot of different ways of hunting. Some hunt for dowries; others for bankruptcies; on one side there's the hunt for consciences; on the other for victims to be sold, bound hand and foot. The man who comes back with his bag well filled is acclaimed, made much of, received by the world of fashion and distinction. We must be fair to this hospitable place; the city you have to deal with is the most complaisant in the world. If the haughty aristocracies of the European capitals won't take into their company the man who has made his million in an infamous way, Paris opens her arms to him, runs to his parties, eats his dinners, and toasts his infamies."

"But where is there such a girl?" asked Eugène.

"She's right here, and she's yours."

"Victorine?"

"That's it!"

"What do you mean?"

"She's already in love with you, already your little Baroness de Rastignac!"

"But she hasn't a penny," Eugène went on in amazement.

"Hasn't she? In a couple of words the whole thing will be perfectly clear to you. Her father is an old scamp who is believed to have killed one of his friends during the Revolution. He's one of those fellows I spoke of who are perfectly indifferent to opinion. He's a banker, the senior partner in the house, Frederic Taillefer and Co. He has an only son, to whom he means to leave his fortune, to the injury of Victorine. As for me, I hate that kind of injustice. I'm like Don Quixote; I like to defend the weak against the strong. If it were God's will to take his son from him, Taillefer would recognize his daughter. He'd want some sort of heir; that's one of the crazy instincts that Nature gives us. He can't have any children now; I know that. Victorine is sweet and a nice girl; she'll wind her father around her finger. He'll have so much affection for her he'll be whirling like a top. She'll be so much moved by your loving her that she won't forget you; she'll marry you. My part in all this is the part of Providence, I'm going to shape God's will. I've a friend for whom I have done a great service, a colonel in the Army of the Loire who has just been given a place in the Royal Guard. He pays attention to what I advise; and he's become an ultra-royalist; he's not one of those idiots who stand by their convictions.

"If there's one more piece of advice I have to give you, my dear fellow, it's not to stand by your convictions any more than by your words. When you're asked to, sell them. A man who boasts that he never changes his convictions is a man who undertakes always to move in a straight line, a ninny who believes in infallibility. There are no such things as principles, there are only events; there are no such things as laws, there are only circumstances; and the superior person unites himself with events and circumstances so that they will serve his interests. If there were fixed principles and laws, nations wouldn't be changing them just as lightly as we change a shirt. A man isn't required to be better than a whole nation. The man who has done the least for France is a national idol, venerated because he's seen everything as in the color red, and all he's good for, at most, is to be put in the machinery section over at the Conservatory and a label stuck on him reading La Fayette; while the prince who is stoned by everyone, and whose contempt for mankind is so great that he'll spit out any oath that any one asks him for, this man, Talleyrand, was the one who prevented the partition of France at the Congress of Vienna. We should hang garlands on him, but we throw mud at him. Oh, I know how things go; I know the secrets of a great many men. Enough. I'll have an unshakable conviction the day that I meet three men who agree about the realization of a principle, and I'll wait a long time for that! You can't find in the courts three judges who have the same opinion about a clause in the law. Let's come back to my friend. He'd put Jesus Christ back on the cross if I told him to. Just one word from Papa Vautrin, and he'll pick a quarrel with that rascal who doesn't send so much as a hundred sous to his poor sister, and . . ."

At this point Vautrin got up, stood like a fencer on guard, and went through the motions of delivering a lunge. "And he'll do it on the quiet," he added.

"How horrible!" exclaimed Eugène. "You're just joking, Monsieur Vautrin?"

"Now, now, don't get excited!" Vautrin went on. "Don't act like a child! Or, if you want, go ahead and get angry, lose your temper! Call me a scoundrel, a rascal, a bandit, only take care you don't call me a deceiver or a spy! Come on, let yourself go. I forgive you; it's natural at your age. I used to be like that! But think the thing over. You'll do something worse one day. You'll make up to some pretty woman and take money from her! You've thought of it! For how are you going to carry out your idea and succeed unless you get paid for loving? Virtue is indivisible, my boy; you either have it or you don't. Take this idea of repenting for one's sins; it's a pretty system which allows you to feel innocent of a crime just because you've made an act of contrition! Seducing a woman in order to set your foot on a certain step in the social ladder, getting the children in a family squabbling among themselves, all the infamous things that are done, behind the door or otherwise, for pleasure or for personal gain, how do they rank as acts of faith, hope and charity? Why is there a prison sentence of a mere two months for a dandy who in a single night robs a child of half his fortune, and the penitentiary for the poor devil who takes a thousand-franc note under aggravating circumstances? That's the way our laws are. There isn't one clause in them that doesn't fall into absurdity. The man in the yellow gloves, the dandy with his deceitful language, committed an act which was a murder though no blood was shed and indeed he left something of his own life behind; the robber opened a door with his jimmy—two deeds of night! The only difference between what I'm proposing to you and what you'll be doing some day is that there's no blood for you to shed in this. How can you believe in any fixed principles in this sort of world? You must learn to despise mankind and to crawl through the holes that are left in the network of the Code. The secret of large fortunes which have no perceptible explanation is a crime that has been forgotten because it was neatly done."

"Stop, I won't listen to any more of this. You'd make me doubt my own self. Right now, my feelings give me the only guidance I can trust."

"As you wish, my dear boy, I thought you were made of stronger stuff," said Vautrin. "I won't say any more. One last word, though." He looked hard at Eugène. "You know my secret."

"A young man who refuses your proposition will be easily capable of forgetting what it was."

"That's well put. I like that. Another fellow, you know, would not be so scrupulous. Remember what I want to do for you. I give you two weeks. Then you can take it or leave it."

"A man of iron," Eugène said to himself, as he watched Vautrin going off tranquilly, his cane under his arm. "He put to me crudely just what the Viscountess de Beauséant wrapped up in the forms of polite discourse. He tore my heart with claws of steel. Why is it I want to go to Madame de Nucingen's? He guessed my motives the moment I had conceived them. In a few words, this bandit told me more about virtue than I'd learned before from men and books together. If I don't get rid of my ideas of virtue, won't I have robbed my sisters?" and with this question he laid his sack on the table, sat down, and remained lost in a whirl of thought. "To be faithful to virtue, that's a sublime martyrdom. Ah! everyone may believe in virtue, but who really is virtuous? The idol of the nations is liberty; but what nation on the earth has liberty? The skies of my youth are still cloudless; but to strive to be rich or great means, doesn't it, lying, deceiving, climbing roughshod over others, flattering and dissembling? Means agreeing to be the toady of those who have lied, deceived, and climbed? Before you can be their accomplice you have to be their servant. I won't do it. I mean to work nobly and in a pious spirit; I mean to work day and night, and owe my fortune only to my hard work. It will be the slowest made of all fortunes, but every night I'll be able to go to bed without one evil thought. What could be finer than to contemplate one's life and see that it's absolutely pure? My conduct toward life will be like that of a young man toward the girl he's engaged to marry. Vautrin showed me what happens when a marriage is ten years old. The devil! My head is swimming. I won't think any longer. One's heart is the true guide."

Eugène was aroused from his reverie by big Sylvie's voice announcing his tailor, before whom he was glad to appear carrying his two sacks of silver. When he had tried on his evening clothes, he put on his new garments for wear in the daytime, and was wholly metamorphosed. "I'm as good as the Count de Trailles. I've the appearance of a gentleman at last."

"You asked me," said Père Goriot, coming into Eugène's room, "whether I knew where the Baroness de Nucingen was going to a party."

"Where?"

"Well, next Monday she's going to the Marshal Carigliano's ball. If you manage to go there, you'll be sure and tell me whether my girls had a good time, how they were dressed, in short everything about them."

"How did you find this out, Père Goriot?" asked Eugène, leading him to a chair by the fire.

"Her maid told me. I know everything they do through Thérèse and Constance," he continued with a happy expression. The old man was like a lover who was still young enough to delight in the stratagem which enabled him to follow his mistress without her suspecting his knowledge. "You, you will see them," he said, naïvely expressing the grievous envy he felt.

"I'm not sure," Eugène replied. "I'm going to the Viscountess de Beauséant's to ask her if she will introduce me to the marshal's wife." Eugène felt happy at the thought of showing himself in the presence of the viscountess dressed as he proposed to be in the future. What moralists call the abysses of the human heart are no more than the deceptive notions, the involuntary impulses of personal interest. These dramatic climaxes, the theme of so many moralizing declamations, arise from calculations we make to secure our pleasures. When he saw himself well attired, well shod and well gloved, Eugène forgot his virtuous resolution. Youth does not dare to look at itself in the mirror of conscience when it is leaning toward injustice; maturity has already seen its image there at such a moment—in this lies all the difference between these two periods in life.

It was now some days since the two neighbors, Eugène and

Père Goriot, had become good friends. Their secret friendship had its root in the psychological reasons which had engendered the opposite feeling on Eugène's part toward Vautrin. The bold philosopher who will one day work out the effects of our feelings in the physical world will doubtless find more than one proof of their materiality in the relations they make between us and animals. What student of physiognomy is quicker to divine character than a dog is in perceiving whether a stranger is fond of him or not? *Hooked atoms,* a proverbial expression which is on everyone's lips, expresses a fact that has lodged in language to give the lie to the philosophic nonsense we find in those who enjoy making discoveries in the refuse of primitive words. One feels that one is loved. Feeling is impressed on everything and traverses space. A letter is a spiritual thing; it is a faithful echo of the speaking voice; so much so that finer souls esteem it among the richest treasures of love. Père Goriot, whom his unreflecting feelings raised to sublimity of the canine sort, had scented in Eugène's heart compassion, admiring kindness and the sympathies of youth. This union in its present early stage had not as yet led to the exchange of any confidences. If Eugène had made plain his wish to see the Baroness de Nucingen it was not because he counted on the old man to introduce him to her; his hope was rather that some chance remark would serve his end. Père Goriot had spoken to him of his daughters only by way of elaboration of what he had said publicly the day of the two visits.

"My dear Sir," he had said the following day, "how could you have thought that the Countess de Restaud was angry with you because you had mentioned my name? My two daughters are very fond of me. I am a happy father. It is just that my sons-in-law have treated me badly. But I have tried to spare the two darlings from any suffering because of my quarrels with their husbands, and have preferred to see them only in private. The mystery this leads to gives me a thousand delights that other fathers who can see their daughters when they want can't understand. I can't, do you follow me? So I go on fine days to the Champs Elysées after asking their maids if my daughters are driving. I wait to see them pass; I admire their dress; and as they go by they give me a little smile which warms me just as if it were a bit of warm sunlight. I stay at my place, for they will come back that way. I see them again! Being out in the open has done them good; they have rosy cheeks. All around me I hear the murmur: 'There's a beautiful woman!' That delights my heart. Aren't they of my flesh and blood? I'm fond of the horses that draw their carriages; I'd like to be the little dog held in their lap. I live by their pleasures. Everyone has his own way of loving; mine, besides, does no harm to anyone. Why do people talk of me? I'm happy in my own fashion. Is there anything against the law in my going to see my daughters in the evening just when they are leaving to go to a ball? How disappointed I am if I get there too late and am told that they have left. One night I waited till three in the morning to see Nasie, whom I hadn't seen in two whole days. I almost burst with joy. Please speak of me only to say how good my daughters are to me. They'd like to bury me under all sorts of gifts; but I stop them, I say to them: 'Keep your money! What would I do with it? I need nothing.' And really what am I? A nasty corpse whose spirit is wherever my daughters are. When you've seen the Baroness de Nucingen, you'll tell me which of them you like better," the old fellow added after a moment's silence, noting that Eugène was getting ready to leave. He was starting for the Tuileries to pass the time until the hour for presenting himself at the Viscountess de Beauséant's.

This walk was fatal to him. Some women singled him out by their glances. He was so handsome, so young, and his elegance was in such good taste! Realizing that he was the object of an attention that amounted almost to admiration, he thought no more of the sisters and the aunt whom he had reduced to such straits, nor of his virtuous scruples. He had seen passing over his head that devil who is so easily mistaken for an angel, Satan with the diapered wings, sowing rubies, casting arrows of gold on the façades of palaces, clothing women in purple, and giving a foolish splendor to thrones, however humble they might have been in the beginning; he had listened to the god of noisy vanity, whose pinchbeck seems to be a symbol of power. Vautrin's advice, for all its cynicism, had settled in his heart, as in the memory of a virgin there may be engraved the base profile of an old dressmaker who has told her: "You'll have gold and love in heaps." After a leisurely stroll, Eugène called at the Viscountess de Beauséant's toward five o'clock, and was dealt one of those dreadful blows against which the hearts of the young are defenseless. Until now he had found the viscountess full of the polished amenity, the mellifluous grace which aristocratic upbringing cultivates but which attain their completeness only if they issue from the heart.

As he came in, the viscountess made a curt gesture and said in an abrupt tone: "Monsieur de Rastignac, it is impossible for me to see you, just now at least. I'm engaged. . . ."

For one who was observant (and Eugène had quickly become so) this phrase, this gesture, and the look that went along with them, the inflection of the voice, were the history of a character and of the habits of a class. He could see the iron hand under the velvet glove, the personal force, the egoism under the forms of politeness, the wood beneath the varnish. At last he heard the "I, the King" which stretches from the canopy of the throne as far as the humble roof of the least of the gentry. Eugène had been too ready to believe in the noble nature of this woman, taking her word for it. Like all those who are in difficulties he had signed in good faith the delightful pact which binds the beneficiary and the benefactor, the first article in it, when the hearts of both are distinguished, being a declaration of absolute equality. Beneficence, which unites two souls and makes them one, is a heavenly passion as far from being understood, and as rare, as true love. Both are the luxuries of fine spirits. Eugène was eager to go to the Duchess de Carigliano's ball. So he bowed beneath the storm.

"Madame," he said in a voice full of emotion, "if I hadn't something important to ask about I shouldn't have come to bother you. Won't you be so kind as to see me later? I'll wait."

"Very well, come and have dinner with me," she replied, a little ashamed of the hardness with which she had spoken, for she was really just as kind as she was great.

Although he had been touched by this sudden shift in tone, Eugène said to himself as he went off, "Keep on climbing, put up with everything. What must other women be like, if the best of them erases in a moment the promise of her friendship and leaves you in the corner like an old shoe? It has to be everyone for himself. It's true that her house isn't a shop, and that it puts me in the wrong that I need her help. As Vautrin said, you have to be like a cannon ball." His bitter thoughts were dispersed by the pleasure that he looked forward to in dining at the viscountess's. Thus by a sort of fatality the smallest events in his life conspired to push him forward in the career in which, according to the terrible sphinx of the Maison Vauquer, he would have to conduct himself as if he were on a battlefield and kill so that he should not be killed, deceive so that he should not be deceived, check his conscience and his heart at the entry and put on a mask, play pitilessly, and, as in ancient Sparta, grasp his fortune unseen so that he might win the crown.

When he returned to the Beauséant house he found the viscountess full of that gracious kindness which had marked her in all their earlier meetings. They went together to the dining room, where the viscount awaited his wife. There the table shone in all that splendid luxury which, as everyone knows, was carried to the highest point in the period of the Restoration. The Viscount de Beauséant, like many other *blasé* men cared little any longer for any pleasures except those of the table; in gourmandise he was of the school of Louis XVIII and the Duke d'Escars. Accordingly, there was in his dining room the double splendor of viands and trappings. Never had Eugène seen such a spectacle; it was the first time he had dined in a house where social greatness was hereditary. Fashion had just brought to an end the suppers which had formerly ended balls in the time of the Empire, when soldiers had to keep up their strength for the contests which awaited them within doors as well as without. So far Eugène had gone only to balls. The aplomb which was later on to mark him in so notable a degree, and which he was already beginning to acquire, prevented him from showing open amazement. But at the sight of the silver with its sculptured figures, of the thousand refinements of the sumptuous table, and in the presence of service carried on without the least noise, it was hard for a man gifted with a vivid imagination not to prefer the constant elegance of such a mode of life to the life of privations which he had intended to endure beginning on the morrow. His thoughts carried him back for a moment to the boarding-house, and he felt such disgust that he swore to himself that he would leave it in January, just as much to make sure of living in a cleanly abode as to shun Vautrin, whose broad hand he now seemed to feel on his shoulder. If you think of the thousand forms, open and concealed, that corruption takes on in Paris, you marvel, if you have good sense, at the aberration which leads the State to establish schools there and so to gather youth; at the fact that pretty women can live there without being injured; how it can be that the gold at the lenders' shops doesn't take wings and magically fly away. How extraordinary that there are so few crimes, and even misdemeanors, committed by young men! What respect they deserve for the patience with which they subdue their desires and are almost always victors over them! Treated by a great artist the struggle between the poor student and the city of Paris would be one of the most dramatic subjects to be found in our modern civilization.

The viscountess looked at Eugène as if to bid him speak, but in vain; he would say nothing in the presence of her husband.

"Are you going to take me to the play at the Italiens tonight?" the viscountess asked her husband.

"You know how much I'd like to do as you ask," he replied, with an air of mock gallantry which did not deceive Eugène, "but I've arranged to meet some one at the Varieties."

"His mistress," she thought.

"Adjuda won't be with you then this evening?" the viscount asked.

"No," she replied with a touch of ill humor.

"Well, if you absolutely must have an escort, why not go with Monsieur de Rastignac?"

The viscountess smiled at Eugène and said, "It would be very compromising for you."

"*Le Français aime le péril, parce qu'il y trouve la gloire.* That was Monsieur de Chateaubriand's opinion," replied Eugène with a bow.

A few minutes later, sitting beside the viscountess, he was being whirled to the fashionable theatre in a coupé, and he began to believe in a fairy godmother when he entered a box facing the stage and found himself the cynosure of all the lorgnettes, along with the viscountess whose dress was a thing of exquisite beauty. He was moving from one enchantment to another.

"You wish to talk to me," the viscountess said to him. "Ah, there is the Baroness de Nucingen, just three boxes from ours. Her sister and the Count de Trailles are on the other side."

As she spoke, the viscountess was looking at the box where Mademoiselle de Rochefide should have been, and when she did not see the Marquis d'Adjuda there, her expression took on an extraordinary animation.

"How charming she is!" said Eugène, when he had found the Baroness de Nucingen.

"Her eyebrows are too light."

"Yes, but what a pretty slender figure she has."

"Her hands are large."

"But her eyes are beautiful."

"Her face is too long."

"But that gives her distinction."

"How lucky for her that it does. Look at the way she picks up and lays down her lorgnette. Every motion she makes gives away the Goriot in her," the viscountess said, to the great astonishment of Eugène.

The truth was that the viscountess was surveying the whole gathering through her lorgnette; but although she did not seem to be paying any attention to the Baroness de Nucingen, she noted every gesture the other woman made. It was an assemblage of extraordinary beauty, and Delphine de Nucingen was not a little flattered that she had the whole attention of the young, handsome and elegant cousin of the Viscountess de Beauséant. He had eyes for no one else.

"If you go on looking at her like that, you will create a scandal. You'll never be successful, if you use such headlong methods."

"My dear cousin," said Eugène, "you've done so much for me already. If you would only finish what you've begun, I've just one more thing to ask, something which would give you so very little trouble, and mean so much to me. I'm already at her feet."

"So soon?"

"Yes."

"At that woman's?"

"Could I hope to be successful at another's?" he asked, giving his cousin a piercing look. "The Duchess de Carigliano is intimate with the Duchess de Berry," he went on after a pause. "You are sure to see her. Won't you be so kind as to speak of me to her and take me to her ball next Monday? I shall be able to meet the Baroness de Nucingen there, and I'll begin my first skirmish."

"Of course," she replied. "If you feel drawn to her already, your affairs of the heart are prospering excellently. There is de Marsay in the Princess Galathionne's box. The baroness is in agony; she isn't hiding her anger. There's no better time to address a woman, particularly a woman who is a banker's wife. Those ladies from la Chaussée d'Antin all love revenge."

"And what would you do in such a case?"

"I should suffer silently."

At this moment the Marquis d'Adjuda entered the viscountess's box.

"I've botched my business in my haste to be with you here," he said, "and I tell you so that it won't be a vain sacrifice."

The glow that animated the viscountess's face taught Eugène the signs by which he might distinguish genuine love, and not confuse it with the grimaces of the coquettes of Paris. He marveled at his cousin, fell silent, and gave up his place to the marquis, sighing as he did so, "How noble, how sublime is a woman who can love as she loves! And this man would betray her for a doll! How could anyone think of betraying her?" There was a childish rage in his heart. He wanted to fall at her feet; he craved the power of a demon so that he might carry her off in his heart, as an eagle seizes and bears off to his eyrie a young kid still unweaned. He felt humiliated that in this great gallery of beauty, he had no picture of his own, no mistress that was wholly his. "The sign of power," he said to himself, "is to have a mistress and a position that is almost royal." And the look he gave the Baroness de Nucingen was such as a man who has been insulted might give his adversary in the duel. His cousin turned toward him to thank him for his consideration with all the warmth she could express in the nodding of an eye. The first act was over.

"Do you know the Baroness de Nucingen well enough to introduce Monsieur de Rastignac to her?" she asked the Marquis d'Adjuda.

"Why, she would be delighted to see him," he said.

The handsome Portuguese rose, took Eugène's arm, and in a moment they were in the baroness's box.

"Madame," said the marquis, "I have the honor to introduce to you the Chevalier Eugène de Rastignac, a cousin of the Viscountess de Beauséant. You have made so strong an impression on him that I wished to make his happiness complete by bringing him close to his idol."

These words were uttered with a certain air of raillery which covered the element of brutality in the thought, and, covered, as it was here, such a notion never displeases a woman. The Baroness de Nucingen smiled, and bade Eugène take the seat her husband had occupied before going out a moment earlier.

"I scarcely venture to suggest that you stay with me," she said. "Anyone so lucky as to be in the Viscountess de Beauséant's company does not care to leave it."

"But," said Eugène in a whisper, "it seems to me that if I were to think of pleasing my cousin, I should stay with you. Before the marquis joined us, we were speaking of you and of the distinction that marks your person." He was now speaking in his ordinary tone of voice.

The marquis left.

"So you are going to stay with me?" asked the baroness. "We shall have a chance to become acquainted. What the Countess de Restaud has told me of you has made me very eager to see you."

"She must be a great hypocrite; she has forbidden me entrance to her house."

"What do you mean?"

"Madame, I shall be frank and tell you why. But I ask for all your indulgence in confiding to you a secret like this. I am your father's fellow-lodger. I did not know that the countess was his daughter, I was indiscreet enough to speak of him, quite innocently, and by doing so I angered your sister and her husband. You can't imagine in what bad taste the Duchess de Langeais and my cousin found this filial disloyalty. I told them what had happened, and they laughed as if they were mad. It was after this that my cousin, in contrasting you with your sister, spoke of you so highly, and told me how kind you were to my neighbor, Monsieur Goriot. And how indeed could you not love him? He adores you so passionately that I am already jealous of him. We spoke of you this morning two full hours. Then, while I was still thinking of what your father had told me, when I was at dinner with my cousin I said to her that you could not be as beautiful as you were affectionate. No doubt it was to foster such warm admiration that the Viscountess de Beauséant brought me here, saying to me, with her usual grace, that I should see you."

"And so," said the banker's wife, "I already owe you a debt of gratitude. It won't be long before we are old friends."

"I know that friendship with you could not be a common emotion," Eugène replied. "Still I don't wish ever to be your friend."

Such silly phrases, stereotyped for the use of beginners, always have charm for women and show up in their emptiness only when they are read in cold blood. The gestures, the accents, the glances of a young man add incalculably to them. The Baroness de Nucingen thought that Eugène was charming. Then, unable, like any other woman, to say anything to questions raised as boldly as these, she replied to something else.

"Yes, my sister puts herself in the wrong by the way she acts toward our poor father, who has been like a god to us. It is only because my husband has strictly forbidden me to see my father except in the daytime that I yielded the point. But for a long time it has made me unhappy. I have often wept over it. Such violent commands, following upon the brutalities of marriage, have been one of the main reasons for the unhappiness in my home. I am sure that of all the women in Paris I am the one who is happiest in the eyes of the world and unhappiest in reality. You must think me mad to speak to you like this. But you know my father and therefore you cannot be a stranger for me."

"You can never have met anyone," said Eugène, "who had a more eager wish to be yours. What do all women wish for? Happiness," he went on in a voice which penetrated to the soul. "Yes, and for a woman happiness lies in being loved, adored, in having a kindred spirit to whom she can confide her desires, her longings, her disappointments and her joys, to whom she can show herself in the full nakedness of her being, with her pretty little defects and her beautiful excellences, and this without any fear of betrayal. Believe me this devoted heart, always ardent with love, is to be found only in a young man full of illusions, capable of dying at the faintest nod from you, utterly ignorant of the world, and with no wish to know anything of it because you are becoming the whole world for him. You will laugh at my naïveté but here I am, just arrived from the depth of one of the provinces, absolutely fresh, without one contact with the corruption of the world; and I had meant to remain innocent of love. I happened to see my cousin; and she has let me come too close to her heart; she has allowed me to divine the myriad treasures of passion; like Chérubin I am in love with all women until I can devote myself to one. When I saw you the moment I came into this place, I felt myself drawn toward you by an irresistible current. I had thought about you so much! But I did not dream that you were so beautiful as you really are. The Viscountess de Beauséant told me that I must not look at you so constantly. She does not know what power of attraction there is in those lovely red lips, that pale complexion, and those eyes with all their gentleness. I know that I talk madly, but let me talk."

Nothing pleases women more than hearing such sweet words addressed to them. The most pious of them will listen to them even when she must not reply. When he had made a beginning in this fashion Eugène went on with the stream of compliments in a voice which was amorously soft; and the baroness encouraged him with her smiles while she glanced from time to time at de Marsay who stayed in the box of the Princess Galathionne. Eugène did not leave the baroness's side till her husband came to take her away.

"Madame," said Eugène, "I shall have the pleasure of calling on you before the Duchess de Carigliano's ball."

"Since Matame infites you," said the baron, a stout Alsatian with a round face suggesting a dangerous subtlety, "you are sure to pe velcome."

"My plans are coming along," Eugène reflected, "since she did not bridle much when I said to her: 'Will you love me well?' The beast is under my control; I have only to leap on, and assert my mastery." And he went to salute the Viscountess de Beauséant who was now rising from her place and withdrawing with the marquis. He had not realized that the baroness had not been giving him her attention and was awaiting a letter from de Marsay, one of those decisive letters that wound the very soul. In the highest happiness because of his supposed victory, Eugène accompanied the viscountess to the peristyle, where everyone was waiting for the carriages.

"Your cousin is a different man," the Portuguese said to the viscountess after Eugène had left them. "He is going to break the bank. He is as slippery as an eel, and I think he'll go far. Only you could have caught a woman for him just at the moment when she needs to be comforted."

"Oh," said the viscountess, "we must see whether she still loves the man who is deserting her."

Eugène returned to the Rue Neuve-Sainte-Geneviève on foot, forming the most attractive projects. He had noted closely the attention with which the Countess de Restaud had looked at him, when he was in his cousin's box and when he was in her sister's, and he foresaw that her house would no longer be forbidden to him. So four important relationships (for he planned on pleasing the wife of the marshal) were about to be his, in the very heart of the society of Paris. Without being very clear about the means, he surmised in advance that in the complicated play of interests in this world, he must fasten himself firmly to a wheel in order to raise himself to the top of the machine, and he felt that he had the force to do this. "If the Baroness de Nucingen interests herself in me, I will show her how to master her husband. This husband of hers is coining money; he can help me to amass a fortune in a trice." He did not say this to himself crudely; he was not yet enough of a politician to figure out a situation, judge it and calculate it; these ideas floated on the horizon of his mind in the form of little clouds. If they did not have the bitterness of Vautrin's ideas, still if they had been placed in the crucible of conscience they would have produced no very pure residuum. It is by a series of such tamperings with moral principle that men finally come to adopt the flaccid ethics professed by our present age, an age in which it is rarer than ever before to encounter those men who stand four square, those admirable wills that never yield to evil and to whom the least deviation from the line of rectitude appears a crime. Magnificent images of integrity such as lend their power to two masterpieces, Molière's *Alceste,* and Jeanie Deans and her father in the novel of Walter Scott. Perhaps the contrasting work which paints the sinuous ways in which a man of the world, a man of ambition who gets the better of his conscience as he seeks to move along the very verge of evil in order to achieve his aim without sacrificing appearances, would be neither less beautiful nor less dramatic.

By the time he had reached the door of the boarding-house, Eugène had fallen in love with the Baroness de Nucingen. She had pleased him by slender form and birdlike delicacy; he recalled everything about her: the intoxicating sweetness of her eyes, the fine silky texture of her skin beneath which he had almost seen the blood flowing, the enchanting music of her voice, the blondness of her hair. Perhaps the fascination was aided by the walk he had taken, making his blood flow more quickly. He knocked roughly at Père Goriot's door.

"My friend," he said, "I have seen Madame Delphine."

"Where?"

"At the Italiens."

"Was she enjoying herself? Come right in." And the old man who was in his nightshirt opened the door and quickly went back to bed. "Tell me about her," he bade Eugène.

This was the first time that Eugène had been in Père Goriot's room, and he could not repress a gesture of stupefaction at seeing in what hideous destitution he found the father of that daughter whose toilette he had so recently been admiring. There were no curtains at the window; the wallpaper was hanging loose at many places because of the dampness, and where it had shriveled one could see the plaster yellowed by smoke. The old man lying on the bed had but one thin cover, and to keep his feet warm a strip made of mere tatters from Madame Vauquer's worn-out dresses. The floor was damp and covered with dust. Opposite the window stood an old rosewood dresser with swelling lines and drawer handles of twisted copper adorned with leaves and flowers, and an old washstand, the top being only wood, with a wash-basin, pitcher and shaving instruments. His shoes lay in a corner; at the head of his bed was a night table, lacking a marble top and a door. At the side of the mantel, in which there was no trace of fire, stood the square table whose lower bar Père Goriot had used when he was twisting the silver porringer. The rest of the poverty-stricken furniture consisted of a rickety desk on which his hat now lay, two straight chairs, and an armchair with its straw seat stove in. A canopy, hanging from the ceiling over the bed by a mere rag, held up a wretched mass of fabrics with white and red squares. The most destitute porter was beyond a doubt better off in his garret than Père Goriot at Madame Vauquer's. The aspect of the room struck a chill to one's heart, and made it shrink; it was like the worst cell in a prison. Fortunately, Goriot did not notice the expression on Eugène's face as he set his candle down on the night table. The old man turned over and lay on his side, the covers up to his chin.

"Well, which do you like better, the Countess de Restaud or the Baroness de Nucingen?"

"The Baroness de Nucingen," Eugène replied, "for she is fonder of you."

Eugène spoke warmly, and the old man reached an arm from beneath the covers and shook his hand. "Thank you, thank you," he said with feeling. "And what did she say about me?"

Eugène repeated what the baroness had said, adding to the force of her words, and the old man listened as if he were hearing God's own word.

"The dear child! Yes, yes! She is very fond of me! But you mustn't believe what she said about Anastasie! The two sisters are jealous of each other, you see, another proof of their affection! The Countess de Restaud loves me dearly too. I know she does. A father knows his children as God knows us all; he goes right to the heart and can interpret hidden meanings. They are equally affectionate. Oh, if I had had kind sons-in-law, I should have been only too happy. There can't be any complete happiness here on earth of course. If I only could have lived in the same house with them, just hearing their voices, knowing they were there, seeing them come and go, as I used to do when they lived with me, then my heart would have leapt with joy. Did you think they were well dressed?"

"Yes," Eugène replied, and went on, "Monsieur Goriot, how is it that with your daughters so rich and comfortable you can be living in such a shambles as this?"

"Oh, well," said Goriot, with an affectation of indifference, "what good would it do me to be better off? I can't very easily explain these things to you; I'm not able to put together even a couple of words in the proper way." He struck his hand on his heart and said, "This is all that matters. My life is in my daughters. If they enjoy themselves and are happy, and well dressed, and if they walk on carpets, what does it matter, the stuff I put on me, and the sort of place I sleep in? I'm not cold if they are warm; I can't be bored if they are amused. The only worries I have are their worries. When you are a father, when you hear a child of yours cooing, you will say to yourself: 'This is made of my flesh!' You will feel every drop of your blood respond to these little creatures, who are the fine flower of your substance. That's what they are! You'll think you are stirring when they walk. I hear their voices everywhere. One look from them, if it is sad, is enough to make my blood run cold. Some day you will appreciate that one can be much happier in their happiness than in one's own. I can't explain that to you; there are inward stir rings that spread happiness throughout one's whole being. In a word, I have three lives. Shall I tell you a very odd thing? Well, when I became a father I understood God. The whole of Him is everywhere, since the creation came from Him. That, my friend, is the way I am with my daughters. Only I love my daughters better than God loves the world, for the world isn't as fine as God, and my daughters are finer than I. They are so close to my spirit that I had a notion you would see them tonight. Good God!

if a man would make my little Delphine as happy as a woman is when she is really loved, I'd shine his boots, and run his errands. Through her maid I've found out that this little de Marsay is a dirty dog. I've wanted to strangle him. Imagine his not loving such a jewel of a woman, with the voice of a nightingale, and built like a model. Where were her eyes when she married that heavy Alsatian lump? Both of them should have had young men, handsome and very lovable. Well, they did as they wished."

Père Goriot was sublime. Never before had Eugène seen him so illumined with the fires of paternal love. It is very notable how feelings have the power to infuse a new quality into a creature. No matter how rough a creature may be, the moment it expresses a strong and genuine affection, it exhales a particular fluid which changes tne expression of the face, and gives animation to the gestures and color to the voice. Often by the effect of passion the stupidest of beings can rise to an eloquence of idea if not of language and seem to move in a luminous sphere. There was now in the voice and gestures of this old fellow the communicative power which distinguishes the great actor. Are not our fine feelings the poems of our will?

"Well," said Eugène, "perhaps you won't be sorry to hear that she's certainly going to break off with de Marsay. The good-for-nothing has left her to tag after the Princess Galathionne. As for me, tonight I fell in love with Madame Delphine."

"You did?" said Père Goriot.

"Yes. She didn't dislike me. We talked love for a whole hour, and I'm to go and see her on Saturday, the day after tomorrow."

"Oh, what affection I'd feel for you, my dear boy, if you pleased her. You are good; you wouldn't torture her. If you betrayed her I'd cut your throat; that would be the first thing. A woman doesn't love twice, do you know that? But what silly things I'm saying. You must be cold here. Good God, you heard her voice? What message did she give you for me?"

"None," said Eugène—to himself. "She told me," he said aloud, "that she sent you a nice daughterly kiss."

"Good-bye, neighbor; sleep well, and may your dreams be beautiful; mine are fixed by that message. May God aid you to all your desires. Tonight you've been a good angel to me: you bring me the atmosphere of my daughter."

"The poor man," Eugène said to himself as he was going to bed, "it's enough to move a heart of stone. His daughter thought about him as much as about the Grand Turk."

After this talk Père Goriot found in his neighbor an unexpected confidant, a friend. Between them there had come into being the only relationship which could bind the old man to another male. Passions never err in their calculations. Père Goriot saw that he could come a little closer to his daughter Delphine; he saw that she might be more pleased to see him, if she came to like Eugène. Moreover, he had confided to Eugène what was one of his reasons for grief. The Baroness de Nucingen, whose happiness he sought a thousand times daily, had never known the joys of love. There was no doubt that Eugène was, to use the old man's own expression, one of the nicest young men he had ever seen, and he seemed to foresee that Eugène could give his daughter all the pleasures of which she had been deprived. So the old fellow began to feel a friendship for his neighbor, a friendship that went on growing, and without which it would certainly have been impossible for us to know the outcome of this story.

The next morning at breakfast the attention with which Père Goriot looked at Eugène (he sat beside him), the few words he said to him, the change in his expression which ordinarily resembled a plaster mask, surprised the boarders. Vautrin, who now saw Eugène for the first time since their long discussion, appeared to be trying to pierce to his very soul. As he recalled this man's scheme, Eugène, who during the night had been surveying the vast prospect which now opened before him, could not help thinking of Mademoiselle Taillefer's dowry, or looking at Victorine as a most virtuous young man may look at a great heiress. By chance their eyes met. The poor girl thought—how could she help it?—that he looked charming in his new attire. The glance they exchanged was significant enough for Eugène to feel sure that he was the object of these obscure desires which rise in every girl, to be projected toward the first seductive man she meets. A voice cried out within him, "Eight hundred thousand francs!" But he quickly returned to his memories of the night before and thought that his calculated passion for the Baroness de Nucingen was the antidote for his involuntary evil thoughts.

"Yesterday evening Rossini's *The Barber of Seville* was at the Théâtre des Italiens. I'd never heard such delightful music," he said. "Good Lord, how nice it would be to have one's box there!"

Père Goriot seized the idea in flight as a dog seizes on his master's slightest movement.

"You're just like roosters, you men," said Madame Vauquer. "You can do everything you want."

"How did you get home?" asked Vautrin.

"I walked," said Eugène.

"I'm not like that," the tempter went on. "I shouldn't care for half pleasures; I'd go there in my carriage, sit in my box and ride home in comfort. Everything or nothing, that's my motto."

"And a good one," said Madame Vauquer.

"Perhaps you'll be going to see the Baroness de Nucingen," Eugène whispered to Père Goriot. "She'll certainly be eager to see you; she'll want to know a thousand little things about me. I've found out that she'd do anything to be invited to the house of my cousin the Viscountess de Beauséant. Don't forget to tell her that I'm too fond of her to fail to secure for her that pleasure."

Eugène quickly left for the law school; he was bent on being as little as he could in that hateful boarding-house. He loafed almost all day, a victim of that fever that affects young men whose hopes are too high. Vautrin's notions were turning his thoughts toward the life of society just at the moment when he met his friend Bianchon in the Luxembourg Gardens.

"What's given you that serious look?" said the medical student, taking his arm to walk up and down in front of the palace.

"I'm being tortured by evil thoughts."

"What kind of thoughts? You can cure thoughts."

"How do you do it?"

"By giving in to them."

"You may laugh; you don't know what it's all about. Have you read Rousseau?"

"Yes."

"Do you remember that passage in which he asks the reader what he would do if he could become wealthy by killing an old Chinese mandarin, without leaving Paris, just by an act of will?"

"Yes."

"Well then?"

"Oh, I'm on my thirty-third mandarin."

"Don't joke about it. Come, if it were proved to you that the thing was possible and that all you'd need to do would be nod your head, would you do it?"

"Is your mandarin very old? Oh, well, young or old, healthy or paralytic, good Lord . . . Oh, the devil! Well, no."

"You're a decent fellow, Bianchon. But suppose that you love a woman enough to sell your soul for her, and she needs money, a lot of money for her clothes, for her carriage, in short, for all her notions?"

"But you're taking my reason away from me, and you want me to use it."

"Well, Bianchon, I'm mad, cure me. I have two sisters, angels, beautiful and innocent, and I want them to be happy. How can I get in the next five years the two hundred thousand francs they'll need for dowry? You know that there are situations in life when you have to gamble for high stakes and not use up your luck in winning pennies."

"But the question you put to me is the question that everybody has to face at the beginning of life, and you want to cut the Gordian knot with a sword. To act in that way, you must be Alexander the Great or you'll go to the penitentiary. As for me I'm quite content with the simple little life I'm going to make for myself somewhere in my part of the country where I'll just stupidly follow in my father's practice. Human affections can be just as fully satisfied in the smallest circle as in the most immense. Napoleon couldn't eat two dinners and he couldn't have any more mistresses than a medical student has when he is an interne at the Capucins. Our happiness, my dear friend, lies between the soles of our feet and our occiput; and whether it costs a million a year or just a hundred louis, the intrinsic satisfaction is just the same. I decide that the Chinaman should be let live."

"Thanks, you've done me good, Bianchon. We'll always be friends."

"Listen," said the medical student, "as I came away from Cuvier's lecture room at the Jardin des Plantes, I saw the Michonneau and the Poiret sitting on a bench in the park and talking to a man whom I noticed last year at the time of the riots at the Chamber of Deputies, and who looked like a detective disguised as an honest bourgeois living on his income. Let's keep a watch on that couple; I'll tell you why. Good-bye, I've got to go and put in an appearance when my name is called in the four-o'clock roll."

When Eugène got back to the boarding-house, he found Père Goriot waiting for him.

well dressed. No one can put on a new garment without every one else having something to say about it.

"Tchk! Tchk!" said Bianchon, clicking his tongue against his palate as if he were urging a horse to start.

"Rigged out like a duke and peer of the realm," said Madame Vauquer.

"Are you going out in quest of a heart?" asked Mademoiselle Michonneau.

"Cock-a-doodle-do!" cried the painter.

"My compliments to your wife!" said the man from the Museum.

"Have you a wife?" asked Poiret.

Vautrin spoke next with the comic volubility and accent of a barker: "How much is this marvel, won't you tell me, gentlemen? Two cents? No. Nothing at all. It's a relic of the furnishings for the Great Mogul, and all the sovereigns of Europe, including the Gr-r-r-r-r-and Duke of Baden, wanted to see it! Step right in! Go to the smaller wicket! Come, let's have the music now! Boom, la, la, trin la la, boom, boom! You with the clarinet, that was a false note," he went on with a voice grown hoarse. "I'll rap you over the fingers."

"Good Lord, what a treat that man is," said Madame Vauquer to Madame Couture. "I'd never be bored with him."

Amid the laughs and jokes for which this speech so comically declaimed was the signal, Eugène did not miss the furtive glance of Mademoiselle Taillefer who leaned over to whisper a few words in Madame Couture's ear.

"There's the cab," said Sylvie.

"Where can he be dining?" asked Bianchon.

"At the Baroness de Nucingen's."

"Monsieur Goriot's daughter," said Eugène.

At the introduction of this name every one turned toward the old vermicelli maker who was looking at Eugène with a sort of envy.

Eugène reached his destination in the Rue Saint Lazare, one of those slight houses with thin columns and scamped porticoes that are the Parisian conception of the *pretty*,—a true banker's house, full of costly notions, of stucco and stairways with landings in mosaics of marble. He found the Baroness de Nucingen in a small drawing room hung with Italian paintings and with the general air of a café. She was dejected. The efforts she made to hide her low spirits interested Eugène all the more because her mood was not feigned. He had supposed that his presence would make this woman happy and he found her in despair. The disappointment piqued his vanity.

"I've very little right to be in your confidence," he said, after he had teased her about her preoccupied air, "but if my being here is a bother to you, I trust you won't hesitate to tell me so frankly."

"I want you to stay," she replied. "I'd be alone if you were to leave. Nucingen is having dinner out; and I don't care to be alone. I need diversion."

"Why, what's wrong?"

"You'd be the last person I'd tell," she said emphatically.

"I want to know. So I've some relation to what you're keeping secret?"

"Perhaps. No," she resumed, "these differences within a family should be buried from view. Didn't I tell you the day before yesterday? I'm unhappy. Chains of gold are the heaviest of all."

When a woman tells a young man she is unhappy, the young man, if he is intelligent, well dressed and provided with fifteen hundred francs worth of idleness, will inevitably think what Eugène was now thinking, and become smug.

"What can you want?" he asked. "You're young, beautiful, loved and wealthy."

"Don't let's talk about me," she said with an ominous shake of her head. "We'll have dinner together; we'll go and hear the most delightful music. Do you like the way I look?" She rose and showed off a dress of white cashmere with chintz figures, all in the most expensively elegant manner.

"I wish you were wholly mine," said Eugène. "How charming you are!"

"You'd have a poor bargain," she said with a bitter smile. "Nothing here points to misfortune, and yet, despite appearances, I'm absolutely desperate. My worries make me sleepless, I'll soon be ugly."

"Oh, that's impossible," said Eugène. "But I'm curious to know what troubles there may be that a devoted love would not wipe out."

"Ah, if I told you, you'd run from me," she said. "The only sort of love you have for me now is that sort of gallantry that is current among men; but if you really loved me, you'd sink into a pit of despair. You see, I must not tell. Please, let's talk of something else. Come and see my own rooms."

"No, let's stay here," Eugène replied, sitting down beside the baroness on a sofa in front of the fire and boldly taking her hand.

She let him keep it, and even pressed it against his in one of those gestures of concentrated strength which reveal unusually strong feeling.

"Listen," Eugène said to her, "if you have any worries you must tell me them. I want to prove to you that I love you for what you are. Either you'll tell me straight out what your troubles are so that I can free you from them, even if I have to kill half a dozen men, or else I'll walk out of here and never come back."

"Very well, then," she said, a prey to a despair so strong that she struck her hand against her forehead, "I'll put you to the proof this very instant. Yes," she was now speaking to herself, "there's no other solution." She rang.

"Is the baron's carriage ready?" she asked the footman.

"Yes, Madame."

"I shall take it. Get mine ready for him, and my horses. Do not serve dinner till seven o'clock."

"Come on!" she said to Eugène, who began to feel that he was dreaming as he sat in the Baron de Nucingen's carriage beside the baron's wife.

"To the Palais Royal," she said to the coachman. "Stop near the Théâtre Français."

While they were on the way she seemed upset and refused to answer any of Eugène's thousand questions; he did not know what to make of such dumb, impenetrable resistance.

"She'll get away from me in a moment more," he reflected.

When the carriage stopped the baroness looked at him in a way that repressed the mad things he was about to say, for he was now beside himself.

"You really love me?" she asked.

"Yes," he answered, hiding the anxiety which possessed him.

"You won't think anything bad about me, no matter what I may ask of you?"

"No."

"Are you prepared to obey me?"

"Blindly."

"Have you ever gambled?" she asked in a voice that trembled.

"Never."

"Oh, I can breathe again. You'll be lucky. Here's my purse. Go on, take it. There are a hundred francs in it, all that this woman who is so happy possesses. Go up into a gambling place. I don't know just where they are, but I know there are some in the Palais Royal. Stake the hundred francs on the game they call roulette and either lose it all or bring me back six thousand francs. I'll tell you what my worries are when you get back."

"I hope the devil takes me if I understand anything of what I'm going to do, but I'm going to obey you," he said, feeling happy at the thought: "She's compromising herself with me; she won't be able to refuse me anything."

Eugène took the pretty purse, and, after asking a peddler of old clothes where the nearest gambling place was, hurried to Number 9. He went upstairs, let an attendant take his hat, went in and asked where the roulette table was. Amid the astonishment of the habitués, the usher took him up to a long table. Without the least embarrassment, followed by all the spectators, Eugène asked where he should place his bet.

"If you put a louis on one of these thirty-six numbers, and it wins, you'll have thirty-six louis," said a white-haired man of respectable appearance.

Eugène threw down his hundred francs on the number which corresponded with his age, twenty-one. A cry of amazement went up before he got his bearings. He had won without knowing it.

"Take up your money," the old gentleman said to him. "You don't win twice by that system of yours."

Eugène took up a rake that the old gentleman held out to him and drew toward him the thirty-six hundred francs, and still without any idea about the game placed them on the red. The gallery looked at him enviously, seeing that he went on playing. The wheel turned, he won again, and the banker gave him another thirty-six hundred francs.

"You now have seven thousand two hundred francs," the old gentleman whispered to him. "If you will trust me, you'll go away, the red has won eight times running. If you're charitable you will recompense this piece of wise counsel by relieving the indigence of one who was a prefect under Napoleon and is now in the direst need."

Eugène whose head was still in a whirl, let the old man take ten louis, and then went away with the seven thousand francs, still without any notion of the game, but stupefied by his luck.

"Ah, ha!" he said to the Baroness de Nucingen, showing her

the seven thousand francs, when the door of the carriage had closed, and then, "Where are you going to take me now?"

Delphine hugged him wildly and gave him a kiss that was warm without being passionate. "You've saved me!" she cried. Tears of joy ran down her cheeks. "I'm going to tell you everything. You'll be my friend, won't you? You think I'm rich, rolling in riches, that I lack for nothing or seem to! Well, let me tell you that the baron doesn't leave me a single cent; he pays for the upkeep of the house, and for the carriages, and boxes at the theatre; he gives me an allowance for dress that isn't enough; he is deliberately plunging me into secret poverty. I'm too proud to beg anything of him. Shouldn't I be the vilest of creatures if I purchased his money at the price he'd demand? You may ask how, when I've a fortune of seven hundred thousand francs, I've let myself be fleeced? Through pride, through indignation. We're so young, so simple when we marry! The word I'd have had to say to get money from my husband burned my lips. I never dared say it. I used up what I'd saved, and what my poor father gave me. Then I fell into debt. Marriage has been for me the most dreadful disillusionment conceivable. I can't speak of it to you; it's enough to say that I'd rather throw myself out of the window than live with Nucingen in any other fashion than with separate rooms. When I had to tell him of my young woman's debts, for jewelry, for things that happened to catch my fancy— my poor father had made us accustomed to getting everything we wanted—I went through martyrdom; but finally I mustered up my courage and told him. Hadn't I a fortune of my own? Nucingen lost his temper; he told me that I'd ruin him; said the most horrible things. I wished I was a hundred feet under the earth. Since he had taken my dowry he paid; but he stipulated that my personal expenses come out of an allowance, and I resigned myself to this, in order to have peace. Since then I have wanted to satisfy the amour propre of a certain person that you know. Even if he has deceived me, I'd be wrong not to acknowledge the nobility of his character. But it's true that he has deserted me in a shabby fashion! A man should never desert a woman if at some time when she was desperate he's tossed her a heap of gold! A man ought to go on loving her always! You're young, only twenty, you've a fine pure soul, you'll ask me how a woman can take money from a man? Good Lord, isn't it natural to share things with the person to whom we owe our happiness? When one's given everything, is one to stop over a fraction of the everything? Money takes on importance only when the emotion is dead. Doesn't love bind one for life? What woman if she believes she's loved foresees separation? Men swear eternal love to us, how then can there be distinction of interests? You don't know what I suffered today when Nucingen refused to let me have six thousand francs, although he gives as much every month to his mistress, a dancer at the Opéra. I wanted to kill myself. The maddest ideas ran through my head. There were moments when I envied the lot of a servant, of my maid. It would have been mad to go to my father. Anastasie and I have sucked him dry. My poor father would have sold himself if he could find anyone who thought him worth six thousand francs. I should have been driving him to desperation in vain. You've saved me from shame and death. I was mad with pain. Oh, I owed you this explanation; I've been absolutely insane with you. When you left me just now, and I'd lost sight of you, I thought of slipping off on foot. . . . Where to? I don't know.

"That's the life of half the women in Paris: external luxury, cruel anxieties within. I know poor creatures who are even more unfortunate than I am. There are even women who have to get the merchants they deal with to give them faked bills. Others have to steal from their husbands. Some men can be made to think that cashmere dresses worth a hundred louis are worth only five hundred francs, and others that cashmere dresses worth only five hundred francs are worth a hundred louis. There are poor women who have to starve their children to be able to buy a dress. I at least haven't fallen to any of these odious deceits. This is my last ordeal. Some women sell themselves to their husbands in order to rule, but I at least am free! I could get Nucingen to cover me with gold, and I'd rather cry in the arms of a man I can respect! Ah, tonight the Count de Marsay won't have the right to think of me as a woman he has paid."

She buried her face in her hands so that Eugène would not see her tears, but he took away her hands so that he might look at her. She seemed sublime.

"Mixing money with feelings is horrible, isn't it? You won't love me any more," she said.

Such a mixture of right feeling, the source of women's greatness, with misdeeds which the present constitution of society forces them to commit, greatly upset Eugène; he spoke gently and comfortingly to her as he admired her beauty. She was so naïvely indiscreet in her outcry of grief.

"You won't use this against me," she said. "Promise me that."

"Ah, I'm incapable of doing that," he replied.

She took his hand and with a gesture full of gratitude and charm placed it on her heart. "Thanks to you I'm free and gay again. An iron hand was pressing against me all the time. Now I mean to be careful and spend nothing. You'll like me the way I'll be from now on, won't you, my friend? Keep this," she bade him, taking only six of the bank notes. "I really owe you a thousand crowns, for I considered that I was to share with you half and half." Eugène held back as tenaciously as a virgin protecting her honor. But when the baroness said to him, "I shall count you my enemy if you aren't my accomplice," he took the money. "It will be an investment in case of bad luck," he said.

"That's what I was afraid you'd say," she cried out, suddenly growing pale. "If you want me to be anything to you, swear to me that you'll never go back to a gambling place. Good God, if I were to be the agent of your corruption! I'd die of grief."

They had arrived. The contrast between such indigence and such luxury made Eugène's head whirl, and the sinister ideas of Vautrin came back and resounded in his ears.

"Sit down there," said the baroness, pointing to a sofa beside the fire; they were in her bedroom. "I'm going to write a very difficult letter. Give me your advice."

"Don't write at all," Eugène said. "Slip the notes in an envelope, address it, and send it by your maid."

"Why, you're a darling," she said. "Oh, that's what comes of being properly brought up. That's pure Beauséant," she went on with a smile.

"How charming she is!" Eugène thought as he fell more and more under her spell. He looked about the room which expressed the voluptuous elegance of a wealthy courtesan.

"Do you like it?" she asked, as she rang for her maid. "Thérèse, take this to the Count de Marsay and give it into his own hands. If he isn't home bring me back the letter."

Before she left Thérèse gave Eugène a mischievous smirk. Dinner was ready. Eugène took the baroness's arm and she led him to a dining room, where he found once more the luxury which he had admired at his cousin's table.

"Whenever there's a performance of Italian opera, you'll come for dinner and go with me."

"I could grow accustomed to such a pleasant life if it could only last; but I'm merely a poor student who still has his way to make."

"It will be made," she said with a laugh. "You'll see, everything will work out; I never expected to be so happy."

It is in the nature of women to prove the impossible by the possible, and to demolish facts by presentiments. When the Baroness de Nucingen and Eugène entered her box at the

Théâtre des Bouffons, her happiness made her so beautiful that everybody began to gossip in that slanderous way against which women are defenseless and which often gains credence for rumors of wicked doings that are gratuitously invented. When one gets to know Paris, one doesn't believe a word that is said there, and one doesn't say a word about what is done. Eugène took the baroness's hand and they communicated by pressures more or less lively as they shared together the sensations that they had from the music. For them it was an intoxicating evening, and the baroness insisted on driving Eugène as far as the Pont Neuf on his way homeward, and all the time she struggled to prevent his taking a single kiss, although she had lavished kisses upon him at the Palais Royal. Eugène reproached her for such inconsistency.

"A while ago," she said, "it was gratitude for devotion I hadn't hoped to find; now it would be a promise."

"And you don't want to promise anything, ungrateful woman." He grew angry. With one of those gestures of impatience which overjoy a man in love she gave him her hand to kiss, and he took it with an ill humor which she found delightful.

"Until Monday, at the ball," she said.

As he continued his way home on foot under a beautiful moon, Eugène fell into serious thought. He was both happy and dissatisfied; happy because of an adventure whose probable resolution would give him one of the prettiest and most elegant women in Paris, and one whom he desired; dissatisfied because his projects for making his fortune had miscarried. He now felt to the full the reality of the undecided thoughts which had filled his mind two days before. Failure always emphasizes the force of one's claims. The more Eugène enjoyed Parisian life the less content he was to stay in his poverty and obscurity. He played with the thousand-franc note in his pocket as he raised a thousand specious arguments which would justify him in using it for his own purposes. At last he reached the Rue Neuve-Sainte-Geneviève, and when he had mounted the stairs he saw a light still burning. Père Goriot had left his door open and his candle alight so that Eugène might not forget to "tell him about his daughter," as he put it. Eugène concealed nothing from him.

"What's this!" Goriot cried out in desperate jealousy. "They think I'm ruined; I still have an income of thirteen hundred livres. Good God, the poor child, why didn't she come here? I should have sold the bonds, dipped into the capital, and taken out an annuity. Why didn't you come and tell me the plight you were in, my dear fellow? How could you have been so heart less as to risk her poor little hundred francs? It's enough to cut one to the very soul. So that's what sons-in-law are like? If I had them in my power I'd wring their necks! Good God, she wept?"

"With her head against my waistcoat."

"Oh, give it to me," said Père Goriot. "So there were tears on it, my daughter, my dear Delphine's tears, and she never cried when she was little. Oh, I'll buy you another; don't wear it again; leave it with me. According to the contract she has a right to the income from her fortune. Ah, I'll go and see Derville —he's a lawyer—tomorrow. I'll insist that her fortune be invested. I know the laws, I'm an old fox, and I know how to sharpen my teeth again."

"Here, Père Goriot, here are a thousand francs that she wanted to give me from what we won. Keep them for her, in the waist-coat."

Goriot looked at Eugène, stretched out his hand and a tea dropped on it.

"You'll succeed in life," the old man said, gripping Eugène' hand. "God is just, you know that? I know what integrity is and I can assure you that there are few men like you. Will you too, be my dear child? Go, and sleep. You can sleep; you aren' yet a father. She wept, and I was quietly having my meal here, like an idiot, while she was in pain—I who would sell Father, Son and Holy Spirit if I could spare the two of them a tear!"

As Eugène went to bed he reflected, "I think I'll be an honest fellow all my life. There's a pleasure in obeying the inspirations of one's conscience."

Perhaps it is only those who believe in God who do good in secret, and Eugène believed in God.

The next evening, when it was time for the ball, he went to the Viscountess de Beauséant's, and she accompanied him, and introduced him to the Duchess de Carigliano. He was most cordially received, and then joined the Baroness de Nucingen. Delphine had prepared for the party in such a way as would make her attractive in everyone's sight, and in this way more attractive to Eugène whose look of admiration she awaited impatiently though she thought she hid her impatience. For a man who can conceive the feelings of a woman such a moment is full of delight. Who is there who has not enjoyed holding back his opinion, coquettishly hiding his pleasure, searching for a revelation in the anxiety he is causing, delighting in the fears which he can later dissipate by a smile? In the course of this party Eugène estimated the strength of his position and understood that he had standing in society as the acknowledged cousin of the Viscountess de Beauséant. The conquest of the Baroness de Nucingen—he was supposed to have completed this already—placed him on such a height that all the young men looked on him with envy, and in surprising some of them in expressions of this, he for the first time enjoyed the pleasures of smugness. As he passed from one drawing room to another, as he made his way through the groups, he heard his luck discussed and envied. The women predicted he would have success. Delphine, in her fear of losing him, promised that tonight she would not refuse him the kiss she had contested so hard the last time they were together. During the ball Eugène received several invitations. He was introduced by his cousin to a number of women who had all some claims to fashion and whose houses were thought agreeable; he was now a part of the highest and most splendid society in Paris. It was natural that this evening should have had for him the charm of a brilliant debut; and he was to remember it even in his old age, as a young girl remembers the balls in which she won her triumphs.

When the next morning at breakfast, in the presence of the other boarders, he was telling Père Goriot of his successes, Vautrin began to smile in a devilish way.

"And you think," said that fierce logician, "that a young man in society can live in the Maison Vauquer, in the Rue Neuve-Sainte-Geneviève? At a boarding-house which is the acme of respectability from every point of view, no question of that, but which is everything but fashionable? It's cosy; it's beautiful in a solid way; it's proud to be the castle *pro tem* of a Rastignac; but after all it's in the Rue Neuve-Sainte-Geneviève, and is innocent of luxury, since it's a purely patriarchal sort of place. My young friend," he went on in a paternally mocking manner, "if you mean to shine in Paris, you have to have a tilbury and three horses for driving out in the day time, and a coupé for the evening; that is nine thousand francs for your carriages alone. You would be unworthy of your fate if you spent as little as three thousand francs at your tailor's, six hundred francs at your perfumer's, a hundred crowns at your shoemaker's and the same at your hatter's. Your laundry will run to a thousand francs. Young men who are popular in society can't afford to be anything short of absolutely impeccable in their linen. Isn't this what is most often inspected in their attire? Love is like religion; there must be fine linen on the altar. This brings us to fourteen thousand francs. I won't even mention what you spend in gambling, bets and making presents. You can't get along with less than two thousand francs for pocket money. I've led that sort of life; I know what it costs. Add to these primary necessities, three hundred louis for grub, a thousand francs for a perch. Come, my boy, it'll mean twenty-five thousand francs a year in pocket, or you'll fall into the mud, and get laughed at, and lose your future, your successes and your mistresses. I've forgotten the valet and the groom! Are you going to use Christopher as the bearer of your love notes? Will you write them on the kind of paper you use now? It would be suicide. Believe what an old man full of experience tells you!" he said, his bass tones growing stronger. "Either bury yourself in a garret and take hard work for your wife, or choose another way."

Vautrin winked and nodded toward Mademoiselle Taillefer so as to remind Eugène, summing it up in a single glance, of the tempting idea he had sown in his heart to corrupt him.

For several days Eugène led the most dissipated life. Almost daily he had dinner with the Baroness de Nucingen, and then took her out into society. He returned home at three or four o'clock in the morning, and rose at noon to dress and accompany Delphine to the Bois whenever it was fine weather, lavishing his time without taking account of its value, and breathing in all the instruction and all the charm that lies in luxury, with an ardor like that of the impatient calyx of a female palm tree for the fruitful pollen of her love. He gambled for high stakes, lost or won a great deal, and became accustomed to the costly mode of life of young men in Paris. Out of his first winnings he had sent fifteen hundred francs to his mother and sister, accompanying the repayment with handsome presents. Although he had said he meant to leave the Maison Vauquer, he was still living there at the end of January and did not see how he was to get out of the place. Young men are almost all subject to a law which seems inexplicable, but which has its reason in the simple fact of their youth, and in the sort of frenzy with which they hurl themselves upon pleasure. Rich or poor, they never have money for the necessities of life, when they can always find it to satisfy their whims. Extravagant with whatever can be had on credit, they are out-and-out misers about anything that has to be paid for in cash, and they seem to make up for what they don't have by squandering all they can lay hands on. To illustrate very simply, a student always takes better care of his hat than of his suit. The large scale of profit makes a tailor essentially a creditor, while the modest sum the hatter makes renders him one of the most intractable fellows with whom the student has to do. The young man sitting in the balcony of a theatre and flaunting before the lorgnettes of pretty women a dazzling waistcoat, probably is wearing no socks. The hosier, like the hatter, is among his purse's foes.

Eugène had come to this point. His purse was always empty to Madame Vauquer, always full when his vanity bade him make a purchase; it had the maddest ups and downs. If he were to leave the stinking wretched pension, where periodically his social pretentions were humiliated, he would have to pay a month's rent to his landlady, and buy furnishings for his apartment, an apartment fit for a dandy to live in. And this was always impossible. But to get the money he needed for his gambling, Eugène knew how to proceed. He would buy watches and gold chains at his jeweler's at a stiff price which he met out of his winnings, and he would take them to the pawnshop, that grim and quiet friend of youth. Such inventiveness and audacity deserted him when he was merely trying to pay for board and lodging, or to buy some little things that were needed for the successful progress of his fashionable life. There was no inspiration in a vulgar necessity, or in debts contracted for needs that had already been met. Like most of those who have lived such an insecure life he waited till the last moment to meet those bills which are sacred in the eyes of the bourgeois, just as it was with Mirabeau, who would pay for his bread only when the bill came to him in the menacing form of a draft.

About this time Eugène had lost all his winnings, and fallen into debt. He was beginning to understand that it would be impossible to continue living on his new scale without fixed resources. But, although he groaned over the harassing annoyances of his precarious state, he felt he was unable to renounce the pleasures it brought, and was determined to go on with it at any cost. The happy accidents on which he had counted to make a fortune had become mere dreams, and the solid obstacles were increasing. When he had learned the domestic secrets of the Nucingen household, he saw that to use his love as a means of making a fortune, he would have to be perfectly shameless and give up the noble ideas which are the absolution for the faults of youth. If the life he had adopted was externally magnificent, it was gripped by the vise of remorse, and its ephemeral pleasures were bitterly expiated by lasting anguish. He had adopted it, he wallowed in it, making for himself, like La Bruyère's absent-minded man, a bed in the mire of a ditch; but so far, again like the absent-minded man, he had dirtied only his clothes.

"So the mandarin's been killed?" asked Bianchon one night as they left the table.

"Not yet," Eugène replied, "but he's in the throes."

The medical student took this as a joke, but he was wrong. This was the first time in many days that Eugène had dined at the boarding-house, and he was thoughtful during dinner. Instead of leaving at dessert, he stayed in the dining room sitting beside Mademoiselle Taillefer, and from time to time looking at her in an expressive way. Some of the boarders were still at table cracking nuts, others walked about carrying on the discussions they had begun during the meal. It was like almost every evening: everyone left when he felt like it, depending on how much interest he took in the conversation, or on how much torpor his digestion made him feel. In winter the dining room was seldom empty before eight o'clock, when the four women would be left to themselves to make up for the silence imposed on them by their sex in the midst of the crowd of men.

Vautrin was struck by Eugène's preoccupied air and stayed on, although at first he had seemed to be in a hurry to leave; he managed it so that he was out of Eugène's angle of vision and that Eugène might believe he had left. Then, instead of going out along with the last of the other male boarders, he slyly took up his stand in the drawing room. He had penetrated what was going on within Eugène's heart and he expected some decisive step. It was true that Eugène had come to that perplexed situation which many young men have known. Whether she was in love with him, or just coquetting with him, the Baroness de Nucingen had made him endure all the agonies of a genuine passion, bringing into play every resource of feminine diplomacy known to Paris. After she had compromised herself in the eyes of society to make sure of her grip on the cousin of the Viscountess de Beauséant, she continued to hold back from him the rights which he seemed to others to enjoy.

For the last month she had been teasing Eugène's senses so much that she had made an impression on his heart. In the early phase of the liaison Eugène had thought he was the master, but the baroness had now become the stronger by the help of a tactic which stirred in Eugène all the feelings good and bad that belong to the two or three personalities that are to be found in a young man in Paris. Was she acting deliberately? No; women are always sincere, even in the midst of their greatest falsities, because they are yielding to a natural instinct. Perhaps after she had let the young man assume such a power over her so quickly, after she had shown him such an excessive affection, Delphine was obeying a sense of dignity which led her either to take back the concessions she had made or at least to take pleasure in leaving them in abeyance. It is so natural for a Parisian woman, at the very moment when her passion is her guide, to delay her capitulation, to test the heart of the man to whom she is about to entrust her future!

All the baroness's hopes had just been betrayed in her first adventure, and her fidelity to a young egoist had been trampled on. She had good reason for mistrust. She may perhaps have seen in Eugène's manners, now that his quick success in society had made him smug, a sort of disrespect for her, bred of the odd features in their relationship. She certainly wished to cut an important figure to so young a man, and after for so long being humble toward the man who had deserted her she wished to retain dignity and power with her new admirer. She was unwilling that Eugène should think her an easy conquest, precisely because he knew that she had belonged to de Marsay. And finally, after she had been the victim of the degrading tastes of an out-and-out monster, a true libertine for all his youth, she took such delight in moving about in the flowery regions of love, it was for her so charming to survey all its aspects, to listen again and again to its gentle stirrings, to be caressed by breezes which were chaste. The true love was charged with the shortcomings of the false. Such illogical things will be all too common so long as men fail to appreciate how many flowers are cut down in the heart of a young girl by the first strokes of betrayal.

Whatever her reasons were, Delphine was playing with Eugène, and enjoyed playing with him, because she was sure of his love and just as sure that she could end his unhappiness whenever in her royal feminine pleasure she thought the moment had come. His self-respect made Eugène unwilling that his first contest should end in a defeat, and he persevered in his pursuit like a huntsman who is determined to shoot a partridge on the opening day of his first season. His anxieties, his wounded self-respect and his despair, true or assumed, linked him more and more closely to this woman. Everyone thought that the baroness already belonged to him, and he was no nearer success than on the first day he had seen her. He did not know that a woman's coquetry is sometimes more profitable than her love is pleasant; he used to fall into foolish rages. If the season in which a woman refuses to yield to love gave to Eugène the pleasures of the first fruits, these were as costly to him as they were green, tart and delightful to taste. Sometimes in his penniless state, with no future in view, he would override the appeals of his conscience and think about the chances of wealth which Vautrin had shown him to be possible in a marriage with Mademoiselle Taillefer. At present his poverty was so clamorous that he yielded almost involuntarily to the artifices of the terrible sphinx-like man whose glance so often fascinated him. When Poiret and Mademoiselle Michonneau left to go upstairs, Eugène, thinking that except for Madame Vauquer and Madame Couture (who was knitting woolen sleeves and dozing by the stove) he was now alone with Victorine, looked at her so tenderly that she lowered her eyes.

"Are you worried about anything?" Victorine asked him, after a moment's silence.

"What man isn't?" Eugène replied. "If young men could be sure they were loved with a devotion that would make up for the sacrifices they are always ready to make, perhaps they'd never be grieved."

Mademoiselle Taillefer's reply was a glance whose meaning could not be mistaken.

"You think you can be sure of your heart today, but would you be able to say that it would never change?"

A smile played about the poor girl's lips, like a ray coming from the very soul, and her face shone so beautifully that Eugène was frightened at having started into being so deep an emotion.

"Could it be that if tomorrow you were wealthy and happy,

if an immense fortune came to you out of the sky, you would still love the poor young man who had won your favor during the days of your poverty?"

The reply was a pretty inclination of her head.

"A young man who is very unfortunate!"

Another nod.

"What silly things are you young people saying now?" asked Madame Vauquer.

"Don't bother us," Eugène replied. "We understand each other."

"So there seems to be an engagement between the Chevalier Eugène de Rastignac and Mademoiselle Victorine Taillefer?" Vautrin boomed out, as he suddenly disclosed himself at the dining-room door.

"Oh, how you frightened me!" said Madame Couture and Madame Vauquer in chorus.

"I could do worse," said Eugène with a laugh, though Vautrin's voice had given him the most painful feeling he had ever known.

"No disagreeable jokes, gentlemen!" said Madame Couture. "Victorine, we'll go upstairs."

Madame Vauquer went out along with her guests so that, passing the evening in their rooms, she could economize a candle and a fire. Eugène was left to face Vautrin alone.

"I was sure that you would come to it," Vautrin said with imperturbable composure. "But I want you to know that I've my scruples like anyone else. Don't make up your mind in the twinkling of an eye. You're not quite yourself tonight. You're in debt, and I want you to be guided not by despair or passion of any sort, but by reason. That's the way I want you to do as I advised. Perhaps you need a thousand crowns or so. Here they are, take them if you want."

The diabolic man took his wallet from his pocket, and from it drew three notes and flashed them right before Eugène's eyes.

It was a most painful situation for Eugène. To the Marquis d'Adjuda and the Count de Trailles he had debts of honor amounting to a hundred louis. He did not have the money, and dared not go that evening to the Countess de Restaud's, where he was expected. It was to be one of those quiet evenings, when though all that is served is tea and cake, six thousand francs can be lost at whist.

Eugène could scarcely hide his intense nervousness as he replied, "After what you've told me of your project, surely you must understand that it's impossible for me to be indebted to you."

"That's what I hoped you'd say. I'd have been sorry if you had answered in any other way," the tempter replied. "You're a fine young fellow, scrupulous, proud as a lion and gentle as a girl. You're the sort of prey the devil could enjoy. I like young men of your kind. After two or three more meditations on high politics you'll see the world as it is. The superior person should play a few scenes which display his virtue and so give a sop to all his notions and at the same time win the applause of the ninnies out in front. You'll be mine in a few days. Ah, if you'd become my pupil, there's nothing you couldn't attain. You couldn't have a wish that wouldn't be fulfilled in an instant, no matter what you might long for: honor, fortune, women. Everything civilization offers would be yours to savor. You'd be our spoiled darling, our Benjamin, my lot would kill themselves, every one of them, to do your pleasure. Every obstacle in your way would be obliterated. If you still have scruples, I suppose you think I'm a rascal? Well, a man who had as much integrity as you think you have kept up till now, M. de Turenne, used to have little dealings with brigands and he didn't think they compromised him. So you don't want to be under an obligation to me? Don't let that stop you!" and he smiled. "Take these scraps, and on this," he drew out a stamped sheet, "just scribble: *I.O.U the sum of three thousand five hundred francs, payable in a year's time.* And put down the date. The interest is steep enough to relieve your conscience; call me a usurer, and consider that you've no need to feel any gratitude. I don't mind your despising me today, for I'm sure you'll love me later. You'll find in me immense abysses, some of those huge concentrated emotions that ninnies call vices; but you'll never find any cowardice, or any ingratitude. I'm no pawn and no bishop, nothing short of a rook!"

"What sort of man can you be?" Eugène cried. "You were created to torture me!"

"Not at all. I'm a good fellow, one who's willing to dirty himself to keep you out of the dirt for the rest of your life. You ask yourself why I'm so devoted to you? Well, I'll tell you why some day; I'll whisper it into your ear. I gave you a shock when I first showed you how the social order operates, how the machine runs, but your first terror will pass, just like that of the conscript on his first battlefield, and you'll become accustomed to the idea of considering men as soldiers resolved to die in the service of those who've crowned themselves kings. Times have changed a lot. The old way was to hire a ruffian, and say to him: 'Here are a hundred crowns, go and kill Monsieur So-and-so,' and to have a quiet supper after arranging that a man should be put underground for a trifle. But my way is to offer to give you a grand fortune in return for a nod of the head which doesn't compromise you in any way, and still you hang back. The world is getting soft today."

Eugène signed the note and exchanged it for the money.

"Good! Now let's be reasonable," Vautrin went on. "I mean to leave in a few months for America, to start planting tobacco. I'll send you a friendly gift of cigars. If I make money I'll help you out. If I don't have children, and I probably won't, for I'm not inclined to leave a copy of myself here, I'll bequeath my fortune to you. Isn't this being a man's friend? The fact is that I'm very fond of you. I have a longing to devote myself to someone else. I've done that already. You must understand, my dear boy, that I live on a plane higher than that of other men. Actions to me are only means; my mind is on the goal. What is a man to me? Just that!" and he clicked his thumbnail against one of his teeth. "A man is everything or nothing. He's less than nothing when he's a person like Poiret; he can be squashed like a louse, he'll be flattened out, and he'll stink. But when a man is like you, he's a God—not a machine covered with so much skin, but a theatre in which the noblest feelings are aroused, and I live only by feeling. What is a feeling if not a world in a thought? Look at Père Goriot. For him his two daughters are the whole universe; they are the thread which guides him through creation. Well, for me, after digging down to the very core of life, there exists only one real feeling, the friendship between one man and another. I know *Venice Preserved* by heart. Pierre and Jaffier, that's the passion that's at my heart. Have you known many men who if a comrade were to say to them: 'Come, we've a corpse to bury!' would be tough enough to go and do it without breathing a word and boring you with moral maxims? I've done that. I wouldn't speak this way to everyone. But you are a superior person; one can say anything to you; you can understand. You're not going to paddle about for long in the swamps, among the filthy beasts who are all about us here. Well, I've said what I had to say. You'll marry. Let's use our blades! Mine is steel and won't ever soften! Ha! Ha!"

Vautrin left the room without staying to hear the negative reply Eugène was shaping, so that he might put the latter at his ease. He seemed to foresee the little gestures of reluctance, the struggles with oneself which men undertake to look well in their own eyes, and which serve to help them justify to themselves their evil acts.

"Let him do what he wants, I certainly won't marry Mademoiselle Taillefer," Eugène told himself.

He suffered from the discomfort of a moral fever as he thought of making a pact with this man who filled him with horror, but nevertheless was taking on a greater stature in his mind both for the cynicism in his ideas and for the boldness with which he carried on his struggle with society. Then he dressed, called for a cab, and went to the Countess de Restaud's. For the last few days she had been far more considerate toward him, seeing that every step he took brought him nearer to the summit of society and that one day his influence promised to be formidable indeed. He paid his debts to the Marquis d'Ajuda and the Count de Trailles, played at whist a good part of the night and won back what he had lost. He was superstitious, like most men who still have their way to make and are more or less fatalists, and in his run of luck he discerned (because he wished to) heaven's blessing on his perseverance in staying in the path of virtue. The next morning, he asked Vautrin at once if he still had the note, and when it was produced he paid back the three thousand francs, with a natural pleasure which he did not try to conceal.

"Everything is going well," said Vautrin.

"But I'm not your accomplice," Eugène insisted.

"I know, I know," Vautrin replied, interrupting him. "You're still being childish. You're hanging around the doorway."

Two days after this, Poiret and Mademoiselle Michonneau were sitting on a bench in the sun, in a lonely alley in the Jardin des Plantes, and talking with the man who had so rightly made the medical student suspicious.

"Mademoiselle," said Monsieur Gondureau, "I can't see why you have these scruples. His Excellency the Minister of Police of the kingdom . . ."

"Ah, His Excellency the Minister of Police of the kingdom." Poiret echoed.

"Yes, His Excellency is interesting himself in the matter," said Gondureau.

It will seem improbable to everyone that Poiret, that super-annuated clerk, unquestionably a man who, however barren of ideas, was a pattern of bourgeois virtues, should have gone on listening to the self-styled gentleman of means from the Rue de Buffon when at the word *police* the disguise was shorn away and the agent from the Rue de Jerusalem appeared from beneath it. Nevertheless, nothing could have been more natural. Everyone will better understand the species to which Poiret belonged in the vast genus of ninnies by an observation that certain students have already made, but which has had to wait till this moment for publication. There is a pen-pushing species, confined in the budg-et between the first degree of latitude where the annual wage is twelve hundred francs—a sort of administrative Greenland—and the third degree, which begins with the somewhat less marrow-freezing wages of three to six thousand francs, a temperate region, where gratuities are quite at home and flourish despite the diffi-culties in the way of their cultivation. One of the characteristic traits which best reveal the feeble narrowness of life among this subaltern tribe is a sort of involuntary, automatic, instinctive re-spect for the Grand Lama of each ministry, known to the clerk by an illegible signature and under the title "His Excellency the Minister," which in the eyes of the tribe represents a sacred power against whose word no question may be raised. Like the Pope in the minds of Catholics, His Excellency is administratively in-fallible for the clerical species; the radiance he casts gives a luster to all his acts, all his words, and all the words spoken in his name; covers every substance with embroidery and gives legal sanction to every action it ordains; the word *excellency* is proof that the intentions are pure and the will holy; it is a passport for ideas which otherwise would be sharply rejected. What poor clerks would never do in their own interests, they speed to carry out the moment the word *excellency* is uttered. Government offices have their form of passive obedience, just as the Army has; the system stifles conscience, annihilates a man's character and in the end turns him into a cog in the governmental machinery. So it was that Monsieur Gondureau, who seemed to be a judge of human nature, had quickly perceived that Poiret was one of these bureaucratic ninnies, and now brought out at just the right moment as an open sesame the talismanic word *excellency*. He opened fire from his batteries and stunned Poiret whom he thought of as the male analogue of the Michonneau, just as the Michonneau struck him as the female analogue of Poiret.

"Oh, now that you say that His Excellency personally, His Excellency the Minister . . . Oh, but this is a very different thing!" said Poiret.

"You hear what this gentleman says, and you seem to trust his judgment," said the self-styled gentleman of means, turning now to Mademoiselle Michonneau. "Well, His Excellency is now in a state of absolute certainty that the man who calls himself Vautrin, living in the Maison Vauquer, is a convict who has escaped from the penitentiary at Toulon, where he goes by the name of *Cheat-death*."

"Cheat-death you say?" remarked Poiret. "He's very lucky if he deserves that name."

"He does," went on the agent. "The nickname comes of the luck he's had never to lose his life, no matter how bold the venture he was involved in. This man is dangerous, you see! He has powers that put him far out of the ordinary. His conviction itself was a thing which has given him among the men of his sort a tremendous honor. . . ."

"Is he a man of honor, then?" asked Poiret.

"After his own fashion. He agreed to shoulder the blame for a crime that another had committed, a forgery carried out by a very handsome young man of whom he was very fond, a young

Italian who was a bit of a gambler and who has since that time gone into the Army and made a fine record."

"But if His Excellency the Minister of Police is sure that Monsieur Vautrin is Cheat-death, why does he need my help?" Mademoiselle Michonneau asked.

"Yes, indeed," said Poiret, "if in fact the Minister, as you were so obliging as to tell us, is certain, so to speak . . ."

"Certain isn't quite the right word; but he suspects. You'll understand if I put it this way. Jacques Collin, called Cheat-death, is trusted by all the men in the three penitentiaries, who've made him their agent and banker. He makes a lot of money in carrying out their commissions; only a man of unusual talent could succeed in that sort of business. The so-called Vautrin," the agent went on, "is given the money these criminals have; he invests it, and keeps it for them; he is ready to pass it over to any who escape; or when they make wills, he gives it to their families; or else, when they give him a direction, to their mistresses."

"Their mistresses! You mean their wives," Poiret corrected him.

"No, sir. The convict usually has only illicit relations, and we call the women concubines."

"They all live then in a state of concubinage?"

"That's what it comes to."

"But this is a horrible state of affairs and His Excellency should not tolerate it. Since you have the honor to see His Excellency, it is for you, and you seem to have the good of the people at heart, to inform him of the immoral mode of life of these men who are giving a very bad example to the rest of society."

"But the Government doesn't put them there to be models of all the virtues."

"That's so, but still let me . . ."

"Let the gentleman speak, darling," said Mademoiselle Michonneau.

"You understand me, Mademoiselle," Gondureau went on. "Naturally the Government is concerned to get hold of an illegal treasury which is thought to be very large. Cheat-death has a substantial sum, coming not only from what some of his comrades give him to hold, but also from what is entrusted to him by the Ten Thousand Society. . . ."

"Ten thousand thieves!" Poiret cried out in terror.

"No, the Ten Thousand Society is an association of thieves on the grand scale, men who won't meddle in any affairs where there is less than ten thousand francs to steal. This society consists of the élite among the profession, those who appear directly before the assize court. They know the Code, and never run the risk of a death penalty if they are caught. Collin is their agent, their adviser. Through his immense resources this man has succeeded in creating a police of his own, relations which extend everywhere, and he's been able to envelop them in a mystery we can't penetrate. We've surrounded him with spies for the past year, but we haven't been able to find out what he's up to. His treasury, along with his abilities, is always strengthening the operations of vice, serving as a sort of backlog for crime, and maintaining ready for action an army of rascals who are in a state of perpetual warfare with society. If we can get our hands on Cheat-death and his treasury, we'll cut off the evil at its root. So the expedition after him has become an affair of state and of high policy, one that can honor those who co-operate to make it a success. You, Monsieur Poiret, might be restored to service in the administration; you might become secretary to a police commissioner, and your employment would in no way conflict with your drawing your pension."

"But why," asked Mademoiselle Michonneau, "does not Cheat-death abscond with the treasury?"

"Oh, no," replied the agent. "If he were to steal that, wherever he went he would be followed by a man under orders to kill him.

And then a man can't walk off with a treasury as easily as he can with a girl of good family. Besides Collin is a good fellow; he would be incapable of an act like that; he'd think himself dishonored."

"You are right," said Poiret. "He would be utterly dishonored."

"But there's nothing in all this that explains why you don't simply seize him," said Mademoiselle Michonneau.

"Well, it's like this!" The agent whispered in her ear to stop her friend from making any more interruptions or they would never have done, and continued. "He must have a great deal of money to exercise such power as he does, this downy bird. When he came here Cheat-death put on the semblance of a worthy citizen; he's made himself into a good Paris bourgeois; he's taken a room in a boarding-house which isn't at all showy; the man is shrewd, he'll never be taken off guard. Monsieur Vautrin passes for a respected person who engages in important affairs."

"Naturally," Poiret muttered to himself.

"The minister, in case there was a mistake and the man arrested turned out to be really a Monsieur Vautrin, doesn't want to turn the sentiment of the business world in Paris against him, or public opinion. The Prefect of Police is in a shaky position; he has enemies. If there were a mistake the men who want his post would take advantage of the uproar and the spoutings of the liberals to blast him out of it. The procedure here must be the same as in that affair of Cogniard who pretended to be the Count of Saint Helena; if he had really been the count we should have been in a mess. So one has to be quite sure of the identity."

"Then you'll need a pretty woman," said Mademoiselle Michonneau quickly.

"Cheat-death wouldn't let a woman get close enough to him," the agent replied. "I'll tell you a secret; he hates women."

"I can't see then what I could do to make sure of his identity, supposing that I agreed to help for two thousand francs."

"There's nothing easier. I'll give you a phial which contains a dose of liquid which will bring on a sort of stroke in which there'll be no danger but which will look just like apoplexy. This drug will take effect mixed with coffee or with wine. When it does, you'll have the man put to bed, and you'll undress him to make sure he isn't dying. When you're left alone with him, you'll give him a hard slap on the shoulder and then you'll see the branded letters show up."

"Why, that's nothing at all," said Poiret.

"Well, will you do it?" Gondureau asked the old maid.

"Suppose no letters showed up, should I still get the two thousand francs?" asked Mademoiselle Michonneau.

"No."

"What would the fee be then?"

"Five hundred francs."

"Do a thing of that kind for so little? In the forum of one's conscience the evil is the same, and I have to quiet my conscience."

"I assure you that Mademoiselle Michonneau has a very keen conscience," said Poiret, "besides being a most amiable and intelligent person."

"Well," Mademoiselle Michonneau continued, "give me three thousand francs if he is Cheat-death, and nothing at all if he is an honest citizen."

"All right," said Gondureau, "but on condition that the thing is done tomorrow."

"Not so quickly. I must consult my confessor."

"You're a sly one!" the agent said as he got up. "I'll see you tomorrow. If you need me in a hurry, come to Rue Sainte Anne, at the end of the court of the Sainte Chapelle. There's just one door under the archway. Ask for Monsieur Gondureau."

Bianchon was on his way back from Cuvier's lecture, and the rather peculiar expression "Cheat-death" struck him; he also heard the *all right* of the famous head of the Sûreté.

"Why don't you settle it now? It would make an annuity of three hundred francs," said Poiret to Mademoiselle Michonneau.

"Why?" she asked. "I must think. Suppose Monsieur Vautrin were this Cheat-death. Perhaps it would be more profitable to come to terms with him. Still to ask him for money would mean tipping him off, and he'd be capable of running away without paying a cent. That would be a nasty turn of events."

"Suppose he were tipped off," Poiret continued. "This gentleman has told us that he was watched. But you'd stand to lose everything."

"Moreover, I don't like the fellow," Mademoiselle Michonneau reflected. "Every time he speaks to me it is to say something disagreeable."

"You'd do better to act with this gentleman who made a very good impression on me, besides being well dressed. You'd be acting in obedience to the laws in ridding society of a criminal, however decent he may be. Once a criminal always a criminal. Suppose he took a fancy to murder us all? What the devil? We'd be guilty of all the murders, not to speak of our being the first victims."

Mademoiselle Michonneau was so much concerned with her own thoughts that she could spare no attention for the sentences which dripped from Poiret's mouth, like drops of water from a leaky tap. When the old man had once begun to talk and Mademoiselle Michonneau did not stop him, he went on interminably like a machine set in motion. After broaching an initial subject he was led by his parentheses to speak of quite different topics, and without ever coming to any conclusions. When they reached the Maison Vauquer he had quite lost his way in a series of connecting passages and citations which had led him to relate his testimony in the case of Ragoulleau versus Morin, in which he had appeared as a witness for the defense. As they came in, his companion did not fail to note Eugène talking intimately with Mademoiselle Taillefer, and both so engrossed that they paid not the least attention to the two old boarders passing through the dining room.

"That was how it had to end," Mademoiselle Michonneau said to Poiret. "They'd been making such eyes at each other for the past week."

"Yes," he said. "And so she was found guilty."

"Who?"

"Madame Morin."

"I'm speaking of Mademoiselle Victorine," said Mademoiselle Michonneau, unconsciously stepping into Poiret's room, "and you answer by talking about Madame Morin. Who is that woman?"

"What is Mademoiselle Victorine guilty of?" Poiret asked.

"She's guilty of loving Monsieur Eugène de Rastignac, and she is steering straight ahead without seeing where that will take her, the poor innocent!"

During the day the Baroness de Nucingen had brought Eugène to the point of despair. Without as yet having said anything of it, he was now completely won over in mind to Vautrin although unwilling to examine the motives of the friendship which that extraordinary man had for him, or to consider what the future of a union between them might be. Only a miracle could save him from the abyss into which he had begun to slip in the past hour by exchanging with Mademoiselle Taillefer the tenderest promises. Victorine thought that the heavens were opening before her eyes, and that she was hearing an angel's voice; for her the Maison Vauquer was taking on those fantastic hues that stage decorators apply to sets which represent palaces; she loved and she was loved, or at least she thought she was! And what woman wouldn't have thought so if she had looked at Eugène and listened to him during that hour which had been stolen despite all the vigilant eyes in the house? Arguing against his conscience, aware that he was doing wrong and intended to do wrong, telling himself that he would atone for this venial sin by making a woman happy, he had grown handsomer by his despair, and shone with all the infernal fires that raged in his heart. Happily for him, the miracle took place; Vautrin came in, in high spirits, and perceived what was going on in the souls of the two young persons whose marriage he had arranged by the scheming of his diabolic genius. He disturbed their happiness by singing out in his powerful, bantering voice:

Ma Fanchette est charmante
Dans sa simplicité . . .

Victorine fled, as happy now as she had ever before been unhappy. Poor girl! A clasp of the hand, a cheek just touched by Eugène's hair, a word uttered so close to her ear that she had felt the warmth of the speaker's lips, the embrace of her waist by a trembling arm, a kiss on her neck—these were the marks of the love she had won; and since big Sylvie was near by and might come into this radiant dining room at any moment, they were more fervent, more lively, more pleasing than the finest witnesses to devotion recorded in the most celebrated tales of love. These *menus suffrages,* as they were prettily styled by our ancestors, seemed like crimes to a pious girl who went to confession every second week! In that hour she had lavished richer treasures of soul than she could have mustered later, when she was wealthy and happy, in giving the full possession of herself.

"It's all arranged," Vautrin said to Eugène. "Our two dandies have come to grips. Everything took place in the proper way. A question of opinion. Our pigeon insulted my falcon. They meet tomorrow at the Clignancourt redoubt. At eight-thirty Mademoiselle Taillefer will be heiress to the love and the fortune of her father, while she'll be quietly sitting there dipping her buttered bread in her coffee. Doesn't it sound queer when it's said? This Taillefer sprig is expert with his sword, and as sure of himself as a man with all the trumps; but he'll be done in by a thrust that I've invented—a way of bringing the sword up suddenly and piercing the forehead. I'll show you that stroke, for it's incredibly useful."

Eugène listened with a stupid air, and was incapable of making any reply. Just then Père Goriot, Bianchon and some others came in.

"This is the way I wanted to see you," Vautrin went on. "You know what you're doing. Good, my little eagle; you'll be able to rule men; you're strong, four-square, tough; you have my respect."

He wanted to take Eugène's hand, but this was quickly drawn back. Eugène fell into a chair and grew pale; he imagined he saw before him a pool of blood.

"Ah, so you still have a few tags of virtue left," Vautrin whispered. "Papa has three millions, I know what his fortune is. The dowry will make you as white as a wedding dress and in your own eyes, too."

Eugène's mind was made up. That evening he would go and warn the Taillefers, father and son. It was now that, Vautrin having gone away, Goriot whispered to Eugène, "You're sad, my boy! I'm going to cheer you up." And the old vermicelli manufacturer lit his taper at one of the lamps. Eugène followed him, afire with curiosity.

"Let us go to your room," said the old man who had asked Sylvie for Eugène's key. "This morning you thought she didn't love you, eh?" he went on. "She insisted on your going, and you went away angry and in despair. Stupid boy! She was expecting me. Do you understand? We were to go and finish arranging a jewel of an apartment for you to occupy three days from now. Don't give me away. She wants to surprise you; but I don't want it to be a secret from you any longer. You will be living in the Rue d'Artois, just around the corner from the Rue Saint-Lazare.

You will be living like a prince. We've bought such furniture for you as would be worthy of a bride. We've done a lot of things this last month without letting on to you about any of them. My lawyer has set to work; my daughter will have the interest on her dowry, thirty-six thousand francs a year, and the eight hundred thousand francs I am going to insist on having invested open and above board."

Eugène was silent and paced up and down his miserable untidy room, his arms crossed. Père Goriot took advantage of a moment when his back was turned to place upon the mantelpiece a case of red morocco, on which the Rastignac arms were engraved in gold.

"My dear boy," the poor old man went on, "I'm in this up to my neck. But you will see I had a selfish motive. Your move to this other quarter is an opportunity for me. If I ask you a favor you won't refuse me, will you?"

"What is it you'd like?"

"Above your apartment, on the fifth floor, there is a room which goes with it. I shall live there, shan't I? I am getting old; I am too far away from my daughters. I won't be in your way. But I shall be there. Every evening you will talk to me about her. That won't be a nuisance to you, will it? When you come in, even if I'm in bed, I'll hear you and I'll say to myself: 'He has just been with my little Delphine. He took her to the ball; she is happy because of him.' If I were sick, it would be balm to my heart to hear you come in, move about, go away again. There will be so much of my daughter in you! I'll have only a step to go to reach the Champs-Elysées, where they drive every day; I'll always see them instead of sometimes arriving too late, as happens now. And then perhaps she'll come to stay with you! I'll see her in her morning gown, trotting about, moving as softly as a little kitten. This last month she has become just like the young girl she used to be, gay and charming. Her heart is convalescing; she owes her happiness to you. Oh, I'll do the impossible for you. A little while ago when we were coming back to her house she said to me: 'Papa, I'm very happy.' When they say 'Father' in a formal way they chill my heart; but when they call me 'Papa' I seem to see them again as little girls, and all my memories crowd back. I feel that I am more fully their father. I imagine that they belong to no one yet."

The old man wiped his eyes; he was crying. "It was so long since I had heard that word, so long since she had taken my arm. Why, it must be ten years since I walked by the side of one of my daughters. How nice it is to rub oneself against her dress, to suit my pace to hers, to feel the warmth of her body! This morning I was everywhere with Delphine. I went into the shops with her. And then I brought her back to her house. Oh, keep me near you! Sometimes you'll need someone to do some little thing for you, and I'll be there. Oh, if that big lump of an Alsatian would die, if his gout would have the wit to settle in his stomach, wouldn't my poor daughter be happy! You would be my son-in-law; you would be her confessed husband. Oh, she is so unhappy at missing the pleasures of this world that I absolve her of everything. God must be on the side of fathers who love deeply. She loves you too much," he went on with a nod of his head. "While we were on our way she talked to me about you. 'Father, isn't he good, hasn't he a kind heart? Does he talk about me?' Why, from the Rue d'Artois to the Passage des Panoramas she spoke whole volumes about you. At last she poured her heart out to mine. During all this wonderful afternoon, I was no longer old; I felt as light as a feather. I told her that you had given me the thousand-franc note. The dear girl was moved to tears. What's that on your mantelpiece?" said Père Goriot at last, dying with impatience as he looked at Eugène, who stood motionless.

Completely taken aback, Eugène looked at his neighbor with a stupefied air. The duel which Vautrin had fixed for the next day was in such contrast with the realization of his most cherished hopes that he experienced all the sensations of a nightmare. He turned toward the mantel and saw there the small square case, opened it and found within it a paper which covered a Bréguet watch. On the paper were written the words:

I want you to think of me at every hour because . . .
Delphine.

The last word must have referred to some scene which had occurred between them. Eugène was touched by it. His arms were enameled on the inside of the gold case. The watch, something that he had so long yearned for, the chain, the key, the enameling, answered every wish. Père Goriot was radiant. He must have promised his daughter that he would tell her every detail of the effect the surprise of her gift would produce on Eugène; for he was a sharer in their youthful feelings, and did not seem the least happy of the three. He already loved Eugène, both as Delphine's beloved and for his own qualities.

"You are going to see her this evening; she expects you. The big Alsatian lump is having supper at his dancer's. Oh, what a fool he looked when my lawyer let him have the whole truth about himself! Doesn't he claim that he loves my daughter to the point of adoration. If he touches her, I'll kill him. The idea of knowing that Delphine belongs to . . . (he sighed) would make me commit a crime. But it wouldn't be homicide. The fellow is just a calf's head set on a pig's body. You'll take me along with you won't you?"

"Yes, dear Père Goriot, you know very well how dear to me you are."

"It's clear that *you* aren't ashamed of me. Let me embrace you."

He hugged the student. "You will make her very happy. Promise me you will! You will go this evening, won't you?"

"Yes, indeed. I have to go out on an errand that can't be put off."

"Can I be of any use to you?"

"Yes, to be sure you can. While I am at the Baroness de Nucingen's, you go to Monsieur Taillefer's and ask him to see me for an hour in the course of the evening on a matter of the greatest importance."

"Can it be true, then young man," said Père Goriot with a change of expression, "that you are paying court to his daughter, as those fools were saying downstairs? By heaven, you don't know what a Goriot blow can be! If you are deceiving us, that's what you will get. Oh, it cannot be possible!"

"I swear to you," said Eugène, "that I love but one woman in this world, and I have known the truth of this only for a moment."

"How happy that makes me!" said Père Goriot.

"But," Eugène went on, "Monsieur Taillefer's son is called out to a duel tomorrow, and I have heard that he is to be killed."

"What difference can that make to you?" asked Père Goriot.

"Why, I must tell the father that he must stop his son from going to the . . ."

At this moment he was interrupted by Vautrin's voice, which could be heard singing on his doorstep:

> O Richard, o mon roi
> L'univers t'abandonne . . .

Boum! Boum! Boum!

> J'ai longtemps parcouru le monde
> Et l'on m'a vu . . .

Tra—la—la—la.

"Gentlemen," Christophe called out, "the soup is waiting for you, and every one is at table."

"Come," said Vautrin, "you must take a bottle of my Bordeaux."

"Don't you think the watch is pretty?" asked Père Goriot. "Her taste is good, isn't it?"

Vautrin, Père Goriot and Eugène went down together and because of their lateness had seats side by side. Eugène was extremely cold to Vautrin during dinner, although the latter, so charming in Madame Vauquer's eyes, had never before risen to such heights of wit. He was sparkling in his sallies, and stimulated the whole table. Such assurance, such sang-froid appalled Eugène.

"What have you been up to, today?" asked Madame Vauquer "You're as gay as a lark."

"I'm always gay when business goes well."

"Business?" asked Eugène.

"Yes, indeed. I've delivered an order of goods on which I'll get a large commission. Mademoiselle Michonneau," he asked, noting how intently the old maid was scrutinizing him, "is there something about my features which you dislike? Is that why you stare at me so hard? Just say the word and I'll get the offending member changed, just to please you.

"Poiret," he went on, "you and I won't fight over this, shall we?" And he leered at the old fellow.

"You should pose for a statue of Hercules in jest," said the young painter, "you rascal!"

"And I will, by the Lord Harry," Vautrin replied, "if Mademoiselle Michonneau will pose as Venus of Père la Chaise."

"And what about Poiret?" asked Bianchon.

"Oh, Poiret will pose as Poiret. He'll be the garden god!" cried Vautrin. "His name belongs to the pear family. . . ."

"And you'd look silly," said Bianchon, "between the pear and the cheese."

"This is all foolishness," said Madame Vauquer. "Why don't you give us your Bordeaux? I see a bottle of it peeping out. That will keep up our spirits, not to mention its being good for the stomach."

"Gentlemen," said Vautrin, "our chairwoman calls us to order. Madame Couture and Mademoiselle Victorine will not cry out against your jesting speeches; but respect the innocence of Père Goriot. I propose that we have a little *bottleorama* of Bordeaux, rendered doubly illustrious by the name of Laffitte, if I may say so, and yet make no allusion to politics. Come on, you lump!" he said glancing at Christophe, who did not stir. "Christophe, come now! Don't you know your own name? Christophe, bring on the liquids!"

"Here you are, sir," said Christophe, presenting the bottle.

After he had filled Eugène's glass and Goriot's, he poured a few drops into his own, and sipped it while his neighbors were drinking. Suddenly he made a wry face.

"Damn it, it tastes of the cork. Take this bottle for yourself, Christophe, and go get some more for us. On the right, you remember? There are sixteen of us, bring eight bottles."

"Since you're loosening up, I'll pay for a hundred marrons," said the painter.

There was a volley of exclamations in which everyone took part: "Oh! Ah! ha! Hurrah!"

"Come on, Mère Vauquer, you must offer a couple of bottles of champagne," cried Vautrin.

"What's that you're saying? Why don't you ask me to give you the house? Two bottles of champagne? That means twelve francs. I certainly don't make as much as that, for my part! But if Monsieur Eugène will make us a present of them, I'll offer you cassis."

"That cassis of hers which purges like manna," Bianchon said *sotto voce*.

"Will you be quiet, Bianchon!" said Eugène. "I can't hear the word 'manna' without my heart's being . . . All right, get the champagne. I'll pay for it," he added.

"Sylvie, get some biscuits and little cakes!" said Madame Vauquer.

"Your little cakes are too much grown up," said Vautrin; "they have beards. But as for the biscuits, go ahead."

In a moment the Bordeaux was circulating, the revelers had grown animated; gaiety redoubled. There was wild laughter, and in the midst of it broke out some imitation of various animal sounds. The man from the Museum had the notion of reproducing a street cry which resembled the howling of an amorous cat, and all at once eight voices were shouting out the following phrases: Knives ground! Chickweed for the little birds? —Pastry, Madame, pastry!—China mended!—Oysters here!— Beat your wives, beat your clothes!—old clothes, old lace, old hats for sale!—Cherry ripe! Bianchon was acclaimed victor for the nasal tone in which he cried: Umbrella merchant! In a few moments there was a row that would split your head, a conversation full of riddles, all like a veritable opera, Vautrin being the conductor, although he did not for a moment fail to watch Eugène and Père Goriot, who seemed to be drunk already. Leaning back against their chairs, they both were looking on at the unusual disorder with grave expressions and drinking little. Both were concerned about what they had to do in the course of the evening and yet they felt incapable of getting up from their places. Vautrin, who was following their changes of expression by side glances he flung at them, seized the instant when their eyelids began to flutter and seemed to be on the point of shutting, to lean over and whisper in Eugène's ear, "My lad, you're not clever enough to contend with Papa Vautrin, and he's too fond of you to let you do anything silly. When I've made up my mind about something, only God himself is strong enough to bar my way. Ah, you meant to go and warn Père Taillefer! to do something that would have been a schoolboy's slip! The oven is hot, the flour is kneaded, the bread is in the pan; tomorrow when we begin to crunch it, we'll send some of the crumbs leaping into the air. And you'd stop it being put in the oven? No, no! It's to be baked, all right. If you have some little bit of remorse, that will stop as you digest. While you sleep your little nap, Colonel Count Franchessini will clear for you Michel Taillefer's succession with the point of his sword. In inheriting from her brother, Victorine will have a cold fifteen thousand francs income. I've already made inquiries, and I know that her inheritance from her mother will rise to more than three hundred thousand. . . ."

Eugène heard what Vautrin was saying, but without being able to make any answer; he felt as if his tongue were glued to his palate, and as if he himself were the victim of an irresistible sleepiness. He could no longer see the table nor the revelers except through a luminous mist. The noise soon quieted down, and the boarders left one by one. Then, when all that remained were Madame Vauquer, Madame Couture, Victorine, Vautrin and Père Goriot, Eugène could see, as in a dream, Madame Vauquer busy taking up the bottles one after another and emptying the little that remained in them so as to make some full bottles.

"Ah," said she, "how mad they are! How young!"

This was the last remark Eugène could understand.

"There's no one like Monsieur Vautrin to start this sort of good time," said Sylvie. "Look, there's Christophe, sleeping like a top."

"Good-bye, Mama," said Vautrin. "I'm going to the Boulevard to see Monsieur Marty in *Le Mont Sauvage,* a magnificent play based on *Le Solitaire.* If you wish, I'll take you and these ladies too."

"No, thank you," said Madame Couture.

"What's this!" Madame Vauquer cried out. "You won't go to see a play taken from *Le Solitaire,* a work written by Atala de Chateaubriand, a work that we used to take such pleasure in reading and so pretty that we used to weep like Madeleines d'Élodie under the lindens last summer, in short a moral work which might be instructive for your ward?"

"We are not allowed to go to comedies," Victorine answered.

"Well, they're out for good, those fellows," said Vautrin, giving a comic sort of push to Père Goriot's head and Eugène's.

As he arranged the student's head on the chair in such a way as would allow him to sleep in comfort he kissed him warmly on the forehead, singing:

> *Dormez, mes chères amours!*
> *Pour vous je veillerai toujours.*

"I'm afraid he may be ill," said Victorine.

"Stay and look after him, then," Vautrin replied. "It's your duty as a devoted wife," he whispered in her ear. "This young fellow worships you, and you'll be his nice little wife, I prophesy that. In short," he now spoke aloud, *"they were highly respected throughout the land, lived happily and had many children.* That's how all love stories end. Come, Mama," he said, turning to Madame Vauquer and giving her a hug, "put on your hat, your fine flowered dress, and the countess's scarf. I'm going for a cab." And he left the room, singing:

> *Soleil, soleil, divin soleil*
> *Toi qui fais murir les citrouilles . . .*

"Good Lord, Madame Couture, I want to tell you that man would make me happy living on the rooftops. Look!" she said turning toward the vermicelli maker, "there's Père Goriot right out. That old pest never had the idea of taking me out anywhere

He'll fall to the floor, good Heavens. Isn't it disgusting in a man of his age to lose his reason? You'll tell me that one can't lose what one doesn't have. Sylvie, take him up to his room."

Sylvie seized the old fellow under his arm, got him to walk in this way, and threw him down across his bed like a bundle, with all his clothes on.

"Poor young man," said Madame Couture, lifting Eugène's hair which had fallen over his eyes, "he's like a young girl; he hasn't any experience of liquor."

"Ah, I don't mind saying that in the thirty-one years I've kept a boarding-house," Madame Vauquer said, "I've had a great number of young men pass through my hands, as they say: but I've never seen one as nice or as distinguished as Monsieur Eugène. Isn't he handsome asleep? Take his head on your shoulder, Madame Couture. Ah, ha! It's falling toward Mademoiselle Victorine's; there's a god that looks after the young. If he had leaned back a little more, he would have hurt his head against the back of the chair. The two of them would make a very pretty couple."

"Don't say any more," cried Madame Couture. "How can you say such things?"

"Oh," said Madame Vauquer, "he can't hear. Come along, Sylvie, and help me dress. I'm going to put on my corset."

"Oh, Madame, your large corset! And just after your dinner! You'll have to get someone else to lace you. I don't mean to be your murderess. Why, you'd be doing something so foolish it might cost you your life."

"Pooh! I don't care. I must be worthy of Monsieur Vautrin."

"You certainly must be fond of your heirs!"

"Come, Sylvie, don't argue," said the widow, as she left the room.

"At her age," said the cook, pointing to the widow and looking at Victorine.

Madame Couture and her ward, on whose shoulder Eugène was sleeping, were left alone in the dining room. Christophe's snores resounded through the silent house, and contrasted with the quiet slumbers of Eugène, who was sleeping as gracefully as a child. Happy in being able to perform one of those acts of charity in which all a woman's feelings find expression, and one which allowed her sinlessly to feel the young man's heart beating on her own, Victorine—her expression showed it—was full of a pride that was maternal and protective. In the throng of feelings that pressed in her heart the sharpest one was a tumult of sensuous pleasure in contact with the warmth of another innocent young body.

"Poor dear girl!" said Madame Couture, pressing her hand.

The old lady was pleased by the innocence and simplicity of her expression, crowned by a halo of happiness. Victorine looked like one of those naïve medieval paintings in which the artist has neglected all the accessories and kept the magic of his calm and proud art for the face, yellow in tone, but a yellow with golden tints in which heaven itself seems to be reflected.

"And, Mama, he didn't drink more than two glasses," said Victorine, running her fingers through Eugène's hair.

"Why, if he had been a debauched boy, my dear, he would have carried his wine like the others. His being overcome by it does him credit."

The sound of a cab could be heard outside.

"Mama," said the young girl, "here is Monsieur Vautrin. Please support Monsieur Eugène's head yourself. I shouldn't like to be seen in this position by that man; he says things that defile one's soul, and his glances are as embarrassing as if one's dress were being taken off."

"No," said Madame Couture, "you're wrong. Monsieur Vautrin is a fine sort of man, a little like my late husband, brusque but kind. He may be rough but he means well."

Just then Vautrin came in very softly and looked at the picture formed by the two children gently bathed in the light of the lamp.

"Well, well," he said crossing his arms, "here's a scene that would have inspired beautiful pages in the good heart of Bernardin de Saint Pierre, the author of *Paul et Virginie*. How beautiful youth is, Madame Couture! Poor boy," he went on, looking at Eugène, "sleep on. Sometimes good things happen to one while asleep. Madame," he said, addressing the widow, "what I like in this young man, what moves me, is knowing that the beauty of his soul is in keeping with the beauty of his face. Look, isn't that just like a cherub resting on the shoulder of an angel? Ah, that young man is worthy of being loved! If I were a woman I'd be ready to die (Oh, no! I'd not be so silly as that!) to live, for him! As I admire the two of them there, Madame," he was now speaking in a low voice and bending toward Madame Couture's ear, "I can't help thinking that God created them for each other. The ways of Providence are well hidden; Providence fathoms what is in our bodies, what is in our hearts," he cried aloud. "Seeing you united, my children, united by the same purity, by all human feelings, I say to myself that it is impossible that you should ever again be separated. God is just. Now," he said to the girl, "I think I've seen in your palm lines of prosperity. Do give me your hand. I'm an expert in chiromancy, I've often told fortunes. Come, don't be afraid. Oh, what's this I see? On my word as a man of honor, you will soon be one of the richest heiresses in Paris. You will bring all kinds of happiness to the man who loves you. Your father will ask you to come to him. You'll marry a man of noble birth, young and handsome, and who adores you."

Just then the heavy step of the coquettish Madame Vauquer on her way downstairs interrupted Vautrin's prophecies.

"Here is Mama Vauquer, beautiful as a *starrr,* and tagged out like a carrot. Are we just the least bit stifled?" he asked, putting his hand on the top of her corset. "The twins in front of your heart are in a tight spot, Mama. If you should cry there'd be an explosion; but I'll gather up the fragments with the care of an antiquarian."

"There's a man who knows the idiom of French gallantry," said the widow, leaning forward to whisper in Madame Couture's ear.

"Good-bye, children," Vautrin said, turning toward Eugène and Victorine. "You have my blessing," he continued, laying his hands on top of their heads. "Believe me, Mademoiselle, the good wishes of an honest man are worth something; they should bring you happiness. May God hear them!"

"Good-bye, my dear," Madame Vauquer said to Madame Couture. "Do you think," she added in a whisper, "that Monsieur Vautrin has any intentions on my person?"

"Oh! Oh! Ha! Ha!"

"Ah, mother darling," said Victorine sighing and looking at her hands, when the two women were left alone, "suppose that what our good Monsieur Vautrin said were true!"

"Well, only one thing would need to happen to make it true," replied the old lady. "Your brother would just have to fall from his horse."

"Oh, Mama!"

"Good Lord, perhaps it is a sin to wish ill to your enemy," the widow continued. "Well, I shall do penance for it. But the truth is that I wouldn't be sorry to lay flowers on his grave. What a mean heart he has! He hasn't the courage to speak for his mother, and he keeps her fortune by tricks, to your great loss. My cousin had a large fortune. It is your ill luck that it was never made clear how much she brought with her in the marriage contract."

"My happiness would often be hard to bear if it cost anyone's life," said Victorine. "And if I could be happy only by my brother's disappearance I'd rather always stay here."

"Good Lord, to use the phrase of Monsieur Vautrin," Madame Couture went on, "he is a good man and, as you see, he is full of religion. I was pleased to learn that he's not an unbeliever like the others who show less respect in speaking of God than the devil would. Oh, well, who can say by what paths it pleases Providence to lead us?"

With Sylvie's help the two women finally got Eugène to his room, laid him upon his bed, and the cook loosened his outer clothes so that he might be more comfortable. Before she left, while her protectress's back was turned, Victorine kissed Eugène on the forehead and felt all the happiness that could come of such criminal larceny. She looked about the room, gathered, so to speak, all the thousand happinesses of the day into a single thought, drew a picture of them which she contemplated at length, and fell asleep the happiest creature in Paris. The festive occasion under whose cover Vautrin had got Eugène and Père Goriot to drink wine in which a narcotic had been mixed decided the ruin of its author. Bianchon, half drunk, forgot to question Mademoiselle Michonneau about Cheat-death. If he had uttered that name, he would certainly have put Vautrin (or Jacques Collin, to give this prison celebrity his true name) on his guard. Further, the nickname Venus of Père la Chaise had resolved Mademoiselle Michonneau to deliver the convict to the police just when, in her confidence that Collin would pay well, she was weighing whether it might not be better worth her while to inform him and help him escape during the night. She had just left, accompanied by Poiret, to call on the famous head of the Sûreté in Petite Rue Sainte Anne, under the impression that her business was only with a trusted employee named Gondureau.

The director received her graciously. Then, after a conversation in which every point was worked out exactly, Mademoiselle Michonneau asked for the potion by means of which she was to carry out the test concerning the brand. By a gesture of satisfaction on the part of the great man of the Petite Rue Sainte Anne, as he looked for the phial in a drawer in his desk, Mademoiselle Michonneau divined that in this capture there was something much more important than the arrest of a simple convict. By dint of much ransacking of her brain she arrived at the suspicion that the police hoped, on the basis of disclosures made by informers in the penitentiaries, to be quick enough to lay hands on a considerable mass of money. When she had expressed her conjectures to this foxy fellow, he broke into a smile and sought to give the old maid's suspicions another course.

"You're wrong," he said. "Collin is the most dangerous *brainbox* that has ever been on the side of thieves. That's all. The scoundrels know it very well; he is their banner, their stay, in a word their Bonaparte; they all love him. This scamp will never leave his *nut* on the Place de Grève."

Mademoiselle Michonneau not understanding, Gondureau explained for her the two slang expressions he had used. *Brainbox* and *nut* are two energetic words taken from the idiom of thieves, a class which was the first to feel the need to consider the human head under two aspects. The *brainbox* is the head of the living man, his reflective power, his thought. *Nut,* a contemptuous term, expresses how trivial a thing a head is when it has been cut off.

"Collin is playing with us," he went on. "When we have to do with men of his kind, men like bars of steel triple tested, our game is to kill them if, while they are being arrested, they take a notion to make the least resistance. We count on some violence on Collin's part so that we may kill him tomorrow. In this way we avoid a trial, the costs of feeding and guarding a criminal, and this is a kindness to society. The process of law, the summoning of witnesses, their fees, and the execution, the whole line of things that makes up the legal way of getting rid of these scoundrels costs more than the thousand crowns that you shall have. There is also a saving of time. By thrusting a bayonet right through Cheat-death's belly, we shall prevent a hundred crimes, and avoid the corruption of fifty good-for-nothings who will behave themselves very nicely around the court room. This is police work well done. According to the true philanthropist, this kind of action means the prevention of crime."

"Why, it's a service to the country!" said Poiret.

"That's right!" said the director. "You're coming out with sensible remarks for a change tonight. Yes, of course, we are doing a service to our country. And the world is very unjust in its view of us. We render society very great services, and they are ignored. In a word, it's the nature of a superior man to rise above prejudices, and the nature of a Christian to bend his back to bear the misfortunes that good brings in its train when it is done in unconventional ways. Paris is Paris, do you understand? That is the key to my life. I am your obedient servant, Mademoiselle. Tomorrow I'll go with my men to the Royal Gardens. Send Christophe to the Rue de Buffon, to Monsieur Gondureau's house where I used to be. Monsieur Poiret, I am at your service. If anything should ever be stolen from you, make use of me to get it back. You can count upon me."

"Well," said Poiret to Mademoiselle Michonneau, "you come across idiots that the word 'police' sends into a dither. This gentleman is very agreeable and what he asks of you is as simple as saying good morning."

The morrow was to take its place among the most extraordinary days in the history of the Maison Vauquer. The outstanding event up to this point in the quiet annals of the house had been the meteoric apparition of the pseudo-Countess d'Amber-mesnil. But everything was to fade in the light of the events of this great day which was to form an inescapable part of Madame Vauquer's conversations to the time of her death. The day began with Eugène and Père Goriot sleeping till eleven. Madame Vauquer, who had got back from the Théâtre de la Gaîté at midnight, remained in bed till ten-thirty. Christophe had overslept because of his potations from the bottle Vautrin had given him, and was late in performing his domestic duties. Poiret and Mademoiselle Michonneau did not complain of the delay in serving breakfast. As for Madame Couture and Victorine, they slept late. Vautrin went out before eight o'clock and returned just when breakfast was served. There was no protest, then, when about eleven-fifteen Sylvie and Christophe knocked at all the doors to announce that breakfast was ready. While the two of them were absent from the dining room, Mademoiselle Michonneau, the first to go downstairs, poured the liquor into Vautrin's silver goblet in which the cream for his coffee was then being heated as it stood in the bain-marie along with all the others. The old maid had counted on this peculiar practice of the house to attain her object. It was not easy to assemble the seven boarders. At the very instant when Eugène, stretching his arms, came down, the last of all, a messenger gave him a letter from the Baroness de Nucingen. The letter read:

I'm not angry with you, and I have no false vanity in our dealings, my dear. I waited for you till two in the morning. Waiting for the person one loves! Anyone who has known the torture of it will never impose it on anyone else. I can see that this is the first time you have loved. What can have happened? I am full of anxiety. If I had not been afraid of disclosing the secrets of my heart, I should have gone to find out what was befalling you, good or bad. But to go out at that hour whether on foot or in my carriage would have been sure ruin, wouldn't it? I felt what an unhappy thing it is to be a woman. Restore my peace of mind, explain to me why, after what my father told you, you did not come. I'll be angry, but I'll forgive you. Are you ill? Why do you live so far away? One word, please. You'll come soon, won't you? A word will be enough for me if you're busy. Tell me either that you will rush to see me or that you are ill. But if you were ill my father would have come to tell me. What can have happened?

"Yes, indeed," said Eugène, rushing into the dining room as he crumpled the letter without reading it to the end, "what can have happened? What time is it?"

"Half-past eleven," said Vautrin, as he put sugar in his coffee.

The escaped convict looked at Eugène with that coldly fascinating glance which some men with an extraordinary magnetic power possess and which, it is said, can calm the insane in their asylums. Eugène trembled in every limb. The sound of a cab could be heard in the street, and a servant in Monsieur Taillefer's livery, immediately recognized by Madame Couture, hurried into the room with a frightened look.

"Mademoiselle," he said, "your father is asking for you. A great misfortune has occurred. Monsieur Frédéric has been in a duel and has had a sword wound in his forehead, the doctors despair of his life; you will barely have time to say farewell to him; he has lost consciousness."

"Poor young fellow!" said Vautrin. "I don't see why a man quarrels when he has a sure income of thirty thousand livres. It goes to show that youth does not know how to behave."

Eugène protested.

"What is upsetting you, you great child?" asked Vautrin, as he quietly finished drinking his coffee, an operation which Mademoiselle Michonneau was following too closely to have any feeling for the extraordinary event which had laid its weight on everyone else. "Are there not duels in Paris every morning?"

"I'll go with you, Victorine," said Madame Couture.

The two women hurried away without even shawl or hat. Before she left, Victorine, whose eyes were full of tears, gave Eugène a look which said, "I didn't think that our happiness would make me weep so much."

"Ah, ha, Monsieur Vautrin, so you're a prophet?" said Madame Vauquer.

"I'm everything," said Jacques Collin.

"How queer it is, to be sure," Madame Vauquer went on, slipping from one insignificant phrase about the event to another. "Death takes us without asking us anything about it. Young people often die before the old. How lucky we women are not to be subject to duels; but we have other ills that men don't have. We bring children into the world, and the ailments of childbirth last a long time. How lucky for Victorine! Her father can't avoid adopting her now!"

"That's right!" said Vautrin, with a look at Eugène. "Yesterday she didn't have a cent; today she has a fortune of many millions."

"And you, Monsieur Eugène," said Madame Vauquer, "you've certainly struck it rich."

While this conversation was going on Père Goriot was looking at Eugène and noticed that he had in his hand the crumpled letter.

"You haven't finished reading it! What does that mean? You can't be like the others?" he said.

"Madame Vauquer," said Eugène, looking toward her with such a force of horror and disgust that everyone was taken aback, "I'll never marry Mademoiselle Victorine."

Père Goriot grasped his hand and shook it. He would have liked to kiss it.

"Ah, ha," said Vautrin. "The Italians have the right word for this: *col tempo*."

"I'm waiting for the answer," the Baroness de Nucingen's messenger said to Eugène.

"Say that I'll be there."

The man left. Eugène was so violently exasperated that he was incapable of prudence.

"What can be done?" he said to himself, but in a distinctly audible voice. "There are no proofs."

Vautrin began to smile. The potion had by now reached the stomach and was beginning to take effect. But the convict was so robust that he was able to get up and, looking at Eugène, to say, though in a hollow voice, "Young man, good can befall us while we sleep." And he fell down in a dead faint.

"So there is divine justice, after all," Eugène exclaimed.

"Why, what's this, what can have happened to poor Monsieur Vautrin?"

"It's apoplexy!" Mademoiselle Michonneau cried out.

"Sylvie, run, girl, get the doctor!" said the widow. "Oh, Monsieur Rastignac, go for Monsieur Bianchon and do be quick. Perhaps Sylvie won't be able to find our doctor, Monsieur Grimprel."

Eugène was only too happy for a pretext to get away from the room which now seemed to him a frightful den, and left on the run.

"Christophe, come, run off to the druggist and ask for something that helps apoplexy."

Christophe went off.

"Père Goriot, you must help us to carry him up to his room."

They raised Vautrin from the floor, managed to get him upstairs, and laid him on his bed.

"I can be of no use to you. I'm going to see my daughter," said Goriot.

"You selfish old creature," Madame Vauquer cried out. "I hope you die like a dog."

"Go and see if you have any ether," Mademoiselle Michonneau asked Madame Vauquer, after undoing Vautrin's clothes with Poiret's help.

Madame Vauquer went down to her apartment and left Mademoiselle Michonneau in command of the battlefield.

"Come, take off his shirt and turn him over, and be quick. Show that you can be of some good by sparing me a sight of naked flesh," she bade Poiret. "You're as helpless as a ninny."

When Vautrin had been turned over, Mademoiselle Michonneau gave him a smart slap on the shoulder, and the two fatal letters showed white against the redness of the surrounding skin.

"Well, you've won your reward of three thousand francs mighty quickly!" Poiret exclaimed, holding Vautrin upright while Mademoiselle Michonneau put his shirt back on him. "Ah, what a weight he is," he continued, laying him down again.

"Be quiet. Perhaps there's a strong-box?" the old maid said quickly, and her glance seemed to pierce right through the walls, so sharp was her eye for every least little piece of furniture in the room. "If we could only think of any sort of pretext for opening this desk!"

"Perhaps it would be wrong to do that," Poiret replied.

"No. Stolen money belongs to everybody, and so to nobody. But we haven't time. I hear the Vauquer coming back."

"Here's some ether," Madame Vauquer said. "Good Lord, what a day of excitement this is! That man can't have apoplexy; he's white as a sheet."

"A sheet?" Poiret echoed.

"His heart-beat is regular," said the widow, who had put her hand against his heart.

"Regular?" Poiret asked in amazement.

"He's quite all right."

"Do you think so?" Poiret inquired.

"Why, he looks as if he were just sleeping. Sylvie has gone

for a doctor. Look, Mademoiselle Michonneau, he's sniffing the ether. Oh, it's just a spasm. His pulse is good. He's strong as a Turk. Look, what a muscle he has, there over the belly; he'll live a hundred years. His wig hasn't been displaced. Why, it's glued to his head; he's got false hair, look, the natural color is red. They say that red-haired people are good through and through or else bad to the same degree. He must be one of the good ones?"

"Good for hanging," said Poiret.

"You mean good for hanging around a pretty woman," Mademoiselle Michonneau quickly added. "Get along, Monsieur Poiret. It's a woman's business to look after men when they're not well. Besides, for the good you are doing, you might as well leave us," she went on. "Madame Vauquer and I will look after our dear Monsieur Vautrin very well."

Poiret went away quietly without a protest, just like a dog his master has kicked.

Eugène had gone out to walk, to breathe fresh air; he felt he was suffocating. The crime which had been committed at the hour for which it had been planned, he had intended to prevent the night before. What had happened? What was he to do? He trembled at being an accomplice. Vautrin's composure continued to appall him.

"Suppose Vautrin were to die without regaining the power of speech?" he asked himself. He was moving along the alleys in the Luxembourg Gardens as if he thought himself tracked by a pack of dogs, and seemed to hear their barks.

"Well, have you read the *Pilote*?" Bianchon cried out to him.

The *Pilote* was a radical newspaper, edited by Monsieur Tissot. A few hours after the morning papers came out, the *Pilote* carried the day's news in an edition destined for the provinces. Timing its appearance in this way it had an advantage of twenty-four hours over other sheets in reaching the provincial towns and cities and the countryside.

"There's a wonderful story in it," said Bianchon. "Young Taillefer fought a duel with Count Franchessini of the old guard, who ran his sword two inches into his forehead. So there's little Victorine one of the richest girls in Paris. Oho! if it could have been foreseen! What a lottery death is! Is it true that Victorine was fond of you?"

"Be quiet, Bianchon. I'll never marry her. I'm in love with a maddeningly attractive woman. She loves me. I . . . ."

"The way you say it one would think you were burning to be unfaithful to her. Just show me a woman whom it's worth sacrificing the Taillefer fortune to have."

"Are all the devils in hell after me?" Eugène cried out.

"What's upsetting you? Are you crazy? Give me your hand," Bianchon said. "I want to feel your pulse. You're feverish."

"Please go to Mama Vauquer's," Eugène asked him. "That rascal Vautrin fell down in a dead faint."

"Ah," said Bianchon, as he left Eugène, "you're confirming suspicions I mean to verify."

Eugène's walk was long and solemn. He examined his conscience, turning it inside out. But although he had to pry into dark corners, ask himself many questions and hesitate before answering them, his integrity came out of the sharp and terrible debate sure as a bar of steel, strong enough to resist any pressure. He remembered the confidences Père Goriot had made to him the night before; he recalled the apartment in the Rue d'Artois, chosen so that he might be near Delphine; he took out her letter, reread it, and kissed it. "A love like this will be my sheet anchor," he thought. "This poor old man's heart has been wrung. He never speaks of his sufferings; but who could fail to surmise what they are? Well, I'll look after him as if he were my father; I'll provide him with a thousand pleasures. If she loves me, she'll come often and spend the day and he'll be there. That great Countess de Restaud is a horrible creature; she'd make a porter out of her own father! Dear Delphine! she's kinder to the old man; she deserves to be loved. Oh, how happy I'll be tonight!"

He took out the watch, admired its beauty and continued, "Everything has turned out well for me. When there's real love, lasting love, there can be presents like this. There's nothing wrong in my taking this. Besides, I'm going to be tremendously successful and I'll be able to return what I receive a hundredfold. In this liaison there's nothing criminal, nothing to lead even the most severely virtuous to raise an eyebrow. How many decent people form unions like ours! We're deceiving no one, and it's deception that debases. To lie is to surrender one's soul, isn't it? It's a long time since she separated from her husband. And for that matter I'll tell that Alsatian that he must yield to me a woman whom he can't make happy."

Eugène's struggle lasted a long time. Although victory was to lie with his youthful virtue, still a curiosity that was too strong for him to conquer led him back, as the darkness was falling in the late afternoon, to the Maison Vauquer which he had sworn he would leave forever. What he wanted to know was whether Vautrin was dead. Bianchon had begun by giving him an emetic, and he had then sent off a specimen of the vomit for a chemical analysis at the hospital. He was struck by Mademoiselle Michonneau's insistence that the matter should be thrown away, and his suspicions were thus strengthened. Moreover, Vautrin recovered so quickly that Bianchon could not avoid suspecting some plot against the man who was the life of the boardinghouse. When Eugène returned Vautrin was standing beside the stove in the dining room. The boarders had gathered earlier than usual, eager to hear the news about the young Taillefer's duel, craving all the details of the affair and wondering what influence it might have on Victorine's destiny. They were gossiping aimlessly. Only Père Goriot was absent. As he entered, Eugène's eyes met Vautrin's. Vautrin's composure was complete and his glance went so deep into Eugène's heart and stirred so many evil things there that the young man trembled.

"Well, my dear boy," the convict said to him, "I'm going to get the better of death for quite a while. These ladies tell me that I had a stroke which would have killed an ox, and here I am in the best of health."

"An ox," said the widow Vauquer. "It would have done for a bull."

"Perhaps you're sorry to find me alive?" Vautrin whispered to Eugène, whose thoughts he believed he could read. "That would be the feeling of a man who was devilishly strong!"

"By the way," said Bianchon, "Mademoiselle Michonneau was talking the day before yesterday of a man called Cheat-death. That would be just the right name for you."

The sobriquet struck Vautrin like a thunderbolt. He grew pale and staggered; and his magnetic glance fell on Mademoiselle Michonneau with the strength of a direct shaft of sunlight. Under the impact of that glance her legs lost their strength and she sank into a chair. Poiret quickly moved between Vautrin and the woman, realizing from the tremendous fierceness of the convict's expression that she was in danger. His mask of good nature had vanished, leaving his true character bare; and although the boarders could not yet understand the meaning of the drama that was taking place they were struck dumb and stupefied. Just then the steps of several men were heard, as well as the sound of muskets being grounded on the pavement outside the house. As Collin was instinctively scanning the walls and windows in quest of a means of escape, four men appeared at the door. In front was the head of the Sûreté; the three others were policemen.

"In the name of the law and the king!" one of the police began; his words were drowned in a clamor of astonishment.

Silence soon fell on the room, and the boarders stepped aside at the advance of three of the newcomers, each of whom had his hand on a pistol in a side-pocket. Two gendarmes who had followed the police stood by the door to the drawing room, and two more appeared by the door that led to the stairway. The noise of several soldiers tramping and grounding their muskets could be heard outside. No hope of flight remained with Cheat-death, who was the center of everyone's atention. The head of the Sûreté went up to him, and the first thing he did was to give Vautrin a smashing blow on the head, a blow so violent that it tore the wig off and showed up Collin's head in all its horrible reality. The accompaniment of short brick-red hair brought out in the head and the visage a frightful quality of brute strength mingled with cunning; the outlines of his powerful chest increased the effect; and it was as if Vautrin were now illuminated by the fires of hell. Everyone now understood the whole truth of Vautrin, his past, his present, his future, his implacable ideas, his conviction that his own will was absolute law, the royal power conferred upon him by the cynicism of his thoughts and actions, and the strength of an organization ready to his hand. His face was suffused and his eyes shone like those of a wild-cat. His first movement expressed such savage energy, his voice roared so loud that all the boarders burst out in a cry of terror. At his gesture, and struck too by the general clamor, the police drew their pistols. Collin understood the danger he was in as he saw the weapons glitter in the light and at once gave a proof of the highest power a man can have. A horrible and majestic spectacle! The only proper comparison for his face would be with a huge kettle full of the steaming vapor which is powerful enough to move mountains but dissolves in the twinkling of an eye at contact with a drop of cold water. The drop which calmed his

rage was a thought which came to him with the speed of lightning. He broke into a smile and looked at his wig.

"This isn't one of your polite days," he said to the head of the
Sûreté. And he extended his hands to the police, and nodded to
them that they should come up to him. "Gentlemen of the police,"
he said, "put the handcuffs on me. I call on those present to witness
that I offer no resistance." An admiring murmur, prompted by
the speed with which fire and lava came and went in this human
volcano, echoed through the room. "That spoils your game, you
ruffian," he continued with a firm glance at the celebrated director of the Sûreté.

"Hurry up and take your coat and shirt off," said the director
with marked contempt.

"Why should I?" Collin asked. "There are ladies here. I deny
nothing and I give myself up."

He paused and surveyed the company like an orator who is
about to say something surprising.

"Write it down, Papa Lachapelle," he bade an old man with
white hair who had sat down at the end of the table after drawing from a portfolio the warrant for arrest. "I admit to being
Jacques Collin, known as *Cheat-death,* under sentence of twenty
years in irons; and I've just proved to you that I have a right to
the sobriquet. If I had so much as raised my hand," he said to
the boarders, "those three sneaks would have spattered my blood
about Mama Vauquer's floors. These rascals are specialists in
devising ambushes!"

As she heard this Madame Vauquer began to be sick. "Good
Lord," she said to Sylvie, "it's enough to make one really ill, just
to think that I went with him to the Gaîté last night."

"You must learn to be philosophic, Mama," Collin continued.
"Did you suffer any harm from being in my box at the Gaîté
last night? Are you better than we? There's less infamy branded
on our shoulders than there is lodged in your hearts, you flaccid

units in a cancerous society. Why, the best among you did not repel me." At this point his eyes fixed Eugène's, and he smiled graciously, in sharp contrast with the rough expression his features had worn. "Our little bargain still holds good, that is if you want it to, my dear boy. You understand?" He sang out:

> *Ma Fanchette est charmante*
> *Dans sa simplicité*

"Don't worry," he went on, "I know how to make sure I get my part of the swag. No one would dare to do me, I can tell you."

The penitentiary, with its particular manners and its particular slang, its shifts in a trice from the jesting to the horrible, its frightening sort of greatness, its familiarity and depravity, was summed up in the speech Vautrin had just made, and in the man himself, who was no longer a man, but the example of an entire degenerate nation, a tribe wild and logical, brutal and supple. In an instant Collin had become an infernal poem which represented every human feeling save one, penitence. His gaze was that of Milton's fallen archangel whose will is steadfast for continued war. Eugène's eyes dropped as he accepted the criminal relationship as an expiation for the evil thoughts he had had.

"Who was it that betrayed me?" asked Collin, and his terrifying glance rested on each member of the company in turn. It stopped when he came to Mademoiselle Michonneau. "It was you, you old whore, you're responsible for that dead faint I had, you prying old maid. I'd have to say just two words and your neck would be sawed through within a week. But I forgive you; I'm a Christian. Besides, you weren't the one who disclosed my whereabouts. Who did? Ah, ha, they're searching my rooms!" he shouted as he heard the officers of the Sûreté upstairs opening his drawers and gathering together his belongings. "The birds have flown; they left the nest yesterday. You won't find out a thing. My records are here," and he struck his hand against his fore-

head. "Now I know who got the money. It can't have been anyone but that greedy wretch Thread-of-silk. Isn't that right, Mister
Grabber?" he asked the head of the Sûreté. "It fits too well with
the stay that our bank notes made upstairs. Not a thing left, my
little sneaks. As for Thread-of-silk, he'll be killed within a couple
of weeks, even if you set the whole of the gendarmerie on guard
to save him. What did you give to the Michonnette?" he asked
the police. "A mere thousand crowns? I was worth more than
that, you rotten Ninon de l'Enclos, you tattered Pompadour, you
cemetery Venus. If you'd tipped me off, you'd have had six thousand francs. Ah, you didn't suspect that, you old flesh merchant,
or you'd have come to me instead. Yes, I'd have given that to you
to escape a journey which is going to be an annoyance to me and
will mean a loss of money," he continued, as the shackles were
put on his hands. "These people are going to take pleasure in
dragging my case out endlessly so that it'll be the greatest nuisance
possible for me. If they sent me straight to the penitentiary, I'd
soon be back at my business, despite the little flatfeet of the
Quai des Orfèvres. Down in the penitentiary the whole lot would
turn their very souls inside out to accomplish the escape of their
general, Cheat-death. Is there a single one among you who is
rich as I am to the point of having ten thousand brothers ready
to do anything for you?" he asked proudly. "There's goodness
here," he went on striking his breast, just above the heart. "I've
never betrayed anyone. Look, you old harlot, look at them!"
He was speaking to Mademoiselle Michonneau. "They're terrified
by me, but you simply disgust them. Pick up your booty." He
paused and looked about at the company once more. "What
stupid creatures you are! Have you never seen a convict? A convict of Jacques Collin's sort is a man less cowardly than his
fellows, a man who protests against the injustices of the social
contract, to use the phrase of Jean-Jacques, whose disciple I am
proud to say I am. In a word, I stand alone against the Govern-

ment with its mass of courts, police and budgets, and I can beat the lot of them."

"The devil," said the painter, "what a splendid subject for a painting he makes!"

"Tell me, lackey of my lord the executioner, governor of the *Widow*," that name instinct with terrible poetry that convicts give to the guillotine, he was speaking now to the head of the Sûreté, "won't you be a good fellow and tell me whether it was Thread-of-silk that turned me in? I wouldn't want him to pay for what someone else has done. That wouldn't be just."

Just then the men who had opened and sorted everything that had been found in his room returned and whispered to their chief. The warrant was now drawn up.

"Gentlemen," said Collin, addressing the boarders, "they're about to take me away. You have all been very kind to me during my stay in this house. I shall be grateful. I now bid you adieu. You'll let me send you some figs from Provence." He took a few steps, and then turned about again to look at Eugène. "Good-bye, Eugène," he said in a soft and sad tone which was in singular contrast with the abrupt way he had spoken up till now. "If you should be hard up, I've left you a friend on whose devotion you may count." His shackles could not prevent his assuming the position of a man standing on guard at the beginning of a duel; he called out like a fencing master, "One, two!" and then lunged. "If you get into difficulty, just turn in that direction. Man and money both are at your disposal."

The singular man spoke these last phrases in a tone so jesting that only Eugène and he could grasp what they meant. When the house was empty of agents, gendarmes and soldiers, Sylvie, rubbing vinegar on Madame Vauquer's temples, looked about at the amazed boarders and said, "Well, he was a decent fellow, all the same."

This phrase broke the spell that had been cast on everyone by the copiousness and variety of the feelings stirred by the scene which had just ended. After looking at one another, the boarders all together turned their eyes toward Mademoiselle Michonneau, as gaunt, dry and cold as a mummy, huddled by the stove. She lowered her eyes as if she feared that her shade was not enough to hide the look in them. The face that they had disliked for so long a time they now understood. A murmur so perfectly uniform in tone as to reveal unanimous disgust sounded dully through the room. Mademoiselle Michonneau heard it, but she did not stir. Bianchon was the first to voice the general feeling, leaning over toward his neighbor and saying in a low voice, "I'm getting out of here if that woman is to go on having dinner with us."

In a twinkling of an eye everybody except Poiret supported the position he had taken; and feeling the strength of their united support, Bianchon went up to the old boarder and said, "You're specially friendly with Mademoiselle Michonneau, so you must speak to her and make it plain to her that she must leave at once."

"At once?" Poiret repeated in astonishment.

Then he went over to her and whispered a few words in her ear.

"But I've paid in advance; my money matters to me as much as anyone else's," she said, darting a viper's glance at all the boarders.

"That's no difficulty; we'll collect among us enough to make up to you what you lose," said Eugène.

"You back Collin," she replied, looking at him scrutinizingly and venomously, "and it's not hard to see why."

Eugène jumped at this as if he were about to rush upon her and strangle her. That look of the old maid, with the perfidious implications that he seized in it, had cast a horrible light on his spirit.

"Let her be, you must," the boarders cried out.

Eugène crossed his arms and was silent.

"Let's finish with Miss Judas," said the painter, speaking to Madame Vauquer more particularly. "If you don't put her out, we'll all leave your camp, and we'll spread the facts everywhere; we'll make it known that it's full of convicts and spies. If you do put her out, we'll be silent about this matter, all of us, for it might happen after all in the best of society so long as criminals are not branded on the forehead and not forbidden to disguise themselves as respectable citizens of Paris and act the part of silly jokers like all bourgeois."

When she heard this speech, Madame Vauquer miraculously recovered her strength. She sat up, crossed her arms, opened those clear eyes of hers in which there was no trace of tears.

"Do you want to ruin my house? There's Monsieur Vautrin. Good Lord . . ." She stopped short. "I can't help calling him by the name he bore when he was an honest man. That makes one apartment that is empty, and you want me to have two more at a time when everyone is settled for the season."

"Gentlemen, let's take our hats," said Bianchon, "and go for dinner to Flicoteaux in the Place de la Sorbonne."

In an instant Madame Vauquer estimated which was the more profitable line to take, and then she glided toward Mademoiselle Michonneau. "Come, my dear friend, you don't want my place to be ruined, do you? You see to what extremities these gentlemen drive me; go up to your room for this evening."

"That won't do, that won't," the boarders cried out. "We mean that she's to leave right now."

"But the poor lady hasn't had her dinner," said Poiret in a pitiful tone.

"She can have her dinner wherever she wants," several said in unison.

"Out with the sneak!"

"Out with the sneaks!"

"Gentlemen," said Poiret, suddenly showing the height of courage that love confers on the ovine male, "you should respect a person who belongs to the weaker sex."

"Sneaks have no sex," said the painter.

"What a sexorama!"

"To the doororama!"

"Gentlemen, this is most improper. When someone is told to go, there is a certain politeness that should be observed. We have paid and we shall stay," said Poiret, putting his cap on, and sitting down beside Mademoiselle Michonneau, to whom Madame Vauquer was preaching a sermon.

"Naughty, you naughty boy," said the painter in a comic tone, "go away!"

"If you don't leave, the rest of us will," said Bianchon.

And the boarders moved in a mass toward the drawing room.

"Mademoiselle, what can you be thinking of?" Madame Vauquer cried. "It'll mean my ruin. You can't stay; they will use force."

Mademoiselle Michonneau stood up.

"She's going to go! She's not going to go! She's going to go! She's not going to go!" The exclamations alternated, and the sound of them along with the hostile things that were said about her obliged Mademoiselle Michonneau to go, but not before she had made some private stipulations in a whisper to Madame Vauquer.

"I'm going to go to Madame Buneaud's," she said in a threatening manner.

"Go where you want," said Madame Vauquer, who felt cruelly insulted in the choice of a rival boarding-house which naturally aroused her hatred. "Go to the Buneaud's; the wine would make a goat drunk and the meat is bought at a scrap-counter."

The boarders in absolute silence formed in two files. Poiret looked at Mademoiselle Michonneau so lovingly, he was so obviously uncertain whether to go or stay, that the boarders, delighted by Mademoiselle Michonneau's departure, laughed outright and looked from one to another.

"Hi! Hi! Poiret," the painter called out.

The man from the museum began to sing with comic intonation the opening lines of a ballad which was then well known:

> *Partant pour la Syrie,*
> *Le jeune et beau Dunois . . .*

"Get along, you're dying with the desire to, *trahit sua quemque voluptas*," said Bianchon.

"Every man follows his own girl, a free translation of Virgil," said the tutor.

Mademoiselle Michonneau made a gesture as if she would take his arm, and this Poiret could not resist, so he came forward and supported the old maid. Applause resounded, and there was an explosion of laughter. "Bravo, Poiret! That old Poiret! Poiret Apollo! Poiret Mars! Valiant Poiret!"

Just then a messenger came in and gave a letter to Madame Vauquer who, as soon as she had read it, fell back in her chair.

"There's nothing for me but to burn my house! This is a thunderbolt! Young Taillefer died at three o'clock. I'm properly punished for having wished those ladies good fortune to the detriment of that poor young man. Madame Couture and Victorine ask me to send their things to Monsieur Taillefer's house: the girl is going to live with her father and he will let her keep Madame Couture as a companion. Four apartments vacant, five boarders less!" She sat down, and seemed close to tears. "Disaster has overtaken my house!" she cried.

Suddenly they heard in the street the sound of a cab drawing up in front of the house.

Goriot came in quickly and his face was shining and bright

with joy, so much so that one might have believed he was reborn.

"Goriot in a cab," said the boarders. "It's the end of the world!"

The old fellow hastened to Eugène, who was standing lost in thought in a corner of the room, and took him by the arm. "Come along," he said gaily.

"You haven't heard what has been happening," said Eugène. "Vautrin was a convict. He's just been arrested, and the younger Taillefer is dead."

"Well, what difference does that make to us," Père Goriot answered. "I'm to have dinner with my daughter, at your place, don't you remember? She's waiting for you. Come on!"

He pulled Rastignac by the arm so vigorously that the latter was moving against his will, and it was as if Goriot were abducting a mistress.

"Let's have dinner," said the painter.

Immediately everyone drew up a chair and sat down.

"Good Lord," said big Sylvie, "everything goes wrong today. My mutton stew stuck to the pan. You'll just have to eat it burnt."

Seeing only ten instead of the usual eighteen people at her table, Madame Vauquer could not muster up spirit to say a word; but everyone tried to console and cheer her. The boarders began by speaking of Vautrin and the day's happenings, but they soon let the conversation follow its usual devious course and were talking about duels, prison, justice, amending the law. Soon they were a thousand miles from Jacques Collin, Victorine, and her brother. If there were but ten, they made noise enough for twenty, and seemed to be more numerous than usual. This was the sum of the difference between this dinner and that of the night before. The customary indifference of this self-centered little world, which in the diurnal goings on of Paris would have another prey to devour the next day, got the upper hand, and even Madame Vauquer was finally able to bring herself to cherish hope, a creed preached lustily by big Sylvie.

On into the evening that day was destined to be a fantasma-
goria for Eugène, whose strong character and sound head were
yet not sufficient to enable him to sort out his ideas as he sat beside Père Goriot in the cab; the old man's talk revealed a most
unusual happiness and echoed powerfully in his ear like words
heard in a dream, so many emotions had the young man experienced.

"It was settled this morning. The three of us are going to have
dinner together. Together! Do you understand what that means?
It's four years since I had dinner with Delphine, my little Delphine. I'm going to have her to myself for a whole evening.
We've been at your apartment since this morning. I took my coat
off and worked like a laborer. I helped to carry the furniture.
Ah, you don't know how delightful she can be at table. She'll be
thoughtful of me. She'll say: 'Papa, take some of that, it's good!'
And then I'm not able to eat a thing. Oh, it's so long since I have
been as happy with her as we shall be tonight."

"Well," Eugène said, "today everything has been turned upside down, it seems."

"Upside down?" Père Goriot commented. "Why things were
never so fine. I don't see a single face in the street that isn't gay;
people are shaking hands and embracing one another; they're
as happy as if they were going to have dinner with their daughters, to lick their chops over such a good little dinner as she
ordered when I was with her from the chef at the Café des
Anglais. But, you know, if she's there chicory is as sweet as
honey."

"I think I'm beginning to get my senses back," said Eugène.

"Drive faster, coachman!" bade Père Goriot, opening the front
window. "If you go faster I'll give you a hundred sous extra, provided you get me to the address you know within ten minutes."
When he heard this, the coachman began to shoot across the city
with the speed of lightning.

"He barely moves, this coachman," said Père Goriot.

"Where is it you're taking me?" asked Eugène.

"To your home," said Père Goriot.

The cab drew up in the Rue d'Artois. The old fellow was the first to get out and he tossed ten francs to the coachman with the prodigality of a widower who in the first paroxysm of his delight pays heed to nothing.

"Come, let's go up," he said to Eugène, as he led him through a courtyard and conducted him to the door of an apartment on the third floor at the back in a house which was newly built and of fine aspect. There was no need for Père Goriot to ring. Thérèse, the baroness's maid, opened the door. Eugène saw that it was a delightful bachelor's apartment, consisting of a hall, a little sitting room, a bedroom and a study, and that there was a view over a garden. In the sitting room, furnished and decorated in a fashion which would bear comparison with the prettiest and most graceful rooms one could think of, Eugène could see, by the light of some candles, that Delphine was rising from a sofa by the fireside, and laying her fan upon the mantel. She said to him in a voice full of affection, "You had to be brought here. You're a person who doesn't understand anything."

Thérèse left the room. Eugène took Delphine in his arms, and, folding her in a close embrace, he wept with happiness. This final contrast between what he had seen and what he saw now, in a day which had brought so many irritations both to his head and his heart, made him break down completely.

"I was sure, for my part, that he loved you," said Père Goriot in a whisper to his daughter, while Eugène lay on the sofa so exhausted that he could not say anything or even understand how this final stroke of the magic wand had operated.

"You must come and look," the Baroness de Nucingen said to him, as she took him by the hand and led him into a bedroom

in which rugs and furniture and even the smallest details resembled, as he could see, Delphine's own, though on a smaller
scale.

"There isn't a bed," said Eugène.

"No," she said, blushing and gripping his hand.

Eugène looked at her closely, and, young as he was, he understood how much of genuine modesty there is in the heart of a
woman who is in love.

"You are the kind of person who ought to be worshipped forever," he whispered in her ear. "We understand each other so
well that I'll dare to tell you the keener and more sincere love is,
the more it ought to be veiled and mysterious. Let's not tell anyone our secret."

"So, I'm to be no one, I suppose," scolded Père Goriot.

"You know very well that you are *we*. . . ."

"Ah, that's what I hoped you'd say! You won't pay any attention to me, promise? I'll come and go like a good fairy who is
everywhere and whom you know to be around although you
don't see him. Well, now, Delphinette, Ninette, Delly, wasn't I
right when I told you, 'There's a pretty apartment in the Rue
d'Artois; let's furnish it for him.' You didn't want to. It's I who
am the author of your happiness just as I'm the author of your
life. Fathers must always be giving if they mean to be happy. To
be always giving, that's the essence of being a father."

"What's this you say?" asked Eugène.

"She didn't want to do it; she was afraid there'd be silly talk,
as if the world's opinion were worth one's happiness! The truth
is that every woman dreams of doing what she has done. . . ."

There was no one to hear Père Goriot. The baroness had led
Eugène into the dressing room where the sound of a kiss echoed,
however lightly it may have been given. This room too was in
keeping with the elegance of the apartment, in which, indeed,
nothing was lacking.

"Have we done it the way you would have liked?" she said, as they returned to the sitting room for dinner.

"Yes, you've done it only too well. Alas, luxury as complete as this, the realization of so many beautiful dreams, the poetry of young and elegant life—I am so sensitive to all this that I can't feel I don't deserve them; but I can't accept them from you and I'm still too poor. . . ."

"So you're already resisting me," she said with a touch of an authoritative manner mingled with jest, and wrinkling her face in the pretty way women have when they wish to laugh away some scruple so that it may more easily be dissolved.

But Eugène had examined his conscience too gravely that day; and the arrest of Vautrin, revealing to him the depth of the abyss into which he had almost fallen, had too much reinforced his nobler feelings and his sense of delicacy; he could not yield to the caressing way in which the baroness was trying to refute the scruples of his honor. He felt immensely sad.

"What's this?" she said. "You'd refuse? Do you know what such a refusal means: that you doubt the future; that you don't dare bind yourself to me! You're afraid you'll betray my love for you? If you love me, and I love you, why do you draw back from accepting such trifling obligations? If you knew the pleasure I had in busying myself with this bachelor's apartment, you wouldn't hesitate and you'd ask my forgiveness. I had money which was yours, and I used it well. That's all there is to it. You think you're being big, and you're being small. You ask a lot more from me. ('Ah!' she exclaimed as she observed Eugène looking at her passionately.) And you're so formal about silly little trifles. If you don't love me, why, then, don't accept! My fate lies in a single word. Speak! Father, give him some good reasons," she added, turning toward her father after a pause. "Does he suppose that I'm less fastidious than he is about our honor?"

Père Goriot looked on at this pretty quarrel with the fixed smile of a drug addict.

"You child, you're just beginning life," she continued, seizing Eugène's hand. "You've come to a barrier which a great many people can't surmount. A woman's hand opens it before you, and you draw back. But you're going to be a success; you'll make a splendid fortune; success is written on your forehead. Can't you give me back then what I'm lending you today? In olden days, didn't ladies give their chevaliers, armor, sword, helmet, coat of mail and horse, so that they could go forth and fight in their lady's name at tournaments? Well, Eugène, the things I'm offering to you are the arms of our age, the tools a man has to have if he is going to be anybody. The garret where you live now must be a pretty place if it's anything like Papa's. Come, shall we not have our dinner now? Do you want to make me sad? Answer me!" she said, shaking his hand. "Good God, Papa, make him decide, or I'll leave and never see him again."

"I'll make him decide," said Père Goriot, emerging from his state of ecstasy. "My dear boy, you're going to borrow money from usurers, aren't you?"

"I'll have to," Eugène replied.

"Well, it's settled then," said the old fellow, drawing out a miserable wallet, the leather all scuffed with wear. "I've turned usurer. I've paid all the bills; here they are. You don't owe a cent for anything that's here. It doesn't amount to very much, five thousand francs at the most. So I lend them to you. You won't refuse me. I'm not a woman. Just give me an I.O.U. on a scrap of paper and you can repay me some time in the future."

There were tears in Eugène's eyes and in Delphine's, as they looked at each other in surprise. Eugène stretched out his hand and grasped the old fellow's.

"Well, why not? Aren't you my children?" asked Goriot.

"But my poor father," asked the baroness, "how did you do it?"

"Oh, so that's what you want to know?" he continued. "When I had argued you into setting him up here near you and saw you buying things as if for a bride, I said to myself: 'She'll be in trouble.' The lawyer says that the suit to force your husband to restore your fortune will take more than six months. Good. I realized the capital which has provided my income of thirteen hundred and fifty francs; and with fifteen thousand francs, I took out an annuity of twelve hundred, which is well secured, and with what remained of my capital I paid the dealers from whom you were buying. Upstairs I have a room worth fifty crowns a year. I can live like a prince on forty sous a day, and I will still have something over. I never wear anything out; I scarcely need anything in the way of clothing. For a couple of weeks now I've been laughing to myself and thinking how happy you both would be! And aren't you?"

"Oh, Papa, Papa," said the baroness, leaping on her father's knees. She covered his face with kisses, rubbed her blonde hair against his cheeks, and her tears fell on that old face, now so radiant and joyous. "My dear father, what a father you are! No, there aren't two fathers like you under the sun. Eugène already was so fond of you; what will he feel now?"

It was ten years since Goriot had felt his daughter's heart beating by his. "My children," he said, "Delphine, you will make me die of joy! My poor heart is breaking. Come, Eugène, after this you owe me nothing at all!" The old man seized his daughter in so wild and frantic an embrace that she said, "Oh, you're hurting me!"

"I have hurt you!" he said and grew pale. He looked at her with an expression of pain that transcended humanity. To give an adequate picture of this Christ of paternity, one would have to compare him with those paintings in which the princes of the palette have rendered the Saviour's sufferings for the sake of mankind. Père Goriot gave a gentle kiss to the waist that his fingers had pressed too hard. "No, no," he went on, "I didn't hurt you!" and he smiled as he questioned her remark, "It was you who hurt me by crying out. Actually it cost a bit more," he said, kissing his daughter's ear very gently as he whispered into it, "but we have to deceive him or he'd be angry."

Eugène could not speak for wonder at the old man's boundless devotion, and as he looked at him he registered that naïve admiration which in the young is born of faith.

"I'll make myself worthy of all that you've done," he said.

"Oh, Eugène, what you've said is very beautiful," said the Baroness de Nucingen, kissing him on the forehead.

"For you," said Père Goriot, "he refused Mademoiselle Taillefer and all her millions. Yes, indeed, she loved him, and now that her brother is dead she's rich as Croesus."

"Oh, why do you speak of that?" Eugène cried out.

"Eugène," Delphine whispered in his ear, "now I've a regret for tonight. Ah, I'll love you so much, and forever."

"This is the finest day I've had since you both were married!" said Père Goriot. "God may make me suffer as much as may please Him, so long as it isn't through you, and I'll say: 'In February of this year I was for a moment happier than men can be through their whole lives.' Look at me, Fifine!" he said to his daughter. "She's very beautiful, isn't she? Now tell me, have you come across many women with such pretty color and a little dimple like hers? You haven't, have you? Well, I'm the one who made this darling of a woman. And from now on since you are going to make her happy she'll become a thousand times more beautiful. I can endure going to hell, neighbor; if you must have my seat in paradise, you may, I give it to you. Come let's have dinner," he continued, not knowing any longer what he was saying. "Everything is ours."

"Poor Father!"

"If you knew, my child," he replied, getting up and going to her, taking her head and kissing her between the plaits of her hair, "how cheaply you can make me happy! Come and see me sometimes, when I'm upstairs; it will only be a step. Promise me that you will; say it!"

"I will, Father dear."

"Say it again."

"I will, dear Father."

"Now be quiet. I'd make you say it a hundred times if I did as I wanted to. Let us have dinner."

The whole evening was given up to childishness of this sort, and Père Goriot was not the least mad of the three. He lay down at his daughter's feet that he might kiss them; he looked into her eyes for minutes at a stretch; he rubbed his head against her dress; in short he did as many wild things as the youngest and most affectionate lover.

"You see?" said Delphine. "When my father is with us, we must do as he wishes all the time. Sometimes it will certainly be a nuisance."

Eugène, who had already felt several impulses of jealousy, could not blame her for what she said, although it contained the principle of all ingratitude.

"And when will the apartment be finished?" asked Eugène, looking about the room. "We'll have to part tonight?"

"That's so, but tomorrow you'll come and dine with me," she said in a subtle manner. "Tomorrow is one of our days for the Italiens."

"And I'll go to the pit," said Père Goriot.

It was midnight. The Baroness de Nucingen's carriage was waiting. Père Goriot and Eugène returned to the Maison Vauquer, talking of Delphine with a growing enthusiasm which produced a curious rivalry of expression between two violent passions. Eugène could not hide from himself that the father's love, unsullied by any personal interest, overwhelmed his own both by its persistence and its magnitude. The idol was always pure and beautiful for the father, and his adoration drew strength from all the past as well as from the future. They found Madame Vauquer by her stove all alone, except for Sylvie and Christophe. The old landlady sat there like Marius amid the ruins of Carthage. She had been waiting for the two boarders who still remained to her, lamenting with Sylvie. Beautiful as the lamentations are that Lord Byron has put in the mouth of Tasso, they are far inferior in truth of feeling to those which escaped from the lips of Madame Vauquer.

"There'll be but three cups of coffee to make tomorrow morning, Sylvie. Ah, my house is deserted. It's enough to break one's heart. What is my life without my boarders? Nothing at all. Here's my house denuded of its people. What life has a house without its company? What have I done that heaven should thrust all these disasters upon me? I bought beans and potatoes for twenty. And the police in my house! We'll have to eat potatoes and nothing else. And I'll really have to send Christophe away."

Christophe who had been asleep started up and said, "Madame?"

"Poor fellow, he's just like a mastiff," said Sylvie.

"It's the dead season. Everyone has a room. Where can I possibly hope to find boarders? I'll go mad. And that witch of a Michonneau taking Poiret away from here! What can she have done to him to get him to follow her about like a poodle?"

"Oh, you know," said Sylvie, shaking her head, "those old maids know lots of tricks."

"Poor Monsieur Vautrin whom they've made a convict of," the widow went on. "Well, I can't help it, Sylvie, I don't yet believe it's so. A man as gay as he was, a man who took brandy in his coffee and paid fifteen francs a month extra for that, and he always paid cash and to the last sou."

"And he was so generous," said Christophe.

"There's some mistake," said Sylvie.

"There can't be. He confessed," Madame Vauquer continued. "And to think that all this has happened in my house, in a quarter where there's not a cat stirring. Upon my word, I think I'm dreaming. For you know we've seen Louis XVI meet with his accident, we've seen the emperor fall, then come back and then fall again, and all that was in the order of possible things; but a respectable boarding-house runs no dangers; a nation can get along without a ruler, but people have to eat; and when a respectable woman, one who was born a de Conflans, serves dinners that are good in every way, why, unless it's the end of the world. . . . But that's just what it is, the end of the world."

"And to think that Mademoiselle Michonneau, who is responsible for all this evil that has befallen you, is going to get, according to what we hear, a thousand crowns income for her life."

"Don't mention her, she's nothing but a rascal!" said Madame Vauquer. "She's going to stay at the Buneaud's, besides. But she's capable of anything. She must have done some dreadful things in her life; she's committed murder, and robbed, too, in her time. It was she who should have gone to prison instead of that poor dear man."

It was at this moment that Eugène and Père Goriot rang the bell.

"Ah, here are the two who are still faithful to me," said the widow with a sigh.

But the two faithful ones had but a faint recollection of the disasters which had befallen the boarding-house, and they very quickly told their landlady that they were going to live in the Chaussée d'Antin quarter.

"Ah, Sylvie," said Madame Vauquer, "that was my last trump. Gentlemen, you've given me a death-blow. I feel it in my stomach; it's as stiff as a board. This day has added ten years to my age. I'll go mad, on my word I will! What shall I do with the beans? Well, if I'm going to be alone here you must leave to-morrow, Christophe. Good-bye, gentlemen. Good night."

"What's wrong with her?" Eugène asked Sylvie.

"Good Lord, everyone has left because of the business today. It's affected her head. Why, I hear her crying! It'll do her good to have the weeps. This is the first time I've ever known her to do so in all the time I've been her servant."

The next day, Madame Vauquer had reasoned herself into a better state of mind. If she seemed to grieve like a woman who has lost all her boarders and whose life has been turned upside down, she was in full possession of her faculties. It was clear that the grief was a real one, a deep grief, a grief caused by what comes of one's interests being injured and one's habits broken. It is certain that the look a lover casts at the place his mistress lives as he leaves it is no sadder than the look that came to Madame Vauquer's eye as she surveyed the empty table. Eugène comforted her by saying that Bianchon whose interneship was to end in a few days was sure to take his room; that the man who worked at the museum had often expressed his desire to have Madame Couture's apartment; and that in the course of a few days she would again have a full company of boarders.

"May God hear your wish, but misfortune has taken up residence here! Before ten days are out someone will die, you will see," she said with a mournful glance around the room. "Who will be the victim?"

"It's a good thing we're getting away from here," said Eugène to Père Goriot in a very low voice.

"Madame," said Sylvie, running in with a frightened expression, "it's three days since I last saw Mistigris."

"Ah, if my cat is dead, if he's left us, I . . ."

The poor widow did not finish the sentence; she put her hands together and lay back in her chair crushed by the frightful omen.

Toward noon, when the postmen reach the quarter of the

Panthéon, Eugène received a letter in an elegant envelope, sealed with the Beauséant arms. It enclosed an invitation for the Baron and Baroness de Nucingen to the great ball which had been announced a month before and which was to be given in the Beauséant mansion. Along with the invitation was a little note for Eugène:

I thought you would be glad to undertake to carry my wishes to the Baroness de Nucingen; I am sending you the invitation for which you asked me, and I shall be delighted to make the acquaintance of the Countess de Restaud's sister. So bring this pretty person to my house and be sure that you do not give her all your affection, for I have a right to expect a great deal of it in return for my affection for you.

The Viscountess de Beauséant

"Well," Eugène thought to himself, as he reread this note, "my cousin tells me clearly enough that she doesn't want the Baron de Nucingen."

He went at once to Delphine, happy to be able to give her a delight for which he would certainly be rewarded. The Baroness de Nucingen was in her bath. Eugène waited in her boudoir, a prey to the impatience that is natural in a young man who is ardent and in a hurry to possess a mistress he has desired for two whole years. An emotion such as this does not come twice in the life of a young man. The first woman who wins a man's attachment, the first real woman, that is to say, the first who comes before him in the magnificent accompaniments of Parisian society, never has a rival. Love in Paris is quite unlike any other kind of love. Neither men nor women there are deceived by the gilded commonplaces which everyone utters as a decent screen for affections which pretend to be disinterested. In this area a woman must not only satisfy the heart and the senses, she is perfectly aware that she has greater obligations to fulfill toward the thousand vanities of which life consists. In Paris, particularly, love is essentially boastful, bold, spendthrift, pretentious, insincere and dazzlingly expensive. All the ladies of Louis XIV's court envied Mademoiselle de la Vallière the eagerness of passion which made that great prince forget that his cuffs cost a thousand crowns apiece when he tore them to assist the Duke de Vermandois's entry into this world. What then may be expected of the rest of humanity?

Be young and wealthy and have a title, go beyond this if you can: be sure that the more incense you burn before your idol, the more favorable the idol will be toward you, if indeed you have an idol. Love is a religion and its rites are more costly than those of any other religion; love passes quickly, like an urchin who likes to see as he passes the proof of the devastation he works. The luxury of feeling is the poetry of garrets; without this wealth what would became of love? If there are exceptions to these Draconian laws in the Parisian code, they are found in solitude, in souls who have not let themselves be mastered by social doctrines, souls who live near some fountain whose waters are clear and fleeting, but never-ending; souls faithful to their green shade, happy to listen to the language of the infinite which for them is written in every object and which they find again in themselves as they patiently wait for their wings, pitying those who are earthbound. But Eugène, like most young men, meant to present himself in the lists of society fully armed; he had already caught its fever, and perhaps he already felt within himself the power to dominate it, but as yet without knowing either the means or the end of this ambition. If one is without a pure and sacred love which can fill one's life, the thirst for power can become a fine quality; one has only to abandon self-interest and to set as one's object the greatness of one's country. But Eugène had not yet come to the point where a man can contemplate the course of life and sit in judgment upon it. He had not yet succeeded in shaking off completely the fresh and fragrant ideas which envelop as with green branches the youth of those who are reared in the provinces. He had been hesitating to cross the Parisian Rubicon. However he may have burned with curiosity, he had kept, up to now, some remnants of devotion to the happy life that the true gentleman leads in his château. On the evening before, however, he had lost his last scruples at the sight of his apartment in the Rue d'Artois. When he began to enjoy the material privileges of fortune, as he had long enjoyed the moral privileges of aristocratic birth, he sloughed off the skin of a provincial and quietly established himself in a position from which the future promised well. So, waiting for Delphine, sitting comfortably in this pretty boudoir of hers, which was also becoming in some sense his, he was already very far away from the Eugène who had come to Paris the year before, so far that as he surveyed his past self telescopically he began to wonder if he were now the same being.

"Madame is now in her bedroom," Thérèse came to tell him, and at the words a tremor ran through him.

He found Delphine leaning back on a sofa set beside the fire, and looking fresh and rested. When he saw her stretched out on waves of muslin, he could not avoid comparing her to those beautiful Indian plants in which the fruit appears in the heart of the flowers.

"Well, here we are!" she said, and her voice was full of emotion.

"Guess what I bring you," said Eugène, sitting down beside her and taking her arm to kiss her hand.

As she read the invitation the Baroness de Nucingen's delight was patent. The eyes she turned toward Eugène were full of tears, and she threw her arms around his neck to draw him toward her, in a wild excess of satisfied vanity.

"And it's to you—" ("Darling," she whispered in his ear, "but Thérèse is in my bathroom and we must be careful.") "—that I owe this happiness? Yes, I'll call this a form of happiness. When I get it through you it's more than just a triumph of vanity. No one has been willing to introduce me to this circle. You think that I'm petty, frivolous, light-headed, at this moment, like a Parisian woman; but you must feel that I'm ready to sacrifice everything for you, and that if I want to enter the Faubourg Saint-Germain more ardently than ever, it is because I shall find you there."

"Don't you think," said Eugène, "that the Viscountess de Beauséant is strongly implying that she does not wish to see the Baron de Nucingen at her ball?"

"Yes, you're right," said the baroness, handing the letter back to Eugène. "Women of her kind are mistresses of the art of impertinence. But it doesn't matter; I shall go. My sister will be there; I know that she's planning a magnificent costume. Eugène," she continued, lowering her voice, "she is going in order to explode horrible suspicions. You don't know the stories that are being told about her! Nucingen came to tell me this morning that it was openly talked about at the Club. Good Lord, the things that the honor of a woman and a family may hang on! I felt that I was touched, attacked, wounded, through my poor sister. According to some people, the Count de Trailles has signed drafts for a hundred thousand francs; they had almost all come due, and he was just about to be sued. In this extremity she is believed to have sold her diamonds, those magnificent diamonds which you've perhaps seen her wearing and which came to her from the dowager Countess de Restaud. In short, for the past two days this has been the talk of the town. So I can understand why Anastasie is having a lamé dress made and why she wants to be the cynosure of all at the Viscountess de Beauséant's, by appearing there in all her glory, wearing the diamonds. But I don't want to be outshone by her. She has always tried to eclipse me; she has never been kind to me although I have helped her in so many ways and would always let her have some money when she had none. But let's talk no more about society; today I want to be completely happy."

At one o'clock in the morning Eugène was still at the Baroness de Nucingen's; and when she lavished on him a lover's farewell, the farewell which is so full of the promise of joys to come, she said to him, in melancholy mood, "I'm so afraid, so superstitious, call my presentiments what you like, that I tremble at the idea that I shall pay for my happiness by some frightful catastrophe."

"What a child you are!" said Eugène.

"So it's I who am the child tonight," she said, laughing.

Eugène returned to the Maison Vauquer sure that he would be leaving it the next day; on his way he gave himself over wholly to those delightful dreams that all young men have while their lips retain the taste of pleasure.

"Well!" said Père Goriot when Eugène passed his door.

"Well," Eugène replied, "I'll tell you everything tomorrow."

"You'll tell me absolutely everything, won't you?" the old fellow cried out. "Go to bed. Tomorrow we are to begin our happy life."

The next day Goriot and Eugène were ready to leave the boarding-house and only waiting for their porter to appear, when toward noon the Rue Neuve-Sainte-Geneviève resounded with the noise of a carriage which stopped right in front of the Maison Vauquer. The Baroness de Nucingen stepped down and asked if her father was still in the house. When Sylvie replied that he was, she quickly went upstairs. Eugène was in his room, but his neighbor did not know it. At breakfast he had asked Père Goriot to take his things when he left the house, telling him that they would meet in the Rue d'Artois at four o'clock. But while the old fellow had been away looking for a porter, Eugène, who had been able to answer the roll call very early, had come back without anyone seeing him, so that he might settle his accounts with Madame Vauquer. He did not wish to have Goriot do this for him, since the old man would in his fanaticism no doubt have paid for Eugène as well as for himself. The landlady had gone out. Eugène went upstairs to his room to see if he had forgotten anything, and congratulated himself on doing so when in the drawer of his table he came on the uncompleted I.O.U. he had given to Vautrin and which after he had redeemed it he had carelessly thrown there. Since he had no fire he was going to tear it into little bits, when, recognizing Delphine's voice, he refrained from making any sound and stopped short so that he might hear what she said, thinking that she should have no secret from him. Then, from the very first words he found the conversation between father and daughter so interesting that he could not help listening.

"Ah, Father," she said, "thank Heaven that you had the idea of asking for an accounting of my fortune soon enough to prevent my being ruined. Is it all right for me to speak?"

"Yes, the house is empty," said Père Goriot in a tone which showed he was not himself.

"Why, what's the matter, Father?" asked the Baroness de Nucingen.

"You've just dealt me a body blow. It's as if you had hit me with an axe. May God forgive you, child," said the old man. "You don't know how much I love you; if you knew you wouldn't have said a thing like that so abruptly, above all if things are not desperate. What can have been so urgent that you couldn't wait a few minutes, and instead of coming to me here have come to the Rue d'Artois?"

"Oh, Father, what control can one be expected to have just after news of a catastrophe comes? It's driven me mad. Your lawyer has discovered a little sooner than was anticipated the misfortune which would have certainly burst upon me later on! Your long experience in business is going to be necessary to us, and I hurried to find you just like a drowning person clutching at a straw. When Monsieur Derville saw that Nucingen was bringing up a lot of technical objections he threatened him with a lawsuit and told him that a judge would quickly issue an order. Nucingen came to my apartments this morning and asked me if I was determined to ruin him and myself also. I told him that I knew nothing about the matter, that I had a fortune and ought to have possession of it, and that everything concerning the matter should be referred to my lawyer, for I was absolutely ignorant and could not understand anything at all that had to do with such proceedings. Wasn't this what you had advised me to say?"

"Very good," Père Goriot commented.

"Well," Delphine went on, "he told me just how his business stood. He has thrown all his capital and mine into enterprises that are barely under way, and for which a great deal of money had to be advanced. If I were to force him to hand over my dowry, he would have to go into bankruptcy; while on the other hand if I consent to wait a year he engages on his honor to give me back a fortune twice or three times as large as the dowry by investing my capital in land speculations. At the end of the year I would be in full control of all my funds. Father dear, he was quite frank; he frightened me. He asked my pardon for his conduct, he gave me my liberty, and agreed to my doing just as I like on condition that I leave him absolutely free to conduct his business under my name. He promised, as proof of his good faith, to call in Monsieur Derville every time I wanted him to do so to make sure that the documents by virtue of which he would make me owner were rightly drawn up. In short, he delivered himself to me, tied hand and foot. He asked for the direction of the household for two years longer, and begged me to spend no more on myself than he allows me. He convinced me that all he would be able to do would be to keep up appearances, that he had parted with his dancer and that he would

229

..eed to exercise the strictest economy in secret, if he was to tide himself over until the term when his speculations are completed, with unimpaired credit. I was harsh with him; I questioned everything he said so that I might make him desperate and thus learn more. He showed me his books, and he even cried. I've never seen a man in such a state. He lost his head and spoke of killing himself; he ranted and raved. He made me feel sorry for him."

"And you believe all those fairy tales?" cried Père Goriot. "He's an actor. I've had business dealings with Germans; they are almost always honorable, and extremely straightforward; but if underneath the air of honesty and good faith any of them sets out to be cunning and false, he's worse than a man of any other race. Your husband is taking advantage of you; he's hard pressed; he pretends to be done for; but he means to be more the master in your name than he ever was in his own. He's going to profit by the emergency so that he'll be immune to all the risks of his business. He's as cunning as he is treacherous; he's a thoroughly bad fellow. No, no, I'm not going to the graveyard leaving my daughters destitute of everything. I still know something about business. He's engaged his funds in enterprises, his interest in them is represented by some securities, receipts, contracts? Well, let him show these, and settle with you. We'll select the soundest of the speculations, we'll run the risks, and we'll have the titles in our name—*Delphine Goriot, married woman, separated in her estate from the Baron de Nucingen.* Why, does he take us for idiots, this fellow? Does he believe that I could endure for two days the idea of leaving you penniless, without bread? I wouldn't endure it for one day, for one night, for two hours. If it were true I wouldn't survive the knowledge. What! I've worked for forty years of my life, carried sacks on my back, sweated my strength out, deprived myself of everything all my life long, and all for you, my angels, who made every labor and every burden easy; and now my fortune and my life would go up in smoke! It would make me die mad. By everything that is most sacred on earth and in Heaven, we are going to get this all made clear, see that the books are right, check the accounts, and examine all the enterprises! I won't sleep, I won't lie down, I won't eat till I am sure that your fortune is all there. Thank God it's in your own name. You'll have Monsieur Derville as your lawyer. Fortunately he's a man of integrity. By Heaven, you shall keep your nice little million, your fifty-thousand livres income to the end of your days, or I'll make a stir in Paris. Ah! Ah! If the tribunals should fail to do us justice I'd go to the higher courts. Knowing that you were safe and well looked after in respect of money, that was the thought that calmed my worries and lightened every shadow. Money is life. Money is all-powerful. What does that big hulk of an Alsatian think he's putting over? Delphine, don't grant him a penny's worth of a concession! What a beast he is, tying you up in this fashion and making you unhappy. If he needs you, we'll hold him in, and see that he goes straight. Good Lord, my brain is on fire; there's something boiling hot in my head. My Delphine cast out in the street! Oh! My Fifine! You! On my word! Where are my gloves? Look, we must go at once. I mean to see everything, the books, the speculations, the bank accounts and the files, and right now! I won't feel tranquil again till I'm absolutely sure that your fortune is in no danger whatever, till I see it with my own eyes."

"Father dear, we must be prudent. If you acted with the least grain of a vengeful spirit in this, any too hostile intention, it would mean my ruin. He knows you, and he thought it was perfectly natural that, egged on by you, I was anxious about my fortune; but I swear to you, he has it in his hands and there he means to keep it. He's perfectly capable of fleeing with the capital, and leaving us in the lurch. He's enough of a rascal for that! He is quite aware that I wouldn't so dishonor the name I bear as to take him to court. He's both strong and weak. I've looked into everything fully. If we push him too far I'm ruined."

"So he's an out-and-out scoundrel?"

"Well, Father," she said, throwing herself on a chair in tears, "yes, he is. I didn't want to admit it to you because I wanted to spare you the grief of feeling that you had married me to a man of that sort. His surreptitious life, and his conscience, his body and soul, they're all in harmony. It's frightful! How I hate and despise him! No, indeed, respect for this degraded man is impossible after what he has said to me. A man who could throw himself into such commercial transactions as he has described to me has not an atom of delicacy, and the reason I'm so afraid is that I've pierced right to the depths of his mind. He's my husband and yet he frankly proposed to give me complete freedom of action—you know what that means?—if in case of misfortune he could use me as a straw man, as a mere legal instrument in his hands."

"But there's the law! There's a Place de Grève, for sons-in-law of this sort!" cried Père Goriot. "Why I'd guillotine him myself if there were no executioner."

"No, Father, there's no law to restrain him. Listen, and in a few words I'll tell you what he said, stripped of the circumlocutions in which he swathed it: 'Either you let me carry out my speculations to their conclusion, or else everything is lost and you haven't a penny; you're ruined, I can have no other accomplice but you.' Isn't that clear? He still clings to me. My integrity as a woman makes him feel easy; he knows that I shall let him keep his own fortune and be satisfied when mine is returned to me. It is a criminal and fraudulent association and I have to agree to it, or else face ruin. He's buying my conscience; and the price is leaving me perfectly free to belong to Eugène. 'I leave you free to commit any faults that you have a mind to, and you leave me free to commit any crimes I have a mind to,

in the way of ruining poor folk!' Is that clear enough for you?
Do you know what he means by a business operation? He buys
vacant land under his own name, then he has houses built by
straw men. These men enter into transactions with all sorts of
men in the building trades, for which payment will be made at
the end of a long term, and the straw men undertake for a
trifling sum to give a discharge to my husband, who thus becomes
the owner of the houses while the straw men settle with the builders they've taken in by going into bankruptcy. The name of the
Nucingen company was used to dazzle the eyes of the poor
builders. I understood what he meant. And I also understood
that to prove, in case of need, that enormous sums had changed
hands, Nucingen has sent securities in a considerable amount
to Amsterdam, London, Naples, Vienna. How could we get
possession of these?"

Eugène heard the dull thud of Goriot's knees striking the
floor; no doubt he had fallen.

"My God, what have I done to you? My daughter handed
over to this wretch. There's nothing he can't force her to do if
he wants! Forgive me, Delphine," the old man cried.

"Yes, I've fallen into an abyss, and perhaps it's your fault,"
said Delphine. "We have so little intelligence about things when
we marry. What do we know of the world, business, men, morals?
Fathers should think for us. My dear Father, I'm not blaming you
for anything, forgive me for the word. I'm altogether to blame
in this. No, don't cry, Papa," she said, kissing his forehead.

"Don't you cry either, Delphine darling. Let me kiss away
your tears. I'll be myself again and disentangle the wretched mess
of business your husband has contrived."

"No, leave it to me; I'll be able to work out a scheme that
will get the better of him. He loves me; so I'll make use of my
dominion over him and get him to invest some of the capital at
once in properties. Perhaps I'll induce him to buy back Nucingen

in Alsace in my name; he likes the notion. But you must come tomorrow and examine the books and the business. Monsieur Derville is quite ignorant of anything that has to do with commerce. No, don't come tomorrow. I don't want to be ill. The Viscountess de Beauséant's ball will be the day after tomorrow, I must take care of myself so I'll be rested and beautiful for it, and be a credit to my dear Eugène! Come let's look at his room."

Just then a carriage drew up in the Rue Neuve-Sainte-Geneviève and in the stairway the Countess de Restaud could be heard asking Sylvie, "Is my father in?" This saved Eugène in the nick of time; he was already planning to throw himself on his bed and pretend he was asleep.

"Oh, Father, have you heard about Anastasie?" asked Delphine, recognizing her sister's voice. "It seems that very odd things have been happening in her household too."

"What's this?" said Père Goriot. "This is going to be the end of me. My poor head won't stand a double disaster."

"Good morning, Father," said the countess, coming in to his room. "Oh, you're here, Delphine!"

She seemed embarrassed at meeting her sister.

"Good morning, Nasie," said the baroness. "Do you think it so odd that I should be here? *I* see my father every day."

"Since when?"

"If you came, you'd know."

"Don't badger me, Delphine," said the countess in a sad tone. "I'm very unhappy. I'm ruined, my poor father. Yes, quite ruined this time!"

"What is wrong, Nasie?" cried Père Goriot. "Tell us everything, child. She's so pale. Delphine, come, help her. Do be kind to your sister. I'll love you all the more if that's possible!"

"My poor Nasie," said the Baroness de Nucingen, getting her sister to sit down, "do speak. In us you see the only two people who will always love you enough to forgive you everything.

You know the affections that unite a family are the ones that you can rely on most." She gave her salts to smell, and the countess recovered.

"It will kill me," said Père Goriot. "Come," he went on, stirring his fire of clods, "come up to the fire, both of you. I'm cold. What's wrong, Nasie? Tell us quickly; you're killing me."

"Well," said the poor woman, "my husband knows everything. Just imagine. You remember, Father, that draft of Maxime's some time ago? Alas, it wasn't the first. I had already paid a number of them. Toward the beginning of January the Count de Trailles seemed to me very depressed and worried. He said nothing; but it is so easy to read in the heart of those one loves; a mere nothing is enough to tell one. And then one has presentiments. In short he was more loving, more affectionate than I'd ever seen him, and I was happier and happier. Poor Maxime, he was mentally bidding me good-bye. He has told me; he was going to blow his brains out. But I tormented him so much, I begged him so hard, I knelt before him for two whole hours! He told me that he owed a hundred thousand francs. Oh, Papa! A hundred thousand francs! I was insane! You didn't have them; I'd used up everything. . . ."

"No," said Père Goriot, "I shouldn't have been able to get them for you unless I went out and stole them. But I should have gone out, and I will go out. . . ."

The two sisters paused at these words, uttered in so lugubrious a tone, sounding like a death rattle, and expressing the agony of paternal feeling reduced to impotence. What selfishness could have been cold enough to be insensitive to this cry of despair which, like a stone thrown into a chasm, reveals its depth?

"I made up the sum by disposing of what did not belong to me, Father," said the countess, bursting into tears.

Delphine was moved and wept, her head on her sister's breast.

"So it's all true," she said to her.

Anastasie bowed her head; the Baroness de Nucingen took her in a warm embrace, kissed her affectionately and drew her to her heart. "Here, you shall always be loved, and no matter what you may do, never condemned," she said.

"My angels," said Goriot in a weak voice. "Why must your union come only out of disaster?"

"To save Maxime's life, in short, to save all my own happiness," the countess went on, encouraged by such evidences of warm and heartfelt affection. "I went to the usurer you know, a man who must have been made in hell, a man nothing can touch, Monsieur Gobseck, taking the family diamonds which mean so much to the Count de Restaud, his diamonds, mine, all of them, and I sold them. Sold them, you understand! He was saved. But it means my death. Restaud knows all."

"Through whom? How? I'll kill him," cried Père Goriot.

"Yesterday I was summoned to his room. I went. 'Anastasie,' he said in a tone (oh! the tone was enough, I guessed everything) 'where are your diamonds?' 'In my room,' I said. 'No,' he said, looking at me hard, 'they are over there on my dresser.' And he showed me the case which he had covered with a handkerchief. 'You know where they come from?' he said to me. I fell on my knees. I cried, I asked him what death he would prefer to have me die."

"You actually said that!" exclaimed Père Goriot. "By the blessed name of God, whoever harms either of you so long as I live can be sure that I'll burn him bit by bit. Yes, I'll tear him into pieces." He was silent; the words died on his lips.

"My darling, he actually asked me to do something which is harder than dying. May Heaven keep any other woman from hearing what I heard."

"I'll assassinate that man," said Père Goriot quietly. "But he has but one life, and he owes me two. Well, what did he say?' he continued, turning toward Anastasie.

"Well," the countess went on after a pause, "he looked at me, and 'Anastasie,' he said, 'I'll bury everything in silence; we shall stay together; we have children. I won't kill the Count de Trailles; I might miss him, and if I tried to get rid of him by another means than a duel I might get on the wrong side of the law. If I were to kill him in your arms, I should dishonor all the children. I don't mean that they should perish, nor that their father should, nor that I should. I'm going to impose two conditions on you. Answer me: Are any of the children mine?' I said, 'Yes.' 'Which?' he asked. 'Ernest, our eldest.' 'Good,' he said. 'Now swear to me that you will obey me in one particular from now on.' I swore. 'You shall sign away your property when I ask you to do so.'"

"Don't sign," cried Père Goriot. "Never sign that. Ah, ha, Restaud, you don't understand how to make a woman happy. She goes looking for her happiness where it can be found, and you punish her for your silly incapacity. . . . But he'll have to deal with me, I'm on the watch; he'll find me on his path. Nasie, you can be confident. Ah! He is anxious about his heir! Good, good! I'll seize that heir of his, who's my grandson. I've a right to see the little toddler, haven't I? I'll stow him in my village; I'll take good care of him, you can be sure. I'll bring that monster to terms, when I tell him: 'Now for it! It's between you and me. If you want to have your son, give my daughter back her fortune, and let her manage it as she may wish.'"

"Father!"

"Yes, Father. Ah! I'm a true father. This rascal of a lord isn't going to mistreat my daughters. Good Heavens, I don't know what's running through my veins. I've the blood of a tiger; I'd like to eat these two men. Oh, my children, so that's how your life goes? I'll die of it. What will you do when I am no longer here? Fathers should live as long as their children. Oh, God, how ill Your world is managed. And yet You have a son, according to what is told of You. You should prevent our suffering through our children. My dear angels, what's this, it's only to your sufferings that I am indebted for your coming? Am I to know you only through your tears? Very well, yes, I see that you love me. Come and tell your woes to me; my heart is big; it can contain them all. Yes, indeed, no matter how you may pierce it, the tatters would make new hearts for fathers. I wish I could take your miseries upon me, and suffer in your stead. Ah! when you were little you were happy. . . ."

"That was the only good part of our lives," said Delphine. "Where are the times gone when we used to slide down the sacks in the big attic?"

"Father, I haven't told you all," Anastasie whispered in Goriot's ear so that he started. "The diamonds brought only a hundred thousand francs. An action has been begun against Maxime. We have only twelve thousand francs more to pay. He's promised me to be good and to gamble no more. His love is all I have left in the world, I've paid for it so dearly that I'd die if it were lost to me. I've sacrificed for it fortune, honor, children and peace of mind. Oh, can't you at least do something so that he may keep his place in society, and he'll be able to make his way. Now he owes me more than happiness; if he were to go to jail, our children would be left penniless, and my life would be in ruins."

"I haven't got them, Nasie. I've nothing left, nothing left. It's the end of the world. The world is going to crumble away, for sure. Get away and save yourselves before it does. Ah, I still have my silver buckles, and six covers, the first I bought in my life. And I've only twelve hundred francs in an annuity. . . ."

"What have you done with your investments?"

"I realized them, and kept back only this little scrap of income for my own needs. I had to have twelve thousand francs to set up an apartment for Fifine."

"In your house, Delphine?" the Countess de Restaud asked her sister.

"What difference does it make?" Père Goriot went on. "The twelve thousand francs have been used."

"I can guess," said the countess. "For Monsieur de Rastignac. Ah, poor Delphine, stop in time! You see where it has led me."

"My dear, Monsieur de Rastignac is a young man who would be incapable of reducing his mistress to ruin."

"That's very kind of you, Delphine. Considering the crisis I'm in at present, I thought you would not be so cruel, but you never loved me."

"Yes, she does love you, Nasie," cried Père Goriot. "She was telling me she did just a little while ago. We were talking about you and she insisted that you were beautiful and she herself only pretty."

"She! Hers is a cold sort of beauty," said the countess.

"Supposing it's so," said Delphine reddening, "how have you behaved to me? You disowned me; you've had the doors of all the houses I'd like to go to shut in my face; you've never lost the least opportunity to cause trouble for me. For my part, I haven't come to our poor father to abstract his fortune from him one thousand-franc note after another, and bring him down to the state in which he is now living. That's your work, sister. I've come to see him as often as I could; I haven't excluded him from my house, and I haven't come here to lick his boots when I could make use of him. I didn't even know that he had used these twelve thousand francs for me. I have some principles. You know I do. Besides, when Papa has given me presents I haven't ever begged for them."

"You were luckier than I. The Count de Marsay was wealthy, and you know it all too well. You've always been as hard as a stone. Good-bye, I've neither sister nor . . ."

"Don't say that, Nasie," said Père Goriot.

"Only a sister like you could repeat what no one any longer believes. You're a monster," said Delphine.

"Children, children, say no more, or I'll kill myself right in front of you."

"Go, Nasie, I forgive you," said the Baroness de Nucingen, continuing, "you're unhappy. But I'm better than you. To say that to me at the very moment when I felt that I would do anything to aid you, even if it meant going into my husband's bedroom, something I'd never do for myself or for . . . But it's quite in keeping with all the evil you've done me these nine years."

"Children, children, embrace each other," said the father. "You are both angels."

"No, let me go," said the countess, shaking off her father's grasp on her arm. "She has less pity for me than my husband. Wouldn't one think she was the paragon of all the virtues!"

"I'd rather be thought to owe money to the Count de Marsay than to confess that the Count de Trailles cost me more than two hundred thousand francs," the Baroness de Nucingen retorted.

"Delphine!" the countess cried, taking a step toward her.

"I'm going to speak the truth if you're going to slander me," the baroness retorted coldly.

"Delphine, you're a . . ."

Père Goriot darted forward and, clapping his hand over the countess's mouth, prevented her from speaking.

"Good Heavens, Father, what can you have been touching this morning?" said Anastasie.

"Well, it was wrong of me," said the poor father, wiping his hands on his trousers, "but I didn't know you were coming. I'm moving."

He was happy that his daughter was reproaching him, since it deflected her anger from her sister.

"Ah," he resumed, sitting down, "you've broken my heart. I'm dying, daughters. The inside of my head is on fire; it's as if someone held a flame in my brain. Do be kind. You must love each other! You'd kill me otherwise. Delphine, Nasie, come, you were both right and both wrong. Look, Dedel," he went on, turning his tear-stained eyes toward the baroness, "she must have twelve thousand francs; we must get them. Don't look at each other in that way." He knelt down before Delphine. "Ask her to forgive you just to please me," he whispered. "She's the unhappier; come, won't you?"

"Poor Nasie," said Delphine, appalled by the wild and mad look of grief on her father's face, "I was wrong, won't you kiss me?"

"Ah, what salve that is for my heart," cried Père Goriot, "but where are we to get the twelve thousand francs? What if I offered myself as a substitute for military service?"

"Oh, no, no Father," said the two girls, gathering about him.

"God will reward you for that thought; our whole lives would not be enough. Isn't that right, Nasie?" Delphine said.

"And then, my poor father, it would be just a drop in the bucket," the countess remarked.

"But is there nothing I can do with my blood then?" said the old man in despair. "I'll devote myself to anyone who will save you, Nasie; I'll kill a man for him. I'll do like Vautrin. I'll go to the penitentiary. I'll . . ." He stopped short, as if he had been struck by lightning. "There's no way any longer!" he said, tearing his hair. "If I knew where to go and steal—but it's hard to find out where a robbery can be worked. And I'd need time and help to rob the Bank. Well, I must die; there's nothing else for me. No, I'm no longer good for anything. I'm no longer a father. No! She asks me for something, she's in need, and I, wretch that I am, have nothing for her. Ah, you old rogue, you took out an annuity and you had daughters! So you don't love them? Burst, burst, like the dog you are! Yes, I'm lower than a dog; a dog would not act like that. Oh, my head, it's boiling!"

"But, Papa," cried the two young women, standing beside him so that he could not beat his head against the wall, "you must be reasonable."

He was sobbing. Eugène was appalled; he took the draft made out to Vautrin, which bore a stamp permitting an enlargement of the sum for which it was valid; he changed the figure, and made it into a regular draft payable to Goriot's order for twelve thousand francs, and he then entered his neighbor's room.

"Here is all the money you need, Madame," he said, offering the paper. "I was asleep, and was wakened by the sound of your voices, and so I was able to find out how much I owed Monsieur Goriot. Here is the receipt for it; it's negotiable, and I shall faithfully meet it."

The countess took the paper and held it in her hand, quite still.

"Delphine," she said, pale and quivering with anger, fury and rage, "I forgave you everything, God is my witness, but this! This gentleman was there, you knew it, and you were petty enough to take vengeance on me by having me give away my secrets, my life, the life of my children, my shame, my honor. You're nothing to me from now on. I hate you. I'll do you every injury I can. I . . ." Anger cut her short. Her throat was dry.

"But he's my son, our child, your brother, your savior," said Père Goriot. "Kiss him, Nasie. Look, I take him in my arms," he went on, embracing Eugène with a mad fervor. "Oh, my boy, I'll be more than a father to you; I mean to be a family. I wish I were God; I'd set the world at your feet. Come, kiss him, Nasie; he's not a man, but an angel, a real angel."

"Let her be, Father. She's beside herself now," said Delphine.

"Beside myself? And what about you?" the Countess de Restaud asked.

"My children! I'll die, if you go on like this," said the old man, falling on his bed, as suddenly as if he had been struck by a bullet. "They're killing me," he said to himself.

The countess was looking at Eugène who stood motionless, stupefied by the violence of this scene. "Monsieur de Rastignac," she said, and there was inquiry in her look, her gesture and her tone of voice. She paid no attention to her father whose vest Delphine was quickly unbuttoning.

"Madame, I shall pay, and I shall be silent," he answered, without waiting for her question.

"Nasie, you've killed our father," said Delphine, pointing to the old man, who had fainted, as her sister hurriedly left the room.

"I gladly forgive her," said the old fellow, opening his eyes. "She is in a fearful plight which would turn a stronger head than hers. Comfort Nasie, be kind to her, promise your poor father who is dying," he implored Delphine, pressing her hand.

"Why, what's wrong with you?" she asked in terror.

"Nothing, nothing," the father answered. "It will go away. Something is pressing against my forehead, a migraine. Poor Nasie, what a future she'll have!"

Just then the countess returned, threw herself at her father's knees and cried, "Forgive me!"

"Come," said Père Goriot, "what you're doing now is far more painful to me."

"Monsieur de Rastignac," the countess said to Eugène, her eyes full of tears, "grief made me unjust. Will you be my brother?" she went on, giving him her hand.

"Nasie," Delphine said to her, as she squeezed her hand, "darling Nasie, let's forget everything."

"No," she said, "*I'll* remember."

"My angels," Père Goriot cried out, "you're lifting a curtain from my eyes; your voices restore me to life. Embrace each other again. Well, Nasie, will this paper save you?"

"I hope so. Listen, Papa, will you sign it?"

"Why, how silly I am to forget that! But I was not feeling well. Nasie, don't hold it against me. Send someone to tell me that your trouble is over. No, I'll go. No, no, I won't. I can't see your husband again; I'd kill him. As for any attempt on your fortune, I'll be on hand. Be quick, my girl, and make sure that Maxime is careful from now on."

Eugène was stupefied.

"Poor Anastasie always had a dreadful temper, but she has a kind heart," said the Baroness de Nucingen.

"She came back for the endorsement," Eugène whispered to Delphine.

"Do you think so?"

"I wish I didn't. Don't trust her," he replied, raising his eyes as if to confide to God ideas that he did not venture to utter.

"Yes, she always was something of an actress, and my poor father lets himself be taken in by her poses."

"How are you now, Père Goriot?" Eugène asked the old man.

"I'd like to go to sleep," he answered.

Eugène helped Goriot to bed. Then, when the old fellow had gone to sleep with Delphine's hand in his, his daughter left.

"We'll meet tonight at the Théâtre des Italiens," she said to Eugène, "and you'll tell me how he is. Tomorrow you shall move. Let me see your room. How frightful!" she said on going in. "Why, you have been worse off than my father! Eugène, you've been awfully good; and I'd love you more if that were possible; but, my dear boy, if you want to make your fortune, you mustn't go about throwing twelve thousand francs out the window. The Count de Trailles is a born gambler. My sister doesn't want to see it. He would have gone to find his twelve thousand francs where he knows how to lose and win mountains of gold."

A groan brought them back to Goriot's room. The old man seemed to be asleep; but when the two lovers approached they heard these words. "They are not happy!" Awake or asleep, the accent of the words as he said them so struck his daughter's heart that she came up to the miserable bed on which her father lay and kissed him on the forehead. He opened his eyes, saying, "It's Delphine!"

"Well, how are you?" she inquired.

"All right," he said. "Don't worry, I'm going out. Go along, my children, and enjoy yourselves."

Eugène accompanied Delphine as far as her house; but in his anxiety about the state in which he had left Père Goriot he refused to stay for dinner and came back to the Maison Vauquer. He found Père Goriot on his feet, and ready to go down to dinner. Bianchon had taken a seat from which he could get a good look at the vermicelli-maker's face. When he saw him take up his slice of bread and smell it to tell the kind of flour it was made of, he noticed that the movement was made without anything that one could call consciousness of the action, and he made a gesture full of unfavorable meaning.

"Come and sit by me, my friend interne," said Eugène.

Bianchon came over with the greater readiness, since his change of place brought him nearer to the old pensioner.

"What's wrong with him?" Eugène inquired.

"Unless I'm mistaken, he's done for. Something extraordinary must have happened to him. I believe that he's in imminent danger of a grave apoplexy. Although the lower part of his face is normal enough, the upper features are drawn involuntarily toward the forehead. Look! And then his eyes are in that peculiar state which indicates that the serum has entered the brain. Wouldn't you say that they're full of a fine dust? Tomorrow morning I'll be able to tell more."

"Could anything be done for him?"

"Nothing. Perhaps his death could be delayed if some means were found to stimulate a reaction toward his extremities, toward his legs; but if the symptoms do not cease by tomorrow evening, the poor fellow is lost. Do you know what happened to bring on this illness? He must have had a violent shock, something that broke his morale."

"Yes," said Eugène, remembering how the two daughters had carried on a relentless battle over their father's heart. "At least," he reflected, "Delphine loves her father."

That evening at the theatre Eugène took some precautions so that the Baroness de Nucingen should not be alarmed.

"Don't worry," she said, in answer to Eugène's first remarks, "my father is strong. Only we upset him a little this morning. Our fortunes are at stake; just think of the extent of the disaster. It would kill me if your affection did not make me indifferent to what just a little while ago I should have thought to be mortal agony. Today I have but one fear, I can imagine but one misfortune: the loss of the love which has made me feel joy in being alive. Outside this feeling nothing matters to me; there's nothing else in the world that I love. You are everything for me. If I have any happiness in being rich, it's because it helps me to please you more. I'm ashamed, but I'm more a lover than a daughter. Why? I don't know. My whole life is in you. My father gave me a heart; you have made it beat. The whole world may blame me, and it wouldn't matter to me, so long as you—and you have no right to object to this—acquit me of the crimes to which I'm led by a feeling I can't resist. Do you think I'm an unnatural daughter? Oh, no, it's impossible not to love a father as good as ours. How could I prevent his seeing in the end the natural consequences of our lamentable marriages? Why didn't he stop them from taking place? Wasn't it his part to think on our behalf? Today, I know, he suffers as much as we do; but what could we do about it? Comfort him? We could give him no comfort. Our resignation gave him more pain than our reproaches and complaints could. There are situations in life which are bitterness unrelieved."

Eugène was silent, for the naïve expression of a genuine feeling softened him. If the women of Paris are often false, wild with vanity, self-interested, coquettish and cold, it is certain that when they really love they sacrifice to their passion more feelings than other women do; they are made the greater by all their pettinesses, and are raised to sublimity. Eugène was also struck by the deep and judicious intelligence that a woman brings into play to appraise the most natural feelings when privileged affection enables her to see them in perspective. The Baroness de Nucingen was disturbed by his keeping silent.

"What are you thinking?" she asked him.

"I'm still turning over what you've said. Until now I thought that I loved you more than you loved me."

She smiled and steeled herself against the pleasure the words gave her so that the conversation would not pass the bounds prescribed by convention. She had never heard the vibrant phrases of young and sincere love. A few words more and she could not have restrained herself.

"Eugène," she said, changing the subject, "can you be ignorant of what's happening? Tomorrow all Paris will be at the Viscountess de Beauséant's ball. The Rochefide family have agreed with the Marquis d'Adjuda to keep the news from breaking out; but tomorrow the king signs the marriage contract, and your poor cousin doesn't yet know a thing. She won't be able to escape holding her reception; and the marquis won't be there. People talk of nothing else."

"Society laughs at a thing that is infamous, and muddies its fingers in it! Don't you realize that it will kill the viscountess?"

"No, it won't," said Delphine with a smile. "You don't know

that kind of woman. But all Paris will flock to her house, and I'll be there! And I owe that happiness to you, besides."

"But," asked Eugène, "isn't this one of those ridiculous rumors that are always stirring in Paris?"

"We'll know the truth tomorrow."

Eugène did not go back to the Maison Vauquer. He couldn't deprive himself of the pleasure of enjoying his new apartment. The night before he had had to leave Delphine an hour after midnight; but now it was Delphine who left him at two in the morning to return to her house. He slept rather late the following day and waited for her to come to lunch with him toward noon. Young men covet such charming experiences so much that he had almost forgotten Père Goriot. He found it like a long holiday accustoming himself one after another to the elegant things that now belonged to him. The Baroness de Nucingen's presence added a new value to each of them. Nevertheless, as time drew on toward four o'clock the two lovers thought of Père Goriot, recalling the pleasure he was expecting to enjoy by living in this house. Eugène remarked that the old fellow should be brought there quickly if he were about to be ill, and left Delphine to hurry to the Maison Vauquer. Neither Père Goriot nor Bianchon was at table.

"Well, now," said the painter, "Père Goriot is down and out! Bianchon is upstairs with him. The old fellow has seen one of his daughters, the Countess de Restaurama. After she was here, he insisted on going out, and his illness grew worse. Society is about to be deprived of one of its finest ornaments."

Eugène hurried toward the stairs.

"Oh, Monsieur Eugène!"

"Monsieur Eugène, Madame wants to speak to you," Sylvie cried out.

"Monsieur Goriot and you," said the widow to Eugène, "were to leave on the fifteenth of February. Now it's three days past the fifteenth; it's the eighteenth today. You must pay me a month's rent for both, but if you will undertake for Père Goriot's rent your word will be good enough for me."

"Why is this? Don't you trust him?"

"Trust? If the old fellow were to lose his faculties, and then died, his daughters wouldn't give me a penny, and his belongings don't amount to ten francs. This morning he carried off his last silver covers. I don't know why. He was dressed like a young man. God forgive me, but I think he had applied some rouge; he seemed so much younger."

"I'll be responsible for everything," said Eugène, shuddering with horror and fearful of a disaster.

He went up to Père Goriot. The old man was lying on his bed, and Bianchon was beside him.

"Good day, Père," said Eugène.

The old man smiled gently and answered, turning his glassy eyes toward him, "How is she?"

"She's well. And how are you?"

"Not bad."

"Don't tire him," said Bianchon, leading Eugène to a corner of the room.

"Well?" Eugène asked.

"Only a miracle can save him. The serous congestion has occurred; he has mustard plasters; and luckily he can feel them. They are taking effect."

"Can he be moved?"

"It's impossible. He must be left where he is. He must be spared all movement and all emotional excitement."

"My dear fellow, you and I will look after him," said Eugène.

"I've already had my chief at the hospital here."

"Well?"

"He'll be able to tell tomorrow evening. He promised to come after his work at the hospital was over. Unfortunately, this deluded old fellow did something imprudent this morning, and won't say anything about it. He's stubborn as a mule. When I speak to him he pretends he doesn't hear, and he goes off to sleep so that he won't have to answer; or if his eyes are open he begins to groan. Toward morning he went out. He went some place in the city on foot; nobody knows where. He took with him everything he had that was of any value; he was about some cursed business which was too much for his strength. One of his daughters came."

"The countess?" asked Eugène. "A tall dark woman, with a darting eye, beautifully shaped, a pretty foot, and a flexuous figure?"

"Yes."

"Leave me alone with him for a moment," Eugène asked. "I'll make him confess, and to me he'll tell the whole story."

"Meanwhile I'll go and have dinner. But try not to excite him too much; we still have some hope."

"Don't worry."

"They'll have a good time tomorrow," Père Goriot said to Eugène when they were left alone. "They are going to a grand ball."

"What did you do this morning, Papa, that has made you so ill tonight that you must stay in bed?"

"Nothing."

"Anastasie came?" Eugène asked.

"Yes," Père Goriot answered.

"Well, don't hide anything from me. What did she want this time?"

"Ah," he said, gathering his strength to speak, "she was so unhappy. Look, my boy, Nasie hasn't a penny since that business about the diamonds. For this ball, she had ordered a lamé dress which must be as lovely on her as a jewel. Her dressmaker, an infamous creature, wouldn't give her credit, and her maid paid a thousand francs on account for the dress. Poor Nasie has come to that! It broke my heart. Then, the maid, seeing that Restaud had no longer any confidence in Nasie, was afraid she'd lose her money, and she arranged with the dressmaker that the costume should not be delivered till the thousand francs were paid back. The ball is tomorrow, and the dress is ready. Nasie is in despair. She wanted to borrow my covers and pawn them. Her husband insists on her going to that ball to display to all Paris those diamonds which she is supposed to have sold. Can she say to that monster: 'I owe a thousand francs. Pay them'? No. I understood that, it was easy for me to understand. Her sister Delphine will be going in a superb costume. Anastasie should not be outshone by her younger sister. And then she was so lost in tears, my poor daughter! I felt so humiliated yesterday at not having the twelve thousand francs, that I'd have given the rest of my miserable life to redeem that fault. Do you understand? I had been strong enough to endure everything, but that final lack of money crushed me. Oh, I didn't hesitate, I patched myself up and rigged myself out. I sold the covers and some silver buckles and got six hundred francs; then I signed over my annuity for a year for a cash sum of four hundred francs paid by Papa Gobseck. Ah, I'll live on bread; that was enough for me when I was young, and I can still get along on it. At least my Nasie will have a beautiful evening. She'll be so attractive. I have the thousand-franc note under my pillow, there. What good it does me to feel that I have there right under my head what is going to give such pleasure to my poor Nasie! She can get rid of that horrible maid. Did you ever hear of servants who didn't trust their masters? Tomorrow I'll be well. Nasie is coming at ten o'clock. I don't want them to think I'm ill; they wouldn't go to the ball; they'd stay and look after me. Nasie will hug me tomorrow as if I were her child, and her caresses will cure me. And wouldn't I have spent a thousand francs for drugs? I'd rather give them to my Nasie, who can cure everything. I'll be able to comfort her in her grief, at least. That will make up for the wrong I did in buying the annuity. She's at the bottom of the abyss, and I'm not strong enough any longer to pull her up. Oh, I'm going back into trade. I'll go to Odessa to buy grain. Wheat costs only a third as much there as with us. The importation of cereals is forbidden in principle, but the worthy fellows who make the laws didn't remember to prohibit the products of which wheat is the base. Ah, ha! I found that out today! There's a fortune to make in starch."

"He's mad," Eugène reflected, looking at the old man. "Come," he said, "you must rest, don't talk."

Eugène went down for dinner when Bianchon came up. Then the two passed the night watching the sick man in turn, one reading his medical books, the other writing to his mother and his sisters. The next morning the symptoms manifested by the patient were, according to Bianchon, of a favorable kind; but they required the continual attention of which only the two students were capable, the nature of which cannot be detailed without offending the prudish phraseology of our time. The leeches applied to the old man's decrepit body were accompanied by cataplasms, foot baths, and medical proceedings which demanded the strength and the devotion of the two youths. The Countess de Restaud did not come; she sent a messenger for the money.

"I thought she'd come herself, but it's not a bad idea; she would have been anxious," said the father, seemingly happy in this turn of events.

At seven o'clock in the evening, Thérèse came, bringing a letter from Delphine.

What can you be doing, my dear? So soon after I begin to be loved, am I to be neglected? In the confidences exchanged between our hearts you showed too fine a soul not to be one of those

*who are always faithful, understanding all the nuances there are
in emotions. As you said listening to the prayer of Moses: "For
some it's always the same note, for others it is the infinite in
music." Remember that I expect you tonight to go with me to the
ball at the Viscountess de Beauséant's. There is no question that
the Marquis d'Ajuda's contract was signed at court today, and
the poor viscountess learned of it only at two o'clock. Everybody
in Paris will flock to her house just as the crowd throngs in the
Place de Grève when there is to be an execution. Isn't it horrible,
going to see whether this woman will be able to hide her suffering, if she'll die a good death? I certainly should not go, my dear,
if I had already been to her house; but of course this will be the
last time she will receive and all my struggles would have been
in vain. My position is very different from that of others. Besides,
I'm going for your sake, too. I am waiting for you. If you don't
come within two hours, I don't know that I could forgive the
crime.*

Eugène took up a pen and replied:

*I'm waiting for a doctor who will say whether your father
will live any longer. He is dying. I shall come to you with the
decision and I fear that it may be a death warrant. You will see
whether you can go to the ball. A thousand kisses.*

The doctor came at eight-thirty, and if he could not give a
favorable opinion, he did not believe that death was imminent. He
said they must expect relapses and recoveries to alternate, and
that these would determine the fate of the old man.

"It would be better if he died quickly," was the doctor's last
remark.

Eugène entrusted Père Goriot to Bianchon's care, and left to
bring Delphine the sad news which, imbued as he still was with a

sense of family duty, seemed to him to preclude all thought of pleasure.

"Tell her to have a good time anyhow," Père Goriot cried out to him. The old man had seemed to be in a doze, but he sat up erect as Eugène left.

When the young man appeared before Delphine he was overcome with grief. He found her with her hair done, and her slippers on, and, except for her dress, ready for the ball. But just as with a painter the final strokes of the brush take the most time, the final preparations for the ball needed more care than all that had already been done.

"What's this? You aren't dressed?" she asked.

"But, your father . . ."

"My father again," she interrupted him. "It isn't for you to tell me what I owe to my father. I've known my father for a long time. Not a word, Eugène. I won't listen to you till you're dressed. Thérèse has laid everything out for you at your apartment; my carriage is ready; take it; and come back here. We'll talk of my father on our way to the ball. We must start early; if we're caught in the file of carriages, we'll be very lucky if we arrive by eleven o'clock."

"But, Madame . . ."

"Come, not a word!" she said, running into her boudoir for a necklace.

"Look, Monsieur Eugène, you'll make Madame angry," said Thérèse, pushing the young man out, still appalled by such an elegant parricide.

He dressed accompanied by the gloomiest and most disheartening reflections. Society seemed to him to be an ocean of mud in which if a man so much as dipped a foot he was plunged up to his neck. "The crimes committed in it are of the pettiest and meanest sort," he said to himself. "Vautrin is on a grander scale." He saw that the three principal expressions of society

were Obedience, Struggle, and Revolt—The Family, Society
and Vautrin. He did not have the courage to take a firm stand
Obedience was irksome, Revolt impossible, Struggle uncertain.
He was carried back in thought to the bosom of his family. He
recalled the pure emotions of that tranquil life, the days passed
in the midst of those to whom he was dear. Conforming to the
natural laws of the domestic world, these beloved beings found
there a happiness which was complete, continuous, and without
any anguish. But, despite his virtuous thoughts, he lacked the
courage to confess before Delphine the faith of pure souls, bidding her to be virtuous in the name of love. Already his education,
though still in its early stages, had borne fruit. He was already
selfish in loving. His tact had enabled him to recognize the
quality of Delphine's heart. He could appreciate that she was
capable of trampling on her father's body to go to the ball, and
he had not the strength to play the role of a counsellor, nor the
courage to displease her, nor the virtue to break with her. "She
would never forgive my being right in this matter," he said to
himself. Then he took comfort in interpreting in his own guise
what the doctors had said, in thinking that Père Goriot was
not so dangerously ill as he had supposed; in short, he heaped
up the arguments of an assassin in order to justify Delphine.
She was not aware of her father's condition. The old fellow himself would send her back to the ball if she came to see him. It
often happens that social law, strict in its formula, issues a
condemnation where the apparent crime is excused by the countless modifications which are brought into the family unit by
difference in individual characters, and the diversity of their
interests and situations. Eugène was bent upon deluding himself;
he was ready to make a sacrifice of his conscience for his mistress.
In the last two days everything in his life had undergone change.
Woman had introduced various disorders, had eclipsed Family,
had confiscated everything to her own profit. Eugène and Del-

phine had met in the conditions which were ideal for the experience on both sides of the keenest pleasures. Their passion which had undergone so long a preparation had become more intense through what is mortal to passions, possession. When he possessed this woman, Eugène realized that until then he had merely desired her, and it was only after his happiness had been crowned that he loved her. Love is perhaps but gratitude for pleasure. Whether she was ignoble or sublime, he adored her for the voluptuous pleasures which were the dowry he brought her, and for those which he received from her; just as Delphine had for Eugène the same love as Tantalus would have felt for an angel that might have satisfied his hunger or quenched the thirst in his parching throat.

"Well, how is my father?" the Baroness de Nucingen asked him when he had returned, dressed for the ball.

"Very ill, indeed," Eugène answered, "and if you want to prove your affection for me, we'll go to see him at once."

"All right, I agree," she said, "but it shall be after the ball. My dear Eugène, do be nice, and don't preach to me. Come on."

They left. Eugène was silent for part of the ride.

"Well, what's wrong?" she asked.

"I can hear your father's death rattle," he replied in a tone which showed he was angry. And with the fervid eloquence of youth he began to tell the story of the cruel act to which the Countess de Restaud had been moved by her vanity, the mortal crisis that the father's final act of devotion had brought on, and the price that would be paid for Anastasie's lamé dress. Delphine wept.

"I shall look ugly," she thought. Her tears dried. "I shall go and look after my father; I won't leave his bed," she went on.

"Ah, that's the way I wanted you to be," cried Eugène.

The lamps of five hundred carriages lit up the approaches to the Beauséant mansion. There was a gendarme at each side of the illuminated gate. Society was flocking in such a multitude, and everyone was so eager to see this great woman at the moment of her fall that the apartments on the ground floor of the mansion were already packed when the Baroness de Nucingen and Eugène went in. Since the time when the whole court rushed to see the great Mademoiselle, whose lover Louis XIV was seizing, no disaster of the heart had been so striking as the Viscountess de Beauséant's. In this turn of events the last daughter of the almost royal house of Burgundy rose above her misfortune and until the last moment ruled the society whose vanities she had accepted only for the aid they gave in the triumph of her passion. The most beautiful women in Paris adorned the drawing rooms with their dresses, and with their smiles. The most distinguished courtiers, ambassadors, ministers, illustrious men of every kind, their breasts shining with crosses, medals and many-colored cordons, gathered about the viscountess. The orchestra played beneath the gilded ceilings of this palace which for its queen was as empty as a desert. The viscountess stood at the entrance to the first drawing room to receive her so-called friends. Dressed in white, with no ornament in her simply braided hair, she seemed calm and made no show of grief, pride or assumed gaiety. You would have said she was a Niobe in marble. No one could read her soul. The smile she gave her intimate friends was sometimes jesting; but to everyone she seemed to be wholly herself, so fully what she had been at the time when happiness gilded her with its rays, that the least sensitive could not fail to admire her just as young Roman women applauded the gladiator who could die with a smile. Society seemed to have arrayed itself to bid adieu to one of its sovereigns.

"I was afraid that you wouldn't come," she said to Eugène.

"I've come," he replied in a voice full of emotion, for he took her words for a reproach, "so that I might be the last to leave you."

"Good," she said, taking his hand. "You are perhaps the only

257

person here that I can trust. My friend, love only the woman you can love forever. Never abandon a woman."

She took Eugène by the arm and led him to a sofa in the room where people were playing cards.

"Go to the marquis's house," she said. "Jacques, my valet, will take you and will give you a note for the marquis. I am asking for the return of my letters. I trust he will give them all to you. If you are given them, come up to my room. I have arranged to be told."

She rose to go toward her best friend, the Duchess de Langeais, who was approaching her. Eugène left; he inquired for the Marquis d'Adjuda at the Rochefide mansion, where he was expected to spend the evening, and found him there. The marquis took him to his own house, and gave him a box, saying, "They are all there." He seemed to wish to say something to Eugène, either to ask him about the events of the party and about the viscountess, or perhaps to confess that already he was in despair about his marriage—as he was later to be; but a flash of pride shone in his eyes and he had the regrettable strength to be silent on his noblest feelings. "Say nothing to her about me, my dear Eugène," he said. He pressed Eugène's hand with a gesture at once affectionate and sad, and indicated that he should leave. Eugène returned to the Beauséant house, and was ushered to the viscountess's bedroom, where he saw the preparations for a journey. He sat down beside the fire, gazed at the cedar casket, and fell into a deep melancholy. For him the Viscountess de Beauséant had the stature of a goddess in the *Iliad*.

"Ah, my friend," said the viscountess, as she came in, and pressed her hand upon his shoulder.

He saw that his cousin was in tears, her eyes turned upward, one hand quivering, the other raised. She quickly took the box, put it in the fire and watched it burn.

"They are dancing. They all came very punctually, and death

will come later. Hush, my friend," she said, putting her finger on Eugène's mouth as he was about to speak. "I shall never again see Paris or society. At five o'clock tomorrow morning I am going to leave and I shall bury myself in the depths of Normandy. Since three o'clock this afternoon I've had to make all my preparations, sign documents, and attend to my affairs; there was no one I could send to . . ." She paused. "It was certain that he would be at . . ." She stopped short again, crushed by her grief. At moments such as this everything is painful, and there are words that it is impossible to utter. "Anyhow, I was expecting you this evening and counting on you for this last service. I should like to give you an earnest of my friendship. I shall often think of you; you've struck me as good and noble, young and sincere in the midst of a world in which these qualities are exceedingly rare. I hope that you will sometimes think of me. Here," she said, looking around her, "this is the box in which I kept my gloves. Everytime I took them from it to go to a ball or a play, I felt that I was beautiful because I was happy, and when I touched it, it was always to leave some gracious thought in it; there is a great deal of me in that box, there is the whole being of a Viscountess de Beauséant who no longer exists. Accept it. I'll see that it is taken to your apartment in the Rue d'Artois. The Baroness de Nucingen is very charming tonight; you must be very good to her. If we do not see each other again, you may be sure that I shall pray for you, for you have been kind to me. Let us go down. I don't want to let them think that I've been crying. I have eternity ahead of me. I shall be alone in it, and none will ask whether I weep or not. One more look at this room." She paused. Then, after covering her eyes for a moment with her hand, she wiped them, bathed them in cold water, and took Eugène's arm. "Let us go," she said.

Eugène had never felt any emotion as strong as came from his contact with this pain so nobly repressed. When they re

:urned to the party, Eugène made the round of the rooms, in her company, a final and exquisite attention on the part of this gracious being.

He soon laid eyes on the two sisters, the Countess de Restaud and the Baroness de Nucingen. The countess was dazzling, all her diamonds displayed; no doubt the contact with them burned her flesh; she was wearing them for the last time. Whatever the force of her pride and her love, she could not meet her husband's look with composure. Such a spectacle was not calculated to make Eugène's thoughts less gloomy. Under the diamonds of the two sisters he saw the miserable bed of Père Goriot. The viscountess misinterpreted his melancholy bearing, and withdrew her arm from his.

"Come," she said, "I don't want to rob you of a pleasure."

Eugène was soon claimed by Delphine, happy in the effect she was producing, and wishing to lay at Eugène's feet the homage she was winning in the society in which she hoped to take her place.

"What do you think of Nasie?" she asked him.

"She's discounted everything," he replied, "even her father's death."

Toward four in the morning the crowd in the drawing rooms began to thin out. Soon the music was heard no longer. In the main drawing room only the Duchess de Langeais and Eugène were left. The viscountess returned, thinking she would find only Eugène. She had said farewell to the viscount, who went off to bed, saying to her. "You're making a mistake, my dear, in burying yourself at your age! Do stay with us."

When she saw the duchess, the Viscountess de Beauséant could not repress an exclamation.

"I guessed what you were about to do, Clara," said the duchess. "You're leaving for good; but you shall not leave without hearing me out, or without our understanding each other." She took her friend's arm, and led her into the next room, and there, gazing at her with tears in her eyes, she embraced her and kissed her on the cheeks. "I don't want to take leave of you coldly, my dear; my remorse would be too deep. You can count on me as on yourself. You have shown yourself great tonight. I felt that I was worthy of you and I mean to prove it. I've not always been fair to you; I've not been kind. Forgive me, my dear; I want to disavow everything that may have hurt you; I want to take back my words. Our spirits are united now in the same pain, and I don't know which of us will be the more unhappy. The Marquis de Montriveau was not here tonight, do you understand? No one who saw you at this party will ever forget you, Clara. As for me I'm going to make a last effort. If I fail, I'll enter a convent. And where shall *you* go?"

"To Normandy, to Courcelles, to love, to pray until the hour when God takes me from this earth."

"Come, Monsieur de Rastignac," said the viscountess in a voice full of emotion, thinking that she kept the young man waiting. Eugène dropped on one knee, took his cousin's hand, and kissed it. "Antoinette, good-bye," the viscountess continued, "I hope you will be happy." And turning to Eugène: "You are happy, you are young, and you can believe in something. In my moment of taking leave of the world I shall have had, to surround me, like a few specially fortunate persons on their death-beds, feelings that are religious and sincere."

Eugène left toward five o'clock, after having seen the Viscountess de Beauséant to her carriage and received her last farewell, accompanied by such tears as proved that the most aristocratic of persons are not outside the law of the heart and are not exempt from grief, whatever some of those who toady to the common people would have them believe. Eugène returned to the Maison Vauquer on foot through the damp cold night. His education was drawing to a close.

"We shall not be able to save poor Père Goriot," Bianchon said to him when Eugène entered his neighbor's room.

"My dear fellow," said Eugène, after a glance at the sleeping figure, "go, keep the modest destiny to which you consent to limit your desires. I am in hell, and I must stay where I am. Whatever evil you hear of society, believe it; there is no one, not even a Juvenal, who could paint the horror of it, covered though it be with gold and precious stones."

About two o'clock the next afternoon Rastignac was awakened by Bianchon, who had then to leave the house, and had come to ask him to look after Père Goriot, who had become much weaker during the morning.

"The old fellow can't live two days longer, perhaps he has only a few hours left," said the medical student, "but nonetheless we can't give up the fight against his disease. He is going to need things that will cost a good deal. We will be his nurses, but as for me I haven't a penny. I've looked in all my pockets and in all my drawers: result—zero. I took a moment when he was lucid and asked him what money he had: absolutely nothing. How much have you?"

"I've twenty francs left," said Rastignac, "but I'll go and gamble with them, and I'll win."

"What if you lose?"

"Then I'll ask his daughters and their husbands for the money."

"And what if they won't give any?" Bianchon went on. "The most urgent thing just now is not finding money, but putting hot mustard plasters on him, from his feet right up to the middle of his thighs. If he cries out, there's hope. You know how to do that. Besides, Christophe will help you. I'll go to the druggist and make myself responsible for all the medicines we shall be getting from him. It's a pity that the poor man wasn't in a state to be taken to our hospital; he would have been better off there Come, I'll see that everything is ready for you, and don't leave him till I get back."

The two young men went into the room where Père Goriot lay. Eugene was appalled by the change which had taken place in that face, now convulsed, white as a sheet, and dreadfully weakened.

"How are you, Papa?" he asked, leaning down.

Goriot opened dull eyes and looked at Eugène with the closest attention but without recognizing him. Eugène could not bear it, and his eyes filled with tears.

"Bianchon," he asked, "shouldn't there be curtains drawn across the windows?"

"No, things like that don't affect him any longer. It would be more than we can hope for if he were to feel hot or cold. However, we will need a fire in order to heat broths for him and get ready a number of things. I'll send you a few faggots, which will do till we get some firewood. Yesterday and during the night I used up all your firewood and all his, poor fellow. It was so damp the water was dripping from the walls. I could scarcely get the room dried out. It was filthy as a stable. I had Christophe sweep it out I burned some juniper, the stink was so bad."

"Good God!" said Eugène. "What about his daughters?"

"Note, if he asks for a drink, you must give him this," said the interne, pointing to a large white pot. "If he complains, and his belly is hot and hard, get Christophe to help you and give him a . . . you know what. If he should become very excited and talk a lot, if his mind were to wander, let him be. That would not be a bad sign. But send Christophe to the Cochin hospital. My chief, my friend or I would come and apply leeches. While you were sleeping this morning we had a long consultation with a pupil of Gall, a director at the Hôtel-Dieu and one from our place. These gentlemen thought they discerned some curiou symptoms, and we are going to watch the progress of the disease, so that we can throw some light on several matters of considerable scientific importance. One of these gentlemen claims that if the serum presses more heavily on one organ than another, some peculiar facts might come to light. Listen closely, then, if he should speak, so that you may note the kind of ideas his speech reflects: whether it's memory, or discernment, or judgment, material things, or feelings, whether he makes calculations, whether he thinks of the past. In short, be able to tell us exactly what happens. It may be that the serum will affect everything all at once; then he will die in his present mental state, without regaining his reason. Everything is very odd in illnesses such as this. If the bomb were to burst around here," and Bianchon pointed toward the patient's occiput, "there are cases of singular phenomena; the brain recovers some of its faculties and death approaches more slowly. The serum may regress from the brain, and follow courses which are revealed only by autopsy. At the hospital for incurables, there is an old man who has lost his reason in whom the course lay down the spinal column; he is in horrible agony, but he is alive."

"Did they have a good time?" Père Goriot asked, recognizing Eugène.

"Oh, he thinks only of his daughters," said Bianchon. "He repeated more than a hundred times this past night 'They're dancing. She has her new dress.' He called them by their names. He brought me to tears—the devil with it!—with such intonations: 'Delphine, dear little Delphine! Nasie!' On my honor, it was enough to make one burst out crying," the medical student ended.

"Delphine," said the old man, "she's there, isn't she? I was sure she was." His eyes recovered a power of action, though of a deranged kind, and scanned the walls and the door.

"I'll go down and tell Sylvie to get the mustard plasters ready," said Bianchon. "This is the right moment for them."

Eugène remained alone with the old man, sitting at the foot of the bed, his eyes fixed upon that head which was so terrifying and so painful to see.

"The Viscountess de Beauséant is running away; this man is dying," he said. "Beautiful souls cannot stay long in this world. How could great feelings mingle with a society which is petty, mean and superficial?"

Pictures of the party he had so recently returned from recurred to his memory and contrasted with the spectacle of this deathbed. Bianchon quickly re-entered the room.

"Look, Eugène, I've just seen the chief of the hospital and I've run all the way back. If he shows any signs of reason, if he says anything, lay him on a long mustard plaster so that he will be in contact with it from his neck to the small of his back, and send for us."

"My dear Bianchon!" Eugène exclaimed.

"Oh, it's a matter of scientific interest," Bianchon continued with all the ardor of a neophyte.

"I see," said Eugène. "So I'm the only one who will care for this poor old man from affection."

"If you'd seen me this morning, you wouldn't say so," replied Bianchon, without being in the least offended by the remark. "Doctors who have practiced see only the ailment; but, as for me, I still see the sick person, my dear fellow."

He went off leaving Eugène alone with the old man, and fearful of a crisis, which indeed made itself known without delay.

"Ah, it's you, my dear boy," said Père Goriot, recognizing Eugène.

"Are you feeling better?" Eugène inquired, taking his hand.

"Yes, my head felt as if it were in a vise, but it's getting free now. Did you see my daughters? They'll soon be here; they'll hurry to me as soon as they know I'm sick. They took such care of me in the Rue de la Jussienne. Good Lord, I wish my room was fit for their visit. A young man who was here has burned up all my fuel."

"I can hear Christophe," Eugène said. "He's bringing up some wood for you that has been sent by that young man."

"Good, but how am I to pay for the wood? I haven't a penny, my boy. I've given away everything, absolutely everything. I'm dependent on charity. But at least the lamé dress was beautiful, wasn't it? (Oh, what pain!) Thank you, Christophe. God will reward you, my boy. As for me, I haven't anything."

"I'll pay you well, both you and Sylvie," Eugène whispered in the servant's ear.

"My daughters told you that they were going to come, didn't they, Christophe? Go to them again; I'll give you a hundred sous. Tell them that I don't feel well, that I'd like to embrace them, to see them once again before I die. Tell them that, but don't frighten them too much."

Christophe left at a sign from Eugène.

"They will come," the old man continued. "I know them. What grief I'll give to my darling Delphine if I die! And Nasie too. I don't want to die, for I don't want them in tears. Dying, my dear Eugène, means never seeing them again. Where I'm going it will be very dull for me. To be without his children, that's a father's hell, and I've already had my apprenticeship since they were married. My paradise was in the Rue de la Jussienne. Tell me, if I go to Heaven, shall I be able to return to earth as a spirit and be near them? I've heard of such things. Are they true? At this moment I seem to see them as they were in the Rue de la Jussienne. They came downstairs in the morning. 'Good morning, Papa,' they said. I took them on my knees, and played a thousand games and tricks with them. They caressed me so nicely. Every morning we had breakfast together, and we dined together. In short, I was

a father and I took joy in my children. When they were in the
Rue de la Jussienne they didn't use their brains; they knew nothing of the world; they loved me. Good Lord, why did they not
always remain little girls? (Oh, what pain! My head is tearing
apart.) Oh! Oh! Forgive me! My children! I'm in dreadful pain,
and the pain must be very real, for you've hardened me thoroughly against suffering. Good Lord, if I only had their hands in
mine, I wouldn't feel the pain. Do you think they're coming?
Christophe is so stupid. I ought to have gone myself. It's he who
will see them. But you were at the ball last night. Tell me about
them. They didn't know anything of my illness, did they? If they
had, they wouldn't have danced, the little darlings! Oh, I don't
want to go on being ill. They still need me too much. Their fortunes are in danger. And what husbands they have fallen to!
Make me well! Make me well! (Oh! What pain! Oh, oh, oh!)
Don't you see I must get better, for they need money and I know
where to go and make it. I'll go and make macaroni at Odessa. I
know my way about; I'll make millions. (Oh, this pain is more
than I can bear.)"

For a moment Goriot was silent; he seemed to be bending
every effort to gather his strength so as to bear the pain.

"If they were here, I should not be complaining," he said. "Why
should I complain then?"

There was a slight relief, which lasted for a long time. Christophe came back. Eugène who thought that Père Goriot was
sleeping let the servant report aloud on the success of his mission.

"Monsieur," he said, "I went first to the countess's and I wasn't
permitted to speak to her, for she was engaged in some very serious business with her husband. Since I was insistent, the Count
de Restaud came himself and said in so many words: 'Monsieur
Goriot is dying? Well, that is the best thing he can do. I need the
countess here to finish some important business. She will go when
it's over.' He seemed to be angry, that personage! I was about to

leave the house when the countess came into the hall by a door I didn't know of, and said to me: 'Christophe, tell my father that I have business with my husband and can't leave him; it's a matter of life and death for my children; but as soon as it's over I'll come.' As for the baroness, that was another thing! I didn't see her and I wasn't able to speak with her. 'Ah,' her maid told me, 'the baroness came in from the ball at a quarter after five. She's asleep. If I waken her before noon she'll scold me. When she rings I'll tell her that her father is worse. There's never any point in telling bad news in a hurry.' I implored her in vain. Oh, quite, and I asked to speak to the baron, but he had gone out."

"Neither of his daughters would come!" Eugène cried out. "I'll write to them both."

"Neither," the old man echoed, sitting up straight. "They have business; they are asleep. They won't come. I knew they wouldn't. You have to die to know what children are. Oh, my friend, don't marry, don't have children. You give them life, and they give you death. You bring them into the world; they drive you out of it. No, they won't come. I've known they wouldn't for ten years. Sometimes I'd say it to myself, but I didn't dare believe it."

A tear appeared on the red lower lid of each of his eyes, but did not fall.

"Ah, if I were rich, if I had kept my fortune, if I hadn't given it to them, they would be here; they would be licking my cheeks with their kisses. I should be in a mansion, I'd have beautiful rooms, servants and a fire; and they would be in floods of tears, with their husbands, and their children. I'd have all that. But I have nothing. Money gives you everything, even daughters. Oh, where is my money? If I had treasures to leave, they'd be looking after me, changing my bandages; I'd hear them, I'd see them. Ah, my dear child, my only child, I prefer to be deserted and poor. At least, when a pauper is loved, he knows that the love is real. No, I'd like to be rich. Then I'd see them. Good Heavens, who knows? They both have hearts of stone. I loved them too much for them to love me. A father should always be rich; he should keep his children under bridle and spur like wily horses. And I was on my knees in front of them. The wretches! This is the proper climax for their conduct toward me for the past ten years. If you knew what nice attentions they had for me in the first years of their married life. (Oh, what a martyrdom this pain is!) I had just given each of them about eight hundred thousand francs; they couldn't, and their husbands couldn't, be rude to me. They would greet me, saying, 'Father dear, come this way! Father darling, no, that way!' There was always a place laid for me at their tables. Indeed I used to dine with their husbands, and their manner toward me was full of respect. I still had the appearance of having some money. And why was that? I had said nothing about my business. A man who gives his daughters eight hundred thousand francs is a man to look after. And what attentions they showed me, merely for my money! The world is not a nice spectacle. I'm one who has had the opportunity to see that. They used to take me to the theater in their carriages, and I could stay for their parties whenever I wanted to. In short they called themselves my daughters, and they recognized me as their father. I haven't lost my perceptions, you know, and nothing escaped me. Everything struck home, and my heart was pierced. I could tell very well that they were good for nothing, but the evil admitted of no remedy. When I was at their table I was not as comfortable as downstairs here. I had nothing to say. So when some of those people of fashion and rank whispered to my sons-in-law: 'Who is that gentleman?' 'That's the father with the money bags.' 'The devil it is!' And they looked at me with the respect that is the due of money bags. But suppose that I did bore them sometimes; I certainly had to pay for my shortcomings. Besides, who is perfect? (My head is one huge wound!) I'm suffering now, my dear Eugène, what one suffers in dying, but it's nothing in comparison to the pain that shot through me the first time that Anastasie made me feel that I had said something silly that humiliated her; that look of hers made me bleed from every vein. I wished I knew everything, what I did come to know was that I was not wanted on earth. The next day I went to Delphine to seek consolation, and what should happen but that I did something that made her angry. Then I felt as if I had gone mad! For a whole week I didn't know what to do. I didn't dare go to see them for fear of their reproofs. And so I was shut out of my daughters' homes. O God, since You know the suffering and misery that I have endured, since You have counted the dagger thrusts that I have borne in this season which has aged and changed me, whitened my hair and killed me, why do You make me suffer today? I have fully expiated my sin in loving them too much. They took full revenge for my affection; they have torn at my entrails like torturers. Well! What fools fathers are! I loved them so that I went back like a gambler to the table. My daughters were my particular form of vice. The truth is, in a word, that they were my mistresses! They both were always needing something or other, finery of some sort. Their maids would tell me, and I used to buy what they mentioned and bring it so that I would be welcomed when I came to their houses. But they did not fail to give me some little sermons on my behavior in society. Oh, they did not wait for the next day to do so! They began to blush for me. That's what comes of bringing children up well. And yet at my age I could not be expected to go to school! (What dreadful pain! Good God, doctors, doctors! If my head could be opened I'd suffer less.) My daughters, my daughters, Anastasie, Delphine, I want to see them. Send the police for them! Bring them by force! Justice is on my side, everything is on my side, Nature, the civil code. I protest! Our country will perish if fathers are thrust underfoot. That is clear. Society, the world, depend upon paternity; everything will crumble away if children do not love their fathers. Oh, to see them, to hear them, no matter what they would say, if only I could hear their voices, my suffering would be quieted. Delphine, especially. But tell them when they come not to look at me frigidly, as they do. Oh, my good friend, Eugène, you don't know what it is to find a golden look suddenly turned to one of dull lead. Since the time when they ceased to look on me with brightness in their eyes, I've always felt it was winter, and I've known only grief, and have drunk it to the lees. I've lived to be humiliated and insulted. I loved them so much that I accepted every affront they put upon me as the price of the niggardly, shameful little delights that they doled out. Think of a father concealing himself so that he might see his daughters! I gave my life to them, and they won't give me an hour today! I'm hungry and thirsty, my heart is on fire, and they won't come to soothe my last agony, my last, for I can feel that I'm dying. Can it be that they don't know what it means to walk over one's father's corpse? There is a God above, and He will avenge other fathers whatever we may wish. Oh, they will come! Come, my darlings, come and kiss me once more, a last kiss, my viaticum, and your father will pray to God for you and will tell Him that you have been good daughters, and will plead your cause with Him. After all, you are innocent. They are innocent, my friend. Be sure you tell everybody so; don't let anyone harass them about me. Everything is my fault; I accustomed them to walk over me. For I liked that. That's no one's business; it doesn't concern the justice of man or of God. God would be unjust if he condemned them because of me. I didn't know how to behave; I was stupid and resigned my rights. I would have dragged myself along the gutter for them. How could it turn out otherwise? The finest souls would have succumbed to the corruption that comes of such easiness in a father. I'm a scoundrel, and I'm justly punished. I'm the sole cause of the lapses of my daughters; I spoiled them. They're greedy for pleasure now just as they used to be greedy for candy. When they were young girls I always let them have whatever they fancied. When they were fifteen they had a carriage. There was nothing they couldn't have. I'm the only guilty one, but I'm guilty because I loved. Their voices would always open my heart. I hear them; they're coming. Oh, yes, they will come! The law requires that one should come when one's father is dying; the law is on my side. And then it means only a little trip. I'll pay for it. Write and tell them that I have millions to leave them! On my word of honor! I'll go to Odessa and make Italian paste there. I know the trick. In my scheme there are millions to be made. No one has thought of it. The thing won't spoil in transport, as wheat does, or flour. Eh, eh? Starch! There'll be millions in that. You won't be lying! Tell them millions, and even if it's only greed that brings them I'd rather be deceived, for I'll see them. I want my daughters. I am the author of their being! They belong to me!" Here he sat up erect, and Eugène was looking at a head with rumbled white hair, and a face in which every feature conveyed the angriest menace.

"Come, now," said Eugène, "lie down again, my dear Père Goriot. I'm going to write to them. As soon as Bianchon is back, I'll go for them, if they haven't come."

"If they haven't come?" the old man echoed with a sob. "But I shall be dead, dead in a fit of rage, of rage. Rage is coming over me! At this moment I can see my whole life. I've been a dupe! They don't love me; they never loved me. That's clear. If they have not come, they will not come. The longer they've put it off, the less they'll care to give me the pleasure. I know them. They've never been able to divine anything of my grief and suffering, or my needs, and they won't divine that I'm dying; they don't even have any real understanding of my affection for them. Yes, I know I've made such a habit of sacrificing my life's blood for them that what I was doing had lost its value in their eyes. If they had asked me to let them tear out my eyes I should have said: 'Tear them out!' I'm too much of a fool! They think that all fathers are like theirs. One must always make sure that one is appreciated at one's proper value. Their children will avenge me. But it's in their interest to come here. Warn them that their conduct is deciding what their own deathbeds shall be! They are committing all crimes in this one. You must go! You must! And you must tell them that not to come is equivalent to parricide. They've committed enough crimes without adding that one. Cry out as I do: 'Nasie! Delphine! Come to your father who has been so good to you and who is in such pain!' Nothing, nobody. Am I to die like a dog? That's my reward, desertion. They are hussies, rascals. I curse and abominate them; and I shall rise from my coffin at night to curse them anew, for I am right, am I not, my friends? Their conduct is very wicked, is it not? What am I saying? Didn't you tell me that Delphine was here? She is the better of the two. You, Eugène, are my son; you must love her, and be a father to her. The other is very unhappy. And their fortunes! Oh, my God, I'm dying, the suffering is a little too much; cut off my head and leave me only my heart."

"Christophe, go for Bianchon!" Eugène called out, appalled by the character the cries and lamentations of the old man were taking on, "and bring back a cab for me."

"I'm going for your daughters, my dear Père Goriot. I'll bring them back to you."

"By force, by force! Call out the guard, call out the soldiers. Anything! Everything!" he said and turned a last fully conscious look on Eugène. "Tell the Government, tell the Crown Prosecutor that they must be brought to me. I insist on it!"

"But you have cursed them!"

"Who told you so?" said the old man in stupefaction. "You know very well that I love them. I adore them. If I see them, i!

273

will make me well. Come, my good neighbor, my dear boy, go for them. You are kind. I should like to show that I appreciate what you have done, but I've nothing to give you but the blessings of a dying man. Ah, I should at least like to see Delphine, to bid her make up my debt to you. If the other cannot come, at least bring Delphine. Tell her that you will love her no longer if she won't come. She loves you so much that she will come. Give me something to drink. I'm on fire. Put something on my head. If it were the hand of one of my daughters, that would save me. I can feel it would. . . . My God, who will make new fortunes for them if I die. I want to go to Odessa for them, to Odessa and make paste."

"Drink this," said Eugène, raising the dying man and taking him in his left arm while with the other he gave him a cup of gruel.

"I am sure you love your father and your mother," said the old man, seizing Eugène's hand with his own, now so weak. "Do you realize that I am going to die without seeing my daughters? Always to be thirsty, and never to drink; that's the way I've lived for the last ten years. . . . My sons-in-law have killed my daughters. Yes, I've had no daughters since they were married. Fathers, you must make the Parliament pass a law on marriage. The fact is that you mustn't marry your daughters off if you love them. A son-in-law is a scoundrel who spoils a daughter through and through; he defiles everything. No more marriage! That's what takes our daughters away from us, and then we don't have them with us when we die. Make a law on the death of fathers. This is dreadful! I mean to be avenged! It is my sons-in-law who prevent them from coming. Kill them! Restaud shall die; the Alsatian shall die; they are my murderers! They shall die or they shall give me back my daughters! Ah, it's all over with now! I'm dying without them! Without them! Nasie, Fifine, come, you must come to me! your father is going. . . .'

"My dear Père Goriot, you must not excite yourself. Come, be quiet. Don't let yourself be upset. Don't think."

"Not seeing them, that's the real death pang!"

"You're going to see them."

"Really!" the old man cried out, his mind now wandering. "Oh, to see them! I shall see them! Hear their voices! I'll die happy. Well, I no longer ask to go on living, living no longer had any meaning for me, my sorrows were growing worse and worse. But to see them, to touch their dresses, ah, just their dresses, it's so little; but I'll smell something of theirs. Let me touch their hair. . . ."

His head fell back on the pillow as if he had been hit by a hammer. His hands moved wildly across the covers as if in search of his daughters' hair.

"I give them my blessing," he said, making an effort, "my blessing."

Suddenly his strength left him. Just then Bianchon came in. "I came on Christophe, and he is getting a cab for you." Then he looked at the sick man, and raised his eyelids. The two students could see that the eye was dull and without warmth. "He won't recover consciousness this time, I think," said Bianchon. He took the pulse and put his hand over the old fellow's heart.

"The machine is still running; but in his state it's a misfortune. He'd be better off if he died."

"There's not the least doubt of that," said Eugène.

"What's wrong with you? You're as white as death."

"My friend, I've just been hearing wails and lamentations. There is a God! Oh, yes! There is a God, and He has made a better world for us to go to, or this earth of ours is without meaning. If it hadn't been so tragic I should break out weeping, but I feel such a sense of oppression over my heart and my stomach."

"Look, a lot of things will be needed. Where are we to get the money for them?"

Eugène drew out his watch.

"Take this, and pawn it. I don't want to stop on my way, for I'm afraid to lose a single minute, and I'm only waiting for Christophe to set out. I haven't a penny, and I'll need money here to pay the cabman when I get back."

Eugène rushed down the stairs, and set out for the Countess de Restaud's house in the Rue du Helder. On the way, his imagination, struck by the horrible spectacle he had just witnessed, was adding more and more warmth to his indignation. When he had reached the entry and asked for the countess, he was told that she could not be seen.

"But," he told the footman, "I've come from her father who is dying."

"Sir, we have received from the count the strictest orders."

"If the count is at home, tell him in what state his father-in-law is, and inform him that I must absolutely speak to him this very instant."

Eugène waited a long time.

"Perhaps he's a dying at this moment," he thought.

The footman led him to the first drawing room and here the Count de Restaud received him, standing by a mantel in which there was no fire and without inviting him to sit down.

"Your father-in-law," said Eugène, "is dying at this moment in a miserable hole without a penny for fuel; he is on the very point of death and he is asking to see his daughter. . . ."

The count replied frigidly, "You must have noticed that I have very little affection for Monsieur Goriot. He has compromised his character with the countess; he is the reason why my life is in ruins. I regard him as the foe of my peace of mind. Whether he lives or dies is perfectly indifferent to me. Those are my feelings concerning him. Society may condemn me for them, but I despise opinion. Just now I have more important things to accomplish than bothering what may be thought of me by fools or people I don't care about. As for the countess, she is in no state to leave the house. Besides, I won't allow her to do so. Tell her father that as soon as she has carried out her duty toward me, and toward my child, she will go to see him. If she loves her father, she can be free to go to him in a few moments. . . ."

"It is not my place to judge your conduct; you are master of your wife; but I can count upon the integrity of your word. Just promise me that you will tell her that her father has not a day to live, and has already cursed her because she was not at his bed-side."

"Tell her this yourself," the Count de Restaud replied, struck by the indignation with which Eugène had spoken.

Led by the count, Eugène entered the drawing room in which the countess usually sat. He found her bathed in tears and huddled in her chair, looking like a woman who wished to die. He pitied her. Before she looked up at him, she cast at her husband glances full of fear which told the story of a complete prostration of her strength, crushed by moral and physical tyranny. The count nodded, and she took from his gesture an encouragement to speak.

"Monsieur de Rastignac," she said, "I heard all that you said. Tell my father that if he knew the situation that faces me, he would forgive me. I did not reckon on this torture; it is more than I can endure, but I'll resist to the very end." She was speaking to her husband. "I am a mother. Tell my father that despite appearances," she cried out in despair to Eugène, "my conduct toward him is irreproachable."

Eugène took his leave of husband and wife, divining the horrible crisis in which the woman stood, and withdrew in a state of stupefaction. The count's tone had convinced him that his effort had been useless, and he understood that Anastasie was no longer free. He hurried to the Baroness de Nucingen's house, and found her in bed.

"I'm ill, my poor friend," she told him. "I took cold on the way home from the ball. I'm afraid I may get pneumonia. I'm expecting the doctor. . . ."

"Even if you were at the point of death," Eugène broke in, "you should drag yourself to your father's side. He is calling for you! If you could hear the least of his cries, you would lose all sense of your own illness."

"Eugène, perhaps my father is not so ill as you say; but it would fill me with despair to be the least bit in the wrong in your eyes, and I'll do as you wish. As for my father, I know he would die of grief if my illness became fatal because I went out now. Well, I'll go as soon as the doctor comes. Ah, why haven't you your watch?" she asked, missing the chain. Eugène blushed. "Eugène, Eugène, if you've already sold it or lost it . . . Oh, that would be very bad of you."

Eugène leaned over Delphine's bed, and whispered in her ear, "Do you want to know? Very well, I'll tell you. Your father hasn't enough money left for the shroud in which he'll be laid out tonight. Your watch is in pawn. I had nothing else left."

Delphine quickly leaped out of bed, ran to her desk, and taking up her purse, gave it to Eugène. She rang and cried out, "I'm going, I'm going, Eugène. Let me get dressed; oh, what a monster I'd be! Go on, I'll be there before you are! Thérèse," she cried to her maid, "tell the baron I want him to come up this very instant. I must speak to him."

In his happiness at being able to tell the dying man that one of his daughters would be with him, Eugène reached the Rue Neuve-Sainte-Geneviève in a state not much short of joy. He fumbled in the purse for money to pay the driver. The purse of so rich and elegant a lady held only seventy francs. When he had reached the head of the stairs he could see Père Goriot, supported by Bianchon, and receiving a treatment from the hospital surgeon as the physician looked on. Caustics, the final resource of science, a useless resource, were applied to his back.

"Do you feel them?" asked the physician.

Père Goriot had caught a glimpse of Eugène. "They're coming, aren't they?" he asked.

"He may recover," said the surgeon. "He can speak."

"Yes," answered Eugène, "Delphine is following me."

"Why," said Bianchon, "he was talking of his daughters and crying out for them the way a man at the stake is said to cry out for water."

"Stop," said the physician to the surgeon, "there's nothing more we can do. The case is hopeless."

Bianchon and the surgeon laid the dying man flat on his back on the loathsome mattress.

"But we must change the linen," said the physician. "Even if there is no more hope, one must respect the human being in him. I'll come back, Bianchon," he said to the student. "If he should complain again, apply an opiate to his diaphragm."

The surgeon and the physician left.

"Come, Eugène, pull yourself together, my boy," said Bianchon, when they were alone. "We must put a clean nightshirt on him, and change his bed. Go and tell Sylvie to bring up linen and to give us help."

Eugène went downstairs and found Madame Vauquer busy laying the table, with Sylvie's help. At his first words, the widow came up to him, assuming the bittersweet manner of a merchant who wishes neither to lose her money nor to anger the customer.

"My dear Monsieur Eugène," she said, "you know as well as I do that Père Goriot hasn't a cent left. To supply linen for a man who is about to turn up his eyes is to lose it, and besides one piece will have to be sacrificed for a shroud. And you owe me already one hundred and forty-four francs; say forty francs for the linen, and a few other little things, like the candle that Sylvie will give you, and it will come to at least two hundred francs, a sum that a poor widow like me is in no state to lose. Heavens, look at it fairly. I've already suffered enough loss these past five days since ill luck has taken up lodgings with me. I'd have given five crowns if the old fellow had left a few days ago when you said he would. This isn't good for my business. For two pins I'd insist on his being taken to the hospital. In short, I just ask you to put yourself in my place. My establishment must come first; it's my very life."

Eugène hurried upstairs to Père Goriot's room.

"Bianchon, where is the money for the watch?"

"On the table, there are three hundred and sixty-odd francs left. Out of what it brought I've paid all that we owed. The receipt from the pawn shop is underneath the money."

"Here, Madame Vauquer," said Eugène, when he had reached the foot of the stairs again, still overcome by horror, "let us settle our accounts. Monsieur Goriot will not be with you long, and I . . ."

"You are right. He will be leaving feet first, poor fellow," she said counting out two hundred francs, with an air that was half gay and half melancholy.

"Let us be quick about it," said Eugène.

"Sylvie, get some linen, and go and help these gentlemen upstairs."

"You won't forget Sylvie," Madame Vauquer whispered to Eugène. "She's been up all last night and the night before."

As soon as Eugène's back was turned, the old creature hurried to her cook and said, "Take the sheets that have been turned, number seven. Good heavens, they're good enough for the dead." These last words were whispered in Sylvie's ear.

Eugène who had already gone part way upstairs did not hear what the old boarding-house keeper said.

"Come," Bianchon said to him, "let us get his nightshirt on. Hold him up straight."

Eugène stood at the head of the bed, and held the dying man while Bianchon took off the shirt. The old fellow made a gesture as if to keep something that he thought was hanging on his breast, and uttered plaintive and inarticulate cries in the manner of an animal that is trying to express some great pain.

"Oh! Oh!" said Bianchon, "he wants that little chain of hair and that medallion that we took off a little while ago when we applied the caustics. Poor man, we must give that back to him. It's on the mantel."

Eugène brought over a chain woven of ash blonde hair, doubtless the hair of Madame Goriot. On one side of the medallion was engraved *Anastasie;* on the other *Delphine.* An image of his heart which always rested on his heart. The locks the medallion held were so fine that they must have been snipped during the infancy of the two girls. When the medallion touched his breast, the old man uttered a long sigh so full of satisfaction that it was frightening to hear it. This was one of the last gasps of his sensibility which seemed to be withdrawing to that unknown center from which our sympathies emanate and to which they return. His convulsed face took on an expression of morbid happiness The two students, struck by the terrible power of a feeling which was so strong that it outlasted thought, were moved to tears, and as these fell upon the dying man he uttered a sharp cry of pleasure.

"Nasie! Fifine!" he said.

"He's still alive," said Bianchon.

"And what does it get him?" asked Sylvie.

"Suffering," said Eugène.

After indicating to his friend that he should do likewise, Bianchon knelt down and put his hands under the calves of the sick man, and Eugène on the other side of the bed also knelt and put his hands under Père Goriot's back. Sylvie was standing there ready, as soon as the dying man had been lifted, to slip the sheets off and replace them by those she had brought. It was the tears, of course, that had deceived him, and Goriot used the final remnant of his strength to stretch out his hands; encountering the heads of the two students on either side of his bed, he grasped them strongly by the hair and he was heard to say in a weak voice, "My angels!" Two words, two murmurs, given a stress by the soul that fled away as he spoke.

"The poor dear man," said Sylvie, touched by this exclamation which expressed a final emotion stirred by the most horrible, the most involuntary of deceptions.

This father's last sigh was to be a sigh of joy, the expression of his entire life; once more he was deceived. Père Goriot was piously put back upon his mattress. From this moment his face retained the painful impress of the struggle waged by life and death in a machine which no longer had that kind of cerebral consciousness from which the human being derives the sense of pleasure and of pain. Its destruction was now but a question of time.

"He will continue like this for some hours, and will die without our being able to tell when. There will not even be a death rattle. His brain must be wholly congested."

Just then the step of a young woman out of breath could be heard.

"She's too late," said Eugène.

It was not Delphine, but Thérèse her maid.

"Monsieur," she said, "a violent scene has just occurred between my mistress and her husband over the money that she asked for to help her father. She fainted; the doctor came; she had to be bled; she was crying out: 'My father is dying, I want to see my father!' Indeed her cries were enough to pierce one's very soul."

"Say no more, Thérèse, even if she were to come now it would be of no use. Monsieur Goriot has lost consciousness."

"The poor dear man, is he as ill as that?" said Thérèse.

"You won't need me any longer," said Sylvie. "I must go down for dinner. It's half past four." At the head of the stairs she almost bumped into the Countess de Restaud.

The countess was like a grave and terrifying apparition. She looked at the deathbed, poorly lit by a single candle, and tears flowed from her eyes as she saw the mask of her father, with the last tremblings of life stirring. Bianchon thought it considerate to withdraw from the room.

"I didn't get away soon enough," the countess said to Eugène.

The student nodded his head in mournful assent. The countess took her father's hand and kissed it.

"Forgive me, Father! You used to say that my voice would call you back from the grave. Well, come back to life for one moment to bless your penitent daughter. Listen to me! This is dreadful! Your blessing is the only one that I may hope to have here below henceforward. Everyone hates me; you alone love me. Even my children will hate me. Take me with you. I will love you and care for you. He doesn't hear. I'm going mad!" She fell on her knees and looked fixedly at what remained of her father with an expression of delirium. "My misery is running over," she said, looking at Eugène. "The Count de Trailles has gone, leaving immense debts behind him, and I've learned that he was deceiving me. My husband will never forgive me, and I have left him master of my fortune. I've lost all my illusions. Alas, how could I have so betrayed the only heart" (she pointed toward her father) "in which I was adored! I didn't appreciate him, I drew away from him, I've done him a thousand meannesses, in my infamy."

"He knew it," said Eugène.

Just then Père Goriot opened his eyes, but this was because of a convulsion. The gesture which disclosed the countess's hope was no less horrible to see than the dying man's eye.

"Could he hear?" she cried. "No," she said to herself, sitting down beside the bed.

Since she expressed the wish to stay by her father, Eugène went downstairs to take a little nourishment. The boarders had already gathered.

"Well," said the painter, "it seems that we have a dance of death going on upstairs?"

"Charles," Eugène replied, "I think you might find some less gloomy theme for your jests."

"So we can't laugh any more here?" the painter continued. "What's wrong, since Bianchon told us that the old fellow won't recover consciousness?"

"Well," said the man from the museum, "he'll die as he lived."

"My father is dead," the countess cried out.

At this terrible cry Sylvie, Eugène and Bianchon ran upstairs and found the Countess de Restaud in a faint. After they had brought her back to consciousness, they carried her to the cab which was waiting. Eugène gave her into Thérèse's care, and gave orders that she be taken to the Baroness de Nucingen's.

"Yes, it is true, he is dead," said Bianchon when he came down again.

"Come, gentlemen, sit down," said Madame Vauquer, "the *t*oup will get cold."

The two students sat down side by side.

"What must we do now?" Eugène asked Bianchon.

"Well, I closed his eyes and laid him in a suitable position. After the doctor from the city hall has verified the death—when we've reported it—he will be sewn into a shroud, and then he will be buried. What did you think of doing with him?"

"He'll never again smell his bread in that odd way of his," said one of the boarders, imitating the old fellow.

"Good Lord, gentlemen," said the tutor, "let Père Goriot be; don't make us eat him any longer; he's had the last sauce a full hour ago. One of the privileges of the good city of Paris is that one can be born here and live and die without any one paying any attention to you. Let's take advantage of the good things of civilization. Sixty people have died today. Do you mean to mourn over the hecatombs of Paris? If Père Goriot has croaked, all the better for him. If you worship him, go and stand watch by his body, and let the rest of us have our meal in peace."

"Oh, yes," said the widow, "so much the better for him to be dead! The poor man would seem to have had plenty of trouble all his life."

This was the only funeral oration for a being who for Eugène exemplified Paternity. The fifteen boarders began to chat in their usual fashion. When Eugène and Bianchon had eaten, the sound of forks and spoons, the laughs that rose out of the conversation, the varied expressions of those gluttonous and indifferent faces, and the general imperviousness froze them with horror. They went out to find a priest who would watch and pray by the corpse during the night. They had to bring the final services for the old fellow within the range of the little money they had. Toward nine o'clock that evening the body was placed on a bare frame with a candle on either side in that bare room, and a priest came and sat beside it. Before he went to bed, Eugène who had asked the cleric for some information concerning the costs of the service to be held and the funeral procession, wrote a word to the Baron de Nucingen and the Count de Restaud, asking them to send their business representatives in order to arrange for all the costs of interment. He sent Christophe with the notes; then he got into bed and went to sleep overcome by fatigue. The next morning Bianchon and Eugène had to go themselves and give notice of the death which was officially verified toward noon. Two hours later neither of the sons-in-law had sent any money; no one had come in the name of either; and Eugène had already had to pay the priest. Sylvie had asked for ten francs for laying the old fellow out and sewing him in his shroud, and Eugène and Bianchon had made calculations and concluded that if the relatives of the dead man were unwilling to do anything they would have scarcely enough money to meet the expenses to come. Bianchon undertook personally to place the old man in a pauper's coffin which he had brought from the hospital, where it could be had at a lower rate.

"Let's play a trick on those rascals," he said to Eugène. "Go and buy a plot for a five-year period at Père la Chaise, and order a service of the third class at the church and at the undertaking establishment. If the sons-in-law and the daughters refuse to pay you for what you advance, place an inscription on the tombstone, 'Here lies Monsieur Goriot, father of the Countess de Restaud and the Baroness de Nucingen, buried at the expense of two students.'"

Eugène did not do as his friend advised until he had made useless calls at the Restaud's and the Nucingen's. He did not get beyond the door. At each house the porter had been given strict orders.

"My master and mistress," they said, "are at home to no one; their father is dead and they are in the deepest mourning."

Eugène knew enough about the society of Paris to be aware that he should not press the point. He felt a strange oppression of the heart when he found he could not see Delphine.

"Sell one of your jewels," he wrote in the porter's room, "so that your father may have a proper burial."

He sealed the note and asked the baron's porter to give it to Thérèse to bring to her mistress, but the porter gave it to the baron and he threw it into the fire. When he had carried out all his plans, Eugène returned to the boarding-house toward three o'clock and he could not refrain from shedding a tear when he saw before the house-door a bier that was barely covered by a black cloth and set on two chairs in the deserted street. A poor hyssop which no one had yet touched lay in a dish of silver plate which held holy water. The door had not been draped in black. This was a case of death among the poor, with no show, no mourners, no friends, no relations. Bianchon, who had to be at the hospital, had left a note for Eugène telling him what he had arranged with the church. He wrote that a mass was beyond their means, that they would have to be content with the less costly vespers, and that he had sent Christophe with a note to the funeral establishment. Just as Eugène was reading the end of Bianchon's scrawl, he noticed in Madame Vauquer's hands the medallion circled with gold which held the locks of the two daughters.

"How could you have dreamed of taking that?" he asked her.

"Why, was it to be buried with him? It's gold," Sylvie commented.

"Of course it must," Eugène replied indignantly. "Let him take with him the only thing he has to stand for his two daughters."

When the hearse came, Eugène had the coffin taken up, opened it and piously placed on the old fellow's breast an image which went back to a time when Delphine and Anastasie were young, virgin and pure, and *did not use their brains,* as their father had put it in one of his outcries on his deathbed. Eugène and Christophe were alone, save for two hired mourners, with the hearse which bore the poor man to Saint Etienne du Mont, a church which was not at all far from the Rue Neuve-Sainte-Geneviève. On the arrival there the corpse was introduced into a low dark chapel in which Eugène looked in vain for Goriot's daughters or their husbands. His only fellow mourner was Christophe who thought he owed a final homage to a man who had been the means of his receiving some large tips. As they waited for the two priests, the server and the beadle, Eugène wrung Christophe's hand without being able to utter a single word.

"Yes, Monsieur Eugène," said Christophe, "he was a fine and worthy man, one who never lost his temper, never did anyone any harm, and never did anything that was wrong."

The two priests, accompanied by the server and the beadle, entered and performed all that could be had for seventy francs in an age in which religion is not wealthy enough to pray unfeed. The clerics chanted a psalm, the *Libera,* the *De Profundis.* The service lasted twenty minutes. There was but one carriage, intended for a priest and a server, and they consented to take Eugène and Christophe with them.

"There is no cortège," said the priest. "We can drive faster, so that we won't be late. It's half-past five."

Meanwhile, just as the body was placed in the hearse, two carriages with armorial bearings, the carriages of the Count de Restaud and the Baron de Nucingen, drew up, empty, and followed the procession to Père la Chaise. At six o'clock Père Goriot's body was lowered into the grave. Around it stood his daughters' servants; they disappeared along with the churchmen as soon as the brief prayer for the old fellow, due him because of the student's money, had been said. When the two gravediggers had thrown a few shovelfuls of earth on the coffin so as to hide it, they stood up and one of them, turning to Eugène, asked for their gratuity. Eugène searched his pocket and found nothing; he had to borrow twenty sous from Christophe. This, so small an event in itself, brought on Eugène a horrible sense of sadness. Daylight was ending. The damp twilight affected his nerves. He bent his gaze on the tomb and dropped upon it the last of his youthful tears, a tear wrung from the pious emotions of a pure heart, a tear such as rebounds from the earth to which it falls, toward the heavens. He crossed his arms and looked at the clouds. Seeing him in this posture, Christophe left him.

Eugène, now wholly alone, took a few steps to gain the highest point in the cemetery, and looked out on Paris winding its length along the two banks of the Seine, in which its lights were beginning to be reflected. His eyes were fixed almost avidly on the area between the column in the Place Vendôme and the dome of the Invalides, the region of that high society in which he had sought to make his way. Upon this humming hive he cast a look which seemed already to suck the honey from it, and he gave utterance to these portentous words: "Between us the battle is joined henceforward."

And as a first act in challenge of Society, Eugène went to dine with the Baroness de Nucingen.

Saché
September, 1834.

EUGÉNIE GRANDET

Translated by Dorothea Walter and John Watkins

TO MARIA

May your name—you whose portrait is the fairest adornment of this work—be like a branch of blessed boxwood, cut from no one knows what tree, but assuredly sanctified by religion and kept eternally fresh and green by pious hands for the protection of the house.

ONE

THE FACES OF THE BOURGEOISIE

IN certain provincial towns there are houses which create a feeling of melancholy equal to that aroused by the gloomiest cloisters, the bleakest moorland, or the most mournful ruins. Perhaps they combine the stillness of the cloister, the barrenness of the moors, and the desiccation of the ruins. The life within them moves so slowly that a stranger would suppose them uninhabited were he not suddenly to encounter the pale, cold gaze of a motionless figure, whose half-monastic face appears above the window ledge at the sound of an unfamiliar footstep. These melancholy elements are present in the physiognomy of a dwelling in Saumur, at the end of a steep street leading to the castle by way of the upper town. This street, now little used, hot in summer, cold in winter, and rather dark in places, is remarkable for its resonant pavement of tiny cobblestones, always clean and dry, for its narrow winding course, and for the tranquillity of its houses, which belong to the old town and are overshadowed by the ramparts.

Houses three centuries old still stand firmly here, though built of wood, and their divers aspects contribute to the picturesqueness which recommends this part of Saumur to the attention of antiquarians and artists. It is difficult to pass by without admiring the enormous joists, their ends carved into fantastic figures, which crown with a black bas-relief the ground floor of most of these houses. Here, wooden cross pieces covered with slate form a design in blue on the fragile walls of a house topped off with a studwork roof, bent with the years, its rotten shingles warped by the alternate action of sun and rain. There, worn and blackened window sills appear, their delicate carvings scarcely visible, seeming too frail for the brown earthenware pot from which spring the pinks or rose-bushes of some poor working girl. Farther on are doors studded with enormous nails, where the genius of our ancestors has traced mysterious inscriptions relating family history—inscriptions of which the meaning will never be recovered. Here a protestant has attested his faith; there a Leaguer has cursed Henry IV; elsewhere some burgher has etched the insignia of his magisterial nobility, the glory of his forgotten sheriffdom. The whole history of France is there.

Next to a tottering house with roughly plastered walls, a monument to the artisan and his plane, rises the town house of a nobleman, where on the arch above the stone doorway may still be seen vestiges of his coat-of-arms, shattered by the various revolutions which since 1789 have disturbed the country. In this street the commercial establishments on the ground-floor are neither shops nor warehouses; lovers of the Middle Ages will find here the communal workshop of our forefathers in all its naïve simplicity. These low-ceilinged rooms, which have neither shop fronts, nor showcases, nor show windows, are deep and dark and without adornment, either inside or outside. The doors, banded roughly with iron, open in two horizontal sections. The upper part folds inwards, and the lower, furnished with a spring-bell, swings continually to and fro. Light and air penetrate into this damp cavern either through the upper half of the door or through the space between the vaulted ceiling and the little wall rising breast-high from the floor. In this space are set heavy shutters, which are taken down in the morning and put up again in the evening and secured by heavy iron bars.

The merchant's wares are set out on this wall. There is no attempt here to lure customers. Depending on the nature of the business, the samples may be two or three small tubs of salt or codfish, a few bundles of sailcloth, cordage, copper wire hanging from the joists above, iron hoops along the wall, or some lengths of cloth on the shelves. You go inside. A girl, neatly dressed, young and sprightly, with a white kerchief and red arms, puts aside her knitting and calls her father or her mother, who comes and sells you what you want—phlegmatically, obligingly, arrogantly, according to disposition—merchandise worth two cents or twenty thousand francs.

You see a man who sells stave-wood sitting in his doorway twirling his thumbs as he gossips with a neighbor. He seems to own only a few old shelf-boards for bottles and two or three bundles of laths. But down by the river his well-stocked lumber yard supplies all the coopers in Anjou. He knows almost to a plank how many casks he can sell if the harvest is good. A spell of sunshine makes him rich, a rainy season ruins him; in a single morning puncheons worth eleven francs have been known to drop to six. In this region, as in Touraine, the ups and downs of the weather dominate commercial life. Wine-growers, landed proprietors, lumber merchants, coopers, innkeepers, and boatmen all lie in wait for a ray of sunshine. They go to bed trembling, afraid of hearing in the morning that there has been a frost during the night. They fear rain, wind, and drought and demand water, heat, and clouds to suit their whim. There is a perpetual duel between the heavens and their terrestrial interests. The barometer now saddens, now calms, and now enlivens their faces. From end to end of this street, formerly the Grand'rue of Saumur, the words: "This is golden weather!" are bartered from door to door. And everyone answers his neighbor with: "It's raining gold coins," knowing full well what a ray of sunshine or an opportune shower may yield him.

At noon on Saturdays, during the fine weather, you can't get a cent's worth of merchandise from any of these good fellows. Each has his vineyard, his little farm, and goes off to spend two days in the country. Since everything in the street—purchases, sales, profits—has been anticipated, the merchants find that they have ten hours out of twelve for jolly gatherings, for gossip, comment, and perpetual spying. A housewife can't buy a partridge without the neighbors asking her husband if it was done to a turn. A young girl can't show her face at the window without being observed by all these idlers. Nothing can be hidden there, just as in those dark, silent, forbidding houses there is no mystery. Life is lived almost always in the open air: every family sits in its own doorway, lunches, dines, and quarrels there. No one can pass along the street without scrutiny. Indeed, in the old days, when a stranger arrived in a country town, he was made fun of from door to door. Hence the witty stories and hence the nickname of "mockers" given to the people of Angers, who excelled in this form of urban pleasantry.

The ancient aristocratic houses of the old town are situated at the top of this street which was formerly inhabited by the local nobility. The gloom-filled house in which the events of this story took place was precisely one of those dwellings, venerable relics of a century in which men and things were characterized by a simplicity that French manners and customs are losing day by day. Follow the windings of this picturesque thoroughfare, whose slightest irregularities awaken memories and whose general effect tends to plunge you into a kind of automatic reverie, and you will come upon a rather dark recess, in the middle of which is hidden the door of the house of Monsieur Grandet. It is impossible to understand the full force of this provincial locution—the house of Monsieur Grandet—without giving the biography of Grandet himself.

Monsieur Grandet enjoyed a reputation in Saumur the causes and effects of which are not readily understood by those who have spent little or no time in the provinces. Monsieur Grandet, still referred to as Old Grandet by certain elderly people now rapidly diminishing in number, was in 1789 a well-to-do master cooper who knew how to read, write, and cipher. When the church properties in the district of Saumur were put up for sale by the French Republic, the cooper, who was forty, had just married the daughter of a wealthy lumber merchant. Armed with all his ready cash and her dowry, armed with two thousand golden louis, Grandet went to the local authorities, and with the help of two hundred double louis given by his father-in-law to the staunch republican who was in charge of the sale of government property, he got for a song, legally if not legitimately, the finest vineyards in the district, an old abbey, and a few farms. As the inhabitants of Saumur were rather luke-warm revolutionaries, Old Grandet passed for a daring man, a republican, a patriot, with a mind which revelled in new ideas, whereas the cooper revelled merely in vineyards. He was chosen a member of the local government of the district of Saumur, and his pacific influence made itself felt both politically and commercially. Politically, he protected the former nobles and did all he could to prevent the sale of their property; commercially, he furnished the republican armies with a thousand or two casks of white wine and accepted in payment some magnificent meadowlands belonging to a community of nuns, which had been reserved as the last parcel.

Under the Consulate, Old Grandet became mayor, governed wisely, and did even better for himself; under the Empire, he became Monsieur Grandet. But Napoleon did not like republicans; he replaced Monsieur Grandet, who was reputed to have worn the red bonnet, by a large landowner of the lesser nobility, a future baron of the Empire. Monsieur Grandet cheerfully relinquished his municipal honors. He had had built, in the interests of the town, some excellent roads which led to his prop-

*r*ties. His house and lands, very favorably assessed, paid modest *t*axes; and since the registration of his various holdings, his vineyards, thanks to constant care, had become "tops" for the region—a technical term used to describe the vineyards which produce the finest wine. He might have asked for the Legion of Honor.

Grandet's retirement from politics took place in 1806. He was then fifty-seven, and his wife about thirty-six. An only daughter, fruit of their legitimate love, was ten. Monsieur Grandet, whom Providence doubtless wished to console for his political disappointment, inherited one after another during the course of this year three fortunes, the extent of which nobody could know—that of Madame de la Gaudinière, née de la Bertellière, Madame Grandet's mother; then that of old Monsieur de la Bertellière, Madame Grandet's grandfather; and finally that of Madame Gentillet, her maternal grandmother. The miserliness of these three old people was so excessive that for a long time they had hoarded their money for the pleasure of contemplating it in secret. Old Monsieur de la Bertellière regarded an investment as an extravagance, finding much higher returns in the sight of the gold itself than in the profits of usury. The town of Saumur, however, estimated the value of these fortunes from the income of the real property. So Monsieur Grandet acquired that new title to nobility which our mania for equality can never wipe out; he became the biggest taxpayer in the district.

He cultivated a hundred acres of vineyard, which in the abundant years yielded seven or eight hundred casks of wine. He owned thirteen farms, an old abbey, in which, for the sake of economy, he had walled up the windows and arches and covered over the stained glass to preserve it, and a hundred and twenty-seven acres of meadowland, where three thousand poplars, planted in 1793, grew and flourished. Moreover, the house in which he lived belonged to him. In this way people counted up his visible fortune. As for his capital, there were only two people who could even attempt to guess its extent. One of them was Monsieur Cruchot, the notary whose business it was to look after Monsieur Grandet's usurious loans; the other was Monsieur des Grassins, the richest banker in Saumur, in whose profits the wine-grower shared discreetly when he was so minded.

Although old Cruchot and Monsieur des Grassins were possessed of that profound discretion which in country towns insures trust and wealth, they were so respectful to Monsieur Grandet in public that the observant could estimate the extent of the ex-mayor's fortune by the degree of obsequious consideration they accorded him. Everybody in Saumur was firmly convinced that Monsieur Grandet had a private treasure, a hiding-place packed with louis, and that he indulged nightly in the ineffable joys afforded by the sight of great masses of gold. The miserly were practically certain of it whenever they looked at the old man's eyes, which seemed to have absorbed the color of the yellow metal itself. The countenance of a man accustomed to drawing enormous interest on his capital, like that of the voluptuary, the gambler, or the sycophant, acquires of necessity certain indefinable characteristics, certain furtive, greedy, mysterious expressions, always quite obvious to the initiated. This secret language is a kind of freemasonry of the passions. Monsieur Grandet, then, inspired the respectful esteem to which a man who never owed anything to anybody is entitled. A skilled cooper and an expert wine-grower, he could guess with the precision of an astronomer whether he ought to manufacture for his vintage a thousand casks or only five hundred. He never failed in any speculation, always had casks to sell when the cask was worth more than its contents, could store his vintage in his wine-rooms and await the moment when he could sell his casks for two hundred francs, while the smaller wine-growers had to let theirs go at five louis. His famous vintage of 1811, judiciously stored and slowly disposed of, brought him in more than two hundred and forty thousand francs.

Financially speaking, there was something of both the tiger and the boa-constrictor in Monsieur Grandet. He knew how to crouch and lie low, watch his prey a long while, and spring upon it; then, opening the jaws of his purse, he would gulp down a heap of gold coins and lie torpid like a snake in the process of digestion, cold, impassive, methodical. Nobody could see him go by without a feeling of admiration mingled with respect and terror. Hadn't everybody in Saumur felt the gash of his polished steel claws? For one person, Lawyer Cruchot had obtained the sum necessary to purchase an estate, but at eleven per cent. For another, Monsieur des Grassins had bills discounted, but at a frightful rate of interest. There were few days on which Monsieur Grandet's name was not mentioned either at the market or in after-dinner conversations in the town. To some, the old wine-grower's wealth was a source of local pride. Often a merchant or an innkeeper would say to strangers with a degree of complacency, "Sir, we have two or three millionaire establishments here; but as for Monsieur Grandet, he doesn't even know himself how rich he is!"

In 1816 the ablest reckoners in Saumur estimated the old man's landed property at close to four millions; but since from 1793 to 1817 he must have drawn an average yearly income of a hundred thousand francs from that property, it was fair to assume that he possessed in actual cash an amount almost equal to the value of his estate. Therefore, when at the end of a game of cards or a discussion about vineyards the conversation turned to Monsieur Grandet, the wiseacres would say: "Old Grandet? Why, Old Grandet must be worth five or six million!"

"You're smarter than I am then, for I've never been able to find out just how much he's worth," Monsieur Cruchot or Monsieur des Grassins would say if they heard the remark.

If a Parisian mentioned the Rothschilds or Monsieur Lafitte, the people of Saumur would ask if they were as rich as Monsieur Grandet. If the Parisian, smiling disdainfully, said yes, they would look at each other, shaking their heads incredulously. So vast a fortune threw a mantle of gold over all the man's actions. If at first certain peculiarities of his life gave occasion for ridicule and laughter, the laughter and the ridicule had long since died away. Monsieur Grandet's most insignificant actions now went unquestioned. His way of speaking, his dress, his gestures, the blinking of his eyes, were law to the countryside, where everyone, after having studied him as a naturalist studies the effects of instinct in animals, had learned to recognize the profound and silent wisdom of his slightest actions.

"It will be a hard winter," they would say. "Old Grandet has put on his fur-lined gloves. We'd better get at the harvest."

"Old Grandet's buying a lot of staves. There'll be plenty of wine this year."

Monsieur Grandet never bought either meat or bread. His farmers brought him every week, as part of their rent, a sufficient quantity of capons, chickens, eggs, butter, and wheat. He owned a mill, and the tenant was bound, over and above his rent, to take a certain amount of grain and bring back the flour and bran. Big Nanon, his only servant, although she was no longer young, baked the bread for the household herself every Saturday. Monsieur Grandet had an arrangement with market gardeners, who were also his tenants, to supply him with vegetables. As for fruit, he harvested so much himself that he sold the bulk of it in the market. His firewood was cut from his own hedges or taken from old clumps of half-rotten trees which he cleared away from the edge of his fields. His farmers hauled it into town for him, already cut, and piled it in his woodshed as a favor, receiving in return his thanks. His only known expenditures were for consecrated bread, his wife's clothes and his daughter's, and the rent for their chairs in church; for light, Big Nanon's wages, and the tinning of his pots and pans; for his taxes, repairs on his buildings, and the costs of his various enterprises. He had six hundred acres of woodland, recently purchased, which he got a neighbor's gamekeeper to look after by promising him compensation. Only after this acquisition did he eat game.

Monsieur Grandet's manners were decidedly plain. He spoke little. He usually expressed himself in brief, sententious phrases uttered in a soft voice. Since the Revolution, when he first began to attract attention, the old fellow had developed a tiresome stutter whenever he had to speak at any length or carry on a discussion. This stammering, the incoherence of his speech, the flood of words in which he drowned his thought, and his apparent lack of logic, attributed to defective education, were in reality assumed, and will be sufficiently explained by certain incidents in this story. Moreover, four sentences, precise as algebraic formulas, usually served to embrace and resolve all the problems of life and commerce: "I don't know. I can't. I don't want to. We'll see about that." He never said yes or no, and never wrote anything down. When he was spoken to, he listened coldly, holding his chin in his right hand and resting his right elbow on the back of his left hand, and reached on all matters conclusions from which he never departed. He deliberated long over the most insignificant deals. When his opponent, after a masterly conversation, had unwittingly revealed his secret aims, he would reply, "I can't make a decision without consulting my wife." His wife, whom he had reduced to a state of complete serfdom, was a most useful screen in business. He never went anywhere, never wanted to give or accept invitations to dinner. He never made any noise and seemed to economize in everything, even in movement. He never interfered with other people's things because of his ingrained respect for property. Nevertheless, in spite of the softness of his voice and the circumspectness of his behavior, the speech and manners of a cooper came out, especially at home, where he let himself go more than anywhere else.

Physically Grandet was five feet in height, thick-set, square, with twelve-inch calves, bony knees, and broad shoulders. His face was round, sunburned, and pitted with smallpox. His chin was straight, his lips thin, and his teeth white. His eyes had the calm, voracious expression that people ascribe to the basilisk. His forehead, crossed by innumerable lines, was not without significant bumps. His yellowish, graying hair was like silver and gold, said some of the young people who did not realize the impropriety of making fun of Monsieur Grandet. His nose, thick at the tip, bore a veined wen, which the common herd said, not without reason, was full of malice. This face revealed a dangerous cunning, a calculated integrity, the egoism of a man accustomed to limit his emotions to the joys of avarice and to the only being who really meant anything to him, his daughter Eugénie, his sole heiress. Attitude, manners, bearing, in short everything about him, demonstrated the complete assurance that comes from unvarying success in all one's undertakings.

Though seemingly mild and obliging, Monsieur Grandet was actually as hard as nails. His dress never varied. He looked just the same today as he had looked since 1791. His stout shoes were tied with leather thongs. He always wore close-knit woollen stockings, short breeches of coarse, brown cloth with silver buckles, a velvet waistcoat with alternate stripes of yellow and puce, buttoned squarely, a big, brown coat with broad tails, a black cravat, and a broad-brimmed Quaker hat. His gloves, as heavy as a policeman's, lasted him twenty months, and to keep them clean, he always laid them down methodically on the brim of his hat, in exactly the same spot. Saumur knew nothing more of this man.

Only six people in the town were privileged to enter Monsieur

Grandet's house. Of the first three the most important was Monsieur Cruchot's nephew. Since his appointment as presiding
judge of the civil court of Saumur, this young man had added to
the name of Cruchot that of de Bonfons, and was working hard
to drop the Cruchot. He was already signing his name C. de
Bonfons. The litigant so ill-advised as to call him Monsieur
Cruchot was soon made aware in court of his blunder. The
magistrate protected those who called him Monsieur le Président,
but favored with his most gracious smiles those flatterers who
referred to him as Monsieur de Bonfons. The judge was thirty-
three and owner of the Bonfons (Boni Fontis) estate, which
brought in a yearly income of seven thousand livres. He expected
to inherit the property of his uncle the notary and that of another
uncle, Abbé Cruchot, a dignitary of the chapter of Saint-Martin
de Tours, both of whom were thought to be very rich. These
three Cruchots, backed by a goodly number of cousins and
allied to twenty families in the town, formed a party, like the
Medicis in Florence long ago; and like the Medicis, the Cruchots
had their Pazzi.

Madame des Grassins, mother of a twenty-three-year-old son,
came assiduously to play cards with Madame Grandet, hoping to
marry her dear Adolphe to Mademoiselle Eugénie. Monsieur
des Grassins, the banker, actively supported his wife's schemes
by incessant services rendered in secret to the old miser and always
arrived on the battlefield at the opportune moment. These three
des Grassins also had their adherents, their cousins, their faithful
allies. In the Cruchot camp, the Abbé, the Talleyrand of the
family, ably seconded by his brother the notary, vigorously disputed the field with the banker's wife and strove to keep the rich
heritage for his nephew the judge. This secret struggle between
the Cruchots and the des Grassins, of which the prize was the
hand of Eugénie Grandet, was of passionate interest to all classes
of Saumur society. Would Mademoiselle Grandet marry His

Honor the judge or Monsieur Adolphe des Grassins? To this question some replied that Monsieur Grandet would not give his daughter to either one of them. The ex-cooper, consumed with ambition, was seeking as son-in-law, they said, some peer of France to whom an income of three hundred thousand francs would make all the Grandet casks, past, present, and future, acceptable. Others replied that Monsieur and Madame des Grassins were noble, and immensely wealthy, that Adolphe was quite a satisfactory swain, and that unless he had a Pope's nephew up his sleeve, so suitable an alliance ought to satisfy an upstart, a man whom all Saumur had seen, adze in hand, and who, moreover, had worn the red bonnet. The more acute pointed out that Monsieur Cruchot de Bonfons was free to go in and out of the house at any time, whereas his rival was received only on Sundays. Some people claimed that Madame des Grassins, more intimate with the women of the Grandet household than the Cruchots, could instill certain ideas into their minds which would sooner or later bring her success. Others replied that Abbé Cruchot was the most insinuating man in the world. Bet a woman against a monk and the struggle is equal. "They're running neck and neck," said a wit of Saumur.

Better informed, the oldest inhabitants of the countryside insisted that the Grandets were much too shrewd to let the money go out of the family, that Mademoiselle Eugénie Grandet of Saumur would marry the son of Monsieur Grandet of Paris, a rich wholesale wine merchant. To this the Cruchotins and the Grassinistes replied, "In the first place the two brothers haven't seen each other more than twice in thirty years. Moreover, Monsieur Grandet of Paris has much more ambitious plans for his son. He's mayor of a borough, a deputy, a colonel in the National Guard, and a magistrate of the commercial court. He disowns the Grandets of Saumur and aspires to an alliance with some ducal family—ducal by the grace of Napoleon." Indeed, there wasn't much that people didn't say about an heiress who was a subject of gossip for fifty miles around, and even in the stage-coaches between Angers and Blois!

At the beginning of 1811 the Cruchotins won a signal victory over the Grassinistes. The estate of Froidfond, noted for its park, its noble manor-house, its farms, rivers, ponds, and forests, and valued at three millions, was put up for sale by the young Marquis de Froidfond, who was forced to convert his property into ready cash. Lawyer Cruchot, Judge Cruchot, and Abbé Cruchot, with the help of their adherents, were able to prevent the property from being sold in small lots. The notary made a splendid bargain with the young man, persuading him that he would have to wage countless lawsuits against the purchasers before he could collect the price of the lots from them. He would do much better to sell to Monsieur Grandet, who was solvent and could pay cash for the property. So the fine marquisate of Froidfond was convoyed down the gullet of Monsieur Grandet, who to the great astonishment of Saumur paid for it on the spot, at the cash discount, after the usual formalities. This deal created quite a stir both in Nantes and in Orléans. Monsieur Grandet took advantage of a cart returning to Froidfond to see his manor. Having cast a proprietary glance over the whole estate, he came back to Saumur, satisfied that he had invested his money at five per cent, and fired with the magnificent idea of rounding out the marquisate of Froidfond by concentrating all his properties there. Then, to replenish his treasury, now nearly empty, he decided to cut down all the trees in his woods and forests and sell off the poplars in his meadows.

It is easy now to understand the full force of the term "the house of Monsieur Grandet," that bleak, cold, silent house in the upper town under the shadow of the walls. The two pillars and the arch forming the bay for the doorway had been built, like the house, of tufa, a white stone peculiar to the banks of the Loire and so soft that it does not usually last more than two centuries. The many irregular cavities, oddly hollowed out by the inclemency of the weather, gave the arch and pillars of the bay a resemblance to the vermiculated stonework characteristic of French architecture and made it look something like the gateway of a jail. Above the arch a long frieze represented the four seasons by figures carved in hard stone but already corroded and blackened. This frieze was surmounted by a projecting plinth on which had grown up at random such plants as yellow pellitory, bindweed, convulvuli, and plantain, and a little cherry tree already quite tall.

The door of the archway was of solid oak, brown, shrunken, cracked in all directions, and, though frail in appearance, was stoutly reinforced by a system of bolts arranged in symmetrical designs. A little square grating, its closely set bars red with rust, in the middle of the small door cut in the larger one, served, so to speak, as motif for a knocker, which was attached to it by a ring and which struck on the grinning head of an enormous nail. This knocker, oblong in shape and of the kind our ancestors used to call a Jack-of-the-clock, looked like a big exclamation point; on examining it attentively an antiquarian would have recognized certain traces of the essentially grotesque figure it had formerly represented, now obliterated by long usage. Through the little grating, designed for the purpose of identifying friends in time of civil war, the curious might perceive, at the end of a dark, slimy vault, a few crumbling steps which led into a garden picturesquely enclosed by thick damp walls oozing with moisture and overgrown with tufts of sickly shrubs. These walls were the ramparts, on top of which flourished the gardens of several neighboring houses.

On the ground floor of the house, the most important room was the "hall." The entrance to it was under the arch of the carriage gate. Few people realize the importance of a "hall" in the small towns of Anjou, Touraine, and Berry. The hall is at one and the same time antechamber, drawing room, office, boudoir, and dining room; it is the center of domestic life, the general living room. There the neighborhood barber came twice a year to cut Monsieur Grandet's hair; there the tenants, the curé, the sub-prefect, and the miller's boy came on business. This room, with two windows looking on the street, had a plank floor; gray panels with ancient moldings covered the wall from top to bottom; the bare beams of the ceiling were also painted gray, and the spaces between them were filled in with white plaster which had turned yellow. An old brass clock, encrusted with arabesques in tortoise-shell, adorned the mantel of the ill-cut white stone fireplace. Above it was a greenish mirror, the edges of which, beveled to show its thickness, reflected a thread of light the whole length of a gothic frame in damascened steelwork. The two copper-gilt candelabras, which decorated either side of the mantel-piece, fulfilled a double purpose: by removing the roses, which served as sockets, the main branch could be fitted into a pedestal of bluish marble tipped with old copper, and this pedestal made a candlestick for everyday use. The old-fashioned chairs were up-holstered in tapestries illustrating the fables of La Fontaine; but you had to know this to recognize the subjects, for the colors were so faded and the figures so riddled with darns that it was difficult to make them out.

In the four corners of the hall were built-in cupboards, buffets of a sort, surmounted by a set of filthy shelves. An old card table, the top inlaid as a chess-board, stood in the space between the two windows. Above this table was an oval barometer with a black border enlivened with gilt bands, where the flies had disported themselves with such abandon that the gilding had become problematical. On the wall opposite the fireplace, two portraits in pastel were supposed to represent Madame Grandet's grandfather, old Monsieur de la Bertellière, as a lieutenant in the French Guards, and the late Madame Gentillet dressed as a shepherdess. The two windows were draped in curtains of red corded silk from Tours, tied back by silk cords with ecclesiastical-looking tassels. These luxurious hangings, so little in keeping with Grandet's habits, had, like the mirror, the clock, the tapestried chairs, and the rosewood corner cupboards, been included in the price of the house.

At the window nearest the door stood a straw-bottomed chair mounted on castors in order to raise Madame Grandet to a height which allowed her to observe the passers-by. A work table of stained cherry wood filled up the embrasure, and Eugénie Grandet's little armchair was alongside. For fifteen years mother and daughter, constantly at work in this one spot, had watched the days flow peacefully by from April to November. On the first day of the latter month they could take up their winter station by the fireplace. It was only then that Grandet would allow a fire to be lighted in the hall, and on the thirty-first of March he had it put out regardless either of the frosts of early spring or those of autumn. A foot-warmer filled with embers from the kitchen fire, which Big Nanon managed somehow to save for them, helped Madame and Mademoiselle Grandet through the chillier mornings and evenings of April and October. Mother and daughter looked after the mending of all the household linen and spent their days so conscientiously at this really menial work that if Eugénie wanted to embroider a collar for her mother, she was forced to sit up late at night, deceiving her father to obtain light. For a long time the miser had doled out candles to his daughter and Big Nanon, just as he gave out every morning the bread and other provisions for daily consumption.

Big Nanon was perhaps the one human creature capable of submitting to her master's tyranny. The whole town envied Monsieur and Madame Grandet. Big Nanon, so named because of her five feet eight inches of height, had belonged to Grandet for thirty-five years. Although her wages were only sixty francs a year, she was considered one of the wealthiest domestics in Saumur. These sixty francs, accumulated over a period of thirty-five years, had recently made it possible for her to invest in an annuity of four thousand francs with Lawyer Cruchot. The outcome of Big Nanon's long and persistent economies seemed enormous. Every servant, seeing the poor sexagenarian thus provided for in her old age, was jealous of her, without giving a thought to the hard servitude by which she had won this security.

At twenty-two the poor girl had not been able to find a place anywhere, so repulsive her face had seemed; and in fact this feeling was quite unjust. Her face would have been very much admired on the shoulders of a grenadier guard; but everything in its proper place. When the buildings on a farm where she had looked after the cows burned down, she was obliged to leave and had come to Saumur, filled with that robust courage which stops at nothing, to look for a position. Old Grandet was then thinking of getting married and was eager to set up house. His attention was caught by this girl, who was being turned away from one door after another. A judge of physical strength in his capacity as cooper, he foresaw the profit to be derived from a female built like a Hercules, planted as firmly on her feet as a sixty-year-old oak on its roots, strong in the hips, square in the back, with the hands of a teamster and an integrity as vigorous as her unblemished virtue. Neither the warts that adorned this martial countenance nor its brick-red hue, neither Nanon's sinewy arms nor her rags, dismayed the cooper, who was still of an age when the heart can be touched. So he clothed, shod, and fed the poor girl, paid her wages, and put her to work without treating her too harshly. At this unexpected reception Big Nanon wept secretly for joy and became sincerely attached to the cooper, who nevertheless exploited her in feudal fashion. Nanon did everything. She did the cooking and the rough washing; she took the fine linen to wash it in the Loire and carried it home on her shoulders. She got up at dawn and went to bed late, prepared the meals for all the grape-pickers during the harvest, and kept an eye on the gleaners, defending her master's property like a faithful dog. In short, filled with a blind confidence in him, she obeyed his most ridiculous whims without a murmur.

In the famous year of 1811, with its incredibly laborious harvest, Grandet decided to give Nanon, after twenty years of service, his old watch, the only present she ever received from him. Although he turned his old shoes over to her—she could wear them—it is impossible to consider the quarterly dividend of Grandet's shoes as a gift, because they were so badly worn. Necessity had made this poor girl so niggardly that Grandet had grown to love her as one loves a dog, and Nanon had let him put a spiked collar round her neck of which she no longer felt the pricks. If Grandet cut the bread a little too parsimoniously, she did not complain; she cheerfully shared in the hygienic advantages resulting from the austere diet of the house, where nobody was ever ill. For after all Nanon was one of the family: she laughed when Grandet laughed, was gloomy when he was, stayed out in the cold or came in to get warm when he did, and worked with him. What sweet compensations there were in this equality! Never had the master reproved the servant either for the apricots or the peaches, for the plums or the nectarines, eaten beneath the trees. "Go ahead and enjoy yourself, Nanon," he would say in the years when the branches bent under the fruit till the farmers were forced to feed it to the pigs.

For a farm girl who in her youth had reaped nothing but ill treatment, for a begger in rags given shelter out of charity, Old Grandet's equivocal laugh was a genuine ray of sunshine. Moreover, Nanon's simple heart, her limited intelligence, had room for only one emotion and one idea at a time. Even after thirty-five years she could still see herself as she was when she came to old Grandet's yard, barefooted and tattered, and she could still hear the cooper asking her, "What do you want, dearie?" And her gratitude was ever young. Sometimes Grandet, reflecting that this poor creature had never heard the slightest word of flattery, that she was ignorant of all the tender feelings a woman inspires and could appear one day before God more chaste than the Virgin Mary herself—Grandet, overcome with pity, would look at her and say, "Poor Nanon!" His exclamation was always followed by an indefinable glance from the old servant. The repetition of these words from time to time had long since formed an unbroken chain of friendship to which each exclamation added still another link. There was something vaguely horrible about this pity lodged in Grandet's heart and accepted with real gratitude by his old servant. Yet this shocking pity so typical of a miser, which brought back so many pleasant recollections of economies to the heart of the old cooper, was for Nanon the sum total of happiness. Who wouldn't say, "Poor Nanon!" God will recognize his angels by the inflection of their voices and by their hidden sorrows.

There were a great many households in Saumur where the servants were better treated but where the masters nevertheless received no satisfaction in return. Hence this other saying: "What ever do the Grandets do for their Big Nanon to make her so attached to them? She'd go through fire and water for them!" Her kitchen, with its barred windows looking into the court, was always clean, neat, and cold—a true miser's kitchen, where nothing must be allowed to go to waste. When Nanon had washed her dishes, locked up the remains of the dinner, and put out her fire, she left her kitchen, which was separated from the living room by a corridor, and went to spin by the side of her employers. A single candle sufficed the family for the evening. The servant slept at the end of this corridor in a wretched little closet lit only by a fan-light. Her robust health made it possible for her to live with impunity in this miserable hole from which she could hear the slightest sound in the deep silence that reigned night and day in the house. Like a watch-dog she must have slept with one eye open, resting and standing guard at the same time.

Other parts of the dwelling will be described as they relate to the events of this history; but the sketch just given of the living room, where all the luxury of the household was displayed, may serve to suggest in advance the bareness of the upper stories.

In the year 1819, at the beginning of an evening in the middle of November, Big Nanon lit the fire for the first time. The autumn had been fine. This particular day marked an occasion never overlooked by the Cruchotins and the Grassinistes. And so the six antagonists were preparing to arrive, fully armed and ready for combat, in the Grandet hall, there to outdo each other in tokens of friendship. That morning all Saumur had seen Madame and Mademoiselle Grandet, accompanied by Nanon, on their way to mass at the parish church, and everyone remembered that this was Mademoiselle Eugénie's birthday. Lawyer Cruchot, Abbé Cruchot, and Monsieur C. de Bonfons, calculating the hour at which dinner would be over, were hurrying to arrive before the des Grassins to be the first to congratulate Mademoiselle Grandet. All three carried enormous bunches of flowers gathered in their tiny greenhouses. The stems of the flowers that the judge intended to present were ingeniously tied with a white satin ribbon adorned with gold fringe.

Early that morning Grandet, following his usual custom on these memorable occasions—Eugénie's birthday and saint's day—surprised her in bed and solemnly proffered his paternal gift consisting, as it had for the past thirteen years, of a rare gold piece. Madame Grandet usually gave her daughter either a winter dress or a summer dress according to the season. These two dresses and the gold coins that she garnered in on New Year's Day and her father's name-day constituted a small capital of about a hundred crowns, which Grandet liked to see her accumulate. Wasn't it merely taking his money out of one strong-box to put it into another, and, as it were, cultivating the avarice of his heiress from whom he occasionally demanded an accounting of her fortune, formerly added to by the La Bertellières?

"It will be your marriage dozen," he would say.

The "dozen" is an ancient custom which still flourishes and is religiously preserved in certain provinces of central France. In Berry and in Anjou, when a young girl marries, her family or that of her husband must give her, according to their means, a purse containing twelve coins or twelve dozen coins or twelve hundred coins of silver or gold. The poorest shepherdess would not think of getting married without her dozen, even if it were made up only of penny pieces. In Issoudun people still talk about a certain dozen consisting of a hundred and forty-four Portuguese gold pieces, which was given to a rich heiress. Pope Clement VII, uncle of Catherine de Medici, on marrying her to Henry II, made her a present of a dozen ancient gold coins of great value.

At dinner, the father, overjoyed at seeing his Eugénie so much prettier in her new dress, exclaimed, "As it's Eugénie's birthday, let's have a fire! It will bring good luck."

"Mademoiselle will certainly be married before the year is out," said Big Nanon, carrying away the remains of a goose, the coopers' pheasant.

"I don't see a suitable match for her in Saumur," replied Madame Grandet, looking at her husband with a timid air which, considering her age, revealed the complete conjugal servitude under which the poor woman suffered.

Grandet looked at his daughter and shouted gaily, "The child's twenty-three today; we'll soon have to get busy."

Eugénie and her mother silently exchanged a significant glance.

Madame Grandet was a thin, dried-out-looking woman, yellow as a quince, awkward and slow, one of those women who seem born to be tyrannized over. She had big bones, a big nose, a big forehead, big bulging eyes, and presented, at first glance, a vague resemblance to those mealy fruits which have long since lost all juice and savor. Her teeth were black and sparse, her mouth was wrinkled, and she had a nutcracker chin. She was a good woman, a true La Bertellière. Abbé Cruchot managed to find opportunities of telling her that she hadn't been too bad-looking, and she believed him. An angelic sweetness, the resignation of an insect tormented by children, a rare piety, a steadfast equanimity of soul, and a kind heart made her universally pitied and respected. Her husband never gave her more than six francs at a time for her personal expenses. Although ridiculous in appearance, this woman, who by her dowry and her legacies had brought Old Grandet more than three hundred thousand francs, had always felt so profoundly humiliated by a dependence and slavery against which the gentleness of her soul forbade her to rebel that she had never asked for a cent nor passed any remark on the papers that Lawyer Cruchot presented for her signature. This stupid and secret pride, this nobility of soul, constantly ignored and wounded by Grandet, dominated her conduct.

Madame Grandet always wore a dress of greenish levantine silk and she usually made it last almost a year. With it she wore a neckerchief of white cotton, a straw hat, and almost always a black taffeta apron. As she went out but little, she was easy on shoes. And she never wanted anything for herself. Grandet, seized sometimes with remorse when he remembered how long a time had passed since the day he had last given his wife six francs, always insisted on pin-money for her in selling the year's harvest. The four or five louis presented by the Dutch or Belgian purchaser of the Grandet vintage made up the bulk of Madame Grandet's annual income. But when she had received the five louis, her husband often said to her, as though they had a common purse, "Can you lend me a few cents?" And the poor woman, delighted to be able to do something for the man desig- nated by her confessor as her lord and master, gave him back, during the course of the winter, the greater part of her pin-money. Whenever Grandet drew out of his pocket the five-franc piece allotted monthly to his daughter for incidental expenses—thread, needles, and clothes—he never failed to say to his wife, after hav- ing buttoned up his waistcoat pocket, "And you, Mother, do you need any money?"

"My dear," replied Madame Grandet, moved by a sense of maternal dignity, "we'll see about that."

What a waste of nobility! Grandet thought he was extremely generous to his wife. Philosophers who come across people like Nanon, Madame Grandet, and Eugénie are perhaps justified in concluding that Providence is by nature essentially ironical.

After this dinner, at which the question of Eugénie's marriage was discussed for the first time, Nanon went up to look for a bottle of black currant brandy in Monsieur Grandet's room and almost fell downstairs.

"Clumsy creature," said her master. "Surely you're not going to start falling downstairs too?"

"It's that step on your staircase, sir, that's given way."

"She's right," said Madame Grandet. "You should have had it fixed long ago. Eugénie almost sprained her ankle on it yester- day."

"Come," said Grandet to Nanon, noticing that she had turned quite pale, "as it's Eugénie's birthday and you almost fell down, have a little drink of black currant brandy to pull yourself to- gether."

"Goodness me, I've certainly earned it," said Nanon. "In my place lots of people would have broken the bottle, but I would rather have broken my elbow than let it fall."

"Poor Nanon!" said Grandet, pouring out the brandy.

"Did you hurt yourself?" Eugénie asked, looking at her with concern.

"No, for I saved myself by falling on my behind."

"All right then," said Grandet. "As it's Eugénie's birthday, I'm going to fix your step for you. You people don't know enough to put your foot in the corner where it's still solid."

Grandet took the candle and, leaving his wife, his daughter, and his servant with no light but that of the brightly burning fire, went off to the bakehouse to get boards, nails, and his tools.

"Do you need any help?" shouted Nanon, when she heard him hammering on the staircase.

"No, no, I'm an old hand at this," replied the former cooper.

Just as Grandet was himself repairing his worm-eaten staircase, and whistling at the top of his lungs in memory of the days of his youth, the three Cruchots knocked at the door.

"Is that you, Monsieur Cruchot?" asked Nanon, peering out through the little grill.

"It is," replied the judge.

Nanon opened the door, and by the light of the fire, which was reflected under the arch, the three Cruchots were able to see the way into the hall.

"Ah, you've come to celebrate," said Nanon, smelling the flowers.

"Excuse me, gentlemen," shouted Grandet, recognizing the voices of his friends. "I'll be right with you! I'm not proud. I'm patching up my own staircase."

"Go to it, go to it, Monsieur Grandet. Every man is mayor in his own house," said the judge sententiously, laughing alone at this allusion which nobody else understood.

Madame and Mademoiselle Grandet got up; whereupon the judge, taking advantage of the darkness, said to Eugénie:

"Do permit me, Mademoiselle, to wish you on this, the occasion of your birthday, a long succession of happy years and the continuation of that good health which you now enjoy."

He presented her with a large bunch of flowers of a kind rarely seen in Saumur; then, taking the heiress by the elbows, he kissed her on either side of her neck with an assurance that embarrassed Eugénie. The judge, who looked like a big rusty nail, thought this was the way to woo a lady.

"Make yourself at home," said Grandet, coming in. "You're right there when it comes to celebrating birthdays, Judge!"

"But with Mademoiselle," replied Abbé Cruchot, armed with his bouquet, "every day would be a holiday for my nephew."

The abbé kissed Eugénie's hand. As for Lawyer Cruchot, he didn't hesitate to kiss her on both cheeks, saying, "How we shoot up! Dear me! Twelve months in every year."

Replacing the candle in front of the clock, Grandet, who never let go of a joke but kept harping on it endlessly when it seemed funny to him, said, "As it's Eugénie's birthday, let's light up the torches!"

He carefully removed the branches of the candelabra, put a socket on each pedestal, took from Nanon a new tallow candle with a twist of paper on the end, placed it firmly in the socket, and lit it. He then went to sit down beside his wife, looking in turn at his friends, his daughter, and the two candles. Abbé Cruchot, a round, chubby little man, with a flat red wig and the face of an old woman addicted to gambling, remarked as he stretched out his feet, which were well shod in stout shoes adorned with silver buckles, "The des Grassins haven't come yet?"

"Not yet," said Grandet.

"I suppose they are coming though?" asked the old notary, twisting up his face, which was as full of holes as a skimming-ladle.

"I think so," replied Madame Grandet.

"Are your grapes all harvested?" Judge de Bonfons asked Grandet.

"Everywhere!" answered the old wine-grower, getting up to pace the length of the room and throwing out his chest with a gesture as proud as the word everywhere.

Through the door of the passageway leading to the kitchen he caught sight of Big Nanon, sitting beside her fire with a candle and getting ready to spin there in order not to intrude on the party.

"Nanon," said he, going out into the passage, "put out your fire and your candle and come in here with us. Good Lord, the hall is big enough for all of us."

"But, Monsieur, you're having company!"

"Aren't you just as good as they are? They're all descended from Adam just like you."

Grandet went back to the judge and said, "Have you sold your vintage?"

"No, by Jove, I'm hanging on to it. If the wine's good now, in two years it will be even better. The wine-growers, as you know, have pledged themselves to keep to the prices agreed on, and this year the Belgians won't get the better of us. If they go away, all right. They'll be back again."

"Yes, but let's be sure we agree," said Grandet in a tone which made the judge quake.

"Could he be making a deal with them?" thought Cruchot.

At that moment a knock at the door announced the arrival of the des Grassins, which interrupted a conversation begun between Madame Grandet and the abbé.

Madame des Grassins was one of those lively, plump little women, all pink and white, who, thanks to the monastic routine of life in the provinces and to the regular habits of a virtuous existence, are still young at forty. They are like the last roses of autumn, pleasant to look at, but whose petals have a suggestion of frost about them and whose perfume is growing weak. She dressed quite well, had her clothes sent from Paris, set the fashion for the town of Saumur, and gave parties. Her husband, a former quartermaster in the Imperial Guard, seriously wounded at Austerlitz and retired, preserved in spite of his respect for Grandet, the free and easy manner of the military man.

"Good evening, Grandet," he said to the wine-grower, giving him his hand, and assuming that air of condescension with which he always crushed the Cruchots.

"Mademoiselle," he said to Eugénie, after having greeted Madame Grandet, "you are as beautiful and wise as ever, and I really don't know what one could wish for you." Then he presented her with a little box, which his servant had brought and which contained heather from the Cape, a plant recently imported into Europe and very rare.

Madame des Grassins embraced Eugénie very affectionately, squeezed her hand, and said, "Adolphe has undertaken to present my little remembrance."

A tall, fair young man, pale and delicate-looking, with quite good manners, who seemed shy, but who had just squandered in Paris, where he had gone to study law, eight or ten thousand francs over and above his board and lodging, now came forward, kissed Eugénie on both cheeks, and handed her a workbox of which all the fittings were of silver gilt—a really shoddy article, in spite of the plate on which the letters E. G. fairly well engraved in Gothic characters might give the impression of careful workmanship. As she opened it, Eugénie experienced one of those unlooked-for and perfect delights which make a young girl blush, quiver, and tremble with pleasure. She looked over at her father as though asking his permission to accept, and Monsieur Grandet said "Take it, daughter!" in a tone that would have done credit to an actor.

The three Cruchots were left dumbfounded by the happy, excited glance flashed at Adolphe des Grassins by the heiress, to whom such lavishness was quite incredible. Monsieur des Grassins offered Grandet a pinch of snuff, took one himself, brushed off the grains that had fallen on the ribbon of the Legion of Honor attached to the buttonhole of his blue frock coat, then looked at the Cruchots with an air which seemed to say, "Parry that thrust if you can!" Madame des Grassins cast her eyes on the blue jars which held the Cruchot bouquets as she looked for their presents with the simulated good faith of a malicious woman. At this delicate juncture Abbé Cruchot let the group sit down in a circle in front of the fire and went to walk up and down at the other end of the room with Grandet. When the two old men reached the embrasure of the window farthest away from the des Grassins, the priest said in the miser's ear, "Those people throw money out of the window."

"What difference does that make if it falls into my cellar?" retorted the old wine-grower.

"If you wanted to give your daughter gold scissors, you could well afford to do so," said the abbé.

"I give her something better than scissors," replied Grandet.

"My nephew's an idiot," thought the abbé, looking at the judge, whose tousled hair added still further to the unattractiveness of his sallow face. "Couldn't he have thought up some little trifle that would have made an impression?"

"Shall we have our usual game of cards, Madame Grandet?" asked Madame des Grassins.

"But since we're all here, we *could* have two tables. . . ."

"As it's Eugénie's birthday, why don't you play lotto all together," said Old Grandet. "These two children can join in." The former cooper, who never played games of any kind, indicated his daughter and Adolphe. "Come, Nanon, set up the tables."

"We'll help you, Mademoiselle Nanon," said Madame des Grassins gaily, delighted at the pleasure she had given Eugénie.

"I've never been so happy in my life," said the heiress. "I've never seen anything so pretty anywhere."

"It was Adolphe who chose it and brought it back from Paris," whispered Madame des Grassins.

"Just keep right on, you damned intriguing female!" said the judge to himself. "If ever you have a lawsuit, you or your husband, you'll never win it."

The notary, sitting in his corner, gazed calmly at the abbé, thinking to himself, "No matter what the des Grassins do, my fortune, my brother's, and my nephew's, add up to eleven hundred thousand francs. The des Grassins have at most only half that amount, and they have a daughter. Let them give what they like; heiress and presents too will all belong to us one day."

By half past eight two tables were ready. Pretty Madame des Grassins had managed to place her son beside Eugénie. The actors in this apparently commonplace but really fascinating scene, provided with gaudy cards with numbers on them and blue glass counters, seemed to be listening to the witticisms of the old notary, who never drew a number without making some remark. But they were all thinking of Monsieur Grandet's millions. The old cooper looked smugly at the pink feathers and fashionable clothes of Madame des Grassins, at the banker's martial countenance, at Adolphe, the judge, the abbé, and the notary, and said to himself, "They're all after my money; they submit to this boredom for the sake of my daughter. Ha! My daughter's not for any of them. But they're all useful as harpoons to fish with!"

This family gaiety in the old gray room, badly lighted by two candles; these bursts of laughter, accompanied by the whir of Big Nanon's spinning wheel and sincere only on the lips of Eugénie and her mother; this paltriness of mind in conjunction with such high stakes; this young girl, who, like those innocent birds, un-

witting victims of the high price put on them, was being hunted
down, hemmed in by a display of friendship of which she was
the dupe; all these things contributed to make the scene a tragi-
comedy. And wasn't it after all a scene common to all times and
all places, but reduced to its simplest terms? The figure of
Grandet, exploiting the false sentiments of the two families, and
making enormous profits out of them, dominated the whole
scene and gave it meaning. Isn't this the only god in which we
believe today, money, in all its power, symbolized in a single
human image? The softer emotions of life occupied only a sec-
ondary place here; they animated the three guileless hearts of
Nanon, Eugénie, and her mother. Yet what ignorance there was
in their simplicity! Eugénie and her mother knew nothing of
Grandet's fortune; they judged the world only in the light of
their own vague notions, and neither valued nor despised money,
because they were used to doing without it. Their feelings, repressed without their knowledge, yet still surviving, and the
isolation of their existence, made them curious exceptions in this
gathering of people for whom only the material things counted.
How terrible is man's estate! There is not one of his joys which
does not spring out of some form of ignorance.

Just at the moment when Madame Grandet won a sum of sixteen cents, the largest amount that had ever been pooled in this
room, and while Big Nanon was laughing with delight to see
her mistress pocketing this great wealth, there was such a re-
sounding knock at the door of the house that the women jumped
out of their chairs at the noise.

"Nobody in Saumur would knock like that," said the notary.

"The idea of anyone banging like that!" exclaimed Nanon.
"Do they want to break down the door?"

"Who the devil can it be?" shouted Grandet.

Nanon picked up one of the two candles and went out, accompanied by Grandet, to open the door.

"Grandet! Grandet!" cried his wife, who, impelled by a vague sense of fear, was rushing toward the door of the room.

The card players looked at each other.

"Should we go too?" asked Monsieur des Grassins. "That knock sounded dangerous to me."

Monsieur des Grassins had barely time to catch a glimpse of a young man accompanied by the stage-coach porter, who was carrying two huge boxes and dragging several suitcases. Grandet turned brusquely toward his wife and said, "Madame Grandet, go back to your lotto. Let me talk to the gentleman." Then he quickly closed the door of the hall, where the excited players resumed their places but without going on with the game.

"Is it anybody from Saumur, Monsieur des Grassins?" asked his wife.

"No, it's a traveler."

"He could only have come from Paris."

"That's true," said the notary, pulling out his old-fashioned watch, which was nearly two inches thick and looked like a Dutch man-of-war. "It's nine o'clock. Bless my soul! The mail coach is never late."

"Is the gentleman young?" asked Abbé Cruchot.

"Yes," replied Monsieur des Grassins. "And he's brought luggage weighing at least three hundred kilos."

"Nanon hasn't come back," said Eugénie.

"It must be one of your relations," said the judge.

"Let's place our bets," cried Madame Grandet gently. "I could tell from his voice that Monsieur Grandet was annoyed. Perhaps he won't like it if he notices that we are discussing his affairs."

"Mademoiselle," said Adolphe to his neighbor, "it must surely be your cousin Grandet, a very handsome young man, whom I saw at a ball given by Baron de Nucingen." Adolphe did not go on; his mother stepped on his foot. Then, asking him aloud for two cents to bet with, she whispered in his ear, "Will you shut up, you silly idiot!"

At that moment Grandet returned without Big Nanon, whose step with that of the porter could be heard on the stairs. He was followed by the traveler, who for the past few minutes had aroused so much curiosity and so intensely preoccupied the imaginations of the card players that his arrival in this house and his descent into the midst of this little world might be compared to that of a snail into a beehive or to the introduction of a peacock into some obscure village farmyard.

"Sit down by the fire," Grandet said to him.

Before sitting down, the young stranger made a graceful bow to the assembled company. The men got up to reply with a polite inclination, and the ladies made a ceremonious curtsy.

"You must be cold, sir," said Madame Grandet. "Perhaps you've come from . . ."

"That's a woman for you!" said the old wine-grower, looking up from the perusal of a letter he was holding in his hand. "Let the young man rest."

"But, Father, perhaps there's something the gentleman would like?" said Eugénie.

"He's got a tongue," replied the wine-grower severely.

Only the stranger was surprised at this scene. The others were used to the old man's tyrannical ways. However, after the exchange of these two questions and answers, the stranger got up, and standing with his back to the fire, lifted one foot after the other to warm the soles of his topboots. Then he said to Eugénie, "Thank you, Cousin, I dined at Tours. And," he went on, looking at Grandet, "I don't need anything. I'm not even tired."

"You've come from the capital, sir?" asked Madame des Grassins.

Charles, as the son of Monsieur Grandet of Paris was called, hearing someone address him, took up a lorgnette that hung by a chain around his neck, applied it to his right eye to examine both what was on the table and the people sitting around it, stared most impertinently at Madame des Grassins, and said, when he had seen everything, "Yes, Madame. You're playing lotto, aunt," he added. "Do go on with your game. It's much too amusing to stop."

"I was sure it was the cousin," thought Madame des Grassins, ogling him from time to time.

"Forty-seven!" shouted the old abbé. "Mark it down, Madame des Grassins, isn't that your number?"

Monsieur des Grassins put a counter on his wife's card. Madame, filled with sad forebodings, was watching now the cousin from Paris and now Eugénie and had forgotten all about lotto. From time to time the young heiress cast a furtive glance at her cousin, and the banker's wife could easily detect in her a mounting surprise or curiosity.

THE COUSIN FROM PARIS

MONSIEUR CHARLES GRANDET, a handsome young man of twenty-two, presented at this moment a singular contrast to the worthy provincials, who, considerably disgusted by his aristocratic manners, were studying them in order to ridicule him. This requires an explanation. At twenty-two young people are still close enough to childhood to drop into childish behavior. In all probability ninety-nine out of a hundred would have behaved just as Charles Grandet did. Some days before, his father had told him to go and spend a few months with his uncle in Saumur. Perhaps Monsieur Grandet of Paris had Eugénie in mind. Charles, who found himself in the provinces for the first time in his life, decided to make his appearance with the authority of a young man of fashion, to flabbergast the whole district by his luxury, to make his visit a memorable event, and to import the latest refinements from Paris. In a word, he intended to spend more time polishing his nails in Saumur than he had ever done in Paris and to affect that studied elegance which a young dandy sometimes discards in favor of a casualness not without charm.

So Charles took with him the handsomest hunting costume, the handsomest gun, the handsomest knife, the handsomest sheath in Paris. He took his collection of elaborate waistcoats. There were all kinds—gray, white, black, scarab-colored; some were shot with gold, some spangled, and some iridescent; some were double-breasted with shawl collars or straight collars and some had turned over collars; and some buttoned all the way up with gold buttons. He took every type of collar and cravat in favor at that time. He took two coats made by Buisson and all his finest linen. He took his beautiful gold-fitted dressing-case, a present from his mother. He took all his elegant knick-knacks, not forgetting a ravishing little writing-case presented to him by the most delightful woman in the world, for him at least, by a great lady whom he called Annette, and who was now traveling maritally, boringly, in Scotland, a victim of certain suspicions which required the momentary sacrifice of her happiness; and a great deal of pretty note paper on which to write her a letter every fortnight. In short it was as complete a cargo of Parisian trifles as he could possibly make it. From the hunting crop which serves to provoke a duel to the beautifully chased pistols which end it, every implement used by a young idler to cultivate the soil of his life was there. His father having told him to travel alone and modestly, he had reserved the coupé for himself, pleased enough not to have to damage a delightful traveling carriage specially ordered to take him to his Annette, the great lady who . . . etc., and whom he was to rejoin the following June in Baden Charles expected to meet scores of people at his uncle's, to hunt in his uncle's forests, in fact to lead the usual life on a country estate. It didn't occur to him to look for his uncle in Saumur, where he had merely inquired about him in asking the way to Froidfond; but hearing that he was in town, he supposed he would find him in some great mansion.

In order to make a suitable first appearance at his uncle's, whether at Saumur or at Froidfond, he had put on his most elegant traveling attire, studied yet simple, really "adorable," to use the word which at that time epitomized the peculiar perfections of people or things. He had just had a hairdresser in Tours recurl his beautiful chestnut hair. He had changed his linen there and put on a black satin cravat which, combined with a round collar, served to frame his fair and smiling face agreeably. A traveling coat, partly unbuttoned, nipped in his waist and disclosed a cashmere waistcoat with a shawl collar under which was a second white waistcoat. His watch, carelessly dropped into a pocket, was attached to one of his buttonholes by a short gold chain. His gray trousers, buttoned at the sides, were set off at the seams with patterns in black silk embroidery. He gracefully twirled a cane whose chased gold knob could not mar the freshness of his gray gloves. Above all, his cap was in excellent taste. Only a Parisian, and a Parisian of the most exalted sphere, could array himself thus without appearing ridiculous and harmonize in fatuity all these fopperies, which besides were carried off with a dashing air, the air of a young man who has a fine brace of pistols, a sure aim—and Annette.

Now if you would understand the mutual surprise of the Saumurois and the young Parisian, and visualize perfectly the radiant gleam cast by the traveler's elegance into the midst of the gray shadows of the hall and of the figures composing this family picture, try and imagine what the Cruchots looked like. All three took snuff, and had long ago ceased to care about the drip from their noses or the little black specks sprinkled over the frills of their dingy shirts with their crumpled collars and yellowing pleats. Their limp cravats twisted into ropes as soon as they tied them round their necks. They had such enormous quantities of linen that they had to have it washed only twice a year; they stored it at the bottom of their cupboards, where time was able to communicate to it its gray and aging hues. These people combined to perfection inelegance and senility. Their faces, as faded as their shabby clothes, as wrinkled as their trousers, seemed worn, shriveled, and contorted. The general negligence of the other costumes, without finish or freshness, as they so often are in the provinces, where people unconsciously cease to dress for each other and begin to consider the price of a pair of gloves, was ın harmony with the slovenliness of the Cruchots. Disgust with fashions was the only subject on which the Grassinistes and the Cruchotins were in perfect agreement.

Whenever the young Parisian held up his lorgnette to investigate the peculiar appurtenances of the hall, the beams of the ceiling, the color of the woodwork, and the specks that the flies had imprinted there in sufficient number to punctuate the *Encyclopédie méthodique* and the *Moniteur,* the lotto players raised their heads and examined him with as much curiosity as they would have shown for a giraffe. Monsieur des Grassins and his son, though not unfamiliar with the appearance of a man of fashion, nevertheless shared in the astonishment of their neighbors, whether they fell under the indefinable influence of the general feeling or whether they concurred in it, seeming to say to their compatriots by glances full of irony, "That's what they're like in Paris." Moreover, they were all quite free to observe Charles at leisure without fear of displeasing the master of the house. Grandet was absorbed in the long letter he was holding, and to read it he had taken possession of the only candle on the table without consideration for his guests or their comfort.

Eugénie, to whom such perfection either of dress or person was entirely unknown, saw in her cousin a creature descended from some heavenly region. She inhaled with delight the fragrance given off by that glossy hair so gracefully curled. She would have liked to touch the satiny kid of those exquisite gloves. She envied Charles his small hands, his complexion, the freshness and delicacy of his features. In short, if it is possible to sum up the impressions that the young dandy produced on an unsophisticated girl perpetually occupied in mending stockings and patching up her father's wardrobe, whose whole life had been spent beneath these dirty rafters without seeing more than one person an hour pass by in this silent street—the sight of her cousin aroused in her heart delicately pleasurable sensations like those excited in a young man by the dreamlike figures of women drawn by Westall in the English "keepsakes," and engraved by the Findens with so deft a burin that we hardly dare breathe on the paper for fear of wafting away these celestial apparitions. Charles drew out of his pocket a handkerchief embroidered by the great lady who was traveling in Scotland. On seeing this beautiful handiwork wrought with love in the hours lost to love, Eugénie looked at her cousin to see if he were really going to use it. Charles's manners, his gestures, the way he held his lorgnette, his affected insolence, his scorn for the workbox which had just given the rich heiress so much pleasure and which he obviously found worthless or ridiculous—in short, everything that shocked the Cruchots and the des Grassins filled her with such delight that before falling asleep she was to dream a long time about this paragon of cousins.

The lotto numbers were being drawn very slowly, but soon the game came to an end. Big Nanon came in and announced in a loud voice: "Madame, you'll have to give me sheets to make the gentleman's bed."

Madame Grandet followed Nanon out of the room. Madame des Grassins then said in a low voice, "Let's take back our pennies and stop playing." Everybody picked up his two pennies from the old chipped saucer where he had placed them; then the whole assembly moved in a body and wheeled round at an angle of ninety degrees toward the fire.

"You've finished?" said Grandet, without looking up from his letter.

"Yes, yes," replied Madame des Grassins, going over to sit beside Charles.

Eugénie, actuated by one of those impulses which are born in the hearts of young girls when a tender emotion first takes up its abode there, left the room to go and help her mother and Nanon. If she had been questioned by a shrewd confessor, she would doubtless have admitted that she was thinking neither of her mother nor of Nanon, but that she was filled with a keen desire to inspect her cousin's room in order to see what she could do for him, just to put something or other there for him, to remedy any oversight, to anticipate all his wants, to make the room as elegant and tidy as possible. Eugénie already believed that she alone was capable of understanding the ideas and tastes of her cousin. She arrived just in time to prove to her mother and Nanon, who were coming back thinking they had done everything, that everything was still to be done. She suggested to Nanon that she warm the sheets with embers from the fire; she herself put a cloth on the table and told Nanon to be sure to change it every morning. She convinced her mother of the necessity of lighting a good fire in the fireplace and persuaded Nanon to bring up a great pile of wood into the corridor, without saying anything to her father. She ran to fetch from one of the corner cupboards in the hall an old lacquered tray inherited from the late Monsieur de la Bertellière, took also a six-sided crystal goblet, a little tarnished spoon, and an antique flask engraved with cupids, and triumphantly placed the whole collection on a corner of the mantelpiece. More ideas had poured into her mind in a quarter of an hour than had ever before occurred to her in her whole life.

"Mama," she said, "my cousin will never be able to stand the smell of tallow. Suppose we buy a wax candle?" And she went off, light as a bird, to get from her purse the five-franc piece that she had received as her monthly allowance. "Here, Nanon," she said, "hurry up!"

"But what will your father say?" This terrifying protest was made by Madame Grandet when she saw her daughter armed with a sugar bowl of old Sèvres china brought back by Grandet from the castle of Froidfond. "And where will you get the sugar? Are you mad?"

"Oh, Mama, Nanon can just as well buy the sugar as the candle."

"But your father?"

"Surely his nephew shouldn't have to go without his glass of sugared water? Besides, he'll never notice."

"Your father sees everything," said Madame Grandet, shaking her head.

Nanon hesitated; she knew her master.

"Go on, Nanon, as it's my birthday!"

Nanon gave a loud laugh on hearing the first joke her young mistress had ever made and obeyed her. While Eugénie and her mother were doing their best to embellish the room Monsieur Grandet had assigned to his nephew, Charles found himself the object of the attentions of Madame des Grassins, who was trying to flirt with him.

"It's very courageous of you, sir," said she, "to give up the pleasures of the capital in winter to come and live in Saumur. But if we don't frighten you too much, you'll see that there's entertainment to be had here too."

She gave him one of those flirtatious glances typical of the provinces, where the women express in their eyes so much coyness and circumspection that they impart to them that delicate concupiscence peculiar to those of ecclesiastics for whom any pleasure is either a theft or a transgression. Charles felt so completely out of his element in this room and so far away from the vast manor and sumptuous existence he had imagined to be his uncle's that as he looked at Madame des Grassins, he began to see in her a faint resemblance to the faces of Paris. He responded gracefully to the overtures made to him, and they embarked very naturally on a conversation during which Madame des Grassins gradually lowered her voice in keeping with its confidential nature. Both she and Charles felt the same need to exchange confidences. So after a few moments of coquettish chatter and semi-serious nonsense, the adroit provincial was able to say to him with no fear of being heard by the others, who were discussing the sale of wines, with which all Saumur was preoccupied for the moment:

"Sir, if you will honor us with a visit, you will certainly give as much pleasure to my husband as to me. Our drawing room is the only one in Saumur where you will meet both the aristocracy of commerce and the nobility. We belong to both groups, who consent to meet only there, and just because they have a good time. My husband—I say it with pride—has the respect of both classes. So we shall try to relieve the boredom of your stay here. If you have to spend all your time at Monsieur Grandet's, good heavens, what will become of you? Your uncle is an old skinflint, who thinks only of propagating his vines; your aunt is a pious soul who can't put two ideas together; and your cousin is a little simpleton, uneducated, common, without a dowry, who spends her time mending dish-towels."

"She's not a bad sort, this woman," said Charles Grandet to himself as he replied to the simperings of Madame des Grassins.

"It seems to me, my dear, that you're monopolizing the young man," said the big, fat banker, laughing.

At these words the notary and the judge made a few more or less malicious remarks; but the abbé looked at them knowingly; and as he took a pinch of snuff and passed his snuffbox round, summed up what was in their minds by saying, "Who is better qualified than Madame to do the honors of Saumur for the young gentleman?"

"Now what do you mean by that, Abbé?" asked Monsieur des Grassins.

"I mean it, sir, in the best possible sense for you, for your wife, for the town of Saumur, and for the gentleman," added the wily old man, turning toward Charles.

Without seeming to pay the slightest attention, Abbé Cruchot had been able to guess at the conversation between Charles and Madame des Grassins.

"Sir," said Adolphe at last to Charles in a manner intended to seem offhand, "I don't know if you remember me at all; I had the pleasure of being opposite you at a ball given by the Baron de Nucingen, and . . ."

"Perfectly, sir, perfectly," replied Charles, surprised to find himself the center of attention.

"This is your son?" he asked Madame des Grassins.

The abbé gave the mother a malicious glance.

"Yes, sir," said she.

"You must have been very young when you were in Paris?" replied Charles, addressing himself to Adolphe.

"Well you know, sir," said the abbé, "we send them off to Babylon as soon as they've been weaned."

Madame des Grassins interrogated the abbé with a glance of amazing penetration.

"You have to come to the provinces," he went on, "to find women of thirty years or so as youthful-looking as Madame, with sons on the point of graduating in law. I can still remember the days when the young men and ladies stood up on their chairs to watch you dance at a ball, Madame," added the abbé, turning toward his female adversary. "For me your triumphs are of yesterday. . . ."

"Oh, the old scoundrel!" said Madame des Grassins to herself. "Has he found me out?"

"It looks as if I'd be quite a success in Saumur," said Charles to himself, unbuttoning his coat, putting his hand in his waistcoat, and looking far into the distance in imitation of the pose given to Lord Byron by Chantrey.

Old Grandet's inattention, or rather the preoccupation into which the reading of his letter had plunged him, did not escape the notice either of the notary or the judge, who were trying to guess at the contents from the almost imperceptible movements of the old man's face, which was strongly illuminated by the candle. The wine-grower had difficulty in maintaining the usual calm of his expression. It is easy to imagine the look that came over his face on reading this tragic letter:

My dear brother: It is almost twenty-three years since we have seen each other. My marriage was the occasion of our last interview, after which we parted on good terms with one another. Naturally, I could hardly foresee that you would one day be the sole support of our family, whose prosperity gave you such satisfaction then. When this letter reaches your hands, I shall no longer exist. In my position I did not wish to survive the disgrace of bankruptcy. I have clung to the edge of the abyss to the last moment, hoping always to be able to keep afloat. I had to let go. The combined bankruptcies of my broker and of Roguin, my notary, have swept away my last resources and left me nothing. I am in the painful position of owing nearly four millions with assets of only one million. The wines I have in storage are subject at this moment to the fall in prices caused by the abundance and quality of your harvest. In three days Paris will say: "Monsieur Grandet was a rogue!" And I, the soul of honor, shall lie in a shroud of infamy. I have stripped my son both of his name, which I have besmirched, and of his mother's fortune. He knows nothing of all this, my unhappy son whom I have idolized. We said a loving farewell to each other. He was unaware, fortunately, that the tide of my life was ebbing out in this last good-bye. Will he curse me one day? My dear brother, the curses of our children are a terrible thing; they can appeal against ours, but theirs are irrevocable. Grandet, you are older than I, you owe me your protection. Act so that Charles may cast no bitter word on my grave! Brother, if I were writing you in my own blood and tears, there vould be less anguish in it than I am putting into this letter; for

I would weep, I would bleed, I would die, I would no longer suf-
fer; but I do suffer and I gaze dry-eyed at death.

From now on you are Charles's father! He has no relatives on
his mother's side, you know the reason. Why did I not heed the
prejudices of society? Why did I yield to love? Why did I marry
the illegitimate daughter of a great lord? Charles has no family
now. Oh, my unhappy son! My son! Listen, Grandet, I have not
come to you to beg for anything for myself; in any case, your
property is perhaps not extensive enough to carry a mortgage of
three millions. But for the sake of my son, mark you, brother, I
clasp my hands beseechingly when I think of you. Dying, I con-
fide Charles to your care, Grandet. And now I can contemplate
my pistol without suffering, in the thought that you will be a
father to him. Charles loved me well; I was so good to him; I
never opposed him; he will never curse me. Besides, you will see,
he is gentle; he takes after his mother; he will never cause you
grief. Poor boy! Accustomed to the enjoyments of luxury, he has
never known the privations to which both you and I were con-
demned by the poverty of our early years. . . . And now he is
ruined and alone. Yes, all his friends will desert him, and it is I
who have brought this humiliation upon him. Ah, would that I
had the strength to fire the shot that would send him to join his
mother in heaven! Madness! I return to my misfortune and that
of Charles. I have sent him to you so that you can break the news
to him gently of my death and his own future. Be a father to
him, but a kind father. Don't tear him away all of a sudden from
his idle life; it would be the death of him. I beg him on bended
knee to renounce all claims which, as his mother's heir, he may
have against my estate. But it's a superfluous plea; he is honorable
and he will realize that he should not appear among my credi-
tors. Persuade him to give up the right to everything he would
inherit from me in due course. Reveal to him the harsh condi-
tions under which he must now live because of me; and if he

still retains some love for me, tell him in my name that all is not lost for him. Yes, work, which saved both of us, can restore the fortune of which I deprived him, and if he is willing to listen to his father's voice, which for his sake would emerge for a moment from the tomb, let him depart, let him go to the Indies. Brother, Charles is an upright and courageous young man; you must give him goods to trade with; he would die rather than not return to you the original capital that you lend him, for you will lend it to him, Grandet! If not you will suffer remorse. Ah, were my child not to find aid nor kindness in you, I would demand of the Lord eternal vengeance on your harshness.

If I had been able to save anything at all, I would have had the right to give him something back out of his mother's estate; but my last monthly payments have absorbed all my resources. I should have preferred not to die uncertain of my son's fate; I should like to have felt the sacred promise implicit in the warmth of your hand; it would have reassured me. But time is running short. While Charles is traveling, I shall be drawing up my balance sheet. I shall try to prove by the good faith of my accounts that my disaster is due neither to guilt nor dishonesty. Am I not doing this for Charles's sake? Farewell, brother. May all God's blessings be yours in the generous guardianship which I entrust to you and which, I doubt not, you will accept. There will ever be a voice praying for you in that world to which we must all adjourn some day and where I have already gone.

Victor-Ange-Guillaume Grandet.

"You were saying?" said Old Grandet, carefully folding the letter into its original creases and putting it into his waistcoat pocket. He looked at his nephew with a humble, timid air under which he hid his emotions and his calculations. "Have you got warmed up now?"

"Yes, quite, my dear uncle."

"Well, where have our women gone?" asked the uncle, already forgetting that his nephew was to stay with them. At that moment Eugénie and Madame Grandet came in again.

"Is everything ready upstairs?" the old man asked them, recovering his composure.

"Yes, Father."

"Well, Nephew, if you're tired, Nanon will show you to your room. Gad, it's no room for a swell! But you'll have to forgive a poor wine-grower who never has an extra penny. The taxes swallow up everything."

"We don't want to intrude, Grandet," said the banker. "You've probably got things you want to talk about with your nephew. We'll wish you good night. Till tomorrow."

At these words the company rose, and each made a characteristic bow. The old notary went to look for his lantern under the arch and came back to light it, offering to accompany the des Grassins on their way. Madame des Grassins had not foreseen the incident which was to end the evening prematurely, and her servant had not arrived.

"Will you do me the honor of accepting my arm, Madame?" said Abbé Cruchot to Madame des Grassins.

"Thank you, Monsieur l'Abbé, but I have my son," she replied tartly.

"Ladies can't possibly compromise themselves with me," said the abbé.

"Do take Monsieur Cruchot's arm," her husband said to her.

The abbé walked off with the pretty lady so quickly that they were soon a few paces in front of the caravan.

"He's a very nice young man, Madame," said he, squeezing her arm. "Well, that's all over and done with as far as we're concerned. You'll have to say good-bye to Mademoiselle Grandet; Eugénie will go to the Parisian. Unless this cousin happens to be enamored of some young lady in Paris, your son Adolphe will find in him the most formidable rival. . . ."

"Oh, come now, Monsieur l'Abbé. That young man won't take long to discover that Eugénie's a little fool, a girl without freshness. Did you notice her this evening? She was as yellow as a quince."

"Perhaps you pointed that out to the cousin?"

"And I certainly didn't hesitate . . ."

"Always sit beside Eugénie, Madame, and you won't need to say much to the young man against his cousin. He'll make his own comparisons. . . ."

"In any case he's promised to dine at my house the day after tomorrow."

"Ah, if you wished, Madame . . ." said the abbé.

"And what would you like me to wish, Monsieur l'Abbé? Are you trying to give me bad advice? I haven't reached the age of thirty-nine, with a spotless reputation, thank God, to compromise it even for the empire of the Grand Mogul. We're both old enough not to have to mince words. For a priest you have really some very incongruous ideas. Shame on you; you're as bad as Faublas."

"So you've read Faublas?"

"No, Monsieur l'Abbé. I meant to say *Les Liaisons Dangereuses*."

"Ah, that book is infinitely less immoral," said the abbé, laughing. "But you're making me out to be as corrupt as the young men of today. I simply wanted to . . ."

"I defy you to say that you weren't trying to put wicked ideas into my head. Surely it's quite obvious. If the young man—and I admit that he's quite attractive—were to make love to me, he'd never notice his cousin. In Paris, I know, there are worthy mothers who do sacrifice themselves in this way for the happiness and prosperity of their children; but we are in the provinces, Monsieur l'Abbé."

"Yes, Madame."

"And," she replied, "I should not want, nor would Adolphe himself want, a hundred millions bought at that price."

"Madame, I said nothing about a hundred millions. That temptation might be too much for either of us. Only I do believe that a virtuous woman can indulge, quite innocently, in a few harmless little coquetries, as part of her social duties, and as . . ."

"Do you think so?"

"Shouldn't people try to be agreeable with each other, Madame? . . . Allow me to blow my nose. I assure you, Madame," he went on, "that he looked at you through his lorgnette with a rather more flattering air than that with which he observed me; but I forgive him for paying homage to beauty rather than to old age. . . ."

"It's quite evident," said the judge in his deep voice, "that Monsieur Grandet of Paris has sent his son to Saumur with highly matrimonial intentions."

"But in that case the cousin wouldn't have dropped in like a bombshell," replied the notary.

"That doesn't mean anything," said Monsieur des Grassins, "The old man's very sly."

"Des Grassins, my dear, I've asked the young man to dinner. You'll have to go and invite Monsieur and Madame de Larsonnière, and the du Hautoys, with the beautiful Hautoy daughter, of course. Let's hope she'll be properly dressed. Her mother, out of jealousy, makes her wear such dreadful clothes. I trust, gentlemen, that you will do us the honor of coming," she added, stopping the procession to turn round toward the two Cruchots.

"Here you are at home, Madame," said the notary.

After having said good night to the three des Grassins, the three Cruchots went on home, applying their provincial genius for analysis to every angle of the great event of the evening, as it affected the respective positions of the Cruchotins and the Grassinistes. The admirable common sense which governed the conduct of these great schemers made both sides realize the necessity for a temporary alliance against the common enemy. Oughtn't they to help each other to keep Eugénie from falling in love with her cousin, and Charles from thinking of her? Would the Parisian be able to withstand the treacherous insinuations, the soft-spoken calumnies, the disparaging praises, the ingenuous denials which would constantly float around him to deceive him?

When the four relatives found themselves alone in the hall, Monsieur Grandet said to his nephew, "We must go to bed now. It's too late to discuss the business which brings you here; we'll choose a suitable moment for that tomorrow. We have breakfast at eight o'clock. At noon we eat a little fruit, and a bit of bread, just a snack, and drink a glass of white wine. Then we dine, like the Parisians, at five. That's the order of the day. If you want to look at the town or its surroundings, you are free to do so. You will forgive me if my affairs do not always permit me to accompany you. You'll probably hear everybody round about saying that I am rich: Monsieur Grandet this and Monsieur Grandet that! I let them talk. Their gossip does my credit no harm. But I haven't a cent, and I work, at my age, like a young journeyman who owns nothing but a cheap plane and two strong arms. You'll perhaps soon discover for yourself what a franc is worth when you have to sweat for it. Come, Nanon, the candles!"

"I hope you'll find everything you need, Nephew," said Madame Grandet, "but if there's anything you want, you can call Nanon."

"My dear aunt, that's most unlikely. I think I have everything with me. Allow me to wish you and my young cousin good night."

Nanon handed Charles a lighted wax taper, a candle from Anjou, very yellow in color, shopworn and so like tallow that Monsieur Grandet, incapable even of suspecting its existence in the house, failed to notice this magnificence.

"I'll show you the way," said the old man.

Instead of going out by the door of the hall which opened on the archway, Grandet went ceremoniously through the corridor separating the hall from the kitchen. A swing door provided with a large oval pane of glass closed this corridor off from the staircase to counteract the cold that poured in. But nonetheless in winter the north wind whistled through it, and in spite of the sand-bags put at the doors in the hall, it was almost impossible to keep the temperature at a comfortable level. Nanon bolted the front door, closed the hall, and let loose from the stable a wolf-dog, whose bark was so hoarse that it sounded as if he had laryngitis. This animal, noted for his ferocity, recognized only Nanon. These two primitive creatures understood each other. When Charles saw the yellowed, smoke-stained walls and worm-eaten banister of the staircase, every step of which trembled under the heavy step of his uncle, his heart sank lower and lower. He thought he was in a hen roost. His aunt and his cousin, toward whom he turned with a questioning glance, were so used to this stairway that, not guessing the cause of his astonishment, they took it for an expression of friendliness and replied with a pleasant smile which filled him with despair. "What the devil did my father send me here for?" he wondered.

On the first landing he saw three doors painted brick red and with no casing. They were imbedded in the crumbling walls and equipped with iron bars fastened with naked bolts, which tapered off like lances as did either end of the long keyhole of the lock. The door at the top of the staircase, opening into the room above the kitchen, was evidently walled up. The only entrance to this room, which Grandet used as an office, was through his bedroom. The single window which let in light from the court was protected on the outside by a heavy iron grating. Nobody, not even Madame Grandet, was allowed to enter; the old man preferred to be alone there like an alchemist at his furnace. There, doubtless, some hiding-place had been very skilfully contrived; there were stored the titles to his estates; there hung the scales for weighing his gold coins; there every night and in secret he made out his receipts, vouchers, and estimates, so that the business men, who always found Grandet with everything in readiness, could imagine that he had a fairy or a demon at his command. There, doubtless, while Nanon snored till the rafters shook, while the wolf-dog kept watch and yawned in the courtyard, while Madame and Mademoiselle Grandet were sound asleep, the old cooper came to cherish, caress, gloat over his gold, and pack it away in casks. The walls were thick, the shutters discreet. He alone had the key to this laboratory, where, it was said, he consulted maps on which his fruit trees were marked, and where he figured out his produce to the last twig of vine, and almost to the last stick of wood.

The entrance to Eugénie's room was opposite this walled-up door. Then, at the end of the landing, were the old couple's rooms, which occupied the whole front of the house. Madame Grandet had a room adjoining Eugénie's, which was entered by a glass door. The master's room was separated from his wife's by a partition and from the mysterious office by a thick wall. Old Grandet had lodged his nephew on the second floor in a high-ceilinged attic above his own room so that he could hear him if he took a notion to go and come. When Eugénie and her mother arrived in the center of the landing, they exchanged their good-night kiss, and, after having taken leave of Charles in a few words, which sounded cold on their lips but were no doubt warmly felt by the daughter, they went into their rooms.

"This is your room, Nephew," said Old Grandet to Charles,

opening the door. "If you have to go out, you must call Nanon. Without her, impossible! The dog would eat you without a word of warning. Sleep well. Good night. Ha, ha, the ladies have made a fire for you," he went on. At that moment Big Nanon appeared armed with a warming-pan. "Well, here's something else!" said Monsieur Grandet. "Do you take my nephew for a woman in confinement? Please take your embers away, Nanon!"

"But, sir, the sheets are damp, and this gentleman is really as delicate as a woman."

"Go on, then, as you've taken it into your head," said Grandet, giving her a shove. "But be careful not to set the place on fire." Then the miser went downstairs, muttering to himself.

Charles stood aghast in the midst of his bags. After having glanced at the sloping walls with their yellow paper strewn with bunches of flowers like that of a cheap country tavern, at a fireplace of grooved limestone of which the sight alone was chilling, at the chairs of yellow wood with varnished cane seats, which seemed to have more than four angles, at the open bedside table big enough to hold a small scout sergeant, at the meager rag carpet at the foot of a canopied bed, the moth-eaten hangings of which quivered as if they were about to fall, he looked seriously at Big Nanon and said, "I say, my dear child, am I really in the house of Monsieur Grandet, former mayor of Saumur, and the brother of Monsieur Grandet of Paris?"

"Yes, sir, and a very pleasant, very kind, and very perfect gentleman. Shall I help you to unpack your bags?"

"I'd be very glad if you would, old trooper! Haven't you served in the marines of the Imperial Guard?"

"Ha, ha, ha!" laughed Nanon. "What's those—the marines of the Guard? Are they salty? Do they go on the water?"

"Come, get my dressing-gown out of that suitcase. Here's the key."

Nanon marveled at the sight of the dressing-gown of green silk with its flowers of gold in an antique design.

"Are you going to wear that to bed?" she asked.

"Yes."

"Holy Mary, what a beautiful altar front it would make for the parish! My dear, sweet sir, do give it to the church, and you'll save your soul. Otherwise it will make you lose it. Oh, how nice you look like that! I'm going to call Mademoiselle to come and see you."

"Come now, Nanon, since Nanon it is, will you keep quiet? Let me go to bed. I'll fix my things tomorrow. And if my gown pleases you so much, you can save your own soul. I'm much too good a Christian not to give it to you when I go away, and you can do anything you like with it."

Nanon stood rooted to the spot, looking at Charles, unable to believe his words.

"Give me that beautiful piece of finery!" she said as she left. "He's already dreaming, the young gentleman. Good night."

"Good night, Nanon."

"What on earth did I come here for?" thought Charles before he fell asleep. "My father's no fool; my journey must have some object. Oh, well, tomorrow's soon enough for serious matters, as some Greek idiot said."

"Holy Mary, how nice my cousin is!" said Eugénie to herself, interrupting her prayers, which she never finished that night.

Madame Grandet had no thoughts at all as she went to bed. Through the communicating door in the middle of the partition, she could hear the miser walking up and down in his room. Like all timid wives she had studied the character of her lord and master. Just as the gull foresees the storm, she had sensed, from certain imperceptible signs, the inward tempest agitating Grandet and, to use her own expression, "played dead." Grandet looked at the door lined with sheet-iron, which he had had put on his office, and said to himself, "What mad idea made my brother bequeath his child to me? A fine inheritance! I haven't fifty crowns to give him. And anyway, what would fifty crowns mean to this fop who stared at my barometer as if he wanted to throw it in the fire?"

As he thought of the consequences of that tragic will, Grandet was perhaps even more disturbed than his brother at the moment of writing it.

"I'm to have that golden gown?" said Nanon, who fell asleep clothed in her altar front, dreaming of flowers and carpets and damasks, for the first time in her life, as Eugénie dreamed of love.

THREE

LOVE IN THE PROVINCES

*I*N the pure and monotonous life of young girls there comes a delicious hour when the sun spills its rays into their souls, when the flowers express their thoughts, when the throbbings of the heart communicate to the brain their warm fecundity and dissolve all ideas into a vague desire—a day of innocent melancholy and soft delights! When babies begin to see, they smile; when a young girl first discerns sentiment in nature, she smiles as she smiled when she was an infant. If light is the first love of life, is not love the light of the heart? This moment revealed to Eugénie the meaning of things here below.

An early riser, like all country girls, she got up in good time, said her prayers, and began to dress, an occupation which was to have a meaning from now on. First she brushed her chestnut hair smooth, then twisted the thick braids on the top of her head with the utmost care, making sure that no loose tresses escaped and giving to her coiffure a symmetry that heightened the timid candor of her features. The simplicity of this arrangement harmonized well with the unsophisticated lines of her face. While she washed her hands several times in plain water, which hardened and reddened the skin, she looked at her lovely round arms and wondered what her cousin did to have such soft white hands and such well-shaped nails. She put on new stockings and her prettiest shoes. She laced her corset straight without skipping a single eyelet. In short, desiring for the first time in her life to look her best, she felt the satisfaction of having a new dress, well made and becoming to her.

When she had finished dressing, she heard the parish clock strike and was surprised to find it was only seven o'clock. Her eagerness to have all the time necessary to dress with care had made her get up too early. Being ignorant of the art of re-arranging a lock of hair ten times over and standing back to study the effect, Eugénie simply crossed her arms, sat down by the window, and gazed at the yard, the narrow garden, and the high walls overshadowing it: a melancholy, circumscribed view, but not devoid of the mysterious beauties peculiar to solitary places and uncultivated nature. Near the kitchen was a well surrounded by a curb and with a pulley fastened to a curved iron rod, to which clung a vine, its leaves faded, reddened, and shriveled by the autumn. From there the twisted stem of the vine reached over to the wall, took hold, ran along the house, and ended at a woodpile, where the wood was stacked as neatly as might be the books of a bibliophile. The stones of the courtyard displayed those dark patches produced through the years by moss, weeds, and lack of use. The thick walls showed their green coating, streaked with wavy brown lines. Finally, the eight steps which dominated the far end of the court and led to the garden gate were broken and buried under tall plants, like the tomb of a knight interred by his widow at the time of the crusades. Above a foundation of worn stones rose a lattice-work door of rotting wood, half falling down with age, and over it creeping vines intertwined at will. On either side of this gate projected the twisted branches of two stunted apple trees. Three parallel alleys, graveled and separated by square beds, where the earth was held in by box borders, made up this garden, which ended at the foot of the wall in a clump of lime trees. At one end were raspberry bushes, at the other a huge walnut tree, which drooped its branches almost into the cooper's office. A clear day and the beautiful autumn sunshine typical of the banks of the Loire were beginning to dispel the hoar frost which the night had laid on these picturesque features, on the walls and on the plants which adorned this garden and this court.

Eugénie found a new charm in the aspect of these things which up to now had seemed so ordinary to her. A thousand confused thoughts were born in her soul and expanded there as the rays of the sun increased in strength outside. And then she experienced that sensation of vague, inexplicable happiness, which enfolds the moral being as a cloud might enfold the physical being. Her reflections were in accord with the details of this curious landscape, and the rhythms in her heart matched the rhythms of nature. When the sun reached a part of the wall from which hung maidenhair ferns, their thick leaves shot with many colors like the throat of a dove, celestial rays of hope lighted up the future for Eugénie, and from now on she loved to gaze upon that stretch of wall, on its pale flowers, its bluebells, its faded grasses, with which were mingled memories as tender as those of childhood. The sound that each leaf made as it fell from its twig into this echoing courtyard gave answer to secret questionings of the young girl, who might have stayed there all day long, oblivious of the passing hours. Then came tumultuous stirrings of the soul. She got up several times, stood in front of her mirror, and looked at her image as an honest author examines his work to criticize and reproach himself.

"I'm not beautiful enough for him!" Such was Eugénie's thought, a humble thought and latent with suffering. The poor girl was unjust to herself, but modesty, or rather timidity, is one of the chief virtues of love. Eugénie was one of those robust young girls, so frequently seen among the lower middle classes, whose charms seem rather commonplace. But if she resembled the Venus de Milo, her features were ennobled by that refinement of Christian feeling which purifies a woman and gives her a distinction unknown to the sculptors of antiquity. She had a very large head with the masculine yet delicate brow of the Jupiter of Phidias and gray eyes to which her chaste life, reflected there in its entirety, lent a radiant light. The features of her round face, at one time pink and white, had been coarsened by an attack of smallpox, which while not severe enough to leave any scars had destroyed the velvety texture of a skin still so soft and fine that her mother's kiss left a momentary red mark upon it. Her nose was a little too broad, but it harmonized with her bright red lips, which with their innumerable tiny lines were full of love and kindness. Her neck was perfectly rounded. The full curve of her modestly veiled bosom attracted the eye and inspired reverie; a well-cut gown would doubtless have added grace, but to the connoisseur the inflexibility of her stately figure had its own charm. Eugénie, tall and sturdy, had nothing of the prettiness which appeals to the masses; but she had that true beauty so easy to recognize, which only the artist fully appreciates. The painter who seeks in this world a model with the heavenly purity of the Virgin, who looks among all womankind for those modestly proud eyes divined by Raphael, those virginal lines, often inborn, but which only a chaste and Christian life can either preserve or bestow—such a painter, in love with his ideal, would suddenly have discovered in Eugénie's face that innate nobility which is unaware of itself; beneath her calm brow he would have sensed a world of love, and in the shape of her eyes and the lowering of her eyelids a suggestion of the divine. Her features, the outlines of her face, neither altered nor wearied by passion, resembled the vague contours of a gentle and distant horizon glimpsed across tranquil lakes. This calm and rosy countenance, haloed with light like a lovely, full-blown flower, was refreshing to the soul, distilled the charm of the spirit reflected in it, and held the attention. Eugénie was still on that shore of life where childhood illusions flower, where daisies are gathered with a zest never to be recaptured. And as she looked at herself in the mirror, still unconscious of what love was, she said, "I'm too ugly. He'll never take any notice of me."

Then she opened the door of her room which led to the staircase and leaned over to listen for the noises of the household. "He's not up yet," she thought, hearing Nanon's morning cough as the good creature came and went, sweeping the hall, lighting her fire, chaining the dog, and talking to the animals in the stable. Eugénie went down at once and rushed up to Nanon, who was milking the cow.

"Nanon, dear Nanon, do make some cream for my cousin's coffee."

"But I'd have had to do that yesterday, Mademoiselle," said Nanon, bursting out into loud laughter. "I can't make cream. Your cousin's a darling, just a darling. You should have seen him in his grand dressing-gown, all silk and gold. I saw him. His linen is as fine as the curé's surplice."

"Nanon, do make us some sweet biscuit."

"And who's to give me the wood for the oven, the flour, and the butter?" asked Nanon, who in her capacity as Grandet's prime minister sometimes assumed a vast importance in the eyes of Eugénie and her mother. "Do I have to rob him, the poor man, to feast your cousin? You ask him for butter, flour, and wood. He's your father. He can give it to you. Oh, there he is now, coming down to give out the provisions . . ."

Eugénie ran off into the garden, dismayed at the sound of her father's footsteps, which shook the staircase. She was already feeling the effects of that excessive modesty and that peculiar awareness of happiness which makes us believe, perhaps not without reason, that our thoughts are engraved on our foreheads and obvious to everyone. Conscious for the first time of the bareness of her home, the poor girl experienced a feeling of vexation at not being able to make it worthy of her cousin's elegance. She felt a passionate desire to do something for him—what, she did not know. Frank and unsophisticated, she allowed herself to be carried away by her angelic nature without questioning her impressions or her impulses. The very sight of her cousin had aroused in her the natural inclinations of a woman, and they were to manifest themselves all the more vigorously, because, having reached the age of twenty-three, she was fully mature both intellectually and emotionally.

For the first time in her life she dreaded facing her father. She realized that he was the master of her fate and felt guilty at not telling him all her thoughts. She began to walk rapidly, astonished at the freshness of the air she breathed in and at the quickening effect of the sunshine, from which she seemed to draw spiritual warmth, new life. While she was trying to think up a way of getting the sweet cake, one of those quarrels as rare as swallows in winter had broken out between Big Nanon and Grandet. Armed with his keys, the old man had come to measure out the necessary provisions for the day.

"Is there any bread left over from yesterday?" he asked Nanon.

"Not a crumb, sir."

Grandet took up a large round loaf, well sprinkled with flour, and molded in one of those flat baskets used for bread-making in Anjou, and was going to cut it, when Nanon reminded him, "There are five of us today, sir."

"That's true," replied Grandet. "But your loaf weighs six pounds. There'll be some left over. Besides, you'll see that these young men from Paris don't eat bread."

"What do they eat then—'spreads'?" asked Nanon.

In Anjou a "spread," in the language of the natives, means anything that goes with bread from the butter on a slice—an ordinary spread—to peach jam, the most refined of spreads; and all those who in their childhood have licked the spread and left the bread will understand the meaning of this phrase.

"No," Grandet replied, "they eat neither spread nor bread. They're practically like marriageable daughters."

Finally, after having planned the menu for the day, the old man was turning toward his fruit store-room, first locking his provision cupboards, when Nanon stopped him to ask, "Sir, would you let me have a little flour and some butter? I'd like to make some biscuit for the children."

"Are you going to pillage the whole house because of my nephew?"

"I wasn't thinking any more of your nephew than of the dog, not any more than you were yourself. Look here, you've given me only six pieces of sugar. I need eight."

"My goodness, Nanon, I've never seen you like this before. What's got into you? Are you running things here? Six pieces of sugar is all you'll get."

"Well, how will your nephew sweeten his coffee then?"

"With two pieces. I'll do without myself."

"You'll do without sugar at your age! I'd sooner buy it for you out of my own pocket."

"Oh, mind your own business."

In spite of the lower price, sugar still remained in the old cooper's eyes the most precious of colonial commodities; to him it was still worth six francs a pound. It had been necessary to use it sparingly under the Empire, and this had become an inveterate habit with him. All women, even the most simple-minded, know dodges for getting their own way. Nanon gave up the sugar to get the biscuit.

"Mademoiselle Eugénie," she shouted out the window, "you want some biscuit, don't you?"

"No, no," replied Eugénie.

"All right, Nanon," said Grandet, hearing his daughter's voice. "Here you are." He opened the flour-bin, gave her a measureful, and added a few ounces of butter to the piece he had already cut.

"I need some wood to heat the oven," said the implacable Nanon.

"Very well, take what you need," he replied sadly. "But then you can make us a fruit tart and you can cook the whole dinner in the oven. In that way you won't have to light two fires."

"Goodness," exclaimed Nanon, "you don't need to tell me that!"

Grandet cast an almost paternal glance at his faithful prime minister.

"Mademoiselle Eugénie," cried the cook, "we're going to have some biscuit."

Old Grandet came back laden with fruit and arranged a plateful on the kitchen table.

"Look at the pretty boots your nephew's got, sir," Nanon said to him. "What leather, and how good it smells! I wonder what you clean it with? Shall I use some of your egg polish?"

"I believe egg polish would spoil that leather, Nanon. Anyway, tell him you don't know how to clean morocco. Yes, it's morocco. He'll buy something for himself in Saumur and bring it to you to shine his shoes. I've heard it said that they put sugar into their polish to make it bright."

"It's good to eat then?" said the servant, putting the boots up to her nose. "Oh, oh, they smell like Madame's eau de cologne. Isn't that funny?"

"Funny!" said her master. "You think it's funny to spend more money on those boots than the man who wears them is worth?"

"Sir," she said, when her master had come back again after locking the store-room, "aren't you going to have beef broth once or twice a week on account of your . . . ?"

"Yes."

"Then I'll have to go to the butcher's."

"Not at all. You can make us chicken broth. The farmers will see that you have plenty. But I'll tell Cornoiller to shoot some crows. That kind of game makes the best broth in the world."

"Is it true, sir, that they eat the dead?"

"You are stupid, Nanon! Like the rest of the world they eat what they can get. Don't we live off the dead ourselves? What are legacies after all?"

Old Grandet, having no more orders to give, pulled out his watch, and seeing that he still had half an hour before breakfast, took his hat, went out to kiss his daughter, and said to her, "Wouldn't you like to go for a walk in my meadows along the Loire? I've got something to do there."

Eugénie went to put on her straw hat, lined with pink taffeta. Then father and daughter walked down the winding street to the square.

"Where are you off to so early in the morning?" asked Lawyer Cruchot as he met Grandet.

"To see something," replied the old man, not fooled by his friend's early morning walk.

Whenever Old Grandet was going to see something, the lawyer knew by experience that there was always something to be gained by going with him. So he accompanied him.

"Come, Cruchot," said Grandet to the notary. "You are one of my friends. I'm going to prove to you how foolish it is to plant poplars on good land. . . ."

"So you consider the sixty thousand francs you pocketed for the ones that were in your meadows on the Loire nothing at all?" asked Lawyer Cruchot, opening his eyes in amazement. "Weren't you lucky! Cutting your trees just at the moment they ran short of white wood at Nantes and selling them at thirty francs!"

Eugénie listened without knowing that she was approaching

the most solemn moment of her life, and that the notary was going to bring down on her head a paternal and supreme sentence. Grandet had arrived at his magnificent meadows along the banks of the Loire; thirty workmen were busy clearing, filling in, and leveling the ground where the poplars had been.

"Look how much land a poplar takes, Lawyer Cruchot," he said to the notary. "Jean," he called out to one of the workmen, "m-m-measure with your r-r-rule in b-b-both directions."

"Four feet by eight," replied the workman, when he had finished.

"Thirty-two feet lost," said Grandet to Cruchot. "I had three hundred poplars in this row, didn't I? Now . . . three h-h-hundred times thirty-t-t-two fee-feet s-s-swallowed up five hundred in hay; add twice as much on the sides—fifteen hundred; as much again for the middle rows. L-l-let's say a thousand bales of hay."

"Well," said Cruchot, to help his friend out, "a thousand bales of that hay are worth about six hundred francs."

"S-s-say t-t-twelve hundred allowing for three or four hundred francs on the second crop. Well, f-f-figure out what t-t-twelve hundred francs a year d-d-during forty years y-y-yields at c-c-compound interest."

"Say sixty thousand francs," said the notary.

"Agreed! That would m-m-make only sixty thousand francs. Well," the wine-grower went on without stuttering, "two thousand poplars forty years old wouldn't bring me in fifty thousand francs. It's a loss. I found that out," said Grandet, getting on his high horse. "Jean," he continued, "fill in the holes except on the Loire side, where you can plant the poplars I bought. By putting them close to the river, they'll nourish themselves at the expense of the government," he added, turning to Cruchot with a slight twitch of the wen on his nose equal to the most ironical of smiles.

"That's clear. Poplars should be planted only on barren ground," said Cruchot, flabbergasted by Grandet's calculations.

"Y-y-yes, sir," replied the cooper with irony.

Eugénie, who was looking at the glorious scenery of the Loire without paying any attention to her father's calculations, soon began to listen to Cruchot's remarks when she heard him say to his client, "Well, so you've brought a son-in-law from Paris. All Saumur is talking about your nephew. I'll soon have to draw up a contract, Papa Grandet."

"You c-c-came out early to tell me that," Grandet went on, accompanying this reflection with a twitch of his wen. "Well, old f-f-friend, I'll be frank with you and tell you what you want to know. You see, I'd sooner throw my d-d-daughter into the Loire than g-g-give her to her c-c-cousin. You c-c-can p-p-publish that. But don't; just let p-p-people talk."

This reply made Eugénie feel faint. The dim hopes which had begun to spring up in her heart suddenly blossomed forth, materialized, as it were, and took shape in a cluster of flowers that she saw mown down and lifeless on the ground. Since the evening before she had become attached to Charles by all those links of happiness which bind soul to soul; from now on suffering was to strengthen them. Is it not the noble destiny of woman to be more affected by the majesty of grief than by the splendors of fortune? How could it happen that paternal feeling had been extinguished in her father's heart? What crime had Charles committed? Mysterious problems! Already her new-born love, in itself so profound a mystery, was being enveloped in further mysteries. She walked back on trembling legs, and when she reached the gloomy street, to her so gay, she felt its sadness, as she breathed in the melancholy which time and things had imparted to it. She was spared none of the vicissitudes of love. At a short distance from the house, she walked ahead of her father and after knocking waited there at the door for him. But Grandet, who had noticed that the notary was carrying an unopened news-paper, said to him, "How do government bonds stand today?"

"You won't listen to me, Grandet," replied Cruchot. "Hurry up and buy some. There's still a chance of making twenty per cent in two years, apart from a high rate of interest—five thousand francs a year on eighty thousand francs."

"We'll see," replied Grandet rubbing his chin.

"Good God!" said the notary, who had opened his paper.

"What's the matter?" cried Grandet.

Cruchot pushed the paper under his nose, saying, "Read this article."

"Monsieur Grandet, one of the most highly respected merchants of Paris, blew out his brains yesterday, after having appeared as usual at the Bourse. He had sent in his resignation to the president of the Chamber of Deputies and had also resigned from his functions as judge of the commercial court. The failures of Messrs. Roguin and Souchet, his broker and his notary, had ruined him. The esteem in which Monsieur Grandet was held and the credit he enjoyed were nevertheless such that he could no doubt have obtained help from other Paris merchants. It is to be regretted that this honorable man should have yielded to a momentary despair, etc."

"I knew it," said the old wine-grower to the notary.

These words made Lawyer Cruchot's blood run cold. In spite of his legal insensibility he felt a chill run down his spine at the thought that the Grandet of Paris had perhaps implored in vain the help of the millionaire Grandet of Saumur.

"And his son, so happy yesterday . . ."

"He doesn't know anything about it yet," replied Grandet with the same composure.

"Good-bye, Monsieur Grandet," said Cruchot, who understood everything now and was off to reassure Judge de Bonfons.

Grandet found breakfast served when he came in. Madame

Grandet was already seated in her raised chair, knitting herself sleeves for the winter. Eugénie flung her arms around her neck and kissed her with that effusiveness which is often the result of a secret grief.

"You can eat now," said Nanon, coming down the stairs four steps at a time. "The boy's sleeping like a cherub. How sweet he is with his eyes shut! I went in and called him. No answer!"

"Let him sleep," said Grandet. "He'll waken soon enough to hear the bad news."

"What's the matter?" asked Eugénie, putting into her coffee the two small pieces of sugar weighing nobody knows how few grams which the old man amused himself by cutting up in his spare time. Madame Grandet, who had not dared ask this question, looked at her husband.

"His father has blown his brains out."

"My uncle?" said Eugénie.

"Oh, the poor young man!" cried Madame Grandet.

"Yes, poor is right," replied Grandet. "He hasn't a cent to his name."

"Why, he's sleeping as if he owned the earth!" said Nanon gently.

Eugénie stopped eating. Her heart contracted as the heart does when, for the first time, pity, aroused by the unhappiness of the one she loves, overwhelms a woman's whole being. The poor girl wept.

"You didn't know your uncle. What are you crying for?" said her father, darting at her one of those looks of a famished tiger such as he doubtless cast on his heaps of gold.

"But, sir," said the servant, "who could help feeling pity for the poor young man sleeping there like a top, unconscious of his fate?"

"I'm not talking to you, Nanon. Hold your tongue!"

Eugénie learned at this moment that the woman who loves must always hide her feelings. She did not answer.

"You'll say nothing of this to him until I get back, I hope, Madame Grandet," continued the old man. "I have to go and straighten out the ditch of the meadows along the road. I'll be back at noon for lunch and shall then discuss my nephew's affairs with him. As for you, Mademoiselle Eugénie, if it's that jackanapes you're crying over, that will do, my girl. He'll be off in no time for the Indies. You'll never see him again. . . ."

Her father took up his gloves from the brim of his hat, put them on with his habitual calm, rubbing them into place by inserting the fingers of one hand between those of the other, and went out.

"Oh, Mama, I'm suffocating!" cried Eugénie when she was alone with her mother. "I've never suffered like this."

Madame Grandet, seeing her daughter turn pale, opened the window and made her breathe the fresh air. "I feel better now," said Eugénie after a moment.

This nervous excitement in a nature which until now had seemed calm and cold reacted on Madame Grandet. Looking at her daughter with that sympathetic intuition with which all mothers are endowed for the objects of their love, she guessed everything. Indeed, the life of the celebrated Hungarian sisters, bound to one another by a freak of nature, had not been more intimate than that of Eugénie and her mother, always together in that window embrasure, together at church, and breathing in the same air as they slept.

"My poor child!" said Madame Grandet, pressing Eugénie's head against her breast.

At these words the young girl raised her head, looked questioningly at her mother, trying to read her secret thoughts, and said, "Why send him to the Indies? If he's unhappy, shouldn't he stay here? Isn't he our closest relative?"

"Yes, my child, it would be quite natural. But your father has his reasons and we must respect them."

Mother and daughter sat down in silence, the one on her raised chair, the other in her little armchair; and both took up their work again. Overcome with gratitude for the admirable understanding shown by her mother, Eugénie kissed her hand, saying, "How good you are, my dear mother!" At these words, Madame Grandet's face, old and faded by long years of sorrow, lighted up with happiness.

"Do you like him?" asked Eugénie.

Madame Grandet replied only with a smile; then, after a moment of silence, she said in a low voice, "Are you already in love with him? That would be wrong."

"Wrong?" replied Eugénie. "Why? You like him, Nanon likes him, why shouldn't I like him? Listen, Mother, let's lay the table for his breakfast." She threw down her sewing. The mother did the same, adding, "Foolish child!" But she was happy to justify her daughter's folly by sharing in it. Eugénie called Nanon.

"What do you want now, Mademoiselle?"

"Nanon, you'll have cream by noon, won't you?"

"Yes, by noon," replied the old servant.

"Well, give him good strong coffee. I've heard Monsieur des Grassins say they make the coffee very strong in Paris. Put a lot in."

"And where do you think I'm going to get it?"

"Buy some."

"And if the master meets me?"

"He's gone to his meadows."

"I'll run now. But Monsieur Fessard already asked me if the Three Wise Men were staying with us when he gave me the wax taper. The whole town will know about our extravagance."

"If your father notices anything," said Madame Grandet, "he's quite capable of beating us."

"Well, then, let him beat us. We'll take his blows on our knees."

Madame Grandet's only reply was to raise her eyes to heaven. Nanon put on her kerchief and went out. Eugénie got out a clean tablecloth, then went to fetch a few bunches of grapes that she had amused herself by hanging on strings across the attic. She walked lightly along the corridor so as not to awaken her cousin and could not help listening at his door to his regular breathing. "Sorrow keeps watch while he sleeps," she said to herself. She took the greenest leaves of the vine, arranged her grapes as coquettishly as an old, experienced head-waiter could have done, and carried them triumphantly to the table. She pillaged the kitchen of the pears counted out by her father and placed them in a pyramid among the leaves. She came and went, running and skipping. She would have been quite willing to sack her father's house completely, but he had all the keys. Nanon came back with two fresh eggs. When she saw them, Eugénie felt like hugging her.

"The farmer from Lande had them in his basket. I asked him for them, and he gave them to me as a favor, the darling."

After two hours of careful preparations during which Eugénie left her work twenty times to go and watch the coffee boil, to listen to the sounds her cousin made as he was dressing, she succeeded in producing a very simple and inexpensive luncheon, which nevertheless was an appalling departure from the established custom of the household. Luncheon was eaten standing. Each took a piece of bread, a fruit or butter, and a glass of wine. As she looked at the table set in front of the fire, at the arm chair drawn up to her cousin's place, at the two plates of fruit, the egg cup, the bottle of white wine, the bread, and the sugar piled up in a saucer, Eugénie trembled in every limb at the very thought of the looks her father would give her, if he were to come in at that moment. She therefore glanced frequently at the clock in order to figure out whether her cousin would be able to get his lunch over before the old man came back.

"Don't worry, Eugénie, if your father comes I'll take all the blame," said Madame Grandet.

Eugénie could not repress a tear.

"Oh, my dear mother," she cried. "I've never loved you enough!"

Charles, who had been wandering round in his room for ages and humming to himself, finally came down. Fortunately it was only eleven o'clock. A true Parisian, he had taken as much pains over his dress as though he had been in the castle of the noble lady who was traveling in Scotland. He came in with that affable, smiling manner so becoming to the young, and it made Eugénie feel both sad and happy. He had taken the destruction of his castles in Anjou as a good joke, and greeted his aunt gaily.

"Did you sleep well last night, my dear aunt? And you, Cousin?"

"Very well, sir. And you?" said Madame Grandet.

"Yes, perfectly."

"You must be hungry, Cousin," said Eugénie. "Sit down at the table."

"But I never breakfast before noon, the time when I usually get up. However, I had so little to eat on the journey that I won't refuse. Besides . . ." he drew from his pocket the most charming of flat watches ever made by Breguet. "Oh, it's only eleven o'clock. I'm up early."

"Early?" said Madame Grandet.

"Yes, but I wanted to put my things away. Well, I'll willingly eat some little thing, a chicken or a partridge perhaps."

"Holy Mary!" cried Nanon when she heard this.

"A partridge?" said Eugénie to herself. She would have been glad to spend her entire savings for a partridge.

"Come and sit down," said his aunt.

The dandy let himself drop into the armchair just as a pretty woman reclines on a sofa. Eugénie and her mother took straight chairs and sat beside him in front of the fire.

"Do you always live here?" Charles asked them, finding the hall even uglier by day than it had been by candlelight.

"Always," replied Eugénie, looking at him, "except during the grape harvest. Then we go to help Nanon and we all live in the abbey of Noyers."

"Don't you ever go anywhere?"

"Sometimes on Sundays after vespers, when it's fine," said Madame Grandet, "we walk out onto the bridge or go to watch the hay being cut."

"Have you a theatre?"

"Go to the play!" cried Madame Grandet. "To see actors! But, sir, don't you know it's a mortal sin?"

"Here, my dear sir," said Nanon, bringing in the eggs, "we'll give you your chickens in the shell."

"Oh, fresh eggs!" cried Charles, who, like people accustomed to luxury, had already forgotten about his partridge. "But that's delicious. Now what about some butter, my dear child?"

"Oh, butter! But then you won't have any biscuit!" said the servant.

"Nanon, bring the butter," cried Eugénie.

The young girl watched her cousin as he cut his bread into strips with as much pleasure as the most sentimental little Paris milliner gets out of seeing a melodrama in which virtue emerges triumphant. It is true that Charles, brought up by a charming mother, his manners perfected by a woman of fashion, had the affected, elegant, dainty gestures of a coquette. The compassion and tenderness of a young girl are truly magnetic. Charles, seeing himself the object of his cousin's and his aunt's attentions, could not help being influenced by the friendly feelings which flowed toward him and, as it were, inundated him. He gave Eugénie a bright, caressing glance full of kindness, a glance which was almost a smile. He became aware, as his eyes lingered on Eugénie, of the exquisite harmony of the features in her pure countenance, of her innocent manner, of the limpid magic of her eyes, where young love sparkled and where desire was unconscious of passion.

"Upon my word, my dear cousin, if you were in evening dress in a box at the opera, I assure you my aunt would be quite right, for you would certainly be the cause of many sins of envy among the men and of jealousy among the women."

This compliment touched Eugénie's heart and made it beat with joy, although she didn't in the least understand it.

"Oh, Cousin, you're making fun of a poor little country girl."

"If you knew me, Cousin, you would know that I despise irony. It shrivels the heart, crushes all feeling. . . ." And he gulped down very prettily his buttered sippet. "No, I'm probably not clever enough to make fun of other people, and this defect does me a great deal of harm. In Paris it's quite possible to murder a man by saying, 'He has a kind heart.' That phrase simply means: 'The poor boy is as stupid as a rhinoceros.' But since I am rich and am known to be able to hit the target at thirty paces with the first shot from any kind of pistol and in an open field, I am safe from irony."

"What you've just said, Nephew, shows that you have a kind heart."

"You have a very pretty ring," said Eugénie. "Is there any harm in asking to see it?"

Charles stretched out his hand as he took off his ring, and Eugénie blushed when she touched her cousin's pink nails lightly with the tips of her fingers.

"Look, Mother, at the beautiful workmanship."

"Oh, there's a lot of gold in it," said Nanon, bringing in the coffee.

"What's that?" asked Charles, laughing.

And he pointed to a high, narrow pot of brown earthenware, glazed on the outside and lined with china. It had a ring of ashes around it, and the coffee grains rose to the surface with the boiling liquid and fell to the bottom again.

"It's boiled coffee," said Nanon.

"Ah! my dear aunt, I shall leave at least one pleasant reminder of my stay here. You are very much behind the times! I'll teach you how to make good coffee in a Chaptal coffee-pot."

He attempted to explain the system of the Chaptal coffee-pot.

"Oh, dear, if it's as complicated as that," said Nanon, "it would take a lifetime. I'd never be able to make coffee like that. I should say not! And who would get the grass for our cow while I was making the coffee?"

"I'll make it," said Eugénie.

"Child!" said Madame Grandet, looking at her daughter.

At this word, which reminded them of the blow about to descend on the unfortunate young man, the three women fell silent and looked at him with an air of pity which attracted his attention.

"What's the matter, Cousin?"

"Hush!" said Madame Grandet to Eugénie who was about to reply. "Remember, dear, that your father is going to speak himself to Monsieur. . . ."

"Say Charles," said young Grandet.

"Oh, you're called Charles. What a beautiful name!" cried Eugénie.

Presentiments of misfortune are nearly always justified. At this moment Nanon, Madame Grandet, and Eugénie, who could not help shuddering at the thought of the old cooper's return, heard the sound of a familiar knock.

"There's Papa," said Eugénie.

She took away the saucer of sugar, leaving a few pieces on the tablecloth. Nanon carried off the egg cup. Madame Grandet sat up like a startled doe. There was a general panic, which astonished and bewildered Charles.

"Why, what's the matter?" he asked

"Father's coming," said Eugénie.

"Well, what about it?"

Monsieur Grandet came in, cast a sharp glance at the table and at Charles; he saw everything.

"Aha! You've made a feast for your nephew. That's good, fine, excellent!" he said without stuttering. "When the cat's away, the mice will play."

"A feast?" thought Charles, unable to conceive of the rules and customs of this household.

"Give me my glass, Nanon," said the old man.

Eugénie brought his glass. Grandet took a horn-handled knife with a wide blade from his waistcoat pocket, cut a slice of bread, took a little butter, spread it carefully, and began to eat standing up. At that moment Charles was putting sugar in his coffee. Old Grandet noticed the pieces of sugar, and looking questioningly at his wife, who turned pale, took three steps forward. Bending down, he whispered in the poor woman's ear, "Where'd you get all that sugar?"

"Nanon brought it from Fessard's; we hadn't any."

It is impossible to imagine the profound interest the three women took in this mute scene. Nanon had left her kitchen and stood looking into the room to see what would happen. Charles, having tasted his coffee, found it bitter, and glanced about for the sugar which Grandet had already put away.

"What do you want, Nephew?" asked the old man.

"The sugar."

"Take some milk," replied the master of the house. "Your coffee will taste milder."

Eugénie brought back the saucer of sugar which Grandet had already put away, and placed it on the table, looking calmly at her father as she did so. Most certainly, the Parisian lady who holds up a silken ladder with her fragile arms to help her lover escape shows no greater courage than Eugénie displayed in putting the sugar back on the table. The lover will reward his mistress when she proudly exhibits her lovely wounded arm, and every bruised vein will be bathed in tears and kisses and healed by the pleasures of love. But Charles was never to suspect the secret of the profound agitations which were breaking his cousin's heart, as she shrank under the old cooper's withering glance.

"You're not eating, my dear."

The poor slave came forward, piteously cut a slice of bread, and took a pear. Eugénie boldly offered her father some grapes, saying, "Do taste my dried grapes, Papa! You'll have some too, won't you, Cousin? I got these nice bunches specially for you."

"Oh, if we don't stop them, they'll pillage the whole of Saumur for you, Nephew. When we've finished, we'll go together into the garden. I have some things to tell you that are none too pleasant."

Eugénie and her mother cast a look at Charles, the significance of which could not escape him.

"What do you mean, Uncle? Since the death of my poor mother . . ." (at these two words his voice softened) "there can be no further misfortune for me."

"Nephew, who can know the afflictions by which the Lord is pleased to test us?" said his aunt.

"Tut, tut, tut, tut," said Grandet. "There you go again with your nonsense. It pains me, Nephew, to see those nice white hands of yours." He showed him the great ham-like fists that

Nature had placed at the end of his arms. "There's a pair of hands made for gathering up coins! You've been brought up to put your feet in the kid from which the wallets are made that we carry our bills in. That's bad, very bad!"

"What do you mean, Uncle? I'll be hanged if I understand a word of it."

"Come," said Grandet.

The miser closed the blade of his knife with a snap, drank the rest of his white wine, and opened the door.

"Be brave, Cousin!"

Chilled by the young girl's tone, Charles followed his dreadful relative, a prey to mortal terrors. Eugénie, her mother, and Nanon went into the kitchen, impelled by an overwhelming curiosity to observe the two actors in the scene about to take place in the damp little garden, where the uncle began by walking silently up and down with his nephew. Grandet did not mind having to tell Charles about his father's death, but he felt a kind of compassion at knowing that he was penniless and was looking for words to soften the expression of this cruel truth. "You have lost your father!" It was easy to say that. Fathers die before their children. But: "You haven't a cent in the world!" All the misfortunes on earth were summed up in those words. And for the third time the old man went up and down the middle alley, the gravel crunching under his feet. At critical moments in our lives our souls retain a strong impression of the places where joys or sorrows overwhelm us. Thus Charles observed with particular attention the box hedges of the little garden, the pale leaves which fluttered down, the crumbling walls, the curiously twisted fruit trees, picturesque details which were to remain engraved in his mind, forever blended with this supreme hour by a trick of memory peculiar to the passions.

"It's very warm, very fine," said Grandet, taking a deep breath.

"Yes, Uncle, but why . . ."

"Well, my boy," replied his uncle, "I have bad news for you. Your father is very ill . . ."

"Why am I here?" said Charles. "Nanon," he cried, "order post horses. Surely I can find a carriage in the district," he added, turning toward his uncle, who remained motionless.

"Horses and a carriage are useless," replied Grandet, looking at Charles, who stared straight in front of him and remained silent. "Yes, my poor boy, you have guessed it. He's dead. But that's nothing. There's something much more serious. He blew out his brains . . ."

"My father! . . ."

"Yes, but that's nothing. The newspapers comment on it though it's none of their business. Here, read this."

Grandet, who had borrowed Cruchot's newspaper, shoved the tragic article under Charles's nose. At that moment the poor young man, still really a child, still at the age when the feelings find natural expression, burst into tears.

"Ah, that's better," said Grandet to himself. "His eyes frightened me. He's crying. He'll be all right now."

"That's not the worst of it, poor boy," Grandet went on aloud, not knowing whether Charles was listening. "That's nothing. You'll get over it. But . . ."

"Never! Never! Oh, poor father!"

"He's ruined you. You haven't a cent left."

"What difference does that make? Where is my father? Father? . . ."

His tears and sobs resounded horribly within these walls and were repeated by the echo. The three women, filled with pity, wept too; for tears are often as contagious as laughter. Charles, without listening to his uncle, escaped into the court, made his way to the stairs, went up to his room, and threw himself across the bed, hiding his face in the sheets to weep in peace away from his relatives.

"We'll have to let the first shower pass over," said Grandet, coming back into the room where Eugénie and her mother had quickly returned to their places and were working with trembling hands after having dried their eyes. "But that young man's no good. He thinks more of the dead than of money."

Eugénie shuddered as she heard her father express himself in this way about the most sacred of all griefs. From that moment she began to judge him. Although muffled, the young man's sobs sounded through the echoing house, and his anguished lament, which seemed to come from the depths of the earth, ceased only toward evening, having gradually grown weaker and weaker.

"Poor young man!" said Madame Grandet.

Fatal remark! Old Grandet looked at his wife, at Eugénie, and at the sugar-bowl. He recalled the extraordinary breakfast served up to the unfortunate youth and stationed himself in the center of the room.

"Well," he said with his usual composure, "I hope you're not going to continue your extravagances, Madame Grandet. I don't give you *my* money to stuff that young fool with sugar."

"Mother had nothing to do with it," said Eugénie. "It was I who . . ."

"Is it because you've come of age," Grandet continued, interrupting his daughter, "that you've decided to oppose me? Remember, Eugénie . . ."

"Father, your brother's son should not, in our house, have to go without . . ."

"Tut, tut, tut, tut," said the cooper on four chromatic tones, "the son of my brother this, my nephew that! Charles is nothing to us. He hasn't a penny; his father went bankrupt. And when this jackanapes has cried himself out, he'll have to make himself scarce. I won't have him turning my house upside down."

"What does it mean to go bankrupt?" asked Eugénie.

"To go bankrupt," replied her father, "is to commit the most dishonorable of all actions that can disgrace a man."

"That must be a very great sin," said Madame Grandet, "and our brother will be damned."

"There you go again with your litanies," he said to his wife, shrugging his shoulders. "To go bankrupt, Eugénie," he went on, "is a kind of theft which unfortunately is protected by the law. People have entrusted their property to Guillaume Grandet on the strength of his reputation as a man of honor and integrity and he has taken it all and left them nothing but their eyes to weep with. The highway robber is to be preferred to the bankrupt. The former attacks you, you can defend yourself, he risks his neck; but the other . . . In a word, Charles is dishonored."

These words reverberated in the poor girl's heart and weighed heavily upon it. Upright in the same way that a flower born in the depths of a forest is delicate, she knew nothing of the maxims of the world, of its specious arguments or its sophisms. She therefore accepted the outrageous explanation of bankruptcy which her father gave her quite deliberately and without making clear to her the difference which exists between an involuntary and a premeditated failure.

"But, Father, couldn't you have prevented this misfortune somehow?"

"My brother did not consult me. In any case he owes four millions."

"But what is a million, Father?" she asked with the innocence of a child who believes it can promptly secure what it wants.

"A million?" said Grandet. "Why, it's a million twenty-cent pieces, and it takes five twenty-cent pieces to make five francs."

"Good heavens!" cried Eugénie. "How on earth could my uncle have had four millions of his own? Could anyone else in France possibly have as many millions?" (Old Grandet stroke his chin and smiled, and his wen seemed to dilate.) "But what will become of my cousin Charles?"

"He'll go off to the Indies, where in accordance with his father's wish he'll try to make his fortune."

"But has he enough money to go there?"

"I'll pay his fare . . . to . . . well, to Nantes."

Eugénie threw her arms around her father's neck.

"Oh, Father, how kind you are!"

She kissed him with such warmth that Grandet, whose conscience was plaguing him a little, was almost ashamed.

"Does it take long to make a million?" she asked him.

"Listen," said the cooper, "you know what a napoleon is. Well, it takes fifty thousand of them to make a million."

"Mama, we'll have some novenas said for him."

"I was thinking of that," replied the mother.

"That's it, always spending money!" cried the father. "Do you think we're made of money?"

At this moment a hollow groan, more doleful than any of the others, resounded through the attic, striking terror into the hearts of Eugénie and her mother.

"Nanon, go up and see that he doesn't kill himself," said Grandet. "Now then," he added, turning toward his wife and daughter, who had gone pale at his words, "no nonsense, you two. I'm going out now. I want to keep an eye on our Dutchmen, who are leaving today. Then I'm going to see Cruchot to talk all this business over with him."

He left. When Grandet had shut the door, Eugénie and her mother breathed more freely. Never before this morning had the young girl felt constrained in the presence of her father; but for the last few hours her feelings and ideas had been changing every moment.

"Mama, how many louis do you get for a cask of wine?"

"Your father sells his at from a hundred to a hundred and fifty francs, sometimes two hundred, I have heard."

"So when he harvests fourteen hundred casks of wine? . . ."

"Goodness, child, I don't know how much that makes. Your father never tells me anything about his business."

"But then father must be rich?"

"Perhaps. But Monsieur Cruchot told me he'd bought Froid-fond two years ago. That may have left him short."

Eugénie, losing track of her father's fortune, got no further with her calculations.

"He didn't even see me, the poor darling!" said Nanon coming back. "He's stretched out on his bed like a calf, crying like Mary Magdalene and even harder! What's the poor young man so unhappy about?"

"Let's go quickly and console him, Mama. And if there's a knock, we'll come downstairs."

Madame Grandet was unable to resist the sweet persuasion of her daughter's voice. Eugénie was sublime; she was a woman now. Together, with beating hearts, they went up to Charles's room. The door was open. The boy neither saw nor heard. Plunged in tears, he uttered inarticulate cries.

"How he loves his father!" said Eugénie in a low voice.

It was impossible not to recognize, from the tone in which these words were spoken, a heart in the grip of unconscious love. Madame Grandet gave her daughter a glance full of maternal understanding, then whispered. "Be careful, you'll fall in love with him."

"Fall in love with him!" repeated Eugénie. "Oh, if you only knew what father said!"

Charles turned round and saw his aunt and cousin.

"I've lost my father, my poor father! If he had only told me his secret troubles, we could have worked things out together. Dear

God! My kind father! I was so sure of seeing him again that I'm afraid I said good-bye to him rather coldly."

His words were interrupted by sobs.

"We'll pray for him," said Madame Grandet. "Resign yourself to the will of God."

"Cousin," said Eugénie, "have courage! Your loss is irreparable. Now you must think of saving your honor . . ."

With that subtle instinct of the woman who is resourceful in everything, even when she consoles, Eugénie was trying to cheat her cousin's grief by making him think of himself.

"My honor? . . ." cried the young man, tossing back his hair with a violent gesture, as he sat up on the bed and crossed his arms. "Yes, that's true. My uncle said my father had gone bankrupt." He uttered a heartrending cry and hid his face in his hands. "Go, Cousin, go! Dear God, dear God, forgive my father! How he must have suffered!"

There was something horribly fascinating in the spectacle of this youthful sorrow, so genuine, spontaneous, and unselfish. There was a modesty in this grief which the simple hearts of Eugénie and her mother understood, when Charles motioned to them to leave him alone. They went downstairs, took up their places near the window in silence, and worked almost an hour without exchanging a word. Eugénie had noticed in the quick glance she cast over the young man's belongings, the glance of a young girl which sees everything in the twinkling of an eye, the pretty trifles of his dressing-case, his scissors and his razors embossed in gold. This glimpse of luxury in the midst of grief made Charles even more appealing to her, perhaps by way of contrast. Never before had so solemn an event or so dramatic a scene touched the imagination of these two beings forever immersed in monotony and solitude.

"Mama," said Eugénie, "we must wear mourning for my uncle."

"Your father will decide about that," replied Madame Grandet.

They relapsed into silence. Eugénie drew her stitches with a uniformity of movement which would have revealed to an observant eye the intensity of her thoughts. This adorable girl's chief desire was to share her cousin's mourning. At about four o'clock a sudden knock at the door made Madame Grandet's heart beat faster.

"What's the matter with your father?" she said to her daughter.

Grandet came in looking very cheerful. After taking off his gloves, he rubbed his hands together hard enough to take the skin off, if the epidermis had not been tanned like Russian leather, except for the perfume of larches and incense. He walked up and down and looked at the clock. Finally his secret escaped him.

"My dear," he said without stuttering, "I've outwitted them all. Our wine is sold! The Dutch and the Belgians were leaving this morning. I walked up and down in the square in front of their inn, pretending I had nothing to do. What's-his-name, you know him, came up to me. The owners of all the good vineyards are holding their wine and plan to wait. I didn't hinder them. Our Belgian was in despair. I could see that and made a deal. He's taking our wine at two hundred francs a cask, half down. I've been paid in gold. The notes are drawn. Here are six louis for you. In three months the price of wine will fall."

These words were uttered in a calm voice but with such profound irony that the people of Saumur, who at that moment were gathered in the market-place, flabbergasted at the news of the sale Grandet had just made, would have shuddered if they could have heard him. A wave of panic would have caused the price of wine to fall fifty per cent.

"You have a thousand casks this year, haven't you, Father?" said Eugénie.

"Yes, girlie."

This affectionate term was the superlative expression of the old cooper's joy.

"That makes two hundred thousand twenty-cent pieces."

"Yes, Mademoiselle Grandet."

"Well then, Father, you can easily rescue Charles."

The amazement, anger, and stupefaction of Belshazzar on seeing the words *Mene, Mene, Tekel, Upharsin* could hardly compare with the cold rage of Grandet, who having dismissed his nephew from his mind now found him lodged in the heart and in the designs of his daughter.

"What's this? Ever since that dandy set foot in my house, everything has gone wrong. You think you can buy sugared almonds and have feasts and junketings. I won't have it. Perhaps at my age I should know how to behave. Furthermore, I don't propose to take advice either from my daughter or anyone else. I'll do the proper thing by my nephew. You don't need to stick your nose into it. As for you, Eugénie," he added, turning toward her, "let me hear nothing more of this or I'll send you to the abbey of Noyers with Nanon, see if I don't. And no later than tomorrow, if you don't look out. Where is the fellow anyway? Has he come down?"

"No, my dear," replied Madame Grandet.

"Well, what's he doing then?"

"He's weeping for his father," replied Eugénie.

Grandet looked at his daughter and could not find a word to say. After all, he was a father too. He walked up and down the room once or twice, then suddenly went upstairs to his office to think over an investment in government bonds. The cutting down of his two thousand acres of forest had brought him in six hundred thousand francs. Adding to this amount the money received for his poplars, his income from the previous year and from the current year, and the two hundred thousand francs

from the deal he had just concluded, he could get together a sum
of nine hundred thousand francs. The twenty per cent to be made
within a short time on the bonds, which were quoted at seventy
francs, tempted him. He figured out his calculation on the news-
paper which gave the account of his brother's death, hearing but
paying no attention to his nephew's moans. Nanon knocked on
the wall to let her master know that dinner was served. As he
came down the last step of the stairs and reached the archway,
Grandet was saying to himself, "I'll do it. It will pay me eight
per cent. In two years I shall have fifteen hundred thousand
francs and withdraw it in gold."

"Well, where's my nephew?"

"He says he doesn't want to eat anything," replied Nanon.
"That's not healthy."

"So much the more saved," retorted her master.

"That's so," she said.

"Bah! He can't keep on crying forever. Hunger drives the wolf
out of the woods."

The dinner was strangely silent.

"My dear husband," said Madame Grandet when the cloth was
removed, "we must put on mourning."

"Upon my word, Madame Grandet, what reason for spending
money will you think up next! Mourning is in the heart and not
in the clothes."

"But you must wear mourning for a brother, and the Church
tells us . . ."

"Buy your mourning out of your six louis. You can give me a
band of crêpe. That will be enough for me."

Eugénie lifted her eyes to heaven without saying a word. For
the first time in her life her generous instincts, slumbering and
long repressed but suddenly aroused, were outraged at every
turn. This evening was outwardly just like a thousand other evenings of their monotonous lives, but it was certainly the most

horrible. Eugénie worked without raising her head, but did not use the workbox scorned by Charles the evening before. Madame Grandet knitted her sleeves. Grandet twiddled his thumbs for four hours, plunged in calculations the results of which were to astound Saumur the next day. No one called on the family that evening. At that moment the whole town was buzzing with Grandet's staggering deal, his brother's failure, and the arrival of his nephew. To satisfy the need of talking over their common interests, all the vineyard owners of the upper and middle class circles of Saumur had gathered at Monsieur des Grassins', where terrible imprecations were being fulminated against the ex-mayor. Nanon was spinning, and the sound of her wheel was the only voice to be heard beneath the dingy beams of the hall.

"We're not wearing out our tongues," said she, showing her teeth which were as large and white as peeled almonds.

"Mustn't wear anything out," replied Grandet, rousing himself from his meditations. He could see the prospect of eight millions in three years and was sailing along that sheet of gold. "Let's go to bed. I'll go and say good night to my nephew for all of us and see if he wants something to eat."

Madame Grandet stood on the landing of the first story to hear the conversation about to take place between Charles and the old man. Eugénie, bolder than her mother, went two steps higher.

"Well, Nephew, you're in trouble. Yes, weep, that's only natural. After all, a father's a father. But we must bear our misfortunes with patience. I'm making plans for you while you weep. I'm a good uncle to you, remember that. Come now, show a little courage. Wouldn't you like a small glass of wine? Wine doesn't cost anything in Saumur. We offer a glass of wine here as they do a cup of tea in the Indies. But," Grandet went on, "you have no light. That's bad, very bad! You must be able to see what you're doing." Grandet walked over to the mantelpiece. "Why, here's a wax candle," he cried. "Where the devil did they dig up a wax candle? These hussies would tear down the ceilings of my house to boil the fellow's eggs."

On hearing these words, mother and daughter slipped into their rooms and burrowed into their beds with the speed of frightened mice scurrying back into their holes.

"Madame Grandet, have you a secret treasure?" asked the old man, coming into his wife's room.

"Wait, my dear, I'm saying my prayers," the poor mother replied in a tremulous voice.

"The devil take you and your God!" muttered Grandet in reply.

Misers do not believe in a life hereafter; the present is everything for them. This thought throws a horrible light on the present day, when, more than at any other time, money controls the law, politics, and morals. Institutions, books, men, and doctrine, all conspire to undermine belief in a future life—a belief on which the social edifice has rested for eighteen hundred years. Nowadays the grave is a transition but little feared. The future which awaited us beyond the *requiem* has been transported into the present. To attain *per fas et nefas* to a terrestrial paradise of luxury and empty pleasures, to harden the heart and macerate the body for the sake of fleeting possessions, as people once suffered the martyrdom of life in return for eternal joys, is now the universal thought—moreover a thought inscribed everywhere, even in the laws which ask the legislator: What do you pay? instead of asking him: What do you think? When this doctrine has passed down from the middle class to the populace, what will become of the country?

"Madame Grandet, have you finished?" asked the cooper.

"My dear, I'm praying for you."

"All right! Good night. We'll have a talk in the morning."

The poor woman fell asleep like the schoolboy who, not having learned his lessons, fears to encounter on awakening the angry face of his master. Just at the moment when, in fear and trembling, she was drawing the sheets around her so as not to hear anything, Eugénie, in her nightgown, with bare feet, crept up to her and kissed her on the forehead.

"Oh, mother darling," she said, "tomorrow I'll tell him it was me."

"No, he'll send you to Noyers. Leave it to me. He won't eat me."

"Do you hear, Mother?"

"What?"

"Well, he is still crying."

"Do go to bed, daughter. You'll catch cold in your bare feet. The floor is damp."

Thus passed the fateful day which was to weigh so heavily on the whole life of the rich yet poor heiress. Her sleep was no longer as deep nor as innocent as it had been until now. It often happens that certain incidents in human life seem, artistically speaking, improbable, although true. Isn't it perhaps that we almost always fail to interpret our spontaneous decisions in the light of psychology because we neglect to explain the obscure reasoning which prompted these decisions? Perhaps Eugénie's profound passion should be analyzed in its most delicate ramifications; for it turned into a disease, certain scoffers would say, and influenced her whole existence. Many people prefer to deny the outcome rather than to estimate the strength of the bonds, links, and ties which secretly weld one action to another in the moral order. So that here Eugénie's past life will serve observers of human nature as a guarantee of her naïve want of reflection and of the impulsiveness of her emotions. Because her life had been so tranquil, feminine pity, that most intuitive of emotions, had sprung forth the more robustly in her soul.

Disturbed by the events of the day, she woke up several times to listen for her cousin, thinking she had heard the sighs which

since the evening before had been re-echoing in her heart. Sometimes she imagined him dying of grief, sometimes she dreamt
he was starving to death. Toward morning she was sure she heard
a dreadful cry. So she dressed and ran with light steps at dawn
to her cousin's room. He had left the door open. The candle had
burned down into the socket of the candlestick. Charles, overcome by nature, had fallen asleep fully dressed sitting in an armchair with his head resting on the bed. He was dreaming as
people dream when they have had nothing to eat. Eugénie could
weep to her heart's content. She could admire that handsome
young countenance, streaked with grief, those eyes swollen with
weeping, and, although closed, still seeming to shed tears. Charles
subconsciously sensed Eugénie's presence. He opened his eyes
and caught her expression of pity.

"Excuse me, Cousin," he said, obviously unaware of the hour
or of where he was.

"There are hearts in sympathy with you here, Cousin, and *we*
thought you might need something. You ought to go to bed.
You're wearing yourself out sitting up like this."

"That's true."

"Well, good-bye."

She ran away, embarrassed but happy that she had come. Only
innocence can venture to be so bold. Virtue, enlightened, can be
as calculating as vice. Eugénie, who had not trembled while she
was with her cousin, could hardly stand up when she got to her
room. Her childlike innocence had suddenly vanished. She considered her action, reproached herself a thousand times. What
will he think of me? He'll think I'm in love with him. That was
exactly what she most wanted him to think. True love has foresight, and realizes that love awakens love. What an event in the
life of this solitary young girl to have gone secretly like this into
a young man's room! Are there not thoughts and actions, where
love is concerned, which for certain souls seem equal to the most

sacred vows? An hour later she went to her mother's room and dressed her as usual. Then they went to their places in front of the window and waited for Grandet with that anxiety which according to temperament chills or warms the heart, contracts or dilates it, when a scene or a punishment is feared. This feeling of anxiety is so natural that domestic animals experience it acutely enough to cry out at a slight tap, whereas they remain silent when they accidentally wound themselves. The goodman came down, but he spoke absent-mindedly to his wife, kissed Eugénie, and took his place at the table without appearing to remember his threats of the evening before.

"What's happened to my nephew? The lad gives no trouble."

"He's asleep, sir," replied Nanon.

"So much the better. He won't need a wax candle," said Grandet facetiously.

This unwonted clemency, this acrid gaiety, astonished Madame Grandet, and she looked attentively at her husband. The goodman . . . It may be well to point out here that in Touraine, Anjou, Poitou, and Brittany the word "goodman," frequently used to describe Grandet, is as often applied to the cruelest of men as to the kindliest, once they have reached a certain age. This title is no indication of individual good-nature. The goodman, then, took his hat and gloves and said, "I'm going to stroll around the market place and find the Cruchots."

"Eugénie, your father certainly has something on his mind."

Grandet, who was a light sleeper, spent half his nights in the preliminary calculations which gave astonishing accuracy to his views, observations, and schemes and assured them of that unfailing success which so amazed the people of Saumur. All human power is a combination of patience and time. The strong will and watch. The life of the miser is a constant exercise of human power in the service of his personality. He relies on two qualities only: self-love and self-interest. But self-interest being

to some extent an established and conscious self-love, the endur-
ing affirmation of a genuine superiority, self-love and self-interest
are two parts of the same whole—egotism. This is perhaps the
reason for the enormous curiosity aroused by misers skilfully
portrayed. Everyone has something in common with these individuals who impinge on all human emotions by concentrating
them all in one passion. Where is the man without desire, and
what mundane desire can be satisfied without money? Grandet
had indeed something on his mind, as his wife expressed it. There
was in him as in all misers a persistent need to compete with
other men, to win their money by legal means. To get the better
of others—isn't that to demonstrate one's power, to acquire the
perpetual right to despise those weaklings who allow themselves
to be devoured here below? Oh, who has ever properly understood the lamb lying peacefully at the feet of God, the most
touching emblem of all terrestrial victims, the symbol of their
future, the glorification of suffering and weakness? The miser
allows this lamb to grow fat, pens him in, slaughters him, cooks,
eats, and despises him. The miser's food is made up of money
and disdain.

During the night the old man's ideas had taken another course
—hence his clemency. He had hatched a plot to make fools of the
Parisians, to rack, gull, pummel them, to keep them hopping,
make them sweat, hope, turn pale. All this he would do to amuse
himself at their expense, he, the former cooper, sitting there in
his dingy hall or going up and down the worm-eaten stairway of
his house in Saumur. He had been thinking about his nephew.
He wanted to save his dead brother's honor without its costing
either himself or his nephew a penny. His funds were invested
for three years; all he had to do now was manage his properties.
He needed some outlet for his malicious energy and he had found
it in his brother's bankruptcy. Not having anything at the moment to squeeze between his paws, he wanted to crush the

Parisians for Charles's profit and play the part of the good brother at small cost to himself. The family honor counted for so little in this scheme that his good intentions may be compared to the need gamblers feel to see a game well played even though they have nothing at stake in it. The Cruchots were necessary to his plan, but he did not want to go after them. He had decided to make them come to him and to set in motion that very night the comedy of which he had just conceived the plot, so that the next day he would be, without its costing him a penny, an object of admiration to the whole town.

FOUR

A MISER'S PROMISES—VOWS OF LOVE

*I*N her father's absence Eugénie had the happiness of being able to devote herself openly to her cousin's well-being, to lavish on him without fear the treasures of her pity, one of woman's sublime superiorities, the only one she wishes to impose, the only one she forgives a man for letting her assume. Three or four times Eugénie went to listen to her cousin's breathing, to find out if he were asleep or awake. Then, when he got up, the cream, the coffee, the eggs, the fruits, the plates, the glass, everything having to do with his breakfast, was the object of her special care. She ran lightly up the old stairway to listen to the sounds that came from her cousin's room. Was he dressing? Was he still weeping? She went as far as the door.

"Cousin?"

"Yes, Cousin."

"Will you have breakfast in the hall or in your room?"

"Wherever you like."

"How do you feel?"

"My dear cousin, I'm ashamed to say that I'm hungry."

This conversation through the door was for Eugénie a truly romantic episode.

"Well, we'll bring your breakfast up to your room so as not to annoy Father."

She ran down to the kitchen with the lightness of a bird.

"Nanon, go and make up his room."

This stairway so often ascended and descended, in which the slightest sound re-echoed, seemed to Eugénie to have lost its decrepit aspect. It had become luminous, it spoke to her, it was as young as she, as young as the love it served. At last her mother, her kind and indulgent mother, was willing to humor the whims of her love, and when Charles's room was made up, they both went to keep the unhappy youth company. Did not Christian charity require them to console him? These two women derived from religion a goodly number of little sophistries to justify their conduct. So Charles Grandet found himself the object of the most affectionate and tender care. His saddened heart felt keenly the charm of this gentle friendliness, of this exquisite sympathy, which these two women, under perpetual restraint, were able to express on finding themselves free for a moment in the region of suffering, their natural sphere. Exercising the right of a relative, Eugénie began to put away the linen and the toilet articles her cousin had brought with him, and could marvel to her heart's content at each luxurious trifle, at the knick-knacks of silver and chased gold that she came across and which she held in her hand for a long time on the pretext of examining them. Charles could not help being deeply touched by the solicitude of his aunt and cousin. He was familiar enough with Paris society to know that in his present plight he would have encountered there only cold and indifferent hearts. Eugénie appeared to him in all the splendor of her peculiar beauty, and he now admired the simplicity of manner at which he had laughed the night before. And when Eugénie took from Nanon the china bowl of coffee to serve it to her cousin with unconcealed emotion and a look of affection, the eyes of the Parisian youth filled with tears. He took her hand and kissed it.

"Well, what is it now?" she asked.

"Oh, these are tears of gratitude," he replied.

Eugénie turned abruptly toward the fireplace to take the candlesticks.

"Here, Nanon, take them away," she said.

When she looked at her cousin, she was still flushed, but at least her glance could dissemble and hide the excessive joy which filled her heart. But their eyes expressed the same feeling as their souls merged in a single thought; the future was theirs. This tender emotion was all the more precious to Charles in the midst of his great sorrow because it was so unexpected. A knock at the door recalled the two women to their places. Fortunately they were able to get down the stairs quickly enough to be back at work when Grandet entered. If he had met them under the archway, it would have been enough to arouse his suspicions. After lunch, which the old man ate standing up, the keeper, who had not yet received the promised indemnity, arrived from Froidfond with a hare, some partridges shot in the park, some eels, and two pike contributed by the millers.

"Well, well, good old Cornoiller, he comes in the nick of time. Is it fit to eat?"

"Yes, my dear generous sir, they were shot just two days ago."

"Come, Nanon, get a move on," said the old man. "Take them away. They'll do for dinner. I'm entertaining the two Cruchots."

Nanon opened her eyes in amazement and looked at everybody.

"Well, but where am I to get lard and spices?" she asked.

"My dear," said Grandet, "give Nanon six francs and remind me to go to the cellar and get some good wine."

"Well then, Monsieur Grandet," continued the keeper, who had come prepared with a harangue for the purpose of settling the question of his wages, "Monsieur Grandet."

"Tut, tut, tut, tut," said Grandet, "I know what you want to say. You're a good fellow. We'll see about that tomorrow. I'm too busy today. Give him five francs," he said to Madame Grandet.

He hurried away. The poor woman was only too happy to buy peace at the cost of eleven francs. She knew that Grandet would keep quiet for a fortnight after he had thus taken back bit by bit the money he had given her.

"Here you are, Cornoiller," she said, slipping ten francs into his hand, "some day we'll reward your services."

Cornoiller could say nothing. He went away.

"Madame," said Nanon, who had put on her black kerchief and picked up her basket, "I only need three francs. Keep the rest. I'll manage all right."

"Get a good dinner, Nanon. My cousin's coming down," said Eugénie.

"There's certainly something very extraordinary going on," said Madame Grandet. "This is only the third time since our marriage that your father has invited friends to dinner."

Toward four o'clock, just as Eugénie and her mother had finished setting the table for six people, and the master of the house had brought up a few bottles of those exquisite wines which provincials cherish so lovingly, Charles came into the room. The young man was pale. His gestures, his countenance, his expression, and the sound of his voice possessed an appealing sadness. He was not pretending sorrow, he was really suffering, and the shadow cast by grief over his features gave him that interesting air so attractive to women. Eugénie loved him all the more for it. Perhaps, too, misfortune had brought him closer to her. Charles was no longer that rich and handsome young man dwelling in a world inaccessible to her, but a relative submerged in frightful misery. Misery begets equality. Women have this in common with the angels—suffering humanity belongs to them. Charles and Eugénie understood each other and conversed only with their eyes; for the poor ruined dandy, the

orphan, retired into a corner and sat there in silence, proud
and calm. But from time to time his cousin's gentle and caressing
glance shone on him, forcing him to abandon his sad thoughts,
to go along with her into the regions of hope and the future,
where she was longing to be with him.

At this moment the town of Saumur was more excited by the
dinner Grandet was giving for the Cruchots than it had been
the evening before by the sale of his vintage, though that constituted a crime of high treason against the whole wine-growing
community. If the wily old wine-grower had been giving his
dinner with the same idea in mind as the one which deprived
Alcibiades' dog of his tail, he might perhaps have been considered
a great man; but utterly superior to a town of which he was continually making game, he paid no attention to Saumur. The des
Grassins soon learned of the sudden death and probable bankruptcy of Charles's father. They resolved to visit their client that
very evening to sympathize with him in his misfortune and show
their friendship, trying at the same time to discover the motives
which had decided him, under such circumstances, to invite the
Cruchots to dinner. At five o'clock Judge C. de Bonfons and his
uncle the notary arrived, dressed up to the nines. The guests
sat down to table and began to eat heartily. Grandet was solemn,
Charles silent, Eugénie speechless, and Madame Grandet spoke
no more than usual, so that the dinner was properly funereal.

When they got up from table, Charles said to his aunt and
uncle, "Permit me to retire. I must begin a long and painful
correspondence."

"Certainly, Nephew."

After Charles had gone and the old man was sure that he could
hear nothing and would be deep in his letter-writing, he looked
slyly at his wife.

"Madame Grandet, what we are going to talk about would be

Greek to you. It's half past seven. You ought to go and tuck yourself up in bed. Good night, Daughter."

He kissed Eugénie, and the two women went out. Now began the scene in which old Grandet, more than at any other moment in his life, applied the skill he had acquired in dealing with men, which often earned for him from those whom he had nipped a little too sharply the nickname of "the old skinflint." If as mayor of Saumur he had had higher ambitions, if by some fortunate circumstance he had reached the upper levels of society and been sent to take part in congresses where the affairs of nations were treated, and if he had there made use of the genius with which his self-interest had endowed him, there is no doubt that he would have been magnificently useful to France. But perhaps it is equally probable that, away from Saumur, the old man would have cut but a poor figure. Perhaps there are minds which like certain animals can no longer reproduce when transplanted out of their native climates.

"J-j-judge, y-y-you were s-s-saying that b-b-bankruptcy . . ."

The stutter affected for so many years by Grandet and accepted, like the deafness he complained about in rainy weather, as quite natural, became on this occasion so wearisome to the two Cruchots that as they listened to the wine-grower they unconsciously made faces in an effort to help him finish the words over which he was deliberately hesitating. Here it might be well to tell the story of Grandet's stuttering and deafness. Nobody in the province had better hearing or could pronounce Anjou French more distinctly than the crafty wine-grower. In spite of all his shrewdness he had once been taken in by an Israelite, who in the course of the discussion applied his hand to his ear like a trumpet on the pretext of hearing better and jabbered so hopelessly in his search for words that Grandet, a victim of his humanity, felt obliged to suggest to this cunning Jew the words and ideas the Jew seemed to be searching for, to complete himself the arguments of the said Jew, to say what the Jew himself should have said, in short to be the Jew instead of being Grandet. The cooper emerged from this strange encounter having concluded the only deal of which he ever had to complain during the whole course of his business career. But if he lost out financially, morally he learned a good lesson and later reaped the benefits of it. So he ended by blessing the Jew who had taught him the art of wearing out the patience of his commercial antagonist and making him constantly lose sight of his own idea in trying to express his opponent's. No other deal had ever required as this one did the assistance of the deafness, the stammering, and the obscure circumlocutions in which Grandet enveloped his thoughts. In the first place, he did not want to shoulder the responsibility of his own project; neither did he wish to declare himself or make his real intentions clear.

"M-m-monsieur de B-B-Bonfons . . ." For the second time in three years Grandet called the Cruchot nephew Monsieur de Bonfons. The judge could believe he had been singled out to be the astute old fellow's son-in-law. "Y-y-you were s-s-saying that b-b-bankruptcies c-c-can in ce-certain cases be pre-pre-prevented b-b-by . . ."

"By the commercial courts themselves. It happens every day," said Monsieur C. de Bonfons, seizing upon old Grandet's idea or thinking he had guessed it and affectionately eager to explain it to him. "Listen!"

"I-I-I'm listening," replied the old man humbly, assuming the malicious expression of a child who is laughing up his sleeve at his teacher, while seeming to pay the closest attention.

"When an important and highly respected man like, for instance, your late brother in Paris . . ."

"M-m-my b-b-brother, yes."

"Is threatened with insolvency . . ."

"They c-c-call it insolvency? . . ."

"Yes, when his failure is imminent, the commercial court, to which he is answerable (note this carefully), has the power, by a decree, to appoint receivers. Liquidation is not bankruptcy, you know? When a man goes bankrupt, he is dishonored; but when he liquidates, he remains an honest man."

"That's very d-d-different, if it doesn't c-c-cost any m-m-more," said Grandet.

"But a liquidation can be put through even without the help of the court. For," said the judge, taking a pinch of snuff, "how is bankruptcy declared?"

"Yes, I n-n-never thought of that," replied Grandet.

"First," replied the magistrate, "by filing a declaration of bankruptcy in the record office of the court. This must be done by the merchant himself or by his duly registered agent. Secondly, at the request of the creditors. But supposing the merchant does not file a declaration and that no creditor asks the court for a decree declaring the aforementioned merchant bankrupt, what happens then?"

"Y-y-yes, l-l-let's see."

"Then the family of the deceased, his representatives, his heirs, or the merchant himself, if he is not dead, or his friends, if he is in hiding, liquidate his business. Perhaps you would like to liquidate your brother's affairs?" asked the judge.

"Ah! Grandet," cried the notary, "that would be a fine thing to do. There's honor in the depths of our provinces. If you were to save your name, for it is your name, you would be . . ."

"Noble," said the judge interrupting his uncle.

"Of course," replied the old wine-grower, "m-m-my b-b-broth-er's n-n-name was Grandet j-j-just like mine. That's c-c-certain. I don't d-d-deny that. A-a-and this l-l-liquidation might be, in m-m-many ways, v-v-very advant-t-tageous t-t-to the interests of m-m-my n-n-nephew, of whom I'm v-v-very f-f-fond. We'll have to s-s-see about that. Those P-P-Paris rogues would b-b-be too

much for m-m-me. I b-b-belong to Sau-m-mur, you see. M-m-ny
v-v-vines, my d-d-drains, and . . . then my b-b-business to look
after. I've n-n-never given a n-n-note. What is a n-n-note? I t-t-take
a good m-m-many, but I've n-n-never signed one. They can be
c-c-cashed and d-d-discounted. That's all I know about them.
I've h-h-heard it said that you can b-b-buy up n-n-notes . . ."

"Yes," said the judge. "Notes can be bought in the market at a
discount. You understand?"

Grandet made a trumpet of his hand and applied it to his ear,
and the judge repeated his words.

"Well, then," replied the old man, "there's s-s-something to be
g-g-got out of it? I know n-n-nothing at my age about such
things. I l-l-live here and l-l-look after the v-v-vines. The vines
g-g-grow, and it's the w-w-wine that p-p-pays. The h-h-harvest
comes first, that's what I s-s-say. I have v-v-very important and
p-p-profitable b-b-business at Froidfond. I c-c-can't leave my
h-h-house to get m-m-mixed up in that d-d-devilish m-m-muddle
that's 'way beyond m-m-me. You say that to l-l-liquidate, to
s-s-stop the d-d-declaration of b-b-bankruptcy, I ought to b-b-be
in P-P-Paris. I c-c-can't be in two p-p-places at once, without
b-b-being a little b-b-bird, and . . ."

"I quite understand," cried the notary. "Well, my old friend,
you have friends, old friends, willing to help you out."

"All right, then," thought the old wine-grower to himself.
"Hurry and make up your minds."

"And suppose someone went to Paris and looked up your
brother Guillaume's chief creditor and said to him . . ."

"J-j-just a m-m-moment, now," the old man interrupted. "S-
s-said what? S-s-something like this: Monsieur Gr-Grandet of
Saumur this, Monsieur Grandet of Saumur that. He l-l-loves his
b-b-brother, he l-l-loves his n-n-nephew. Grandet is a g-g-good
relative; he m-m-means to do r-r-right. He got a g-g-good p-p-
price for his v-v-vintage. D-d-don't f-f-file a d-d-declaration of

b-b-bankruptcy; c-c-call a meeting; l-l-liquidate; and then Gr-Grandet will see what he c-c-can do. B-b-better to l-l-liquidate than l-let the l-law stick its n-n-nose in. Eh? Isn't that so?"

"Right!" said the judge.

"Because you see, Monsieur de B-B-Bonfons, a man must l-l-look before he l-l-leaps. If you c-c-can't, you c-c-can't. When there's a l-l-large sum at stake, you m-m-must know the assets and l-l-liabilities if you're not going to be r-r-ruined. Eh? Isn't that so?"

"Certainly," said the judge. "It's my opinion that in a few months we'll be able to buy up the debts for a certain sum and then pay in full by an agreement. Yes, yes, you can lead a dog a long way if you show him a chunk of pork. As long as there has been no declaration of bankruptcy and you hold a lien on the debts, you'll come out of it as white as snow."

"As s-s-snow," repeated Grandet, making an ear-trumpet of his hand once more. "I d-d-don't understand this s-s-snow."

"But listen to what I'm telling you," cried the judge.

"I'm l-l-listening."

"A note is merchandise which rises and falls in price. That's a deduction from Jeremy Bentham's theory about usury. That writer has proved that the prejudice against usurers was foolish."

"Re-e-eally!" said the old man.

"Granted that in principle, according to Bentham, money is merchandise, and that what represents money is equally merchandise," the judge continued, "granted that it is notorious that, according to the usual variations governing commercial matters, the note as merchandise, carrying this or that signature, like any other article, is plentiful or scarce on the market, rises or falls to nothing, the court decrees . . . (oh, how stupid I am, excuse me) I believe you could buy up your brother at twenty-five per cent."

"Y-y-you c-c-call him J-J-Jeremy Ben . . ."

"B:ntham, an Englishman."

"There's a Jeremiah who could save us a lot of lamentations in business," said the notary laughing.

"Those Englishmen s-s-sometimes show some sense," said Grandet. "So according to B-B-Bentham, if my b-b-brother's n-n-notes are w-w-worth, n-n-not w-w-worth anything . . . Yes, I have it r-r-right, haven't I? That seems clear enough . . . The creditors w-w-would be . . . no, would not be. I unders-s-stand."

"Let me explain the whole thing to you," said the judge. "In law, if you hold a lien on all the debts of the Grandet house, your brother or his heirs owe nothing to anyone. Good."

"Good," repeated the old man.

"In equity, if your brother's notes are negotiated (negotiated, you understand the term?) in the market at a reduction of so much per cent, and if one of your friends should turn up and buy them in, the creditors not having been put under any pressure to dispose of them, the estate of the late Grandet would be honorably released."

"That's true, b-b-business is b-b-business," said the cooper. "That's that . . . B-b-but, st-still, you know, it's d-d-difficult. I h·have n-neither the m-m-money n-n-nor the t-t-time n-n-nor . . ."

"Yes, you can't possibly go. Well, I'll go to Paris for you (you'll pay my expenses, of course, a mere trifle). I see the creditors, I talk to them, I get an extension of time, and everything can be arranged if you will add some cash to the assets so as to buy up all title to the debts."

"Well, we'll see about that. I c-c-can't, I d-d-don't w-w-want to c-c-commit myself without . . . He who c-c-can't, c-c-can't, don't you see?"

"That's quite right."

"My h-h-head's in a wh-whirl with all this t-t-talk . . . This is the f-f-first t-t-time in my l-l-life that I've had to th-think of . . ."

"Yes, you're not a lawyer."

"I'm only a p-p-poor w-wine-grower and know n-n-nothing about what you've j-j-just t-t-told me. I'll have to w-w-work it out . . ."

"Well!" replied the judge, preparing to resume his argument.

"Nephew?" said the notary, interrupting him in reproachful tone.

"Yes, Uncle?" replied the judge.

"Let Monsieur Grandet explain what he intends to do. This power of attorney is a pretty serious business. Our dear friend ought to define it adequately, and . . ."

A knock at the door announced the arrival of the des Grassins family. Their entrance and their greetings prevented Cruchot from finishing his sentence. The notary was glad of the interruption, for Grandet was already beginning to scowl at him and his wen indicated that a storm was brewing. In any case the prudent notary did not think it becoming in a judge of the county court to go to Paris to bring creditors to terms and get himself mixed up in a rather shady deal, which conflicted with the code of strict integrity. Moreover, not yet having heard old Grandet express the slightest inclination to pay anything at all, he trembled instinctively to see his nephew involving himself in this affair. He took advantage of the moment when the des Grassins entered to lead the judge by the arm into the window embrasure.

"You've done enough, Nephew; that's quite enough devotion now. Your desire for the daughter is blinding you. Hang it! You don't need to go at it tooth and nail. Let me steer the ship now; you can give me a hand. Do you think it's proper for you to compromise your dignity as magistrate in such a . . ."

He did not finish. He could hear Monsieur des Grassins saying to the old cooper as he shook hands with him, "Grandet, we have learned of the terrible misfortune in your family, the ruin of the house of Guillaume Grandet and your brother's death. We have come to express our sympathy on this sad occasion."

"The only misfortune," said the notary, interrupting the banker, "is the death of the younger Monsieur Grandet. And he would not have killed himself if he had thought of asking his brother's help. Our old friend, who is a man of honor to his fingertips, plans to liquidate the debts of the house of Grandet in Paris. To save him the annoyance of legal proceedings, my nephew the judge has offered to leave at once for Paris, in order to reach an agreement with the creditors and give them proper satisfaction."

These words, corroborated by Grandet's manner as he stood stroking his chin, astounded the three des Grassins, who on their way to the house had roundly slandered Grandet's avarice, practically accusing him of fratricide.

"Oh, I was sure of it," cried the banker, looking at his wife. "Wasn't I just saying to you as we came along, Madame des Grassins, that Grandet is the soul of honor and would never suffer the slightest shadow to rest on his name! Money without honor is a disease. There is honor in the provinces! That's fine, very fine, Grandet. I'm an old soldier, I can't disguise my thoughts, and I say bluntly: By Jove, that's sublime!"

"B-b-but the s-s-sublime comes pretty dear," replied the old man, while the banker shook him warmly by the hand.

"But this, my good Grandet, with no disrespect to the judge," replied des Grassins, "is a purely commercial matter and needs an expert business man. Your agent should be familiar with creditors' bills, disbursements, and the computation of interest. I have to go to Paris on business, and I could take charge of . . ."

"We'll see about t-t-trying to w-w-work it out b-b-between us if p-p-possible but without b-b-binding me to anything I c-c-couldn't do," said Grandet stuttering, "because you see, the judge naturally expects me to pay the expenses of his trip."

The old man did not stammer at all over these last words.

"Oh!" said Madame des Grassins. "Why, it's a pleasure to go to Paris. I'd gladly pay to go myself."

And she made a sign to her husband as though to encourage him to snatch this commission away from their adversaries at any cost; then she looked very ironically at the two Cruchots, who appeared quite crestfallen. Grandet now seized the banker by a button and drew him into a corner.

"I'd have much more confidence in you than in the judge," he said. "Besides, there's something else in the wind," he added, twitching his wen. "I want to invest in government bonds. I want to buy a few thousand francs' worth but I don't want to pay more than eighty. That sort of thing goes down at the end of the month, I'm told. You know all about that, of course, don't you?"

"Good heavens! Then I'd have to withdraw a few thousand francs for you?"

"Not much to begin with. Mum's the word! I don't want anyone to know I'm going to play that game. You can put in a bid for the end of the month. But say nothing to the Cruchots; that will annoy them. As you're going to Paris, we can see at the same time how things stand for my poor nephew."

"Agreed. I'll leave tomorrow by the mail coach," said des Grassins aloud, "and I'll call for your final instructions at . . . What time would suit you?"

"At five o'clock, before dinner," said the wine-grower, rubbing his hands.

They remained together a few moments longer. Des Grassins said, after a pause, slapping Grandet on the shoulder, "It's a fine thing to have such kind relatives."

"Yes, yes, without making any show of it," replied Grandet.

"I am a good r-r-relative. I l-l-loved my brother, and I'll prove it if it d-d-doesn't c-c-cost t-t-oo . . ."

"We'll be going now, Grandet," said the banker, fortunately interrupting him before he got to the end of his sentence. "As I'm going sooner than I expected, I have some business to attend to before leaving."

"Very well. I myself, as a result of our c-c-conversation, m-m-must retire to my r-r-room and d-d-deliberate, as Judge Cruchot says."

"The devil! I'm no longer Monsieur de Bonfons," thought the magistrate ruefully, and his face assumed the expression of a judge bored by an argument.

The heads of the two rival families went off together. None of them gave any further thought to Grandet's betrayal that morning of the whole wine-growing community. But they tried in vain to sound each other out as to what the old man's real intentions were in this new affair.

"Are you coming to Madame Dorsonval's with us?" Madame des Grassins asked the notary.

"We'll go later," replied the judge. "I've promised to drop in on Mademoiselle de Gribeaucourt this evening, and if my uncle doesn't mind, we'll go there first."

"Good-bye for now, then, gentlemen," said Madame des Grassins. And when the des Grassins were a few paces away from the two Cruchots, Adolphe said to his father, "They're good and sore, aren't they?"

"Be quiet, Son," retorted his mother, "they can still hear us. Besides, what you said is not in very good taste and smacks of the law school."

"Well, Uncle," cried the magistrate, when he saw that the des Grassins were at some distance, "I began by being Judge de Bonfons, and ended up as a mere Cruchot."

"I noticed that that annoyed you; but the wind favored the

des Grassins. And what a fool you are for all your cleverness!
. . . Let them set sail on old Grandet's 'we'll see,' and wait a bit,
my boy; you'll get Eugénie in spite of that."

In a few moments the news of Grandet's magnanimous resolve
was reported simultaneously in three different houses, and this
fraternal devotion was the only subject of conversation in the
whole town. Everyone forgave Grandet for the sale he had made
in spite of the agreement subscribed to by all the wine-growers.
They admired his sense of honor and praised a generosity of
which they had not believed him capable. It is characteristically
French to become enthusiastic, angry, or impassioned over the
meteor of the moment, the fad of the hour. Can it be that
humanity in the mass, nations, have no memory?

When old Grandet had closed the door, he called Nanon.

"Don't loose the dog and don't go to bed. We have some work
to do together. At eleven Cornoiller should be at the door with
the carriage from Froidfond. Listen for him so that you can keep
him from knocking, and tell him to come in quietly. The police
regulations forbid noise at night. Besides, the whole neighborhood need not know that I'm going on a journey."

Having said this, Grandet went up to his laboratory, where
Nanon heard him rummaging, moving about, pacing to and fro,
but with caution. He evidently did not want to waken his wife
or his daughter, and above all had no desire to attract the
attention of his nephew, whom he had begun to curse when he
saw a thread of light under his door. In the middle of the night,
it seemed to Eugénie, preoccupied with the thought of her cousin,
that she heard the moan of a dying man, and for her that dying
man could only be Charles. He was so pale and despondent when
she last saw him. Perhaps he had killed himself. She wrapped
herself quickly in a robe, a kind of cloak with a hood, and was
on the point of leaving her room; a bright light coming through
the chinks of the door made her think of fire; but she was soon

reassured when she heard Nanon's heavy step and the sound of her voice above the whinnying of several horses.

"Is Father carrying off my cousin?" she wondered, opening the door with care to prevent it from creaking but just enough to see what was going on in the corridor.

Suddenly her eye encountered her father's; his gaze, though vague and unnoticing, struck terror to her heart. The old man and Nanon were yoked together by a thick pole, the ends of which rested on their right shoulders. From it hung a stout rope to which was attached a small keg of the kind Grandet amused himself by making in the bakehouse in his spare moments.

"Holy Virgin! How heavy it is!" said Nanon in a low voice.

"What a pity it's only copper coins!" replied the old man. "Be careful not to knock over the candlestick."

This scene was illuminated by a single candle placed between two rails of the staircase.

"Cornoiller," said Grandet to his honorary keeper, "have you got your pistols?"

"No, sir. Mercy, what's there to fear for your copper coins?"

"Oh, nothing," said old Grandet.

"Besides, we'll drive fast," replied the keeper. "The farmers have picked out their best horses for you."

"All right, all right. You didn't tell them where I was going?"

"I didn't know."

"Good. Is the carriage strong?"

"Strong, master? Oh, sure, it could carry three thousand pounds. How much do those old kegs of yours weigh?"

"Gracious," said Nanon, "I ought to know. They must weigh a good eighteen hundred."

"Will you hold your tongue, Nanon! You can tell my wife I've gone to the country. I shall be back for dinner. Drive fast, Cornoiller. We must get to Angers before nine o'clock."

The carriage drove off. Nanon bolted the big door, unchained the dog, and went to bed with a bruised shoulder. But nobody in the neighborhood suspected either Grandet's departure or the object of his journey. The old man's vigilance never relaxed. Nobody ever saw a penny in this house full of gold. After having learned in the morning, from the gossip of the river front, that gold had doubled in price because a large number of ships had been commissioned in Nantes, and that speculators had arrived in Angers to buy it, the old wine-grower, by the simple expedient of requisitioning horses from his farmers, was able to go there and sell his gold and bring back in the form of treasury notes the amount necessary to purchase his bonds, having increased it by the favorable exchange.

"Father's going away," said Eugénie, who had heard everything from the top of the staircase. Silence had fallen over the house again, and the distant rumbling of the carriage, gradually growing fainter, no longer re-echoed through slumbering Saumur. Just then Eugénie felt in her heart, even before she heard it, a cry which sounded through the walls and seemed to come from her cousin's room. A band of light, slender as the blade of a sword, shone from the crack in the door and cut horizontally across the banisters of the old staircase. "He's suffering," she said, going two steps higher. Another moan and she was on the landing outside his room. The door was ajar, she pushed it open. Charles was sleeping. His head hung over the side of the old armchair, and his hand, from which the pen had fallen, nearly touched the floor. The young man's irregular breathing, a result of the position in which he had fallen asleep, suddenly terrified Eugénie, and she went at once into the room. "He must be very tired," she said to herself, as she caught sight of a dozen or so letters already sealed. She read the addresses: To Messrs. Farry, Breilman and Company, carriage makers; to Monsieur Buisson.

tailor, and so on. "No doubt he's been settling all his affairs so that he can leave France soon," she thought. Her eyes fell on two open letters. The words with which one of them began: "My dear Annette . . ." made her feel faint. Her heart pounded, her feet were nailed to the floor. "His dear Annette! He loves and is loved! No more hope! What does he say to her? . . ." These ideas flashed through her mind and heart. She could see the words everywhere, even on the bricks of the floor, in letters of fire. "Give him up so soon! No, I won't read this letter; I ought to go away. But what if I were to read it? . . ."

She looked at Charles, gently raised his head, and placed it against the back of the chair, and he let her do so like a child, which, though asleep, yet recognizes its mother and accepts her kisses and ministrations. Like a mother Eugénie raised the limp hand and like a mother she gently kissed his hair. "Dear Annette!" A demon kept shrieking these two words into her ear. "I know that I may be doing wrong, but I'm going to read that letter," she said, turning away her head, for her deep sense of honor upbraided her. For the first time in her life good and evil wrestled in her heart. Until now she had never had to blush for anything she had done. Passion and curiosity won out. At each phrase, each sentence, her heart throbbed, and the acute pang of desire that filled her as she read made the pleasures of first love still more enticing.

My dear Annette: Nothing could ever have separated us but the great misfortune which has now overwhelmed me and which no human foresight could have avoided. My father has killed himself; his fortune and mine are irretrievably lost. I have been left an orphan at an age when, because of the nature of my education, I might still be considered a child. And yet I must rise up like a man out of the abyss into which I have been plunged. I have just spent half the night in reviewing my situation. If I wish to leave France an honest man, and there can be no doubt of that, I have not a hundred francs of my own to try my luck in the Indies or in America. Yes, my poor Anna, I am going to seek my fortune in those deadly climates. Under those skies it is easily and quickly made, they tell me. As for remaining in Paris, I could not. Neither my soul nor my countenance are made to bear the insults, the indifference, the disdain which await the ruined man, the son of a bankrupt! Good God! To think of owing two million francs! . . . I should be killed in a duel the first week. Therefore I shall not return. Your love, the tenderest and most devoted which ever ennobled the heart of a man, cannot draw me back. Alas, my beloved, I have no money to go to you, to give and receive a last kiss from which I might derive the necessary strength for my enterprise . . .

"Poor Charles, I did well to read the letter! I have gold, I'll give it to him," said Eugénie.

She wiped away her tears and went on reading.

Until now I had never thought of the miseries of poverty. If I have the hundred louis required for the journey, I shan't have a single penny for trading-goods. But no, I shall have neither a hundred louis nor one louis. I shall not know how much money I have left until my debts in Paris have been settled. If I have nothing, I shall go quietly to Nantes and ship as a common sailor. I shall start in over there as have other energetic young men who were penniless but have returned rich from the Indies. Since this morning I have calmly faced my future. It is more dreadful for me than for anyone else, I who have been spoiled by an adoring mother, indulged by the kindest of fathers, and favored, on my entrance into society, with Anna's love! I have known only the flowers of life; this happiness could not last. Nevertheless, my dear Anna, I possess more courage than a thoughtless young man

*might have been expected to have, above all a young man used
to the sweet ways of the most delightful woman in Paris, cradled
in the joys of family life, on whom all things smiled at home and
whose wishes were law to a father ... Oh my father, Annette, he
is dead ...*

*Well, I have thought over my position and yours too. I have
aged a great deal in twenty-four hours. Dear Anna, if to keep me
near you in Paris, you were to sacrifice all the pleasures of luxury,
your beautiful clothes, your box at the Opera, we should still not
have enough for my extravagant way of living. Besides I could
never accept such a sacrifice. So today we must part forever.*

"He's leaving her, Holy Virgin! What joy! . . ."

Eugénie trembled with happiness. Charles stirred and a chill of
fear ran through her. But fortunately for her, he did not waken
and she went on reading:

*When shall I return? I do not know. The climate of the Indies
quickly ages a European, especially a European who has to work.
Let us look ten years ahead. In ten years your daughter will be
eighteen. She will be your constant companion, your keeper. Society will be cruel to you, your daughter perhaps even crueller.
We have seen examples of these harsh social condemnations and
of the ingratitude of young daughters. Let us take warning from
them. Cherish in the depths of your soul as I shall cherish in mine
the memory of these four years of happiness, and be faithful, if
you can, to your poor friend. I cannot demand this of you, however, because you see, my dear Annette, I must adapt myself to
my situation, take a middle-class view of life, and work things
out realistically. Therefore I must think of marriage, which becomes one of the necessities of my new existence. And I must admit that I have found here in Saumur, at my uncle's, a cousin
whose manners, face, wit, and heart would please you, and who,
furthermore, seems to me to have ...*

"He must have been very tired to have stopped writing her," said Eugénie to herself when she saw that the letter stopped short in the middle of this sentence.

She was justifying him! How was it possible for this innocent young girl to recognize the lack of warmth discernible in this letter? To piously brought-up young girls, pure and unsophisticated, everything is love from the moment they set foot in the enchanted regions of love. They walk there surrounded by the celestial light projected from their own souls, which casts its rays on their lover. They color him with the flame of their own feelings and attribute to him their most beautiful thoughts. A woman's mistakes almost always arise from her belief in the good or her faith in the true. In Eugénie's heart the words, "My dear Annette, my beloved," echoed like the sweetest language of love, and charmed her soul as in her childhood the divine notes of the *Venite Adoremus* repeated by the organ had charmed her ear. Furthermore, the tears still visible in Charles's eyes bore witness to all those noble qualities of the heart by which young girls are rightly won. How could she know that if Charles loved his father so much and mourned him so sincerely, this tenderness was much less the result of his goodness of heart than of paternal indulgence? By gratifying their son's every whim, by lavishing on him all the pleasures of wealth, Monsieur and Madame Guillaume Grandet had kept him from making those ugly calculations of which most sons and daughters are more or less guilty when, faced with the delights of Paris, they form desires and conceive schemes which to their annoyance they see constantly postponed and delayed during the lifetime of their parents. The father's liberality had implanted in the son's heart a genuine and unquestioning filial love.

Nevertheless, Charles was a true child of Paris, taught by its customs and by Annette herself to calculate everything, already an old man under the mask of youth. He had received the frightful education of that society, where, in a single evening, are committed in thought and in word more crimes than the law punishes in the courts, where the noblest ideas are assassinated by a witticism, where an individual is considered strong only in so far as he sees things clearly; and there, to see things clearly means to believe in nothing, neither in feelings, nor in men, nor even in events—for events are fabricated there. There, to see clearly, you must weigh your friend's purse every morning, you must know how to hold yourself adroitly above whatever may happen; never allow yourself to admire anything spontaneously, neither works of art nor noble deeds, and establish personal interest as the basis of all your actions. After a thousand follies, the great lady, the beautiful Annette, forced Charles to think seriously; she talked to him of his future, while running a perfumed hand through his hair; as she rearranged a curl, she taught him worldly wisdom. She made him at once effeminate and materialistic—a twofold corruption, but delicate, refined, and in the best of taste.

"You're awfully simple-minded, Charles," she would say to him. "I shall have a hard time teaching you to understand the ways of the world. You've behaved very badly toward Monsieur des Lupeaulx. I know he's not very honorable, but wait until he's lost his power. Then you can despise him as much as you like. You know what Madame Campan used to tell us? 'Children, as long as a man is a minister, adore him; if he falls, help to drag him to the gutter. Powerful, he is a kind of god; fallen, he is beneath Marat in his sewer, because he is alive and Marat is dead. Life is a series of combinations, and you must study and understand them if you are to succeed in always maintaining a favorable position.'"

Charles was too much a man of fashion, he had always been too happy with his parents, too much admired by the world, to have noble ideals. The grain of gold dropped into his heart by his mother had been beaten thin on the Parisian anvil; he had stretched it too far and it was to be worn through by friction. But Charles was only twenty-one. At that age the freshness of youth seems inseparable from candor of soul. The voice, the glance, the face itself seem in harmony with the feelings. Thus the sternest judge, the most skeptical lawyer, the hardest of usurers, always hesitate to believe in the deterioration of the heart, in the corruption of self-interest, while the eyes are still bathed in limpid purity and no wrinkles mar the brow. Charles had never had occasion to apply the maxims of Parisian morality, and up to this day was still radiant with inexperience. But unknown to himself he had been inoculated with selfishness. The germs of political economy as practised by the Parisian were latent in his heart and would not be slow in flowering there once the idle spectator became an actor in the drama of real life.

Nearly all young girls succumb to the gentle promises implicit in such externals; but even if Eugénie had been as wise and observant as some girls in the provinces are, would she have doubted her cousin, whose manners, speech, and actions were still in harmony with the aspirations of his heart? A mere chance, unhappily, revealed to her the last effusions of true sensibility remaining in this young heart; she heard, as it were, the last breaths of his conscience. She put aside the letter—to her so full of love—and began to contemplate her sleeping cousin with pleasure. She still saw this face in the light of her own youthful illusions about life, and she swore to herself that she would always love him. Then she glanced at another letter, without attaching much importance to this second indiscretion; and if she began to read it, it was only to obtain fresh proofs of the noble qualities which, like all women, she attributed to the man of her choice.

My dear Alphonse: When you receive this letter, I shall be without friends; but I assure you that in distrusting those worldly people who are so fond of using the word, I have never doubted

your friendship. I am therefore asking you to take charge of my
affairs and am counting on you to get as much as you can out of
my possessions. By this time you must know my situation. I have
nothing left and I intend to go at once to the Indies. I have just
written to all the people to whom I believe I owe money, and you
will find enclosed the list, which I have made as complete as pos-
sible from memory. My library, my furniture, my carriages, my
horses, and other odds and ends, will suffice, I trust, to pay my
debts. I do not wish to keep anything except perhaps a few worth-
less trifles which might serve to begin my collection of trading-
goods. My dear Alphonse, I shall send you from here a proper
power of attorney for the sale in case of protest. Please send me all
my weapons. Keep Briton for yourself. No one would want to pay
what that noble beast is worth, and I prefer to give him to you
like the customary mourning ring that a dying man bequeaths to
his executor. Farry, Breilman and Company have built me a very
comfortable traveling carriage but they have not yet delivered it.
Try and persuade them to keep it and not ask for any indemnity.
If they refuse to accept this arrangement, do what you can to
avoid anything that might reflect on my good faith in my pres-
ent circumstances. I owe the islander six louis, lost at cards. Don't
fail to pay . . .

"Dear cousin!" said Eugénie putting down the letter and running softly back to her room with one of the lighted candles.
With a thrill of pleasure she opened the drawer of an old oaken
chest, one of the finest examples of the Renaissance period, on
which could still be seen, partly effaced, the famous royal sala-
mander. From it she took a large purse of red velvet with golden
tassels, edged with tarnished gold thread, an inheritance from
her grandmother. She felt its weight with great pride and began
to count over with delight the forgotten items of her little hoard.
First she took out twenty Portuguese coins, still new, struck in

the reign of John V in 1725. At the present rate of exchange they were actually worth five lisbonnines or a hundred and sixty-eight francs sixty-four centimes each, but their conventional value was a hundred and eighty francs on account of the rarity and beauty of the said coins, which shone like the sun. *Item,* five genovines or hundred-franc pieces from Genoa, another rare coin worth eighty-seven francs on the exchange, but a hundred francs to collectors. She had inherited them from old Monsieur de la Bertellière. *Item,* three gold quadruples, Spanish, of Philip V, struck in 1729, given her by Madame Gentillet who always repeated the same phrase with each gift: "This dear little canary, this yellow boy, is worth ninety-eight francs! Take good care of him, my darling; he'll be the flower of your treasure." *Item* (these were valued most highly by her father, the gold in them being twenty-three carats and a fraction), a hundred Dutch ducats, struck in the year 1756 and worth nearly thirteen francs each. *Item* (a great curiosity . . . a species of medals almost sacred to misers), three rupees with the sign of the Scales, and five rupees with the sign of the Virgin, all in pure gold of twenty-four carats; the magnificent coins of the Great Mogul, each of which was worth by mere weight thirty-seven francs, forty centimes, but at least fifty francs to those connoisseurs who love to handle gold. *Item,* the napoleon of forty francs received two days before, which she had put carelessly into her red purse.

This treasure consisted of new and virgin coins, real works of art. Old Grandet often asked about them and liked to see them from time to time in order to point out to his daughter their intrinsic merits, such as the beauty of the milled edges, the brightness of the face, the richness of the letters, whose sharp ridges were not yet worn down. But she did not think of these rarities, nor of her father's mania, nor of the danger she ran in parting with a treasure so dear to him. No, she was thinking of her cousin, and figured out, after making a few mistakes, that she possessed about five thousand eight hundred francs in actual value, which might be sold to collectors for close to six thousand francs. At the sight of all this wealth she began to clap her hands like a child forced to express its overflowing joy in artless physical movements. Thus father and daughter had both counted their fortune, he to go and sell his gold, Eugénie to fling hers into the sea of love. She put the coins back into the old purse, picked it up, and ran unhesitatingly upstairs. Her cousin's secret misery made her oblivious of the hour and the proprieties; moreover, she was fortified by her conscience, her devotion, and her happiness.

Just as she appeared on the threshold of the door, holding the candlestick in one hand and her purse in the other, Charles awoke, saw his cousin, and remained speechless with surprise. Eugénie came forward, set the candlestick down on the table, and said in a trembling voice, "Cousin, I must ask your forgiveness for a great wrong that I have done you; but God will pardon me this sin, if you will wipe it out."

"What is it?" said Charles, rubbing his eyes.

"I read those two letters."

Charles blushed.

"How did it happen?" she went on. "Why did I come up here? Really, I don't remember. But I am tempted not to feel too much remorse at having read these letters, since they have revealed to me your heart, your soul, and . . ."

"And what?" asked Charles.

"And your plans, your need of a sum . . ."

"My dear cousin . . ."

"Hush, hush, Cousin, not so loud, don't let's waken anyone. Here," she said, opening her purse, "are the savings of a foolish girl who has no wants. Take them, Charles. This morning I did not know what money was; you have taught me. It's only a means, that's all. A cousin is almost a brother; you can surely borrow your sister's purse."

Eugénie, half woman and half child, never dreamed of a refusal, and her cousin remained silent.

"Oh, you wouldn't refuse?" asked Eugénie, whose heart could be heard beating in the intense silence.

Her cousin's hesitation humiliated her; but the situation in which he found himself appeared all the more vividly to her mind and she bent her knee.

"I shall not get up till you've accepted the gold," said she. "Answer me, Cousin, I implore you. I must know that you respect me, that you are generous, that . . ."

As he heard this cry of noble despair, the boy's tears fell on his cousin's hands, which he had caught in his own to keep her from kneeling. When she felt these warm tears, Eugénie seized her purse and emptied it out on the table.

"Oh, you will, won't you?" she said, weeping for joy. "Don't be afraid, Cousin, you'll be rich. This gold will bring you luck; some day you'll be able to give it back to me. Besides, we'll be partners. I'll accept any conditions you make. But you really shouldn't value this gift so highly."

Finally Charles was able to express his feelings.

"Yes, Eugénie, I should be very small-minded indeed if I could not accept. However, gift for gift, trust for trust."

"What do you mean?" she asked anxiously.

"Listen, my dear cousin, I have here . . ." He interrupted himself to point to a square box in a leather case standing on the bureau. "I have something there which is as precious to me as life itself. That case was a present from my mother. Since this morning I have been thinking that if she could rise from the grave, she would herself sell this gold which in her fondness she lavished upon me; but if I were to do it, it would seem to me a sacrilege."

Eugénie gripped her cousin's hand convulsively as he uttered these last few words.

"No," he added after a slight pause, during which they exchanged a liquid glance of tenderness, "no, I neither want to destroy it nor risk losing it on my travels. Dear Eugénie, I'll leave it in your care. Never did friend confide more sacred possession to friend. Be the judge of that yourself." He went over and took the box out of its leather case, opened it and sadly displayed to his awe-struck cousin a dressing-case, in which the workmanship of the gold fittings gave them a value far above their weight.

"What you are admiring now is nothing," he said pressing a spring which opened a secret compartment. "For these are worth more to me than anything else in the whole world." He took out two miniatures, two masterpieces of Madame de Mirbel, richly set in pearls.

"Oh, what a beautiful woman! Isn't that the lady you were writing to . . ."

"No," said he smiling, "this lady is my mother, and here is my father—your aunt and uncle. Eugénie, I ought to beg you on my knees to watch over this treasure. If I were to perish and lose your little fortune, this gold would repay you, and you are the only person to whom I could leave these two portraits. You are worthy of this trust; but destroy them rather than let anyone else have them after you . . ." Eugénie was silent. "Oh, you will, won't you?" he added engagingly.

Hearing her own words repeated by her cousin, she glanced at him for the first time with the look of a woman in love, one of those looks in which there is almost as much playfulness as depth of feeling. He took her hand and kissed it.

"Angel of purity! Where we are concerned, money counts for nothing, does it? For us the feeling that lies behind it will be everything from now on."

"You are like your mother. Was her voice as soft as yours?"

"Oh, much softer . . ."

"Yes, for you," she said dropping her eyelids. "Come, Charles, go to bed. I insist. You are tired. Good night."

She gently withdrew her hand from her cousin's, who accompanied her to her room with a light. As they stood upon the threshold of her door, he exclaimed: "Oh, why am I ruined?"

"What does it matter?" she replied. "My father is rich, I'm sure of it."

"Poor child," replied Charles, advancing a step into her room and leaning against the wall, "if he were, he wouldn't have let my father die; he wouldn't leave you in this penury; in fact, he would live quite differently."

"But he owns Froidfond."

"And what's Froidfond worth?"

"I don't know, but he owns Noyers too."

"Nothing but a poor farm!"

"He has vineyards and meadows . . ."

"Not worth mentioning," said Charles with a disdainful air. "If your father had as much as twenty-four thousand francs a year, would you have to live in this cold, bare room?" he added, moving his left foot forward. "There's where you'll keep my treasures," he said, pointing to the old cupboard as if to hide his thoughts.

"Go to bed," she said, preventing him from entering the disordered room.

Charles withdrew and they smiled good night to each other.

Both fell asleep dreaming the same dream, and from then on Charles began to scatter a few roses over his grief. The next morning Madame Grandet found her daughter taking a walk with Charles before breakfast. The young man was still sad, as became a poor devil who had plumbed the depths, so to speak, of his misfortunes and, on measuring the height of the abyss into which he had fallen, had apprehended the whole burden of his future life.

"Father won't be back before dinner," said Eugénie, noticing the anxious look on her mother's face.

It was easy to see from Eugénie's manner, from her expression, and from the unusual sweetness which softened her voice that she and her cousin were in complete agreement. Their souls were ardently wedded, perhaps even before experiencing the full strength of the feelings which united them one to another. Charles remained in the hall and his melancholy was respected. Each of the three women had work to do. As Grandet had forgotten to look after his affairs, a great many people came on business: the roofer, the plumber, the mason, the laborers, the carpenter, the crofters, the farmers, some to arrive at an agreement about repairs, others to pay their rent or collect what was owed to them. So Madame Grandet and Eugénie were obliged to come and go, listening to the interminable speeches of workmen and country folk. Nanon took in the quit-rents in her kitchen. She always awaited her master's orders to know what should be kept for the house and what should be sold on the market. Like many country gentlemen, the old man made a habit of drinking his inferior wine and eating his spoiled fruit. Toward five in the evening Grandet came back from Angers, having received fourteen thousand francs for his gold and carrying in his wallet treasury notes which would yield interest until the time came for him to pay for his bonds. He had left Cornoiller in Angers to look after the horses, which were almost foundered, and bring them back slowly after having given them a good rest.

"I have come back from Angers, my dear," he said. "I'm hungry."

"Haven't you eaten anything since yesterday?" shouted Nanon from the kitchen.

"Nothing," replied the old man.

Nanon brought in the soup. Des Grassins came for his client's instructions just as the family sat down to table. Old Grandet had not even noticed his nephew.

"Just go on with your dinner, Grandet," said the banker. "We can talk while you're eating. Do you know what gold is worth in Angers? They've come to get it for Nantes. I'm going to send some."

"Don't send any," replied the old man, "they've got enough already. We're much too good friends for me to let you waste your time."

"But gold is worth thirteen francs fifty centimes there."

"Say rather *was* worth."

"Where the devil did it come from?"

"I went to Angers last night," replied Grandet in a low voice. The banker quivered with surprise. Then there began a whispered conversation between the two, during which des Grassins and Grandet looked several times at Charles. It was no doubt just when the former cooper told the banker to invest the sum which would bring him in a hundred thousand francs a year that des Grassins betrayed his surprise a second time.

"Monsieur Grandet," he said to Charles, "I'm leaving for Paris, and if you have any errands . . ."

"None, sir, thank you," replied Charles.

"Thank him better than that, nephew. Monsieur des Grassins is going to settle the affairs of the house of Guillaume Grandet."

"Is there some hope then?" asked Charles.

"Why," cried the cooper with a convincing assumption of pride, "aren't you my nephew? Your honor is ours. Isn't your name Grandet too?"

Charles got up, suddenly embraced old Grandet, turned pale, and left the room. Eugénie looked at her father with admiration.

"Well, good-bye, my dear des Grassins. Good luck to you. And get the best of those fellows if you can!" The two diplomats shook hands; the cooper conducted the banker to the door; then, having closed it, he came back and said to Nanon, throwing himself into his armchair, "Get me some black currant brandy!" But too much excited to stay in one place, he got up, looked at the portrait of Monsieur de la Bertellière, and began to sing, doing what Nanon called his dance steps:

> *Dans les gardes françaises*
> *J'avais un bon papa.*

Nanon, Madame Grandet, and Eugénie stared at each other in silence. The wine-grower's hilarity always frightened them when it reached a climax. The evening was soon over. Old Grandet chose to go to bed early; and when he went to bed, everybody else in the house had to go too, just as when Augustus drank, Poland was drunk. Then Nanon, Charles, and Eugénie were just as tired as the master. As for Madame Grandet, she slept, ate, drank, and moved in accordance with her husband's will. However, during the two hours consecrated to digestion, the cooper, more facetious than he had ever been, uttered a number of his favorite maxims, a single example of which will give the measure of his mind. When he had finished his brandy, he looked at the glass.

"No sooner have you put your lips to a glass than it's empty! Such is life. You can't have your cake and eat it. Money can't circulate and stay in your purse. That would be too much of a good thing."

He was jovial and benevolent. When Nanon came in with her spinning-wheel, he said, "You must be tired. Put away your hemp."

"Goodness, I wouldn't know what to do with myself!" replied the servant.

"Poor Nanon! Would you like some brandy?"

"Oh, as for brandy, I won't say no to that. Madame makes it a lot better than the apothecaries. What they sell isn't worth much."

"They put too much sugar in it. You can't taste anything," said the old man.

The next day, the family, meeting at eight for breakfast, afforded for the first time a picture of genuine intimacy. Misfortune had promptly established a bond between Grandet, Eugénie, and Charles; Nanon herself was in sympathy with them without knowing it. The four of them were beginning to constitute a real family. As for the old wine-grower, now that his avarice was sated and he was sure of seeing the dandy leave soon without having to pay for anything except his trip to Nantes, he had become almost indifferent to his presence in the house. He left the two children, as he called Charles and Eugénie, free to do as they pleased under the eye of Madame Grandet, in whom he had implicit confidence as far as conventional and religious morality were concerned. The alignment of his meadows and of the ditches bordering on the road, his poplar plantations on the Loire, and the winter work in his vineyards and at Froidfond took up all his time.

For Eugénie the springtime of love had come. Since the nocturnal scene in which she had given her cousin her small fortune, her heart had followed it. Sharing the same secret, they looked at each other with an expression of mutual understanding, which deepened their emotions and made them more exclusive, more intimate, placing the two of them, as it were, beyond and above the realm of ordinary life. Did not cousinship authorize a certain gentleness of tone, a tenderness of look? Thus Eugénie took delight in lulling her cousin's sorrows with the childish playfulness of a newborn love. Are there not sweet parallels between the beginnings of love and those of life? Don't we rock a baby with gentle songs and tender glances? Don't we tell it marvellous tales of a golden future? Does not hope eternally spread its

radiant wings over the child? Does he not weep now tears
of joy and now of grief? Does he not cry for trifles, for pebbles
to build a shifting palace, for flowers no sooner cut than forgotten? Is he not eager to grasp at time, to hasten forward into
life? Love is our second transformation. Love made children
once more of Eugénie and Charles. It was first love, with all its
childish play, and it was all the more precious to these two hearts
steeped in melancholy. In having to struggle from birth against
the gloom of mourning, their love was all the more in harmony
with the provincial severity of this decaying house.

As he exchanged a few words with his cousin by the side of
the well in this silent court or lingered in this little garden, sitting
with Eugénie on a mossy seat until sundown, while they said
sweet nothings to each other or mused in the silence which
reigned between the ramparts and the house, as one does beneath
the arches of a church, Charles understood the sanctity of love;
for his great lady, his dear Annette, had taught him only its
stormy troubles. At this moment he forsook passion as he had
known it in Paris, coquettish, vain, showy, for pure, true love.
Now he liked the house, for its customs no longer seemed so
ridiculous to him. He came downstairs early in the morning in
order to have a few moments alone with Eugénie before Grandet
arrived to dole out the provisions, and when he heard the sound
of the old man's footsteps on the stairs, he slipped away into
the garden. The harmless crime of this morning meeting, which
was a secret even from Eugénie's mother, and which Nanon
pretended not to notice, gave the most innocent love in the
world all the excitement of forbidden pleasures. After breakfast,
when Grandet had gone to see to his properties and projects,
Charles remained with the mother and daughter, experiencing
the unfamiliar pleasures of helping them wind their wool, of
watching them work, and listening to their chatter. The simplicity of this almost monastic existence, which revealed to him

the beauty of these unworldly souls, touched him deeply. He had believed such customs impossible in France and had admitted their existence only in Germany; and even then, only in fiction, in the novels of Auguste Lafontaine. Soon Eugénie came to represent for him the ideal of Goethe's Marguerite before she had sinned. Day by day his glances and his words enraptured the poor girl, who abandoned herself with delight to the current of love. She grasped her happiness as a swimmer seizes the branch of a willow to draw himself out of the stream and lie at rest on its bank. Did not the sorrows of a coming separation sadden the happy hours of these fleeting days? Each day some little circumstance reminded them that they soon must part.

Three days after des Grassins' departure, Charles was taken by Grandet to the civil court, with all the solemnity that country people attach to such occasions, there to sign a waiver relinquishing his right to his father's estate. Ghastly repudiation! A kind of domestic apostasy! He went to Lawyer Cruchot to have two powers of attorney made out, one for des Grassins, the other for the friend entrusted with the sale of his belongings. Then he had to attend to all the formalities necessary to obtain a passport for travel abroad. Finally, when the simple mourning clothes that he had ordered from Paris arrived, Charles sent for one of the Saumur tailors and sold him all his now useless finery. This action pleased old Grandet particularly.

"Ah, now you look like a man ready to sail away and make his fortune," he said to him when he saw him dressed in a coat of heavy black cloth. "Fine! Excellent!"

"I beg you to believe, sir," replied Charles, "that I shall know how to behave in my new situation."

"What's that?" asked the old man, his eyes lighting up at the sight of a handful of gold that Charles showed him.

"Sir, I have gathered together all the buttons, rings, and other superfluous trifles I own which might have some value. Not knowing anyone in Saumur, I was going to ask you this morning to . . ."

"To buy them?" interrupted Grandet.

"No, Uncle, only to recommend an honest man who . . ."

"Give them to me, Nephew. I'll go upstairs and estimate their value and come back and tell you what they're worth almost to a centime. Jeweler's gold," he said examining a long chain, "eighteen to nineteen carats."

The old man stretched out his big hand and carried off the pile of gold.

"Cousin," said Charles, "may I offer you these two buttons? They can be used to fasten ribbons on your wrists. That's a very fashionable kind of bracelet just now."

"I shall be glad to accept them, Cousin," she said, giving him an understanding look.

"My dear aunt, here is my mother's thimble. I've always kept it carefully in my dressing-case," said Charles, presenting a pretty gold thimble to Madame Grandet, who had been longing for one for ten years.

"I can't find words to thank you, Nephew," said the old mother, her eyes filling with tears. "Night and morning I shall add to my prayers the one most urgent for you, the prayer for travelers. If I die, Eugénie will preserve it carefully for you."

"They're worth nine hundred and eighty-nine francs seventy-five centimes, Nephew," said Grandet, opening the door. "But to save you the trouble of selling them, I shall advance you the money . . . in *livres*."

The expression "in *livres*" means, on the banks of the Loire, that crown pieces of six *livres* must be accepted as the equivalent of six francs without any deduction for shortage in weight.

"I didn't dare suggest it to you," replied Charles, "but it was most repugnant to me to peddle my jewelry in the town where you live People should wash their dirty linen at home, Napoleon used to say. I thank you for your kindness." Grandet scratched his ear, and there was silence for a moment.

"My dear uncle," Charles went on, looking anxiously at him, as though afraid of hurting his feelings, "my aunt and my cousin have been good enough to accept a trifling remembrance of me. May I now present you with these cuff links which can no longer be of any use to me? They will remind you of an unhappy youth who, far away, will often think of those who are now his only relatives."

"My dear boy, you mustn't rob yourself like that . . . What have you got, my dear?" he said, turning eagerly to his wife. "Oh, a gold thimble. And you, girlie? Diamond clasps. Well, I'll accept your buttons, my boy," he went on, shaking Charles by the hand. "But . . . you must allow me . . . to pay your . . . yes, your fare to the Indies. Yes, I want to pay your passage. Besides, you see, my boy, in valuing your jewelry I counted only the weight of the gold. Very likely the workmanship is worth something too. So that's settled. I'll give you fifteen hundred francs . . . in *livres*. I can borrow it from Cruchot, for I haven't a red cent here, unless Perrotet, who is behind with his rent, pays me. I think I'll go and see him."

He picked up his hat, put on his gloves, and went out.

"Then you are really going?" said Eugénie with a look of mingled sadness and admiration.

"I must," he said, bowing his head.

For some days past Charles's bearing, manners, and speech had become those of a man who in spite of his profound afflic- tion feels the weight of his great obligations and draws new courage from his misfortune. He no longer sighed; he had become a man. Eugénie had never been more impressed by her cousin's character than when she saw him come downstairs in his plain black clothes, which went so well with his pale face and serious expression. That day the two women put on mourning too and went with Charles to a requiem celebrated in the parish church for the soul of the late Guillaume Grandet.

At lunch Charles received letters from Paris and read them.

"Well, Cousin, are you satisfied with the way your affairs are being managed?" asked Eugénie in a low voice.

"You should never ask such questions as that, Daughter," replied Grandet. "What the devil? Do I tell you about my affairs? Why do you poke your nose into your cousin's? Leave the boy alone."

"Oh, I have no secrets," said Charles.

"Tut, tut, tut, Nephew, you'll soon find out that you must keep a check on your tongue in business."

When the two lovers were alone in the garden, Charles said to Eugénie, drawing her down beside him on the old bench under the walnut tree, "I was right about Alphonse; he's been marvelous. He has handled my affairs prudently and loyally. I don't owe anything in Paris now. My furniture has been sold to advantage, and he tells me he has taken the advice of a sea captain and invested the three thousand francs that remained in a stock of European curiosities which can be turned to good account in the Indies. He has forwarded my baggage to Nantes, where there's a ship loading for Java. In five days, Eugénie, we must say farewell, perhaps forever, but in any case for a long time. My stock of trading goods and ten thousand francs sent to me by two of my friends make a very small beginning. I can't hope to come back for several years. My dear cousin, don't let your future depend on mine. I may perish, and perhaps a good match may turn up for you . . ."

"You love me? . . ." she said.

"Oh, yes, very much," he replied with a depth of tone which revealed an equal depth of feeling.

"I shall wait, Charles. Heavens, my father's at his window," she said pushing her cousin away as he leaned over to kiss her.

She ran off under the archway and Charles followed her. Seeing this, she retreated to the foot of the staircase and opened the swing door; then without quite knowing where she went, Eugénie found herself near Nanon's tiny room in the darkest spot in the corridor. There Charles took her hand, drew her to him, put his arm around her waist, and pressed her gently to his heart. Eugénie no longer resisted; she received and returned the purest, the sweetest, and yet the most wholehearted of kisses.

"Dear Eugénie, a cousin is better than a brother; he can marry you," said Charles.

"So be it!" cried Nanon, opening the door of her lair.

Startled, the two lovers fled into the hall, where Eugénie took up her work again and Charles began to read the litanies of the Virgin in Madame Grandet's prayer book.

"Hm!" said Nanon. "So we're saying our prayers now."

As soon as Charles had announced his departure, Grandet began to pretend that he had his interests very much at heart. He was generous with everything that cost him nothing, took pains to find him a packer, and declared that the man wanted too much for his cases. Finally he insisted on making them himself out of old boards. He got up at dawn to plane, square off, polish, and nail his planks and made out of them excellent boxes into which he packed all Charles's belongings. He undertook to have them sent down the Loire by boat, to insure them, and to get them to Nantes in good time.

After the stolen kiss in the corridor the hours flew by for Eugénie with terrifying rapidity. Sometimes she thought of going with her cousin. Those who have known the most engaging of the passions—that passion which we see cut off every day by age, by time, by mortal illness, by one or another of the vicissitudes of human fate—will understand Eugénie's torments. She often wept as she walked in the garden, which now seemed too

cramped for her as did also the courtyard, the house, and the
town. She imagined herself crossing the vast expanse of the seas.
At length the eve of departure arrived. That morning, while
Grandet and Nanon were away, the precious box containing the
two portraits was solemnly placed in the only drawer of the old
chest having a key, in which the now empty purse reposed. The
concealment of this treasure was accompanied by a goodly number of kisses and tears. When Eugénie put the key in her bosom,
she had not the courage to prevent Charles from kissing the spot.

"It shall never leave that place, my dear."

"Then my heart will always be there too."

"Oh, Charles, you mustn't," she said chidingly.

"Are we not married?" he replied. "I have your promise, accept mine."

"I am yours forever!" they each said, repeating the words twice
over.

No promise made upon this earth was ever more pure.
Eugénie's innocence had momentarily sanctified the young man's
love. Breakfast the next morning was sad. In spite of the gold-
embroidered dressing-gown and a gold cross that Charles gave
her, Nanon herself, at liberty to express her feelings, had tears
in her eyes.

"That poor, sweet, young gentleman who's going over the seas!
May God protect him!"

At half past ten the family set out to accompany Charles to
the coach for Nantes. Nanon had unchained the dog and closed
the door, and insisted on carrying Charles's handbag. All the
merchants of the old street were on the thresholds of their shops
to watch this procession, which was joined in the market-place
by Lawyer Cruchot.

"Be sure you don't cry, Eugénie," said her mother.

"Nephew," said Grandet at the door of the inn, kissing Charles
on both cheeks, "go away poor, come back rich. You'll find your

father's honor safe. That I, Grandet, guarantee. Then it will only be for you to . . ."

"Oh, Uncle, you soften the bitterness of my departure. Surely that is the finest present you could give me!"

Not understanding what the old cooper was about to say when he interrupted him, Charles shed tears of gratitude on his uncle's weather-beaten face, while Eugénie pressed with all her strength her cousin's hand and her father's. Only the notary smiled, admiring the old man's cunning, for he alone had understood Grandet. These four inhabitants of Saumur, surrounded by several people, stood in front of the coach until it left. Then, when it had disappeared onto the bridge and could only be heard rumbling in the distance, Grandet said, "Pleasant journey!" Fortunately Lawyer Cruchot was the only one who heard this exclamation. Eugénie and her mother had gone to a place on the quay from which they could see the coach and were waving their white handkerchiefs, and Charles replied by waving his.

"Oh, Mother, what I would give to have God's power for a single moment!" said Eugénie when she could no longer see Charles's handkerchief.

In order not to interrupt the current of events which take place in the bosom of the Grandet family, we must glance ahead at the various transactions which the old man carried on in Paris through the agency of des Grassins. A month after the banker's departure, Grandet was in possession of a certificate entitling him to an annuity of a hundred thousand *livres* purchased at eighty francs net. The particulars given at his death by the inventory of his property threw no light upon the means suggested by his caution to remit the price of the certificate in return for the certificate itself. Lawyer Cruchot believed that Nanon, unknown to herself, was the trusty instrument by which the money was transported. At about this time, the servant was absent for five days on the pretext of putting something to rights at Froidfond, as though the old man were capable of leaving anything in disorder. As far as the affairs of the house of Guillaume Grandet are concerned, all the old cooper's expectations were realized.

The Bank of France, as everybody knows, possesses exact information about all the great fortunes of Paris and the provinces. The names of des Grassins and of Félix Grandet of Saumur were known there and enjoyed the respect accorded to well-known financial figures whose wealth is based on enormous unencumbered estates. The arrival of the Saumur banker, charged, it was said, with the honorable liquidation of the house of Grandet in Paris, was enough to preserve the late merchant's reputation from the shame of protested notes. The seals were broken in the presence of the creditors, and the family notary went to work at once on the inventory of the estate. Soon after this des Grassins called a meeting of the creditors, who unanimously elected him conjointly with François Keller, the head of a rich banking house, and one of the chief creditors, as liquidators, with full power to protect both the honor of the family and the interests of the claimants. The credit of Grandet of Saumur, the hopes he raised in the hearts of the creditors through des Grassins, facilitated the transactions; there was not a single recalcitrant among them. No one thought of transferring his claims to his profit-and-loss account, and they all said to themselves, "Grandet of Saumur will pay!" Six months went by. The Parisians had redeemed the notes in circulation and kept them at the bottom of their wallets. Thus the cooper had achieved his first objective. Nine months after the first meeting, the two liquidators paid out forty-seven per cent to each creditor. This amount was obtained by the sale of the securities, properties, goods, and chattels belonging to the late Guillaume Grandet and was paid over with scrupulous fidelity. This liquidation was handled with the strictest integrity. The creditors gratefully acknowledged the remarkable and undeniable honor of the Grandets. When these praises had circulated for a suitable length of time, the creditors demanded the rest of their money. They had to write a collective letter to Grandet.

"Now it starts!" said the former cooper, throwing the letter into the fire. "Patience, my dear friends."

In reply to the proposals contained in this letter, Grandet of Saumur requested that all claims against his brother's estate be deposited with a notary, together with receipts for payments already made, on the pretext of checking the accounts and establishing exactly the assets and liabilities. This demand gave rise to innumerable difficulties. Ordinarily a creditor is something of a crank, one day ready to agree to anything, the next breathing fire and slaughter; and suddenly he may become quite accommodating. Today his wife is in good humor, his latest offspring has cut his teeth, everything is going well at home, he doesn't want to lose a penny. Tomorrow it rains, he can't go out, he's melancholy, he says yes to any proposal that might wind up the business. The day after tomorrow he requires guarantees. At the end of the month, he insists on an execution, the hangman! The creditor is like the sparrow on whose tail little children are urged to put a grain of salt; but the creditor in turn applies this image to the claim he can never lay hold of. Grandet had observed carefully the atmospheric variations in creditors, and those of his brother fulfilled all his predictions. Some grew angry and flatly refused to make the requested deposit. "Good! Just as it should be," said Grandet, rubbing his hands as he read the letters des Grassins wrote him on this subject. Others consented to the said deposit only on condition that their rights should be fully guaranteed, renouncing none of them and even reserving the right to declare bankruptcy. This was followed by further correspondence at the end of which Grandet of Saumur agreed to all the conditions. By means of this concession the meeker creditors were able to make the more stubborn ones listen to reason. The papers were deposited, but not without some demur. "This old man," they said to des Grassins, "is making fools of us."

Twenty-three months after the death of Guillaume Grandet, many of the creditors, caught up in the whirl of business in Paris, had forgotten about the recovery of their Grandet debts, or if they happened to think of them merely said, "I'm beginning to believe the forty-seven per cent is all I'll ever get out of that." The cooper had counted on the power of Time, who, he used to say, is not a bad sort of fellow. At the end of the third year, des Grassins wrote to Grandet that in exchange for ten per cent of the two million four hundred thousand francs still owed by the house of Grandet, he had persuaded the creditors to give up the title to their claims. Grandet replied that the notary and the stock-broker whose shameful failure had been the cause of his brother's death were still very much alive! They might now be solvent and ought to be sued in order to get something out of them and reduce the amount of the deficit. At the end of the fourth year the deficit was duly estimated at twelve hundred thousand francs. There were negotiations lasting six months between the liquidators and the creditors, between Grandet and the liquidators. In short, hard pressed to fulfill his agreement, Grandet of Saumur replied to the two liquidators, toward the ninth month of that year, that his nephew, who had made his fortune in the Indies, had indicated to him his intention of paying his father's debts in full himself; he could not take it upon himself to settle them surreptitiously without having consulted him; he was waiting for a reply. Toward the middle of the fifth year the creditors were still held in check by the words "payment in full," which the ineffable cooper, laughing in his sleeve, threw out from time to time. And he never said the words, "Those Parisians," without a sly smile and an oath.

But the creditors were reserved for a fate unexampled in the annals of commerce. When the events of this story require their reappearance, they will be found still in the same position to which Grandet had reduced them. As soon as the bonds reached a hundred and fifteen, old Grandet sold, and withdrew from Paris about two million four hundred thousand francs in gold, which he placed in the little casks along with the six hundred thousand francs of compound interest brought in by his certificates. Des Grassins was now living in Paris. This is why. In the first place he had been elected deputy; then, father of a family but bored by the dullness of Saumur, he became infatuated with Florine, one of the prettiest actresses of the Théâtre de Madame, and there was a recrudescence of the army quartermaster in the banker. It is useless to speak of his conduct; Saumur condemned it as thoroughly immoral. His wife was fortunate in having her property in her own name and in having brains enough to manage the bank in Saumur. The business was carried on in her name in order to repair the breeches made in her fortune by the extravagances of Monsieur des Grassins. The Cruchotins aggravated the false position of the quasi-widow to such an extent that she made a very poor match for her daughter and was forced to give up the idea of an alliance between Eugénie Grandet and her son. Adolphe joined his father in Paris and there became, people say, a proper scamp. The Cruchots triumphed.

"Your husband has no sense," said Grandet as he lent Madame des Grassins a sum of money on good security. "I'm very sorry for you, you're a good little woman."

"Ah, Monsieur," replied the poor lady, "who could have believed that the day he left your house to go to Paris he was going to his ruin?"

"Heaven is my witness, Madame, that up to the last minute I did everything I could to prevent him from going. Judge Cruchot was most eager to replace him; but now we know why he was so determined to go."

Thus Grandet was under no obligation to des Grassins.

FIVE

FAMILY SORROWS

*I*N any situation women have more reasons for sorrow than men and suffer more. Man has his strength and can exercise his power: he acts, moves, thinks, and keeps himself busy; he looks ahead and finds consolation in the future. It was thus with Charles. But woman stays at home. She is left with her grief from which nothing can distract her. She descends to the very depths of the abyss which yawns before her, measures it, and often fills it with her tears and prayers. It was thus with Eugénie. She embarked upon her destiny. To feel, to love, to suffer, to sacrifice will always be woman's fate. Eugénie was to be in all things a woman except in the one thing that consoles for all others. Her happiness, gathered together like the nails strewn on the wall, to use Bossuet's fine simile, would never so much as fill even the hollow of her hand. Sorrows are never long in coming, and for her they came soon. The day after Charles's departure, the Grandet house resumed its ordinary aspect for everyone except Eugénie, who suddenly found it very empty. Unknown to her father, she insisted that Charles's room remain as he had left it. Madame Grandet and Nanon were willing accomplices in this status quo.

"Who knows, he may come back sooner than we think?" she said.

"Oh, I would like to have him here," replied Nanon. "I quite liked having him round! He was such a dear, sweet young man, almost as pretty as a girl with his curly hair." Eugénie looked at Nanon. "Holy Virgin, Mademoiselle, you have the eyes of a lost soul! You mustn't look at people like that."

From that day Mademoiselle Grandet's beauty took on a new character. The solemn thoughts of love which slowly filled her soul, the dignity of a woman beloved, gave to her features that kind of radiance that painters render by a halo. Before the coming of her cousin, Eugénie could be compared to the Virgin before the conception; when he had gone, she was like the Virgin mother; she had conceived love. These two Marys, so different and so well depicted by certain Spanish painters, together compose one of the most brilliant of the symbolic figures in which Christianity abounds. As she was returning from mass the day after Charles's departure, for she had made a vow to go to mass every day, Eugénie bought in the town bookstore a map of the world which she tacked up beside her mirror in order to follow her cousin on his voyage to the Indies, to be able to feel herself somehow present, morning and evening, in the vessel which was carrying him there, to see him, to ask him a thousand questions, to say to him: "Are you well? Are you unhappy? Do you really think of me as you look at the guiding star whose beauty and usefulness you have taught me?" Then, in the morning, she would sit pensively beneath the walnut tree on the worm-eaten bench covered with gray moss where they had said so many foolish, tender things to each other, where they had built so many castles in Spain, dreamed such pretty dreams of their life together. She thought of the future as she looked at the little bit of sky the walls allowed her to see, then at the old house and the roof above Charles's room. In short, hers was that lonely love, that true, persistent love that permeates every thought and becomes the substance, or, as our fathers would have said, the very stuff of life. When the so-called friends of old Grandet came in the evening to play cards, she was gay, she pretended; but all through the morning she talked of Charles with her mother and Nanon. Nanon had discovered that she could sympathize in the sufferings of her young mistress without failing in her duty toward her old master. And she would say to Eugénie, "If I had had a man of my own, I would have . . . followed him to hell . . . I would have . . . why . . . I'd have been ready to die for him. But . . . I've never had one. I shall die without knowing what it means to live. Would you believe it, Mademoiselle, that old Cornoiller, who's really quite a decent sort, is always hanging round me, because of my money, just like those who come sniffing round the master's hoard and paying court to you. I can see it, for I'm still sharp enough, though I'm as big as a church. Well, Mademoiselle, I like it, even if it isn't love."

Two months went by. This domestic life, once so monotonous, was now enlivened by the consuming interest of the secret which bound these three women even more closely together. For them Charles still lived and moved beneath the grim, gray rafters of the hall. Morning and evening Eugénie opened up the dressing-case and looked at her aunt's portrait. One Sunday morning she was surprised by her mother as she was absorbed in trying to trace Charles's features in those of the portrait. Madame Grandet was then admitted into the terrible secret of the exchange that had taken place between Charles and Eugénie.

"You gave it all to him!" said the horrified mother. "What will you say to your father on New Year's Day when he asks to see your gold?"

Eugénie's eyes grew fixed, and the two women sat in mortal terror through half the morning. They were so disturbed that they missed the high mass and only went to the low mass. In three days the year 1819 would be over. In three days would begin a terrible drama, a bourgeois tragedy without poison, or dagger, or spilt blood, but as far as the actors were concerned, crueler than all the horrors enacted in the illustrious family of the Atrides.

"What's to become of us?" said Madame Grandet to her daughter, letting her knitting lie in her lap.

The poor woman had suffered so much anxiety for the past two months that the woolen sleeves she needed to get through the winter were not yet finished. This domestic detail, though apparently insignificant, had sad results for her. After one of her husband's dreadful outbursts of anger she broke into a cold sweat which, because she lacked those very sleeves, brought on a severe chill.

"I was thinking, my poor child, that if you had told me your secret, we would have had time to write to Monsieur des Grassins in Paris, and he could have sent us gold coins like yours, and although Grandet knows them well, perhaps . . ."

"But where would we have got so much money?"

"I would have used my own property. In any case Monsieur des Grassins would have . . ."

"It's too late now," replied Eugénie in a hollow, broken voice, interrupting her mother. "Don't we have to go tomorrow morning and wish him a happy New Year in his room?"

"But, Daughter, why shouldn't I go and see the Cruchots?"

"No, no, that would be handing me over to them and putting ourselves in their power. Besides, I've made up my mind. What I did was right, and I don't regret it. God will protect me. May His holy will be done! Ah, if you had read his letter, you would think only of him, Mother."

The next morning, the first of January, 1820, the wild terror to which mother and daughter were a prey suggested to them the most natural of excuses for not going solemnly into Grandet's room. The winter of 1819 to 1820 was one of the harshest of that epoch. The snow lay deep on the roofs. As soon as Madame Grandet heard her husband moving about in his room, she said to him, "Grandet, get Nanon to make a small fire in my room;

the cold is so sharp that I'm freezing under the bed-clothes. I've reached an age when I need a few comforts. Besides," she added after a slight pause, "Eugénie ought to come in here to dress. The poor child might fall ill from dressing in her room in such weather. Then we'll go and wish you a happy New Year beside the fire in the hall."

"Tut, tut, tut, tut, such a speech! What a way to begin the year, Madame Grandet! You've never talked so much. And yet I hardly think you've been eating bread soaked in wine." There was a moment's silence.

"Very well," continued the old man, who probably had some reason of his own for agreeing to his wife's request, "I shall do what you wish, Madame Grandet. You're really a good woman, and I don't want anything to happen to you at your time of life, though, in general, the la Bertellières are made of iron. Huh, isn't that so?" he cried, after a pause. "Well, I've forgiven them. We got their property in the end." And he coughed.

"You're gay this morning, Monsieur," said the poor woman gravely.

"Oh, I'm always gay . . .

> *Gai, gai, gai le tonnelier,*
> *Raccommodez votre cuvier!"*

he added, coming into his wife's room fully dressed. "Yes, bless my soul, it certainly is cold all right. We'll have a good breakfast my dear. Des Grassins has sent me a pâté de foie gras with truffles! I'm going now to get it at the coach office. There ought to be a double napoleon for Eugénie enclosed," the cooper whispered in her ear. "I have no more gold, my dear. I still had a few old coins; I don't mind telling you that; but I had to let them go in business." And to celebrate the New Year, he kissed her on the forehead.

"Eugénie," cried her mother, "I don't know which side of the bed your father got out of, but he's in good humor this morning. Oh, we'll manage all right."

"What's got into the master this morning?" asked Nanon, coming into her mistress's room to light the fire. "First of all he said to me: 'Good morning, happy New Year, you big silly! Go and make a fire in my wife's room, she's cold.' Was I dumbfounded when I saw him holding out his hand to give me a six-franc piece which is hardly worn down at all! Look, Madame, just look at it! Oh, the kind man! He's a good man, that's a fact. There are some people who the older they get the harder they get. But he, he's getting as sweet and mellow as your black currant brandy. He's a good, good man . . ."

The secret of Grandet's joy lay in the complete success of his speculation. Monsieur des Grassins, after deducting the amount which the old cooper owed him for the discount on a hundred and fifty thousand francs in Dutch notes, and for the surplus which he had advanced to make up the sum required for the purchase of the bonds, which were to bring in a hundred thousand francs a year, had now sent him by mail coach thirty thousand francs in silver coin, the balance of his first half year's interest, informing him also that the bonds had gone up in value. They were then quoted at eighty-nine; the leading capitalists bought, at the end of January, at ninety-three. For the last two months Grandet had been making twelve per cent on his capital; he had checked over his accounts, and would in future receive fifty thousand francs twice yearly, without incurring any taxes or costs for repairs. He understood at last what it meant to have money invested in bonds, a thing which provincials have been extremely loath to do, and he could see himself, before five years were up, possessor of a capital of six millions, which would have increased without much trouble and which, added to the value of his landed properties, would form a colossal fortune. The six francs given to Nanon were perhaps the reward of an immense service that the servant, all unawares, had rendered her master.

"Oh, oh, where's old Grandet going, running about so early in the morning as if there were a fire?" said the merchants, who were busy opening up their shops. Then, when they saw him coming back from the quay followed by a porter from the coach office wheeling a barrow loaded with full sacks, one said, "Water always flows into the river; the old fellow was going for his gold."

"It comes in from Paris, from Froidfond, and from Holland!" said another.

"He'll end by buying the whole of Saumur," cried a third.

"He pays no attention to the cold; he's always thinking of business," said a wife to her husband.

"Hey! Hey! Monsieur Grandet, if that's a nuisance to you," said a cloth merchant, his nearest neighbor, "I'll take it off your hands."

"Oh, it's just copper coins," replied the wine-grower.

"Silver," said the porter in a low voice.

"If you want me to treat you right, you'd better keep a check on your tongue," said the old man to the porter as he opened his door.

"Oh, the old fox, I was sure he was deaf," thought the porter. "He seems to be able to hear all right when it's cold."

"Here's twenty sous as a New Year's present, but mum's the word!" said Grandet. "Now run along. Nanon will bring back your barrow. Nanon, have the linnets gone to mass?"

"Yes, sir."

"Come, get a move on! To work," he shouted, loading her up with sacks. In a few moments the coins were carried up to his room, where he locked himself in.

"When breakfast is ready, you can knock on the wall. Take the barrow back to the coach office."

The family were not having breakfast till ten.

"Your father won't ask to see your gold here," said Madame

440

Grandet to her daughter as they came back from mass. "You can pretend to be very chilly. Then we'll have time to replace your little treasure before your birthday . . ."

As Grandet came downstairs, he was thinking of turning the silver from Paris into gold as soon as possible and of his admirable speculation in government bonds. He had decided to invest his income in this way until the bonds went up to a hundred francs. A fatal train of thought as far as Eugénie was concerned. As soon as he entered the room, the two women wished him a happy New Year, his daughter by throwing her arms affectionately around his neck, Madame Grandet gravely and with dignity.

"Well, well, my child," he said, kissing his daughter on both cheeks. "I am working for you, you see. I want to make you happy. One needs money to be happy. Without money, nothing doing! Look, here's a brand-new napoleon. I sent to Paris for it. On my word of honor, there isn't a speck of gold here. You're the only one who has any gold. Show me your gold, girlie."

"Oh, it's too cold. Let's have breakfast," replied Eugénie.

"All right, after breakfast then, eh? It will help our digestion. Good old des Grassins, he sent us the pâté anyway," he replied. "Well, go ahead and eat, children; it won't cost us anything. He's doing very well, des Grassins, I'm quite pleased with him. The old magpie's helping Charles out, and for nothing, too. He's straightening out the affairs of the poor deceased Grandet very well indeed. M-m-m, M-m-m!" he said with his mouth full, after a pause, "this *is* good! Do eat some, my dear! This will keep you going for at least two days."

"I'm not hungry, I'm feeling poorly, you know that."

"Oh, rubbish! You can stuff yourself with no fear of kicking the bucket; you're a la Bertellière, you're pretty solid. You may be a bit yellow, but I like yellow."

The condemned man perhaps awaits an ignominious and public death with less horror than Madame Grandet and her daughter contemplated the events which were to follow this family breakfast. The more gleefully the old wine-grower talked and ate, the heavier grew the hearts of these two women. But the daughter had something to support her in this crisis: she drew strength from her love.

"For him, for him," she said to herself, "I would suffer a thousand deaths."

At this thought she looked at her mother, her eyes shining with courage.

"Clear all this away," said Grandet to Nanon, when, toward eleven o'clock, breakfast was over. "But leave us the table. We'll be able to look at your little treasure all the more comfortably," he said, looking at Eugénie. "Little! Faith, no! You possess in actual value five thousand nine hundred and fifty-nine francs, and forty from this morning; that makes six thousand francs less one. Well, I myself will give you that franc to make up the round number, for, you see, girlie . . . Well? What are you listening for, Nanon? Get out of here and go on with your work," said the old man. Nanon disappeared.

"Listen, Eugénie, you must give me your gold. You won't refuse your old daddy, will you girlie, eh?" The two women were silent.

"I've no more gold. I did have some, but I haven't got it any longer. I'll give you six thousand francs in *livres,* and you'll invest them as I tell you. You mustn't think of your dozen any more. When I marry you off, which will be soon, I'll find you a husband who'll be able to give you the finest dozen ever heard of in the province. Now listen to me, little girl. A fine opportunity has turned up. You can invest your six thousand francs with the government, and every six months you'll get two hundred francs in interest, without having to worry about taxes or repairs or hail or frost or floods or any of those things that plague property owners. Perhaps you're loath to part with your gold, eh, girlie? Bring it

along all the same. I'll pick up some more gold pieces like those
for you, Dutch, Portuguese, Mogul rupees, and genovines; and
along with those I'll give you on your name days, in three years
you'll have made up half of your nice little golden treasure again.
What do you say, girlie? Look up, now. Go and get it, the precious little thing. You ought to kiss me on the eyelids for telling
you the secrets and mysteries of the life and death of money.
Really coins live and swarm like men; they come and go and
sweat and multiply."

Eugénie got up; but after having taken a few steps toward the
door, she suddenly turned, looked her father full in the face, and
said: "I no longer have *my* gold."

"You no longer have your gold!" cried Grandet, starting up
like a horse that hears a cannon fired ten paces off.

"No, I no longer have it."

"You're mistaken, Eugénie."

"No."

"By the shears of my father!"

When the cooper swore this oath, the rafters trembled.

"Good God in heaven! Madame is turning white," cried
Nanon.

"Grandet, your anger will be the death of me," said his poor
wife.

"Tut, tut, tut, tut, you people, you never die in your family!
Eugénie, what have you done with your coins?" he cried, turning on her.

"Sir," said the girl, falling at Madame Grandet's knees, "my
mother is very ill. Look, do not kill her."

Grandet was terrified by the pallor which overspread his wife's
face, usually so yellow.

"Nanon, come and help me to get to bed," said the mother in
a weak voice. "I'm dying . . ."

So Nanon gave her arm to her mistress; Eugénie did the same.

but it was only with infinite pains that they were able to get her upstairs to her room, for she swooned at every step. Grandet remained alone. However, a few minutes later he went up seven or eight steps and cried, "Eugénie, when your mother has gone to bed, you will come downstairs."

"Yes, Father."

After having reassured her mother, she came at once.

"Daughter," said Grandet, "you're going to tell me where your treasure is."

"Father, if you give me presents of which I am not sole mistress, you can take them back," replied Eugénie coldly, taking the napoleon from the mantelpiece and giving it to him.

Grandet eagerly seized on the napoleon and slipped it into his vest pocket.

"I shall certainly never give you anything again. Not even that!" he said, clicking his thumbnail against his front tooth. "So you despise your father, you have no confidence in him, you don't know what a father is? If he isn't everything to you, then he's nothing. Where is your gold?"

"Father, I love you and respect you in spite of your anger; but I humbly ask you to remember that I'm twenty-three. You've reminded me too often that I'm of age for me to forget it. I did what I wanted to do with my money, and you can be sure it has been well invested . . ."

"Where?"

"It's an inviolable secret," she said. "Haven't you your secrets?"

"Am I not the head of the family? Am I not permitted to have my own business?"

"But this is my business."

"There must be something wrong about it if you can't tell your father, Mademoiselle Grandet."

"There is nothing wrong about it, but I can't tell it to my father."

"At least you can tell me when you parted with your gold?"

Eugénie shook her head.

"You still had it on your birthday, didn't you?"

Eugénie, who had become as crafty through love as her father was through avarice, again shook her head.

"But who ever heard of such obstinacy, or such theft?" said Grandet, his voice rising to a crescendo which gradually echoed through the house. "What, here in my own house, my own home, somebody has taken your gold! The only gold there was! And I'm not to know who it is! Gold is a precious thing. The most virtuous girls may make a mistake and give away I don't know what. It happens in the most aristocratic families and even in the middle classes. But to give away gold, for you did give it to someone, didn't you?"

Eugénie made no response.

"Was there ever such a daughter! Am I really your father? If you've invested it, you have a receipt . . ."

"Was I free or not to do as I liked with it? Was it mine?"

"But you're a child!"

"I'm of age."

Flabbergasted by his daughter's logic, Grandet turned pale, stamped, and swore. Then, finding words at last, he shouted, "Wicked serpent of a daughter! Ah, wretched creature, you know that I love you and you take advantage of it. She'd cut her father's throat! Good God, you'd throw our fortune at the feet of that ragamuffin in morocco boots. By the shears of my father! I can't disinherit you, by God, but I curse you, you and your cousin and your children! You'll see that nothing good will come of all this you hear me? If it was to Charles that you . . . But, no, that's impossible. What! Do you mean to say that that contemptible fop has robbed me . . ." He looked at his daughter who remained cold and silent.

'She won't budge, she won't flinch. She's more of a Grandet than I am! At least you didn't give your gold away for nothing, did you? Come, tell me."

Eugénie looked at her father with an ironical glance which offended him.

"Eugénie, you're in my house, your father's house. To remain here you must submit to my orders. The priests tell you to obey me."

Eugénie bowed her head.

"You have wounded me in the thing I hold most dear," he went on, "I don't want to see you again until you are ready to submit. Go to your room. You shall stay there until I give you permission to come out. Nanon will bring you bread and water. Do you hear me? Go!"

Eugénie burst into tears and ran to her mother. After having walked round the garden a few times in the snow, without noticing the cold, it occurred to Grandet that his daughter was probably with his wife. Delighted at the thought of catching her disobeying his orders, he dashed up the stairs with the agility of a cat and appeared in the room. Eugénie lay with her face hidden against her mother's bosom and Madame Grandet was stroking her hair.

"Console yourself, my poor child, your father will get over it . . ."

"She no longer has a father!" said the cooper. "Can it be you and I, Madame Grandet, who have begotten a daughter as disobedient as she is? A fine bringing up, and religious too! Well, you're not in your room? Come, to prison, to prison, Miss."

"Do you intend to deprive me of my daughter, sir?" asked Madame Grandet, her face flushed with fever.

"If you want to keep her, take her away with you. Clear out of the house, both of you. By thunder, where is the gold? What has become of the gold?"

Eugénie got up, gave her father a haughty look, and went into her room. The old man turned the key.

"Nanon," he shouted, "put out the fire in the hall." And he sat down in an armchair at the corner of the fireplace in his wife's room, saying, "She probably gave it to that miserable seducer, Charles, who only wanted her money."

Madame Grandet found in the danger which threatened her daughter and in her love for her sufficient strength to remain outwardly calm, silent, and deaf.

"I knew nothing of all this," she replied, turning her face toward the wall to avoid her husband's furious glances. "Your violence makes me so ill that if I trust my own presentiments, I shall never leave this room alive. You might have spared me at this time. I, who have never caused you any grief, at least as far as I know . . . Your daughter loves you. I believe her as innocent as a babe unborn. So do not make her miserable, revoke your sentence. The cold is very severe. You might be the cause of a serious illness."

"I shall neither see her nor speak to her. She shall remain in her room on bread and water until she has given satisfaction to her father. What the devil! The head of a family ought to know where the gold of his house has gone to. She had perhaps the only rupees in France, then the genovines, the ducats from Holland . . ."

"Sir, Eugénie is our only child, and even if she had thrown them into the water . . ."

"Into the water!" shouted the old man, "into the water! You are crazy, Madame Grandet. When I say a thing, I mean it, you know that. If you want to have peace in the house, make your daughter confess, get it out of her. Women know how to do that sort of thing better than men. Whatever she has done, I won't eat her. Is she afraid of me? Even if she had covered her cousin with gold from head to foot, he's on the high seas, isn't he? We can't run after him . . ."

"Well, sir . . ." Excited by the nervous state in which she was or by her daughter's misfortune, which brought forth all her tenderness and intelligence, Madame Grandet was clever enough to notice the frightful twitching of her husband's wen just as she was on the verge of replying. She changed her mind without changing her tone. "Well, sir, have I ever had any more influence over her than you have? She hasn't said anything to me; she takes after you."

"Good heavens, how your tongue wags this morning! Tut, tut, tut, tut, I believe you're trying to defy me! You're probably in league with her."

He stared fixedly at his wife.

"Really, Monsieur Grandet, if you want to kill me, you have only to keep on like this. I tell you, sir, and were it to cost me my life, I would still repeat it: you are doing your daughter an injustice, she is more in the right than you are. That money belonged to her. She can only have put it to a good use, and God alone has the right to know our good deeds. Sir, I implore you, take Eugénie back into your favor . . . In that way you will lessen the effect of the shock your anger has given me and may perhaps save my life. My daughter, sir, give me back my daughter!"

"I'm clearing out," he said. "My house is not habitable; mother and daughter argue and talk as if . . . Brrr! Pooh! A cruel New Year's gift you've made me, Eugénie," he shouted. "Yes, yes, cry away! You'll be sorry for what you're doing, you hear? What's the good of taking the sacrament twice a month if you secretly give away your father's gold to a good-for-nothing who'll devour your heart when you've nothing else to lend him? You'll see what your Charles is worth with his morocco boots and his supercilious airs. He has neither heart nor soul if he dares to carry off a young girl's treasure without her parents' consent."

When the street door closed, Eugénie left her room and went to her mother.

"You were very brave for your daughter," she said.

"You see, my child, to what forbidden things may lead us? . . . You have made me tell a lie."

"Oh, I'll ask God to punish me alone."

"Is it true," asked Nanon in dismay as she entered, "that Mademoiselle is to have nothing but bread and water for the rest of her days?"

"What does that matter, Nanon?" said Eugénie quietly.

"Oh, do you think I'll eat jam when the daughter of the house is eating dry bread. Never. Not I."

"Not a word about all this, Nanon," said Eugénie.

"I'll keep my mouth shut; but you'll see!"

Grandet dined alone for the first time in twenty-four years.

"So you're a widower now, sir?" said Nanon. "It must be disagreeable to be a widower with two women in the house."

"I'm not talking to you. Keep your trap shut or I'll fire you. What's in that saucepan that I hear boiling on the stove?"

"It's grease that I'm rendering."

"We're having company this evening. Light the fire."

The Cruchots, Madame des Grassins, and her son arrived at eight o'clock, and were surprised to see neither Madame Grandet nor her daughter.

"My wife's not feeling very well, and Eugénie is with her," replied the old wine-grower, whose face betrayed no emotion.

At the end of an hour spent in trivial conversation, Madame des Grassins, who had gone up to pay a visit to Madame Grandet, came down, and everyone asked her, "How is Madame Grandet?"

"Not at all well, not at all," she said. "Her condition seems to me really alarming. At her age you should take every precaution, Papa Grandet."

"We'll see about that," replied the wine-grower absent-mindedly.

They all wished him good night. When the Cruchots were out in the street, Madame des Grassins said to them, "Something's happened at the Grandets'. The mother is very ill and she doesn't know it. The daughter's eyes are red as if she had been crying for a long time. Can they be trying to marry her against her will?"

When the wine-grower had gone to bed, Nanon came silently in her stocking feet to Eugénie's room and showed her a pâté baked in a saucepan.

"Look, Mademoiselle," said the good soul, "Cornoiller gave me a hare. You eat so little that this pâté will last you a good week; and in this cold weather there's no danger of it going bad. At least you won't have to live on dry bread. That isn't healthy at all."

"Poor Nanon," said Eugénie, pressing her hand.

"I've made it very good, very tasty, and *he* never found it out. I bought the lard and the bay leaf out of my own six francs. After all, it's my money." Then the servant hurried away, thinking she heard Grandet.

For several months the wine-grower kept coming to see his wife at different hours of the day without mentioning his daughter's name, or seeing her, or making the slightest allusion to her. Madame Grandet never left her room, and her condition grew worse from day to day. Nothing could soften the old cooper. He was quite immovable, harsh and cold as a mass of granite. He continued to come and go as usual; but he no longer stuttered, talked less, and was harder in business than he had ever been. He often made an error in his calculations.

"Something has happened at the Grandets'," said the

Cruchotins and the Grassinistes. "What can have happened at the Grandet house?" became a stock question at all the evening parties in Saumur. Eugénie went to mass escorted by Nanon. If Madame des Grassins addressed a few words to her as she was coming out of the church, she replied evasively and without satisfying her curiosity. Nevertheless, it became impossible, after two months, to hide either from the three Cruchots or from Madame des Grassins the secret of Eugénie's enforced seclusion. The moment arrived when no pretexts sufficed to explain her continued absence. Then, although it was impossible to discover by whom the secret had been betrayed, the whole town learned that since New Year's day Mademoiselle Grandet had, by her father's orders, been locked up in her room on bread and water and without a fire; that Nanon cooked delicacies for her and brought them to her during the night; and they even found out that the young girl could see and look after her mother only while her father was out of the house.

Grandet's behavior was severely condemned. The whole town outlawed him, so to speak, remembered his treachery and hardheartedness, and excommunicated him. When he passed by, people pointed him out and whispered to each other. Whenever his daughter came down the winding street, accompanied by Nanon, on her way to mass or vespers, all the inhabitants came to their windows to examine with curiosity the bearing of the rich heiress and her countenance, which wore an expression of melancholy and angelic sweetness. Her confinement and her father's disfavor meant nothing to her. Couldn't she look at the map of the world, the little bench, the garden, the stretch of wall, and couldn't she taste again upon her lips the honey left there by love's kisses? For some time she and her father were both unaware that they were the subject of conversations in the town. Pious and pure before God, her conscience and her love helped her to suffer patiently her father's wrath and vengeance.

But one profound grief silenced all others. Each day her mother, that sweet and gentle creature, who grew lovelier from the radiance of her spirit as death approached—her mother was slowly wasting away. Often Eugénie reproached herself with being the innocent cause of the cruel, lingering disease that was destroying her. This remorse, although soothed by her mother, bound her still more closely to her love. Every morning, as soon as her father had gone out, she came to her mother's bedside, and Nanon brought her her breakfast there. But poor Eugénie, sad and troubled by her mother's sufferings, mutely drew Nanon's attention to her mother's face, wept, and dared not speak of her cousin. Madame Grandet always had to say first, "Where is *he*? Why doesn't he write?"

Neither mother nor daughter had any idea of distance.

"Let's think of him, Mother," replied Eugénie, "but don't let's talk of him. You are ill, you come before everything."

Everything meant *him*.

"Children," Madame Grandet would say, "I'm not sorry to die. God has blessed me in allowing me to look forward with happiness to the end of my miseries."

Every word this woman said was pious and Christian. When, during the first months of the year, her husband came to breakfast with her and walked up and down in her room, she would repeat the same words with angelic sweetness, but with the firmness of a woman to whom approaching death lends the courage she has lacked during her lifetime.

"Sir, I thank you for the interest you take in my health," she would reply, when he had made the most perfunctory inquiries, "but if you would render my last moments less bitter and lighten my sufferings, take your daughter back into favor; show yourself a Christian, a husband, and a father."

Whenever he heard these words, Grandet would sit down near the bed with the air of a man who sees a shower approaching and quietly takes shelter under a doorway. He would listen to his wife in silence and make no reply. After the most touching, the most tender, the most pious supplications had been addressed to him, he would say, "You're a bit pale today, my poor wife." Utter forgetfulness of his daughter seemed graven on his stony brow and compressed lips. He was not even moved by the tears which, at his vague replies, always couched in more or less the same words, streamed down his wife's white face.

"May God forgive you, sir," she said, "as I forgive you myself. Some day you will stand in need of mercy."

Since his wife's illness, he no longer dared to make use of his terrible: "Tut, tut, tut, tut!" Nonetheless his despotic nature was not disarmed by this angel of gentleness, whose plainness was slowly vanishing, dispelled by the strength of the moral qualities reflected in her face. She was all soul. The spirit of prayer seemed to purify and refine the coarser features of her face and make them luminous. Who has not observed the phenomenon of this transfiguration on saintly faces where the habits of the soul have finally triumphed over the most graceless features by imprinting upon them that divine illumination which comes from the nobility and purity of elevated thoughts? The spectacle of this transformation, brought about by the sufferings which were consuming the remnants of the physical in this woman, did affect, however feebly, the old cooper, who nevertheless remained adamant. If his language ceased to be contemptuous, his conduct was nevertheless dominated by an imperturbability which maintained his superiority as head of the household. Whenever his faithful Nanon appeared at the market-place, jeers and reproaches against her master whistled about her ears; but although public opinion roundly condemned old Grandet, his servant defended him for the honor of the house.

"Well," she said to the old man's detractors, "don't we all get harder as we grow older? Why shouldn't the old man toughen up a bit too? Shut up with your lies. Mademoiselle lives like a queen. She's alone; well, it's because she wants to be. Besides, my masters have their reasons."

Finally, one evening toward the end of spring, Madame Grandet, wasted even more by grief than by illness, having failed in spite of her prayers to reconcile Eugénie and her father, confided her secret troubles to the Cruchots.

"To keep a girl of twenty-three on bread and water!" cried Judge de Bonfons. "And for no reason! But that constitutes wrongful cruelty; she can protest, in as much as upon . . ."

"Come, Nephew," said the notary, "cut out that legal gibberish. "Don't worry, Madame, I'll bring an end to this imprisonment tomorrow."

Hearing her name mentioned, Eugénie came out of her room.

"Gentlemen," she said, coming forward with a proud dignity, "I beg you not to interfere in this matter. My father is master in his own house. As long as I live in his house, I must obey him. His conduct must not be subjected either to the approval or disapproval of the world; he is accountable only to God. On the strength of our friendship I ask you never to mention this. To accuse my father would be to attack our own reputation. I am grateful to you, gentlemen, for the interest you have shown; but you will oblige me even more if you will put a stop to the insulting rumors which are abroad in the town and of which I have learned by accident."

"She is right," said Madame Grandet.

"Mademoiselle, the best way of preventing people from gossiping is to restore your liberty," replied the old notary respectfully, struck by the beauty which retirement, melancholy, and love had imparted to Eugénie.

"Well, my dear, let Monsieur Cruchot settle this matter, if he is so sure of success. He knows your father and understands how to manage him. If you want to see me happy for the short time I have left to live, you and your father must be reconciled at all costs."

The next morning, following a custom he had adopted since Eugénie's confinement, Grandet went out to walk up and down a few times in his little garden; he had chosen for this walk the hour when Eugénie brushed and arranged her hair. When the old man came to the big walnut tree, he hid behind its trunk, stood there for a few minutes looking at his daughter's long hair, and doubtless vacillated between the thoughts prompted by the tenacity of his character and his desire to embrace his child. Often he remained sitting on the little, worm-eaten, wooden bench, where Charles and Eugénie had sworn eternal love, while she also stole glances at her father through the window or in the mirror. If he got up and resumed his walk, she obligingly sat down at the window and began to examine the stretch of wall where the prettiest flowers hung, where the maiden-hair fern grew from the crevices with the convolvulus and a thick-leaved plant, yellow or white, a *sedum* very common in the vineyards around Saumur and Tours. Lawyer Cruchot came early and found the old cooper, on a lovely June day, sitting on the little bench with his back against the dividing wall of the garden, engaged in watching his daughter.

"What can I do for you, Lawyer Cruchot?" he asked when he saw the notary.

"I've come to talk about a business matter."

"Oh, have you got a little gold to give me in exchange for silver?"

"No, no, it hasn't to do with money but with your daughter Eugénie. Everybody's talking about her and about you."

"What business is it of theirs? A man's house is his castle."

"Agreed. A man may kill himself if he likes, too, and what is worse, throw his money out of the window."

"What do you mean?"

"Why, your wife is very ill, my friend. You even ought to consult Monsieur Bergerin; she's in danger of dying. If she does die without receiving proper care, you'll not be very easy in your mind, I take it."

"Tut, tut, tut, tut, you know what's wrong with my wife! Once these doctors get a foot into your house, they come five or six times a day."

"Well, Grandet, you can do as you like. We're old friends; there isn't anyone else in all Saumur who takes more interest in anything that concerns you than I do. So I had to tell you this. Well, enough of that. You're of age, you know what you should do, of course. In any case this wasn't the reason I came. It's something much more important for you perhaps. After all, you don't want to kill your wife; she's much too useful to you. Think of the situation you would be in toward your daughter if Madame Grandet died. You'd have to render an account to Eugénie, for you and your wife hold your property in common. Your daughter will have the right to insist on a division of property and on the sale of Froidfond. In short, she is her mother's heir and you are not."

These words fell like a thunderbolt on the old man, who was not as well informed in law as he was in business. He had never thought of a division of property.

"Therefore I advise you to treat her kindly," said Cruchot in conclusion.

"But do you know what she did, Cruchot?"

"What?" said the notary, curious to hear the truth and learn the cause of the quarrel.

"She gave away her gold."

"Well, did it belong to her?" asked the notary.

"Everybody says that!" said the old man, letting his arms fall in a tragic gesture.

"Are you going, for a mere nothing, to put obstacles in the

way of the concessions you will be obliged to ask of her on her mother's death?"

"Oh, you call six thousand francs in gold a mere nothing!"

"Well, my old friend, do you know what the inventory and the division of your wife's estate would cost if Eugénie insisted on it?"

"What?"

"Two, or three, perhaps four hundred thousand francs! The property would have to be put up at auction and sold to determine its real value, wouldn't it? Whereas if you are in agreement . . ."

"By the shears of my father!" cried the wine-grower, who grew pale and sat down. "We'll see about that, Cruchot."

After a moment of silence or of agony, the old man looked at the notary and said, "Life is very hard! It is full of troubles! Cruchot," he went on solemnly, "you wouldn't deceive me, would you? Swear on your honor that all this you've been telling me is based on the law. Show me the statute; I want to see the statute."

"My poor friend," replied the notary, "don't I know my own business?"

"It's quite true then? I shall be despoiled, betrayed, killed, devoured by my daughter!"

"She is her mother's heir."

"What's the use of children anyway? Oh, my wife, I love her. She's strong, fortunately. She's a la Bertellière."

"She hasn't a month to live."

The cooper beat his brow, paced up and down, and cast a dreadful look at Cruchot, saying, "What's to be done?"

"Eugénie can purely and simply relinquish her claim to her mother's estate. You don't intend to disinherit her, do you? But to obtain a concession of this kind, you mustn't be harsh with her. What I'm telling you now, old man, is against my own interest. What do I live by, if it isn't liquidations, inventories, sales, and divisions of property?"

"We'll see, we'll see. Don't let's talk about it any more, Cruchot. It wrings my vitals. Have you received any gold?"

"No, but I have a few old louis, about ten of them, I'll give them to you. Make your peace with Eugénie, my good friend. You see, the whole of Saumur is accusing you."

"The scoundrels!"

"Come, the bonds are at ninety-nine. Be content for once in your life."

"At ninety-nine, Cruchot?"

"Yes."

"Eh! eh! ninety-nine," said the old man, accompanying the notary to the street door. Then, too much excited by what he had just heard to remain at home, he went up to his wife's room and said to her, "Come now, Mother, you can spend the day with your daughter. I'm going to Froidfond. Be happy now, both of you. It's our wedding anniversary, my dear wife. Look, here are sixty francs for your altar on Corpus Christi Day. You've been wanting to have one for long enough. Make it a good one! Enjoy yourselves, be happy, get well. Here's to happiness! . . ." He threw the ten six-franc pieces on his wife's bed, took her head between his hands, and kissed her forehead. "My good wife, you're feeling better, aren't you?"

"How can you think of receiving the God of mercy in your house, while your daughter is shut out of your heart?" she said with emotion.

"Tut, tut, tut, tut," said the father in a playful voice, "we'll see about that."

"Merciful heavens, Eugénie," cried her mother flushing with joy, "come and kiss your father. He forgives you!"

But the old man had disappeared. He was off as fast as his legs could carry him to his vineyards, trying to bring order into his confused ideas. Grandet was then just beginning his seventy-sixth year. In the last two years particularly, his avarice had increased as do all the prevailing passions of man. As has been observed in misers, in ambitious men, in all people whose lives have been consecrated to a single dominating idea, his emotion had become fixed on a particular object symbolic of his passion. The sight of gold, the possession of gold had become his mono-mania. His despotic tendency had grown in proportion to his avarice, and to abandon the control of the smallest fraction of his property at his wife's death seemed to him against nature. To declare his fortune to his daughter, to give an inventory of his property both landed and personal for sale by auction? . . . "Why," he exclaimed aloud in the midst of a field where he was examining vine shoots, "it would be like cutting my throat." Finally he made up his mind, came back to Saumur at dinner time, resolved to give in to Eugénie, to coax and wheedle her, so that he might die like a king holding the reins of his millions in his own hands to the last breath. Just as the old man, who happened to have taken his master key, was walking stealthily up the stairs to his wife's room, Eugénie had brought the beauti-ful dressing-case to her mother's bed. The two of them, in Grandet's absence, were enjoying themselves in trying to dis-cover Charles's features in his mother's portrait.

"That's exactly his forehead and his mouth!" said Eugénie, at the very moment the wine-grower opened the door. At the look her husband threw on the gold, Madame Grandet cried, "God have mercy on us!"

The old man leaped on the dressing-case as a tiger springs on a sleeping child. "What's this?" said he, carrying off the treasure and going to the window with it. "Real gold! Gold!" he cried. "A lot of gold! It weighs two pounds. Aha! Charles gave you this in exchange for your pretty coins. Eh! Why didn't you tell me? That was a good bargain, girlie! You're my daughter, all right." Eugénie trembled in every limb. "This belongs to Charles, doesn't it?" the old man went on.

"Yes, Father, it doesn't belong to me. This case is a sacred trust."

"Tut, tut, tut, he took your fortune. We must restore your little treasure."

"Father!"

The old man wanted to get his knife out to pry off a gold plaque and was obliged to set the dressing-case down on a chair. Eugénie sprang forward to get possession of it again; but the cooper, who had kept one eye on his daughter and the other on the case, pushed her so violently with a thrust of his arm that she fell on her mother's bed.

"Monsieur! Monsieur!" cried the mother sitting up in bed.

Grandet had taken out his knife and was about to remove the gold.

"Father!" cried Eugénie, throwing herself on her knees and dragging herself over toward him with her hands raised in supplication, "Father, in the name of all the saints and the Virgin, in the name of Christ who died on the cross, in the name of your eternal salvation, Father, for the sake of my life, do not touch it! This dressing-case is neither yours nor mine; it belongs to an unfortunate relative who entrusted it to me, and I must give it back to him intact."

"Why were you looking at it then if it was given you in trust? Looking is worse than touching."

"Father, don't destroy it or you'll disgrace me! Father, do you hear me?"

"Monsieur, have pity!" said the mother.

"Father!" cried Eugénie in so piercing a voice that Nanon, terrified, ran upstairs. Eugénie leaped on a knife that was within reach and armed herself with it.

"Well?" said Grandet calmly with a callous smile.

"Monsieur, Monsieur, you're killing me!" said the mother.

"Father, if your knife so much as scratches that gold, I shall stab myself with this one. You've already made my mother mortally ill; now you're going to kill your daughter. Go ahead, then, but it will be wound for wound!"

Grandet, who was holding his knife over the dressing-case, looked at his daughter and hesitated.

"Would you really do such a thing, Eugénie?" he asked.

"Yes, she would," said the mother.

"She'll do just what she says!" cried Nanon. "Be reasonable, sir, for once in your life." The cooper looked alternately at the gold and his daughter for a moment. Madame Grandet fainted.

"There, don't you see, my dear master? Madame is dying!" cried Nanon.

"Come, Daughter, don't let's quarrel over a box. Take it!" cried the cooper, hastily throwing the dressing-case onto the bed. "You, Nanon, go and get Monsieur Bergerin. Now, Mother," he said, kissing his wife's hand, "it's all over. We've made it up. Haven't we, girlie? No more dry bread. You may eat anything you like. Ah, she's opening her eyes! Well, Mother, Motherkin. Little Mother, come now! Look, you see I'm kissing Eugénie. She loves her cousin. She can marry him if she wants to. She may keep his case. But go on living for a long time, my dear. Come, try to move. Listen, you shall have the finest altar ever seen in Saumur."

"Oh, how can you treat your wife and daughter so?" said Madame Grandet in a feeble voice.

"I'll never, never do it again," cried the cooper. "You'll see I won't, my dear." He went to his office and came back with a handful of louis that he scattered on the bed. "Here, Eugénie. Here, my dear, this is for you," he said, fingering the coins. "Come on, cheer up, get well. You'll not lack for anything, nor will Eugénie. Here are a hundred louis for her. You won't give these away, will you, Eugénie, eh?"

Madame Grandet and her daughter looked at each other in astonishment.

"Take them back, Father. All we ask for is your love."

"Well, all right then," he said, pocketing the louis. "Let's be friends again. Let's all go down to the hall for dinner and we'll play lotto every night for two sous. Have your fling! Eh, wife?"

"Alas, I wish I could, if it would give you pleasure," said the dying woman, "but I can't get up."

"Poor Mother," said the cooper, "you don't know how much I love you. And you too, Daughter!" He hugged and kissed her. "Oh, how good it is to kiss and make up. My little girl! There, Motherkin, don't you see it's all over now. Go and put that away," he said to Eugénie, pointing at the case. "Go on, don't be afraid. I shall never speak of it again, never."

Monsieur Bergerin, the best known doctor in Saumur, soon arrived. After an examination he declared positively to Grandet that his wife was very ill, but that perfect peace of mind, nourishing food, and great care might prolong her life until the end of the autumn.

"Will it be expensive?" asked the old man. "Will she need medicines?"

"Not much medicine, but a lot of care," replied the doctor, who couldn't help smiling.

"Well, Monsieur Bergerin," replied Grandet, "you're a man of honor, aren't you? I trust you. Come and see my wife as often as you think necessary. Save her for me. I love her very much, you see, although I don't show it, for I keep things to myself and eat my heart out in silence. I'm worried. My troubles began with the death of my brother. I'm spending enormous sums for him in Paris—paying through the nose, in fact! And there's no end to it. Good-bye, sir. If you can save my wife, do so even if it costs me two or three hundred francs."

In spite of Grandet's fervent desire for the recovery of his wife, the possible division of whose estate was like a fore-taste of death to him; in spite of the consideration he showed on all occasions for the slightest wishes of the astonished mother and daughter; in spite of the tender care lavished on her by Eugénie, Madame Grandet rapidly approached her end. Each day she grew weaker and wasted away as do most women attacked by an illness at that age. She was as fragile as the foliage on the trees in autumn. She glowed with a celestial radiance like leaves shot through and gilded by the sun. Her death was worthy of her life. It was a truly Christian death, and is that not to say it was sublime? In the month of October, 1822, her virtues, her angelic patience, and her love for her daughter were particularly noticeable; she passed away without a murmur. Innocent and good, she went to heaven, regretting only the gentle companion of her cheerless life, for whom her last glances seemed to predict a thousand sorrows. She was loath to leave her ewe-lamb, innocent as herself, alone in the midst of a selfish world that would strip her of her fleece and her treasures.

"My child," she said as she was dying, "there is happiness only in heaven. You will know that some day."

The day after her death Eugénie found new reasons for clinging to this house where she was born, where she had suffered so much, where her mother had just died. She could not look at the window and the chair on its castors in the hall without shedding tears. She thought she had misjudged her father, now that she found herself the object of his tenderest care. He came to offer his arm to take her down to breakfast. He looked at her with almost benevolent eyes for hours at a time. He hovered over her as though she were made of gold. The old cooper was so unlike himself, he trembled so before his daughter, that Nanon and the Cruchotins, witnesses of his weakness, attributed it to his great age and were afraid his faculties were giving way; but the day the family put on mourning, after the dinner to which Lawyer Cruchot, who alone knew his client's secret, had been invited, the old man's conduct became clear.

"My dear child," he said to Eugénie, when the table had been cleared and the doors carefully closed, "you are now your mother's heiress, and we have a little business to settle between us. Isn't that so, Cruchot?"

"Yes."

"Is it absolutely necessary to discuss it today, Father?"

"Yes, yes, girlie. I can't bear this uncertainty any longer. I'm sure you don't want to do anything to hurt me."

"Oh, Father . . ."

"Well, then let's settle everything tonight."

"What do you want me to do?"

"My little girl, it's not for me to say. Tell her, Cruchot."

"Mademoiselle, your father does not wish to divide the estate, or sell his property, or pay enormous taxes on the ready money he may possess. Therefore, to avoid this, there must be no inventory made of the whole fortune which you and your father now hold in common . . ."

"Cruchot, are you quite sure of that, before you tell it to a mere child?"

"Leave it to me, Grandet."

"Yes, yes, my friend, neither you nor my daughter would think of robbing me. Isn't that so, girlie?"

"But, Monsieur Cruchot, what should I do?" asked Eugénie impatiently.

"Well," said the notary, "you'll have to sign this deed by which you renounce your rights to your mother's estate and leave your father the use of all the property you hold in common, while you, of course, retain the ownership."

"I don't understand a word of what you say," replied Eugénie. "Give me the deed and show me where I'm to sign."

Old Grandet looked alternately at the deed and at his daughter, at his daughter and the deed, a prey to such violent emotions that he had to wipe the drops of sweat from his brow.

"Girlie," he said, "instead of signing this deed, which would cost a lot to register, if you would purely and simply renounce your rights to your poor, dear mother's estate and rely on me for the future, I would prefer it. I would then give you a nice fat income of a hundred francs a month. Look, you'd be able to pay for as many masses as you like for those for whom you are having them said . . . Eh? A hundred francs a month, in *livres*?"

"I shall do whatever you wish, Father."

"Mademoiselle," said the notary, "it is my duty to point out to you that you're robbing yourself . . ."

"Good heavens," said she, "what difference does that make?"

"Shut up, Cruchot. It's settled, it's settled," cried Grandet taking his daughter's hand and stroking it with his own. "Eugénie, you won't go back on your word, will you? You're an honest girl, hm?"

"Oh, Father . . ."

He kissed her effusively and hugged her until she almost choked.

"There, my child, you've restored your father's life; but you're only giving him back what he gave you. We are quits. That's the way to do business. Life is a business. I bless you! You are a virtuous daughter, who loves her father. You may do whatever you like now. Until tomorrow, Cruchot," he said, looking at the horrified notary. "You'll be sure to draw up the deed of relinquishment and enter it on the records of the court."

The next day, about noon, Eugénie signed the papers by which she herself accomplished her spoliation. However, in spite of his promise, at the end of the first year the old cooper had not yet given a cent of the hundred francs a month he had so solemnly promised his daughter. When Eugénie pleasantly reminded him of this, he could not help flushing. He went quickly upstairs to his office, came back, and presented her with about a third of the jewelry he had taken from his nephew.

"Here, little one," he said with an ironical note in his voice, "do you want this for your twelve hundred francs?"

"Oh, Father, are you really giving them to me?"

"I'll give you as many more next year," he said, throwing them into her apron. "So in a little while you will have all these gewgaws," he added, rubbing his hands, delighted to be able to speculate on his daughter's feelings.

Nevertheless, the old man, though still robust, felt the necessity of initiating his daughter into the secrets of the household. For two consecutive years he had her order in his presence the household menu and receive the rents. He taught her slowly and one after another the names and the capacities of his vineyards and farms. About the third year he had got her so accustomed to all his miserly ways and had so firmly established them in her as habits that he had no fear of entrusting her with the household keys and made her the mistress of the house.

Five years went by without a single memorable event to relieve the monotonous existence of Eugénie and her father. The same actions were performed over and over again with the chronometrical regularity of the pendulum of the old clock. Mademoiselle Grandet's profound melancholy was known to all; but if others could guess at the reason, there was never a word from Eugénie to justify the suspicions that all Saumur entertained regarding the state of the rich heiress's heart. The only people she saw were the three Cruchots and a few of their friends, whom they had gradually introduced into the house. They had taught her to play whist and dropped in every evening for a game. In the year 1827, her father, feeling the weight of his infirmities, was forced to initiate her into the secrets of his landed property, and told her that, in case of difficulties, she was to have recourse to Lawyer Cruchot, whose honesty was known to him.

Finally, toward the end of this year, the old man, then eighty-two, was seized by a paralysis, which made rapid progress. Monsieur Bergerin said there was no hope for him. At the thought that she would soon find herself alone in the world, Eugénie drew closer to her father and clung more tightly to this last link of affection. In her mind, as in that of all tender women, love was her whole world, Charles was not there, and she lavished all her care and attentions on her old father, whose faculties were beginning to weaken but whose avarice instinctively persisted. The death of this man offered no contrast to his life. Early each morning he had himself wheeled between the fireplace of his room and the door of his office, which was no doubt filled with gold. There he remained motionless; but he looked with anxiety, now at the people who came to see him and now at the heavy iron door. He insisted on an explanation of every noise he heard, however slight; and to the great astonishment of the notary, he even heard the watch-dog yawning in the courtyard. He awoke from his apparent torpor on the day and at the hour when the rents were due, when accounts were to be settled with his tenants, or receipts made out. He worked his wheelchair round until he faced the door of his office, made his daughter open it, and saw to it that she herself placed the sacks of money one on top of another in safekeeping and locked the door. Then he returned silently to his place as soon as she had given him back the precious key, which was always kept in his vest pocket where he could feel it from time to time. Furthermore, his old friend the notary, realizing that the rich heiress must necessarily marry his nephew the judge if Charles Grandet did not come back, redoubled his attentions. He came every day to put himself at Grandet's disposal, went at his behest to Froidfond, to the farms, to the meadows, to the vineyards, sold the harvests, and transmuted everything into gold and silver, which was secretly added to the sacks piled up in the office.

Finally the death struggle began. The old man's strong frame came to grips with the forces of destruction. He was determined to sit at the chimney corner, facing the door of his office He drew off and rolled up all the covers that were put over him, saying to Nanon, "Put them away, lock them up, so nobody can steal them." Whenever he could open his eyes, in which all his remaining life had taken refuge, he would turn them toward the door of his office where his treasures lay, and say to his daughter, "Are they there? Are they there?" in a tone of voice which betrayed a kind of panic fear.

"Yes, Father."

"Take care of the gold . . . show me some gold!"

Eugénie would then spread louis on a table, and he would remain for hours on end with his eyes fixed on the coins like a child who, at the moment it begins to see, keeps stupidly staring at the same object. And as with a child, a painful smile would flicker over his face.

"It warms me up!" he would say sometimes, allowing a beatific expression to appear on his countenance.

When the parish priest came to administer the last sacrament, his eyes, which had showed no sign of life for several hours, lit up at the sight of the crucifix, the candlesticks, and the holy-water vessel at which he gazed fixedly, and his wen moved for the last time. When the priest put the gilt crucifix to his lips that he might kiss the Christ, he made a horrible gesture to seize it, and this last effort cost him his life. He called Eugénie, whom he could not see, although she was kneeling in front of him and bathing his cold hand in her tears.

"Give me your blessing, Father!" she asked.

"Take good care of everything. You will render me an account of it in heaven," he said, proving by these last words that Christianity should be the religion of misers.

Eugénie Grandet found herself alone in the world in this house with none but Nanon to whom she could turn with the certainty of being heard and understood, Nanon, the only being who loved her for herself and with whom she could speak of her sorrows. Big Nanon was her good angel. She was now no longer a servant but a humble friend. After her father's death Eugénie learned from Lawyer Cruchot that she possessed an income of three hundred thousand *livres* from landed and personal property in the district of Saumur, six millions invested in bonds at three per cent purchased at sixty francs and now worth seventy-six; also two millions in gold and a hundred thousand francs in silver, not counting the arrears still to be collected. The sum total of her fortune was estimated at almost seventeen millions.

"But where is my cousin?" she asked herself.

The day Lawyer Cruchot presented his client with a final accounting of her inheritance, Eugénie remained alone with Nanon. They sat one at each side of the fireplace in this hall now so empty, where everything was reminiscent of the past from the chair on castors on which her mother used to sit to the glass from which her cousin had drunk.

"Nanon, we are alone . . ."

"Yes, Mademoiselle. And if I knew where he was, the darling, I'd go myself to find him."

"The ocean lies between us," said she.

While the poor heiress was weeping thus in the company of her old servant in this gloomy old house, which was the whole universe to her, nobody between Nantes and Orléans talked of anything but Mademoiselle Grandet and her seventeen millions.

One of the first things she did was to settle an annuity of twelve hundred francs on Nanon, who, as she already had an income of six hundred francs, became a rich matrimonial prize. In less than a month she went from spinsterhood to wifehood under the patronage of Antoine Cornoiller, who was appointed keeper general of the lands and estates of Mademoiselle Grandet. Madame Cornoiller had an immense advantage over her contemporaries. Although she was fifty-nine, she did not look more than forty. Her coarse features had resisted the attacks of time. Thanks to the austerity of her monastic life, she mocked at old age with her bright complexion and her iron constitution. Perhaps she had never looked as well in her life as she did on her wedding day. She had the advantages of her ugliness and looked big, fat, and strong with an expression of happiness on her indestructible features which made some people envious of Cornoiller's luck. "She's dyed in the wool," said the draper. "Quite likely to have children," said the salt merchant; "she's pickled in brine, saving your presence." "She's rich, and that fellow Cornoiller has done well for himself," said another neighbor.

When she came out of the old house, Nanon, who was loved by all the neighborhood, received nothing but compliments as she walked down the winding street to go to the parish church. As a wedding present Eugénie gave her three dozen silver forks and spoons. Cornoiller, astonished at such lavishness, spoke of his mistress with tears in his eyes; he would have been willing to let himself be cut to pieces for her. Madame Cornoiller, elevated by Eugénie to a position of trust, now derived as much satisfaction out of her new duties as out of the possession of a husband. At last she had a larder to open and close, provisions to hand out in the morning like her late master. Then she ruled over two servants, a cook and a maid, whose business it was to mend the household linen and make Mademoiselle's dresses. Cornoiller combined the offices of keeper and steward. Needless to say, the cook and the chambermaid chosen by Nanon were real treasures. Thus Mademoiselle Grandet had four servants who were completely devoted to her. Consequently the farmers hardly noticed the old man's death, so strictly had he established the usages and customs of his administration, which were scrupulously continued by Monsieur and Madame Cornoiller.

SIX

THE WAY OF THE WORLD

*A*T thirty Eugénie had known none of the joys of life. Her pale, sad childhood had slipped by at the side of a mother whose heart, misunderstood and wounded, had known only suffering. Departing this life with joy, she pitied her daughter for having to live and left in Eugénie's soul a touch of remorse and eternal regret. Eugénie's first, her only love was a constant source of melancholy to her. Having spent only a few brief days with her lover, she had yielded him her heart between two kisses furtively given and received; then he had gone away, putting a whole world between them. This love, cursed by her father, had been almost entirely responsible for her mother's death and had brought her only sorrow mingled with frail hopes. Thus, until now, in her struggle for happiness she had wasted her strength and gained nothing. In the life of the soul, as well as in the life of the body, there is both a breathing in and a breathing out; the soul must absorb the feelings of another soul, must assimilate them in order to give them back again more abundantly. Without this glorious human phenomenon, there can be no life for the heart; it cannot breathe; it suffers and wastes away. Eugénie had begun to suffer. In her case wealth was neither a power nor a consolation; she could only exist through love, through religion, and through her faith in the future. Love made her understand eternity. Her heart and the gospels marked out two worlds awaiting her. Night and day she was plunged in the depths of infinite thoughts, which for her perhaps merged into one. She withdrew into herself, loving and believing herself loved. For seven years her passion had colored everything for her. Her treasures were not the millions from which the income was piling up, but Charles's dressing-case, the two portraits hanging above her bed, the jewels recovered from her father and proudly spread out on a layer of cotton wool in a drawer of the cabinet, her aunt's thimble, which her mother had used and which she put on religiously every day to work at a piece of embroidery—Penelope's web, begun solely for the purpose of wearing on her finger that gold so full of memories.

It did not seem likely that Mademoiselle Grandet would wish to get married while she was still in mourning. The genuineness of her piety was well known. And so the Cruchot family, whose policy was wisely directed by the old abbé, were satisfied to encircle the heiress by lavishing upon her the most affectionate attentions. Every evening her drawing room was filled with the most ardent and devoted Cruchotins of the countryside, who did their best to sing the praises of the mistress of the house in every key. She had her court physician, her grand almoner, her chamberlain, her first lady of the bedchamber, her prime minister, and above all her chancellor—a chancellor who was eager to guide her in everything. Had the heiress wished for a train bearer, one would have been found for her. She was a queen, the most adroitly flattered of all queens. Flattery never emanates from great souls; it is the attribute of petty minds, who succeed in making themselves even smaller than they are, the better to enter the vital sphere of the person about whom they gravitate. Flattery implies self-interest. So the people who came every evening to adorn Mademoiselle Grandet's house—they called her Mademoiselle de Froidfond—were marvelously successful in overpowering her with adulation. This chorus of praise, new to Eugénie, made her blush at first; but little by little, however fulsome the compliments, her ear grew so accustomed to hearing her beauty praised that if some newcomer had found her plain, she would have felt this slight much more than eight years earlier. At last she came to like these soft words, which she secretly laid at the feet of her idol. By degrees she got used to being treated as a queen and to seeing her court well filled every evening.

Judge de Bonfons was the hero of this little circle, where his wit, his person, his education, and his amiability were constantly lauded. Someone observed that in seven years he had greatly increased his fortune; that Bonfons brought in at least ten thousand francs a year and was enclosed, like all the Cruchot properties, by the vast domains of the heiress. "Do you know, Mademoiselle," one of the habitual visitors would say, "that the Cruchots have an income of forty thousand francs?" "And then their savings," put in an elderly follower of the Cruchotins, Mademoiselle de Gribeaucourt. "A gentleman from Paris came here lately to offer Monsieur Cruchot two hundred thousand francs for his practice. He will sell it if he is appointed magistrate."

"He plans to succeed Monsieur de Bonfons as judge of the civil courts and is getting ready," replied Madame d'Orsonval; "for the Judge will be made councillor, then presiding judge. He's much too talented not to succeed."

"Yes, he's a very distinguished man," another would say. "Don't you think so, Mademoiselle?"

The judge tried to act in harmony with the rôle he wished to play. In spite of his forty years, in spite of his sallow, unprepossessing face, dry and wrinkled like most judicial countenances, he wore youthful clothes, toyed with a bamboo cane, never took snuff at Mademoiselle de Froidfond's, and always arrived in a white cravat and a shirt whose pleated frill gave him a family resemblance to certain individuals of the genus turkey. He spoke familiarly to the beautiful heiress and called her, "Our dear Eugénie!" In short, except for the number of visitors, the change

from lotto to whist, and the absence of Monsieur and Madame
Grandet, the scene was about the same as the one with which
this story begins. The hounds were still pursuing Eugénie and
her millions; but the pack was more numerous, barked louder,
and beset its quarry more closely. If Charles had arrived from the
depths of the Indies, he would have found the same people and
the same interests. Madame des Grassins, to whom Eugénie was
always kind and courteous, still persisted in tormenting the Cruchots. But, as formerly, Eugénie would still have dominated the
picture; as formerly, Charles would still have been the sovereign
there. Nevertheless there had been some progress. The bouquet
which the judge gave Eugénie on her name day had become a
daily occurrence. Every evening he brought the rich heiress a
large and magnificent bouquet which Madame Cornoiller placed
ostentatiously in a vase and secretly threw out into a corner of the
yard as soon as the visitors had left.

Early in the spring Madame des Grassins tried to disturb the
complacency of the Cruchotins by talking to Eugénie of the
Marquis de Froidfond, whose ruined house might rise again if
the heiress would restore his land by a marriage contract.
Madame des Grassins made much ado about the peerage and the
title of marchioness, and mistaking Eugénie's disdainful smile
for acquiescence, she went around saying that Judge Cruchot's
marriage was by no means as certain as people thought.

"Although Monsieur de Froidfond is fifty," she said, "he
doesn't look any older than Monsieur Cruchot. He's a widower,
he has children, it's true, but he's a marquis, he will be a peer of
France, and where, in these days, can you find a match like that?
I know for a fact that old Grandet put all his money into the
Froidfond estate with the intention of grafting onto that stock.
He often told me so. He was pretty cute, the old fellow."

"Ah, Nanon," said Eugénie one night as she was going to bed,
"how is it that in seven years he has never once written to me?"

While these events were taking place at Saumur, Charles was making his fortune in the Indies. In the first place his trading goods had sold very well. He had quickly realized a sum of six thousand dollars. Crossing the equator had rid him of a great many prejudices. He perceived that the best means of making a fortune in tropical regions as in Europe was to buy and sell men. He went to the coast of Africa and engaged in the slave trade, combining with his traffic in human flesh the sale of such merchandise as could be most advantageously exchanged on the various markets to which his interests led him. He threw himself into business with an energy that left him not a moment of leisure. He was dominated by the idea of reappearing in Paris with all the prestige of a great fortune and of regaining a position even more brilliant than the one from which he had fallen. From knocking about with all kinds of men in all kinds of countries and observing divergent customs, his ideas had changed, and he became skeptical. Having seen what was called virtue in one country condemned as crime in another, he could no longer distinguish between justice and injustice. Perpetually immersed in business, his heart grew cold, contracted, dried up. The blood of the Grandets did not fail of its destiny; Charles became hard and greedy. He sold Chinese, Negroes, swallows' nests, children, artists; he practised usury in the grand style. The habit of cheating the customs made him less scrupulous about the rights of his fellow men.

He then went to Saint Thomas to buy for a song merchandise stolen by pirates and transported it to places where it was needed. If the pure and noble countenance of Eugénie accompanied him on his first voyage, like that image of the Virgin which Spanish sailors place on their boats, and if he attributed his early successes to the magic influence of the prayers and intercessions of this sweet girl, later on the Negresses, the mulattoes, the whites, the Javanese, the dancing girls, the orgies of all kinds and the adventures he had in many countries, completely obliterated the memory of his cousin, of Saumur, of the house, of the bench, of the kiss stolen in the corridor. He remembered only the little garden enclosed by the old walls, because there his hazardous destiny had begun; but he denied his family. His uncle was an old wretch who had filched his jewels. Eugénie had no place either in his heart or in his thoughts, but she did occupy a place in his business as a creditor for the sum of six thousand francs.

This conduct and these ideas explain the silence of Charles Grandet. In the Indies, at Saint Thomas, on the coast of Africa, at Lisbon, and in the United States, the speculator had taken, in order not to compromise his name, the pseudonym of Sepherd. Carl Sepherd could safely show himself everywhere indefatigable, bold, and grasping, like a man who, resolved to make his fortune by fair means or foul, hastens to get the infamy over with in order to become an honest man for the rest of his life. Following this system he made his fortune quickly and brilliantly. So in 1827 he was on his way back to Bordeaux on the *Marie-Caroline*, a handsome brig belonging to a royalist firm. He had with him three solid kegs containing nineteen hundred thousand francs in gold dust, on which he hoped to make seven or eight per cent from the Paris mint. On this brig there was also a gentleman-in-ordinary to His Majesty King Charles X, Monsieur d'Aubrion, an amiable old man who had been foolish enough to marry a woman of fashion whose fortune came from the West Indies. In order to pay for Madame d'Aubrion's extravagances he had gone out to sell her properties.

Monsieur and Madame d'Aubrion of the house of d'Aubrion de Buch, whose last head had died before 1789, had been reduced to an income of twenty thousand francs a year. They had a rather plain daughter whom the mother was resolved to marry without a dowry, her fortune being barely sufficient for her own life in Paris. The success of such an enterprise would have seemed problematical to all society people in spite of the cleverness they might concede to a woman of fashion. Madame d'Aubrion herself, when she looked at her daughter, almost despaired of getting rid of her to anyone, even to a man infatuated with the nobility. Mademoiselle d'Aubrion was as long, thin, and spindly as a dragonfly. She had a disdainful mouth, and over it drooped a nose that was too long, thick at the end, rather yellow in its normal state, but completely red after meals, a kind of vegetable phenomenon more disagreeable in the midst of a pale, dull face than in any other. In short, she was all that a mother of thirty-eight, still pretty and with pretentions, could desire. But to counterbalance these defects, the Marchioness d'Aubrion had given her daughter a very distinguished air, had submitted her to a hygienic routine which temporarily maintained her nose at a reasonable flesh tint, had taught her how to dress with taste, had endowed her with charming manners, had shown her how to cast those melancholy glances which interest a man and make him believe he is going to find the angel he has long sought in vain. She taught her the maneuver of the foot, how to let it peep out at the right moment so that its smallness might be admired just when the nose was so rude as to turn red. In short, she had made the very best she could of her daughter. By means of full sleeves, deceptive padding, billowing skirts carefully trimmed, and tightly laced corsets, she had obtained such curious feminine attributes that she might have exhibited them in a museum for the instruction of mothers.

Charles became very friendly with Madame d'Aubrion, precisely because she wanted to become friendly with him. There were even those who declared that during the crossing the beautiful Madame d'Aubrion neglected no means of capturing so wealthy a son-in-law. When they landed at Bordeaux, in the month of June 1827, Monsieur, Madame, Mademoiselle d'Aubrion and Charles stayed in the same hotel and left together for

Paris. The d'Aubrion town house was loaded down with mort, gages; Charles was to free it. The mother had already mentioned how happy she would be to give up her ground floor to her daughter and son-in-law. Not sharing the prejudices of Monsieur d'Aubrion on the score of nobility, she had promised Charles Grandet to obtain from the good King Charles X a royal ordinance which would authorize him, Grandet, to take the name and arms of d'Aubrion, and by establishing an entailed estate with an income of thirty-six thousand francs a year, to succeed d'Aubrion in the title of Captal de Buch and Marquis d'Aubrion. By uniting their fortunes and living on friendly terms, and by means of sinecures, the house of Aubrion would have a combined income of over a hundred thousand francs a year.

"And when a man has a hundred thousand francs a year, a name, a family, and a position at court, for I shall have you appointed gentleman of the bedchamber, he can become anything he likes," she said to Charles. "You can be anything you choose—master of the rolls, prefect, secretary to an embassy, ambassador. Charles X is very fond of d'Aubrion; they have known each other since childhood."

His ambition aroused by this woman, Charles had played, during the crossing, with all these hopes so skilfully presented to him in the guise of confidences poured out from one heart to another. Believing that his father's affairs had been settled by his uncle, he saw himself all of a sudden anchored in the Faubourg Saint-Germain, where at that time everyone longed to be accepted, and where, in the shadow of Mademoiselle Mathilde's blue nose, he would reappear as the Count d'Aubrion, just as the Dreux reappeared one day as Brézés. Dazzled by the prosperity of the Restoration, which was tottering when he left France, caught up by the splendor of aristocratic ideas, his intoxication, which began on the ship, persisted in Paris, where he resolved to do everything to reach the high position his egotistical mother-in-law had held out to him. With this brilliant perspective before him his cousin no longer counted. He saw Annette again. As a woman of the world Annette strongly advised her old friend to contract this alliance and promised her support in all his ambitious enterprises. Annette was delighted to have Charles marry an ugly and tiresome girl. His stay in the Indies had made him very attractive; his skin was bronzed, his manners had become decided and bold like those of a man accustomed to make quick decisions, to rule, to succeed.

Charles breathed more easily in Paris when he saw that he could play a rôle there. Des Grassins, learning of his return, his approaching marriage, and his fortune, came to talk to him about the three hundred thousand francs still required to settle his father's debts. He found Charles in conference with the jeweler from whom he had ordered his bridal gift for Mademoiselle d'Aubrion and who was submitting the designs. In spite of the magnificent diamonds that Charles had brought back from the Indies, the cost of the settings, together with the plate and the expensive and showy jewelry of the young couple, would come to more than two hundred thousand francs. Charles received des Grassins, whom he did not recognize, with the nonchalance of a young man of fashion who, in the Indies, had killed four men in as many duels. Monsieur des Grassins had already called three times; Charles listened to him coldly, then replied, without having fully understood, "My father's affairs don't concern me. I'm obliged to you, sir, for the trouble you have taken. Unfortunately, it's not really of much use to me. I haven't earned nearly two million francs by the sweat of my brow to fling it at the heads of my father's creditors."

"And what if your father were to be declared a bankrupt in a few days?"

"Sir, in a few days I shall be called the Count d'Aubrion. You can well understand that it would be a matter of complete indifference to me. Furthermore, you know even better than I do that when a man has an income of a hundred thousand francs, his father has never failed," he added, politely edging Monsieur des Grassins toward the door.

At the beginning of August that same year Eugénie was sitting on the little wooden bench where her cousin had sworn eternal love and where she usually breakfasted if the weather were fine. On this fresh and cheerful morning the poor girl was enjoying herself for a while by recalling to mind the great and small events of her love and the catastrophes which had followed it. The sun was shining on that beloved stretch of wall so full of chinks, almost in ruins, which the fanciful heiress had forbidden anyone to touch, although Cornoiller often remarked to his wife that it would fall on them one of these days. At this moment the postman knocked and handed a letter to Madame Cornoiller, who ran out into the garden with it shouting:

"Mademoiselle, a letter!" She gave it to her mistress, asking, "Is it the one you were expecting?"

These words resounded as loudly in Eugénie's heart as they actually re-echoed between the walls of the court and the garden.

"Paris! . . . It's from him . . . He's come back."

Eugénie turned pale and held the letter unopened for a moment. She was trembling so violently that she could not break the seal. Big Nanon stood there with her hands on her hips, and her joy seemed to pour out like smoke through the crevices of her brown face.

"Read it, Mademoiselle."

"Oh, Nanon, why has he come back by Paris when he left from Saumur?"

"Read it, you'll find out."

Eugénie tremblingly broke the seal. A check on the house of Madame des Grassins et Corret of Saumur fluttered out. Nanon picked it up.

"*My dear cousin . . .*"

"I'm no longer Eugénie," she thought. And her heart quailed.

"*You . . .*"

"He used to say 'thou.'"

She folded her arms, not daring to read the letter, and great tears came into her eyes.

"Is he dead?" asked Nanon.

"He wouldn't write if he were," said Eugénie.

She read the whole letter, which was as follows:

My dear cousin: You will learn with pleasure, I am sure, of the success of my enterprises. You have brought me luck, I have come back rich, and I have followed the advice of my uncle. Of his death and of my aunt's I have just been informed by Monsieur des Grassins. It is natural that our parents should die before us and that we should succeed them. I trust that by now you are reconciled. Nothing can resist time, as I am well aware. Yes, my dear cousin, unfortunately for me the day of illusions has passed. What else could you expect? While traveling through many countries, I have reflected on life. When I went away, I was a child; I have come back a man. Nowadays I think of many things that I never dreamed of before. You are free, cousin, and I am still free. There is apparently nothing to prevent the realization of our little plans. But I'm much too honest to hide from you the true state of my affairs. I have not forgotten the promises I made to you; on my long journeys I have always remembered the little wooden bench . . .

Eugénie got up as though she were sitting on live coals and sat down on one of the steps of the court.

. . . the little wooden bench where we swore to love each other forever, the corridor, the gray hall, my attic bedroom, and the night when by your delicate kindness you made my future easier

for me. Yes, these memories have upheld my courage, and I said
to myself that you still thought of me as I often thought of you
at the hour agreed upon between us. Did you really look at the
clouds at nine o'clock? You did, didn't you? I cannot betray so
sacred a friendship; no, I cannot deceive you. At the moment
there is a possibility of an alliance for me which satisfies the conclusions I have come to about matrimony. Love—in marriage—
is an illusion. Today my experience tells me that in marrying one
must obey all the social laws and satisfy all the conventions imposed by the world. Now, there is already a difference in age between us that might perhaps affect your future even more than
mine, my dear cousin. I shall say nothing of your mode of living,
of your education, or of your habits, which are not at all suited to
life in Paris and would hardly fit in with my future plans. It is
my intention to live on a grand scale and entertain a great many
people. And I seem to remember that you like a quiet, peaceful
existence. No, I shall be still franker and make you the judge of
my situation; you have the right to know and pass judgment on it.

I now possess an income of eighty thousand francs a year. This
fortune permits me to marry into the d'Aubrion family, whose
heiress, a young girl of nineteen, brings me her name, a title, the
post of honorary gentleman of the bedchamber to His Majesty,
and a very brilliant position. I confess to you, my dear cousin, that
I am not in the least in love with Mademoiselle d'Aubrion; but
by marrying her I assure my children of a social rank of which
the advantages will one day be incalculable; monarchical ideas are
coming more and more into favor every day. Thus, in the course
of time, my son as Marquis d'Aubrion, with an entailed estate of
forty thousand francs a year, will be able to occupy any position
he chooses in the State. We have obligations to our children.

You see, my dear cousin, how frankly I lay before you the state
of my heart, my hopes, and my fortune. Perhaps after seven years
of separation you have forgotten our childish love; but I have

483

forgotten neither your kindness nor my own promises; I remember them all, even those most lightly given, promises that a less conscientious young man than I am, with a heart less youthful and upright, would not even think of. In telling you that the marriage I am about to make is solely one of convenience and that I still remember our childish love, am I not putting myself entirely in your hands, making you mistress of my fate, and assuring you that if I must renounce my social ambitions I shall gladly content myself with the pure, simple happiness of which you have shown me so touching an example?

"Tum, ta, ta. Tum, ta, tee . . ." Charles Grandet had sung to the tune of *Non più andrai* as he signed himself:

> *Your devoted cousin,*
> *Charles.*

"By thunder! That's doing it properly," he said to himself. And he had looked for the check and added this:

P. S. I enclose a check on the des Grassins bank for eight thousand francs to your order payable in gold which includes the interest and capital of the sum you were kind enough to lend me. I am expecting a case from Bordeaux containing a few things which you must allow me to offer you as a mark of my eternal gratitude. You may return my dressing-case by postchaise to the Hotel d'Aubrion. Rue Hillerin-Bertin.

"By postchaise!" said Eugénie. "A thing for which I would have laid down my life a thousand times!"

Terrible and complete disaster! The ship foundered, leaving neither rope nor plank on the vast ocean of hope! Some women, when they are abandoned, go and tear their lover from the arms of a rival, kill her, and rush to the ends of the earth, to the scaffold, to their tomb. That, no doubt, is fine; the motive of this crime is a sublime passion respected even by human justice. Other women bow their heads and suffer in silence; lifeless and resigned, they weep and pardon, pray and remember to their last breath. This is love, true love, angelic love, proud love, which lives on and dies of its anguish. This was how Eugénie felt after she had read this horrible letter. She raised her eyes to heaven as she thought of the last words of her mother, who, as dying people sometimes do, had looked into the future with a clear and penetrating eye. Eugénie, remembering that prophetic life and death, saw her own destiny at a glance. She could only spread out her wings, reach heavenward, and live in prayer until the day of her deliverance.

"My mother was right," she said weeping. "Suffer and die."

She walked with slow steps from the garden into the hall. Contrary to habit, she did not go through the corridor; but she was reminded of her cousin in the old gray drawing room. On the mantelpiece there was always a certain saucer which she used for breakfast every morning along with the old Sèvres sugar bowl. That morning was to be solemn and eventful for her. Nanon announced the curé of the parish church. A relation of the Cruchots, he had the interests of Judge de Bonfons at heart. A few days earlier the old abbé had urged him to speak to Mademoiselle Grandet, from a purely religious point of view, of her obligation to marry. When she saw her pastor, Eugénie supposed that he had come to get the thousand francs that she gave every month to the poor, and told Nanon to bring them. But the curé began to smile.

"Today, Mademoiselle, I have come to talk to you about a poor girl in whom the whole town of Saumur takes an interest and who, for lack of charity toward herself, neglects her Christian duties."

"Good gracious, Father, you've come upon me at a moment when it's impossible for me to think of my neighbor. I'm completely taken up with myself. I'm very unhappy, and my only refuge is in the Church; her bosom is broad enough to embrace all our woes and her love is so abundant that we can draw upon it without fear of exhausting it."

"Well, Mademoiselle, in concerning ourselves with this girl, we shall be concerning ourselves with you. Listen. If you wish to insure your salvation, there are only two ways open to you: either to leave the world or obey its laws; obey either your earthly destiny or your heavenly destiny."

"Ah, your voice speaks to me at a moment when I was longing to hear a voice. Yes, God has sent you here, Father. I am going to bid farewell to the world and live for God alone, in silence and seclusion."

"My daughter, you must reflect at length on this sudden decision. Marriage is life, the veil is death."

"Well, then, let it be death, a quick death, Father," she said with dreadful eagerness.

"Death! But you have great obligations to fulfill toward society, Mademoiselle. Are you not the mother of the poor to whom you give clothing, wood in winter, and work in summer? Your fortune is a loan that you must return, and you have accepted it as a sacred trust. To bury yourself in a convent would be selfishness; as for remaining an old maid, you must not. In the first place, can you manage your great fortune alone? You might perhaps lose it. You would soon have innumerable lawsuits and become involved in inextricable difficulties. Believe your pastor: a husband could be useful to you. It's your duty to preserve what God has given you. I speak to you as a cherished lamb of my flock. You love God too truly not to find your salvation in the midst of the world of which you are one of the noblest ornaments and to which you set a pious example."

At this moment Madame des Grassins was announced. She came prompted by revenge and a great despair.

"Mademoiselle . . ." said she. "Ah, our curé is here. I shall not say anything. I came to discuss a matter of business with you, and I see that you are in the midst of an important conference."

"Madame," said the curé, "I leave you in possession of the field."

"Oh, Father," said Eugénie, "come back in a little while. I am very much in need of your support just now."

"Yes, my poor child," said Madame des Grassins.

"What do you mean?" asked Mademoiselle Grandet and the curé.

"Haven't I heard of your cousin's return and of his marriage to Mademoiselle d'Aubrion? . . . A woman always has her wits about her."

Eugénie blushed and remained silent; but she made up her mind to assume in the future the impassive countenance that her father had always worn.

"Well, Madame," she replied with irony, "I'm afraid I haven't got my wits about me. I don't understand. You may speak in front of the curé. He's my confessor, as you know."

"Very well, Mademoiselle, this is what des Grassins writes me. Read it."

Eugénie read the following letter.

My dear wife: Charles Grandet has come back from the Indies He has been in Paris for a month . . .

"A month!" said Eugénie to herself, letting her hand fall.

A moment later she went on with the letter.

. . . I had to cool my heels in his waiting room twice before I was allowed to speak to the future Count d'Aubrion. Though all Paris is talking of his marriage and the bans are published . . .

"So he was writing to me just as . . ." said Eugénie to herself. She did not finish, she did not cry out as a Parisian would have done: "The villain!" But her contempt was nonetheless deep for being unexpressed.

. . . This marriage is far from being certain; the Marquis d'Aubrion will not give his daughter to the son of a bankrupt. I went to let him know of the trouble his uncle and I had taken to settle his father's affairs and of the clever maneuvers by which we had been able to keep the creditors quiet until now. And hadn't the little upstart the face to say to me, to me, who for five years have devoted myself night and day to his interests and his honor, that his father's affairs were no concern of his! A lawyer would have the right to demand thirty or forty thousand francs in fees at one per cent on the total of the debts. But patience. There are twelve hundred thousand francs legitimately owing to the creditors, and I shall declare his father bankrupt. I went into the business on the word of that old crocodile, Grandet, and I have made promises in the name of his family. If the Count d'Aubrion cares little for his honor, I care a great deal for mine. So I'm going to explain my position to the creditors. However, I have too much respect for Mademoiselle Eugénie, to whom, in happier days, we had hoped to be allied, to act before you have spoken to her in this matter . . .

At this point Eugénie coldly handed back the letter without finishing it. "I thank you," she said to Madame des Grassins. 'We'll see about that . . .'

"At this moment your voice is exactly like that of your late father," said Madame des Grassins.

"Madame, you have eight thousand one hundred francs in gold to count out to us," Nanon said to her.

"That's true; have the kindness to accompany me, Madame Cornoiller."

"Father," said Eugénie with a noble composure, inspired by

the thought she was about to express, "would it be sinful to remain a virgin after marriage?"

"It's a matter of conscience to which I do not know the answer. If you want to know what the famous Sanchez says about it in his treatise *De Matrimonio,* I shall be able to tell you tomorrow."

The curé departed. Mademoiselle Grandet went up to her father's office and spent the day there alone, refusing even to come down at dinner time in spite of Nanon's pleas. She appeared in the evening at the hour when her regular visitors began to arrive. Never had the Grandet drawing room been as full as it was that evening. The news of Charles's return and his foolish treachery had spread throughout the town. But however keen the curiosity of the visitors, it was not satisfied. Eugénie was prepared for it and allowed none of the cruel emotions that were raging within her to show in her face. She was able to present a laughing countenance in reply to those who tried to express their interest by melancholy looks or words. She was able to hide her unhappiness beneath a veil of politeness. About nine o'clock the games ended and the players left their tables, paid their losses, and discussed the last plays as they came to join those who had been conversing. At the moment when the whole company arose to take their leave, there was a dramatic event which re-echoed in Saumur, through the district, and in the four neighboring prefectures.

"Please stay, Judge," said Eugénie to Monsieur de Bonfons, as she saw him take his cane.

There was not a person in this numerous assembly who was unmoved at these words. The judge turned pale and had to sit down.

"The judge gets the millions," said Mademoiselle de Gribeaucourt.

"It's obvious that Judge de Bonfons will marry Mademoiselle Grandet," cried Madame d'Orsonval.

"That's the best play of the evening," said the abbé.

"It's a grand slam," said the notary.

Everyone had his say, everyone made his pun, all saw the heiress mounted on her millions as on a pedestal. The drama, begun nine years before, had reached its climax. To ask the judge, in front of all Saumur, to remain—wasn't that the same as announcing that she intended to marry him? In small towns the conventions are so rigidly observed that an infraction of this kind amounts to a solemn promise.

"Judge," said Eugénie in a voice filled with emotion, when they were alone, "I know what pleases you in me. Swear that you will leave me free during my whole life, that you will claim none of the rights that marriage gives you over me, and my hand is yours. Oh!" she went on, seeing that he was about to kneel, "I haven't finished. I want to be quite frank with you, sir. In my heart I cherish an inextinguishable love. Friendship will be the only feeling that I can give my husband; I wish neither to offend him nor to transgress the laws of my heart. But you can possess my hand and my fortune only at the cost of a very great service."

"I am willing to do anything," said the judge.

"Here are fifteen hundred thousand francs, Judge," she said, drawing from her bosom a certificate of a hundred shares in the Bank of France. "You must leave for Paris, not tomorrow, not tonight, but right away. Go to Monsieur des Grassins, find out from him the names of my uncle's creditors, call them together, pay all the debts of the estate, both capital and interest at five per cent, from the day they were incurred to the date of settlement. Be sure to get a full receipt signed by a notary in due form. You are a magistrate; you are the only person I can trust in this matter. You are an honest man and a gentleman; I shall embark on the strength of your word and brave the dangers of life in the shelter of your name. We shall be indulgent with each other. We have known each other so long that we are almost like relatives; you would not wish to make me unhappy."

The judge fell at the feet of the rich heiress, his heart throbbing with joy and anguish.

"I shall be your slave!" he said.

"When you have the receipt, sir," she went on, looking coldly at him, "you will take it with all the titles to my cousin Grandet and you will give him this letter. On your return, I will keep my word."

The judge understood he owed Mademoiselle Grandet's consent to a disappointment in love; so he hastened to execute her orders with the greatest possible speed that there might be no reconciliation between the two lovers.

When Monsieur de Bonfons had left, Eugénie sank back in her chair and burst into tears. It was all over now. The judge took the mail coach and was in Paris the next evening. The morning after his arrival he called on des Grassins. The magistrate called the creditors together at the notary's office, where the titles had been deposited, and not a single creditor failed to be present. Although they were creditors, one must do them justice, they were punctual. Judge de Bonfons, in the name of Mademoiselle Grandet, paid them capital and interest. The payment of the interest was one of the most startling occurrences in Parisian business circles of that period. When the receipt had been registered and des Grassins given for his services the fifty thousand francs allocated to him by Eugénie, the judge betook himself to the Hotel d'Aubrion and met Charles just as he was entering his apartment after a stormy scene with his prospective father-in-law. The old marquis had just told him that his daughter could never belong to him until all the creditors of Guillaume Grandet had been paid in full.

The judge handed him the following letter:

Cousin:

Judge de Bonfons has undertaken to place in your hands the quittance for all the sums owed by my uncle and also the receipt by which I acknowledge having received them from you. There has been talk of bankruptcy, and it occurred to me that the son of a bankrupt could not marry Mademoiselle d'Aubrion. Yes, Cousin, you have judged my mind and manners correctly; undoubtedly my acquaintance with the world is slight, I understand neither its calculations nor its customs, and I could not give you the pleasures you seek there. Be happy according to the social conventions to which you have sacrificed our youthful love. To complete your happiness all I can offer you is your father's honor. Farewell, you will always have a faithful friend in your cousin,

Eugénie.

The judge smiled at the exclamation which this ambitious young man was unable to repress when he received the official document.

"We shall announce our marriages at the same time," he said.

"Oh, you are marrying Eugénie? Well, I'm very pleased, she's a good girl. But," he went on, suddenly struck by an illuminating thought, "she must be rich?"

"She had," replied the judge with a mocking air, "almost nineteen millions four days ago, but now she has only seventeen."

Charles looked at the judge thunderstruck.

"Seventeen millions . . ."

"Yes, sir, seventeen millions. When we marry, we shall have together, Mademoiselle Grandet and I, an income of seven hundred and fifty thousand francs."

"My dear cousin," said Charles, recovering a little from the shock, "we can help each other along."

"Agreed," said the judge. "Here is also a little case that I was to give only to you," he added, putting the dressing-case down on the table.

"Well, my dear," said Madame d'Aubrion, entering without paying any attention to Cruchot, "don't take any notice of what poor Monsieur d'Aubrion has just said to you. The Duchess of Chaulieu has turned his head. I assure you, nothing will prevent your marriage . . ."

"Nothing, Madame," replied Charles. "The three millions that my father owed were paid yesterday."

"In cash?" she asked.

"Paid in full, interest and capital, and I'm going to have his name cleared."

"How stupid!" cried his mother-in-law. "Who is this gentleman?" she whispered, when she noticed Cruchot.

"My agent," he answered in a low voice.

The marchioness bowed disdainfully to Monsieur de Bonfons and went out.

"We're already helping each other along," said the judge, taking his hat. "Good-bye, Cousin."

"He's making fun of me, that old cockatoo from Saumur. I feel like letting him have six inches of steel in his belly."

The judge had left. Three days later, Monsieur de Bonfons, back in Saumur, announced his marriage to Eugénie. Six months later, he was appointed councilor of the high court in Angers. Before leaving Saumur, Eugénie melted down the gold of the jewels she had so long cherished and converted them, together with the eight thousand francs from her cousin, into a golden pyx, which she presented to the parish church where she had so often prayed to God for *him*! She divided her time between Angers and Saumur. Her husband, who had shown his loyalty in a political matter, became a judge in the superior courts and finally, after a few years, presiding judge. He was impatiently awaiting a general election in order to get a seat in the chamber. He already had his eye on a peerage, and then . . .

"The King will be his cousin," said Nanon, Big Nanon, Madame Cornoiller, matron of Saumur, when her mistress told her of the dignities which were to be hers. However, Judge de Bonfons (he had finally dropped the Cruchot name altogether), was not to realize any of his ambitious ideas. He died eight days after having been elected deputy of Saumur. God, who sees all and never strikes amiss, was no doubt punishing him for his calculations and the legal shrewdness with which he had drawn up, *accurante Cruchot,* his marriage contract, in which the future couple gave each other, in case they should have no children, their entire property of every kind, landed and personal, without exception or reservation, dispensing even with the formality of an inventory, provided that the omission of the said inventory is not to the disadvantage of their heirs or executors, it being understood that the said gift be, etc. This clause will explain why the judge always treated Madame de Bonfons' wishes with such deference, particularly her desire for solitude. The women quoted Judge de Bonfons as an example of the most considerate of men, pitied him, and often went so far as to censure Eugénie's grief and passion, but as they know so well how to censure a woman, with the most cruel and subtle insinuations.

"Madame de Bonfons must indeed be very ill to leave her husband alone. Poor little woman! Is she likely to get well soon? What's the matter with her anyway? Is it gastritis or cancer? Why doesn't she consult a doctor? She's become quite yellow lately; she ought to consult the Paris specialists. Surely she must want a child? People say she's very fond of her husband; why not give him an heir, in his position? Do you know it's really

dreadful? And if it's the result of a mere whim, it's unpardon.
able. The poor judge!"

Eugénie was endowed with the intuition that the recluse de
velops from perpetual meditation and from the clear-sightedness
with which he apprehends whatever falls within his orbit. Taught
by misfortune and her recent disillusionment to divine what
people were thinking, she knew that the judge desired her
death so that he might find himself in possession of this immense fortune, still further augmented by the estates of his
uncle the notary and his uncle the abbé, whom God, strangely
enough, had seen fit to call to Himself. The poor recluse felt
sorry for the judge. Providence avenged her for the calculations
and for the disgraceful indifference of a husband who respected
the hopeless passion which absorbed Eugénie merely because
it served his purpose. To give life to a child, would that not be
to destroy the hopes of selfishness, the joys of ambition which
the judge cherished? So God flung masses of gold to his prisoner,
who was indifferent to gold and who yearned for heaven, who
lived, pious and good, in holy thoughts, who constantly gave
aid in secret to those in distress.

Madame de Bonfons was a widow at thirty-six, with an income
of eight hundred thousand francs, still beautiful, but with the
beauty of a woman who is nearly forty years of age. Her face
is white, placid, and calm. Her voice is gentle and subdued, her
manners simple. She has the nobility of grief, the saintliness of a
person whose soul has never been sullied by contact with the
world, but also the stiffness of an old maid and the petty habits
which are the result of a narrow provincial existence. In spite
of her income of eight hundred thousand francs, she lives as the
poor Eugénie Grandet once lived, lights the fire in her room
only on those days when her father would have allowed her to
light the fire in the hall and puts it out in conformity with the
program enforced in her youthful years. She is always dressed as

her mother was. The house in Saumur, sunless and cold, always gloomy and melancholy, is symbolic of her life. She carefully accumulates her income, and might perhaps seem parsimonious, had such a charge not been contradicted by the noble use she made of her fortune. Pious and charitable institutions, a home for the aged, and Christian schools for children, a richly endowed public library, bear witness year after year against the avarice of which some people accuse her. The churches of Saumur have been embellished by her. Madame de Bonfons, ironically referred to as Mademoiselle, is looked upon with reverence by most people. And yet that noble heart, moved only by the tenderest feelings, was always to be subject to the calculations of human selfishness. Money was to communicate its cold gleam to this saintly life and teach distrust of feeling to a woman who was all feeling.

"You are the only one who loves me," she would say to Nanon.

This woman's hand heals the secret wounds in many families. Eugénie proceeds on her way to heaven accompanied by a train of good deeds. The greatness of her soul makes up for the narrowness of her education and the petty customs of her early life.

Such is the story of this woman who is in the world but not of it; who, created to be a magnificent wife and mother, has neither husband, nor children, nor family. Lately there has been some question of her marrying again. The people of Saumur are linking her name with that of the Marquis de Froidfond, whose family is beginning to hem in the rich widow as the Cruchots had done in the past. It is said that Nanon and Cornoiller are on the side of the marquis; but nothing could be more false. Neither Big Nanon nor Cornoiller is clever enough to understand the corruptions of the world.

Paris,

September, 1833.